Contents Page

To my wife, who knows all my dreams.

Introduction to Moon Stand Still

In the Eleventh Century, a series of kings from the Saxon and Salian tribes ruled over a vast and unwieldy 'empire' that stretched from the Baltic in the north to the Italian Alps in the south, and from the Rhine in the West to the Elbe in the East. One of these kings, Henry the Third, better known as Henry the Black, tried to establish a kind of imperial peace over this entire area by declaring a unilateral 'Truce of God'. It was a noble but doomed undertaking, applauded by the Church, but frequently ignored or flouted by the myriads of warlords who defended and maintained dukedoms, baronial estates, and small collections of villages and manors across the entire region.

Henry's brief but energetic reign (1039-1056) was characterised by raids, counter-raids, punitive expeditions and dogged campaigns from Friesia to Lorraine, from Bohemia to Poland, and from Hungary to Northern Italy. His reign was all about the search for peace. There is nothing new in that, but Henry had a singular, fixed and determined aim: to rid his kingdom of bloodshed and disorder at whatever level in society, and in whatever corner of the realm he found it. He believed passionately that God – represented by the church on earth –

would uphold his crusade to impose a truce ('Treuga Dei') and then a peace ('Pax Dei') on the citizens of the sprawling empire he struggled to rule.

He failed – some would say, 'of course!' – but his failure has all the quality of high drama springing from the defeat of a noble, but misplaced ideal.

As if that were not enough, monks and chroniclers at the time noted that his reign also seemed to suffer from poor weather, frequent storms and floods, famines, plagues and cattle disease.

At last when Henry appeared to be making some progress in subduing his more defiant warlords, news came that Saxony was under renewed threat from the Liutizen tribes beyond the Elbe.

'Moon Stand Still' begins as Henry's reign reaches this crisis point. The story is set in the area of what later came to be known as Lower Saxony. While some of the figures and place names are fictitious, others did exist. Magdeburg, Meissen, Fulda, Leipzig, Goslar, and Dresdany were known settlements in eleventh century Germany. The Markgrafs (Barons) of Meissen were just beginning to establish themselves as a force to be reckoned with, but I have substituted the name of Ludwig for that of the real Markgraf of the time: Bernhard.

There is no record of the following settlements: Eckerheim, Hochtal, and Weissburg – but I have tried to describe them as if they were actual villages from the period. The 'Scharfgipfel' is also drawn from my own imagination, but such a geographical feature is not completely unknown in Germany.

There is some evidence that wheat harvests were particularly late in eleventh century Europe, probably due to some cyclical climactic changes – this hopefully accounts for the October harvests in Eckerheim, when normally the ground would be prepared for the planting of next season's crops.

While the central characters, Elsa, Markward and Bernhardt, are fictional I have tried to build into them the attitudes, obligations and customs of the period. It was a feudal society, with a strong sense of order despite the constant threat of disorder. Military service and marriage were seen as duties as much as vocations, and yet there is enough evidence in the form of poems, songs and even monastic paintings and illustrations to show us that both chivalry and romance were highly valued by some.

The 'class system' of nobility, townsfolk and peasantry was in many ways entrenched, but this did not prevent 'men of dust' making their way up through the ranks because of their skill, determination and ambition either as soldiers or clerics. In this sense Markward and Wipo represent two such types. However, the uppermost levels of society, where the warlords held sway, were almost exclusively occupied by right of birth, and blood inheritance – not to be achieved by the peasantry.

The campaign beyond the Elbe against the Liutizen was an actual historical event, and I have tried to line it up accurately with the final months of Henry's reign. If the overall mood of the reign was embattled and tragic, as this grim Salian king fought to bring order to an unwieldy empire, I have also tried to reflect the resilience and native optimism of the people over whom he ruled. The eastern 'marches' along the Saxon border were difficult lands to live in and control, but they endured because of the sort of qualities I hope I have highlighted in this tale.

The Two Valleys

The rider eased his horse to a halt in the early evening light, and looked down across the shallow, misty meadow land. A group of houses stood in a straggle along a stream, and there in a fold in the ground was a church with its heavy square tower and shingle-tile roof. There was a mill and mill race almost screened by trees as the stream curved away.

'Home,' he said to himself and patted his horse's neck. 'Come on, boy, we'll see who's there to greet us.'

With a lowering October sky, and with the harvest late most of the villagers would still be in the fields. He trotted down the muddy street glancing right and left at the doorways. There were no children playing. A single dog had run out to meet him, given one bark and skittered away behind a house. A few hens picked and pecked among the ragged gardens – but otherwise all was quiet.

At last he heard the cry of a goose girl somewhere down in the meadow and the honking geese replied. A door swung open on a twisted hinge and an old man shambled out. 'She's home too soon – home too soon!' he muttered to himself, and looked up in surprise when he saw the horseman.

His eyes narrowed as he squinted, and then he broke into a gap tooth grin: 'Aha! It's Markward! It's Markward, isn't it! Home you are, and home from the wars!'

The horseman smiled, and took the old man's hand:

'Well met Wulfstan! I see you still keep the village, and keep it well.'

'Aye, aye my young sir. And I keep it for my lord.' He stepped back, still grinning, and slapped his sides. 'I can't believe it! You're back! And bravely too, with a fine horse, good harness, and a man's beard to boot!'

'I'm back, Wulfstan, for a time at least. But come, now — where are my folks, my mother, my uncle? Where is anyone?'

'Where else but in the fields among the harvest. It's late this year, desperate late, but the winters are slow to come and the summers stray into October.'

He looked up towards the ridges: 'There's a storm coming. From the north. You can smell it. The grains as ripe as it'll ever be and we can't risk it flattened and sodden by a down pour.' He paused and waited as Markward swung down from the saddle.

'You wouldn't have heard.'

'Heard what?'

'Your sister, Brunni, took ill at Stefanstide. The priest said it was a hexe, a curse. The wisewoman said he was a fool, that it was marsh fever and little could be done.'

'She's . . .'

'Oh, still alive, but only just. Your mother hardly leaves her side, and little Albrecht, too. They keep her cool, and fight the sweats, and feed her soup when they can.'

'She's in the house then?' Markward started to move away.

'No, no. A squall last week took the roof. She's in the cruck over there by the elm.' The old man pointed, and then took the horse by the bridle as it tossed its head and started back. 'Whoa there my fine one! Easy now, and I'll find you some fresh hay.'

With a click of his tongue Wulfstan walked the horse along the street, while Markward nodded and then headed towards the cruck.

The girl, her mother and little brother at her side, was deathly pale. She looked tired, but smiled to see her brother and tried to lift herself up. 'I never thought you'd come,' she said.

'I'd always come home, you know I would, little Brunni.' He bent and kissed her on the brow, and then turned to his mother, who stood speechless, wide eyed with joy.

'Markward!' she gasped at last hugging him tight. 'The news was so bad. They said such things . . . the fighting, the plague . . .I thought . . .'

He shook his head and grinned. 'No Mutti, no. I'm here, and home. The Friesians tried, as try they might, but they couldn't stop me. Not ever. But Brunni, I didn't know she'd taken ill.'

'How could you have known? No one leaves the village these days, not since the last muster, and even if they did we would hardly know where to send them with a message. The royal army seems just to wander everywhere like a lost cow.'

Markward gave a short laugh. 'It's true. There were times when we had no idea where we were and less idea where we were going.' He sat down on the edge of the straw mattress and ran his fingers through his sister's hair. Little Albrecht clung to his knee staring up at his big brother. For a time no one spoke. Outside, the goose girl called again, and someone stomped wearily by in the mud.

'It's good to be home, Mutti.'

'And glad it is to have you home! Now come, you must have ridden a long way to get here, and nothing in your belly for sure. There's pottage in the cruck across the way, and the men are coming home from the fields. If they don't have a hare or two for supper I was never born in this village.'

'Thanks, Mutti, but I'll stay awhile with Brunni here.'

'You'll do no such thing my lad. Look at her! All tired out from the excitement of seeing you back safe and sound. It'll bring the fever out again.' She stopped, and frowned:

'You can kiss her goodbye for now, and see her again in the morning.' Markward's mother was smiling, but her hands were on her hips, and he knew that there was no point in arguing.

He grinned, nodded and got to his feet. 'I'm away little sweeting!' he said to his sister as he kissed her forehead. 'Rest up now, and I'll bring you some Michaelmas daisies in the morning.' She smiled and tried to nod, but coughed instead and smiled again, and took her brother by the hand.

Albrecht danced away in front of his brother. 'Come! Come! Markward. I'll show you where the cruck is. I'll show you!'

Outside the folk were coming in from the fields. Wulfstan was greeting them, waving and pointing towards Markward and his little brother. The sun had dipped below the wooded ridge to the West, and a soft, misted light flooded across the little village.

A day later, and Markward, with Albrecht at his side, stood at the edge of the great field, watching as the last of the stooks were hurried into the priest's cart and away to the tithe barn. They would be sheltered there against the rain until the threshing.

'What was it like?' said Albrecht, staring up at his brother.

Markward frowned, and shrugged. 'I try not to think about it, little brother, now that I'm home.'

'Did you fight?'

'We all fought.'

'But did you kill anyone? Did you?'

Markward knelt down and took Albrecht gently by the shoulders. 'Listen, Albi. It's not like fighting with sticks in the meadow. Men fall and bleed. And some die. And every one is a mother's son. And some had sweethearts waiting for

them, and . . .' He stopped. His brother's face had fallen. He
gave him a hug, and stood up.

'But there were things worth remembering, little brother.
Shining warriors and shining swords, and all of us marching
and singing in the sun. Such singing. You should have heard
it, Albi! The old folk songs we sing around the hearth at
night at Michaelmas and harvest time, but these were songs
sung by an army, a forest of men.'

Albrecht's eyes widened. 'Tell me, Markward! Tell me!'

'No, no, I talk too much, and you'll only go running off to
the wars, and leave your mother weeping.'

'Like you did.'

'Aye, aye, like I did, and came home wiser. And it's by the
grace of God I came home at all.'

'Annie the goose girl says that Arnulf and Peter won't be
coming home. She says the Friesians . . .'

'Annie talks a lot, but knows less. Still she may be right.'

For a while they watched the clouds roll in over the far
ridges, and felt the first smattering of rain on their cheeks.

'Won't be long now', said Markward, pulling his cloak
about him. 'We should be for home, anyway. Your mother
made me promise to get you back by midday, and there's
work to do for both of us now the harvest is in.'

'Did you see the king?' said Albrecht suddenly as he
trotted along beside his brother.

'The king? Oh, aye, I saw the king.'

'What's he like?'

'What's he like? He's a king, that's what he's like. But he's
not especially tall or big. And he doesn't dress in fine robes
or wear a great big crown.'

'You saw him, though.'

'I did. We were marching through a burnt out village near
Dordrecht, and he came galloping by with knights all around
him, and a royal banner at the head. They came to a halt at a
crossroads about half a mile ahead, and we caught up with
them. I tell you little Albi, when you see a king, a real king I
mean, a good king and a brave king, your heart just comes

up in your chest. You want to throw back your head and cheer with all your might.'

'Is King Henry a good king, then?'

'He is, though some men may grumble and say not, I tell you he is. Do you know what he did as we came up to him – we, a straggled out bunch of grimy, dusty, ill-fit, half-trained peasants? I'll tell you what he did, he swung off his horse, gave the reins to his squire, and welcomed us like brothers. Bade us sit down, and take our ease, and asked us how things went. The sergeants were none too pleased, I can tell you, but they couldn't do a blind thing about it. And when he ordered a provender wagon to halt, and handed out cheese, bread and wine, their eyes nearly popped out of their sockets. We, all of us felt like laughing, but of course we never did. Just bowed, and tapped the forelock, and wished his majesty well.

'I remember he called us "brave fellows", and said the Empire was nothing without men such as us, and prayed God we would all come safely through the coming battle.'

'A battle?'

'Aye, a battle. In the marshes near Dordrecht where the Rhine meets the sea. Bitter it was.'

'And the King?'

'The King! Henry the Black they call him, and so he is, but it's nothing to do with his heart or soul. Black hair, black beard, and eyes like shining pools of pitch, but the man has a heart of gold.'

'Aha! Markward!' A voice came from behind them. It was Uncle Gart the Hayward. 'A single supper of cheese and bread and wine, and you turn our king into a saint!'

Markward laughed and shook the Hayward by the hand. 'Well met, Uncle! And aye, I do. We judge men by how they act, not what they say.'

'Right enough, right enough! But our good liege lord is a dreamer is he not, with all this talk of peace, and an end to war forever.'

'Maybe so, but he's king enough to fight for it.'

'And we're fools enough to die for it.'

'Not to die for a dream, Gart, but to die for a king.'

The Hayward paused, then grinned. 'You're a minstrel, Markward. The wars have turned your head.'

As they came into the village, Albrecht suddenly squeezed Markward's hand: 'Aunt Helga says you have a sweetheart.'

'Does she now?'

'She does. I heard her talking to the women at the well, and she said you had eyes for a girl at Hochtal.'

'At Hochtal?'

'Yes, Aunt Helga says she's tall and slim with flame red hair.'

'Does she now – well you tell Auntie Helga, she's short and dumpy, and has no hair at all!'

Albrecht looked startled. Gart burst out laughing. He was still chuckling and shaking his head when Markward waved him goodbye by the elm cruck.

'Are the maidens of Eckerheim not good enough for you, that you have to wander the high valley?' Gart called out over his shoulder.

'Maybe I am not good enough for them, uncle,' replied Markward with that awkward smile that not even his mother could translate.

Brunni was not getting any better, and the family was worried. She had scarcely left her bed for days now, and her thin pale body often shook beneath the rough woollen blankets that covered her. The Autumn chill blew through the chinks and cracks of the wattle and daub walls no matter how much Albrecht tried to plug them with clay and straw. Every day Markward went out and cut fresh rushes, and dried them round the hearth, and split logs, and gathered brushwood, and kept the fire crackling and glowing. But the harsh, damp cold crept up through the pounded earth floor and into the trembling little frame of the little girl who lay upon the bed day after day. Still, she had some strength and smiled every time Markward, or his mother or Albrecht came near, and sometimes even spoke a few words. The priest came every second day as the sun was setting. The wisewoman only came if she was asked, and each time she came with herbs, and roots and berries, and a wooden pestle to crush them in.

At last a pedlar happened by who sold potions and cures for a penny and a meal. He said he came from the fever lands near Osnabruck, and their cures were well tried if not assured.

Mutti was uncertain, the priest frowned and the wisewoman just shrugged and hobbled away. It was Markward who nodded, and gave the pedlar a penny, with the promise of two more if the fever went within three days.

The potion stank. It filled the cruck with acrid fumes, and Brunni could scarce take it. In the end Mutti gave it to her mixed with cabbage soup, and the family sat back and waited. The pedlar left, promising to return in three days time.

The first night Brunni tossed and turned and sweated as she had never sweated before. Markward crouched by his sister's bed and muttered curses on the pedlar. Mutti bustled about with rags soaked in water, and Albrecht lay by the hearth staring into the fire. No one slept.

By dawn the sweats had slackened. By noon the shaking had stopped, and when the priest poked his head around the corner at sunset he saw that little Brunni, asleep and calm had colour in her cheeks. Mutti waved him in. Tears of relief were starting from her eyes. Markward and Albrecht were asleep.

'It's a miracle, my daughter,' he said to Mutti as he knelt by the bed.

'If it is, then the pedlar's a saint,' she replied.

There was an awkward pause, but the priest nodded and smiled and put his hand gently on her arm. 'Let the little one rest, daughter, I'll come by in the morning.'

Mutti gave a slight bow and watched him leave.

When the pedlar returned two days later the fever had gone and Brunni was sitting up, laughing and chattering. Markward was happy to pay him the agreed fee and more. Mutti decided that it was time for one of the old hens to go, and soon the cruck was filled with the smell of roast meat, and the sound of feasting. The news of Brunni's recovery had lifted the whole village. The people sang as they threshed the harvest, and the sound of rain drumming on the tithe barn roof (the bishop could afford to buy some old Roman tiles) failed to dampen their spirits.

Dietmar, the Markgraf and lord of the manor, was away with the King's army, but his bailiff came down to the threshing floor with barrels of mead, rounds of cheese, and two sides of salted bacon. The whole village now feasted, and the harvest was declared good.

'Are you back to the King, then?' asked Mutti when she came across Markward down by the stream staring up towards the ridges.

He shook his head: 'Three times the forty days muster in the king's service, and more besides. Henry's a good king, but I've done marching for this year at least.'

'You've a warrant?'

'From the King's provost himself. In a month the campaigning will be over. Winter's almost here. I'm on a pledge to return in the spring.'

'After the planting, surely.'

'Oh, aye. My lord Dietmar made sure of that. But then I must go.' He sighed, and stared at his boots the way he always did when he was struggling to say something. Mutti waited. At last he spoke.

'I go to Fulda. The King's banner will be there.'

'Alongside the bishop's no doubt.'

'No doubt.' He paused again, lost in thought.

'Mutti, I'm away tomorrow for a bit.'

'To Hochtal.'

He looked surprised. 'Aye, to Hochtal. How did you know?'

Mutti gave a short laugh. 'How couldn't I know? Half the village knows. And besides, I knew before your auntie, or any of the gossips at the well.'

She put her hand on her son's shoulder, reaching up as mothers do, and looking into his eyes.

'Listen, my little one. It's been hard here since your father died, and your brother went chasing off to the city. But we won't hold you back. You're a man now. You go where you must. We will always be here, and we'll always welcome you back.'

' Hochtal's not for me, Mutti.'

'But the lassie is.'

'Elsa? Aye, she is, but I hear her heart may belong to another.'

'And you go to find out for sure.'

'For sure.' Markward stooped, picked up a stone and threw it into the stream. 'For sure I will.'

'Well, I'll pack you cheese and bread for your wallet. Wulfstan has been looking after your horse, like a mother with a baby. It would carry you to Hades and back.'

'Well, it'll get me to Hochtal then.' He smiled and gave Mutti a hug.

'I love you Mutti. Whatever happens Eckerheim is my home.'

'You big oaf!' she laughed. 'You who dine with kings and could live in a palace!'

'Why, because I go chasing after a girl from the high valley?'

'No, because you're Markward, and I named you as such, your father and I. We saw the light in your eyes when you were only a suckling, and I knew one day your horse would carry you far.'

Markward picked up another stone and rolled it between his fingers. 'You are as blind as this stone, Mutti, but it's love that makes you so.'

'And blind love sees what others never can,' replied Mutti finishing the proverb. 'You've a good heart, son, don't go breaking it for a girl with flame red hair.'

'Too late, mother mine, too late. But there's always a mending if the girl loves me.'

He hugged Mutti again, pushed the stone into his wallet, and wandered off down to the great barn where Wulfstan kept the horses.

'Oh, wisht ah, wisht,' smiled Mutti to herself as she watched him go. 'I've raised a muckle lad there.'

The next day, Markward saddled his horse and led it out of the great barn.

It was early morning, the villagers were away to the fields to bring in the gleanings, and the children were driving the cattle down to the lower meadow. Mutti had said her goodbyes, and Albrecht had set off early to help with the cows. Brunni stood at the doorway to the cruck and waved.

Markward smiled and waved back.

'I'll bring back you a fine ribbon!' he called. She nodded, laughed and waved again.

He swung up into the saddle and rode away from the village, across the stream and up towards the eastern ridges. Wulfstan, standing by a headland stone of the fallow field watched him go, and shook his head. 'Lads and lassies', he said to himself, and then turned to his work.

The sky was clear, though a mist hung in the valleys, and Markward could feel the morning chill through his cloak. He wore the brigandine tunic he had brought home from the wars. A battered iron casque he had picked up from the field at Dordrecht hung from the saddle. The leather faced buckler he had taken from a Friesian was strapped to his hip, and there on his belt was the broad bladed dagger his uncle had given him the summer before last. But slung from his chest on the heavy leather baldric was the great war-sword he had found among the ruins of an ambush on the road to Goch.

It was almost too big for him, but the balance was superb, and the blade swung smoothly to the flexing of his wrist. Years at the plough had strengthened arm and shoulder, and though the blade was perhaps half a hand too long for Markward, he felt at ease with it. Ranulf, a knight from Goslar, had taught him the basic cuts and parries. In return he had polished and cleaned the knight's hauberk and harness during the Spring campaign. By the end of that Summer with the help of some rough remarks and amused goodwill among King Henry's idle sergeants, Markward had turned himself into a half-decent swordsman. And the horse he now rode, a strong, high-shouldered chestnut hack, made him feel what Wulfstan cheerfully called ' a village knight'.

He rode across a grassy meadow between two groves of birches and began the long climb to the far ridge. From there he would be able to see on the skyline the rocky outcrop called Scharfgipfel. Beyond that, across a wild heathland was the road to Hochtal. If the weather held he would be there in two days.

In late October, along the heathlands of the northern duchies, the icy winds blow in from the Baltic and bend the low stands of laurel, and rowan and birch. After two days in the saddle Markward was cold and tired. But at last, as the pale sun reached the forenoon he saw the jumbled roofs and single spire of Hochtal pushing through the misty rain and smoke.

He could smell fresh bread, dried bracken and cattle dung. He could hear the hollow clang of cow bells and the whistles and hoots of herdsmen. And here and there came the cries of children as they chased the sheep and goats through the late season corn. Hochtal was bigger than Eckerheim. It was more than just a village, but less than a town. Besides the church, it had a mill with grindstones worked by bullocks. It had two tithe barns, a stone manor house where the bailiff lived when his lord was away, a smithy and a bakery. Several of the houses in the village were also made of white plastered stone, timber and thatch, and the 'great farm' which stood just beyond the glebe had a high-walled farmyard and a watch-tower. The manor house stood on high ground to the north of the village, and though the lord's hall was timber framed, it had a round tower with a steep-pitched, tiled roof, and a defended doorway.

Hochtalers were pleased to be called such, and struggled not to look down upon their brethren from neighbouring villages.

Markward took a deep breath and walked slowly into the village, leading his horse. He had been here often enough, usually on market days, and twice when he was on his way to the goose fair at Maibach. Still, he never felt quite comfortable with the folks of Hochtal. It wasn't that they openly resented his presence, it was just that they for the most part simply ignored him, or merely grunted when he greeted them.

Elsa was different, and always had been. Even as a young girl, how many moons ago, she had smiled at him, and teased him for his awkward manner and tousled hair. And because none else would speak to him, he had spoken to her, and then *with* her. And now there came a day when he thought he would 'speak for her' as the Eckerheim saying went.

He at last caught sight of her in the busy market square, by the well. She was helping her father set up a stall. It wasn't a high day, or the normal day for market, but the harvest had been good, and several families including Elsa's had plenty to sell.

How her hair shone, even in this light, and she laughed and tossed her head when a passer-by waved and said something.

For a time Markward stood hesitating, not quite sure what to do, or what to say. As people brushed by him, turning to glance at this stranger, he almost decided to go back to Eckerheim before even Elsa had seen him, or he had spoken to her. Then his horse snorted and ducked its head, and it seemed to jolt him into action.

Before he knew it, he found himself in front of Elsa.

'Hello.' He smiled uncertainly.

She looked up, brightened, and then her face fell. 'It's you.'

'Yes, I came to see you.' He smiled again.

'So I see.' She turned away and busied herself with filling a basket of cabbages.

He reddened with confusion. Her father was standing near a handcart by the stall. Markward could feel his steady gaze, and turned to acknowledge him with a slight bow. It was not returned.

He turned back to Elsa. 'I thought we might talk.'

'Oh, did you now.' She straightened up, and smoothed her dress at her sides, and flicked away a strand of hair from across her eyes. 'Well, let me tell you Markward of Eckerheim, I've little enough to say to you except, be gone!'

Her dark eyes flashed, and as she raised her voice a stir ran through the market place.

Markward took a step back as though he had been struck, and for a moment Elsa's gaze softened. But it was just a moment, and Markward, his heart pounding and his thoughts spinning, never saw it.

'You heard the lassie!' said Elsa's father. Be off now. Go home before I drive you home with the point of my boot.'

A few jeers and laughs came from the small crowd which had gathered to see the fun.

Markward stood, suddenly aware that his hand was resting on the hilt of his sword, and that it was shaking. That old anger that he fought so hard to keep down was boiling up inside him. He knew though, that to stand his ground would be madness. He would be torn to pieces in an instant.

'I'm going,' he said, trying to stop his voice from trembling. 'I wish you well Elsa. I'm sorry if I hurt you, but I wish you well.'

He took his horse's bridle by the bit, and began to lead it back across the square.

'You never came!' she called after him. 'You never came!'

He half-turned. 'I sent word.'

'You sent nothing!'

'I sent word. The provost royal said he was riding this way and would bring your family word. It was the king's warrant, I had to go. It was the muster.'

Elsa clenched her fists. 'You never came. There was no message. I never heard. After all you promised! You promised me you would come, and you left me with nothing. Nothing!' The tears came. Markward started forward, but she held up her hand. 'No ! Go ! I'm promised to another. A man who keeps his promises. A man who will keep me.'

As if a hammer had driven against his chest Markward lurched around and walked slowly from the square. When he reached the edge where a wagon stood piled high with straw someone put a hand on his shoulder. He looked dully into the eyes of a tall, broad-chested young man with jet black hair and huge hands.

He had a strong, rough hewn face, and Markward guessed him for a blacksmith.

'My name is Bernhardt. Elsa and I are to be married before Christmastide.'

Markward said nothing, but gripped the reins tightly.

'You knew Elsa?' the blacksmith asked.

'I knew her. I know her still.'

The blacksmith shook his head slowly and smiled. 'I think maybe her heart was with you once. She talked of you when all I was, was a careless friend.'

Markward glared. He hated this man, and all the more for his quiet words.

He pulled away, but the hand on his shoulder tightened and Markward felt its strength.

'Not yet, I pray you. If you leave in hate, you die in sorrow.'

Markward shook himself free. 'I came as a man, I leave as a man. I will not trade words with one who would steal another's . . .'

'Another's love? You broke her love. You broke it in a twelve month.'

Markward was striding away now, pulling hard on the bridle. He knew if he stayed any longer, his sword would be in his hand and all would be lost. As he reached a cattle trough he steadied his horse, put his foot in the stirrup and swung into the saddle. The blacksmith stood watching him. Elsa, her father and the market square waited silently.

His rage suddenly cleared and he felt a sudden calm. His shoulders sagged and he ran his hand through the chestnut's mane.

'I came back,' he called. 'But you can have her now. 'She loves me not, that much I see.'

Bernhardt the Blacksmith walked slowly towards him, and put his hand on the horse's flank. He spoke quietly.

'I say again, Markward, you broke her love. It hasn't gone, but it is broken, and she will marry me. That much is sure.'

'And I will never come again to this place.'

'That would be wise, and good.'

Markward sighed, nodded, and looked across to where Elsa stood, her father's arm about her shoulder. That flame red hair. He would never forget it. He lifted his hand in farewell, and she half-raised hers as if to reply.

And then he was gone. It seemed as if in a moment of time he found himself outside the village where the ploughed field joined the heathland. He couldn't even remember if he had muttered a goodbye to Bernhardt, but he scarcely cared. He would not be going back. He would never see Hochtal again. Nor Elsa.

He didn't look back. It was almost noon, and the sun still struggled through a thin drizzle and mist. His cloak felt damp and cold. It clung to him, and was heavy about his shoulders. Water droplets covered his hair and dripped across his face. He blinked hard and cursed the day. His horse walked on steadily, brushing through the soaked heaths and glistening grass of the long ridge that led upwards and back to Scharfgipfel. If the weather held he would push on to the edge of the heathland. If it worsened he would turn aside to a shepherd's bothy he had spotted on the way in.

For a time he was lost in his thoughts, struggling to deal with the whirlwind which had struck him in Hochtal. His head down, he gave his horse its head, and hardly knew which way he went.

But then he came to a little rocky stream, the horse hesitated, and he stirred himself, and looked up. Where was he? The weather had closed in. Thick, dark clouds rolled over the heath. Rain, heavy rain, was gathering from the East. Markward urged his horse up the slope beyond the stream and stared into the gloom. There was no sign of the bothy. Perhaps he had passed it. No, he had not ridden far enough. It must be up ahead somewhere.

The wind flapped his cloak and the first heavy drops of rain spattered across the thin trackway he had chosen. He flicked the reins and his horse began a careful trot. 'Easy, lad!' he said leaning over and whispering into its ear. 'We'll find you shelter warm and dry, and maybe some good, fresh straw.'

Hours later and the rain was lashing his back, swirling about him in great drifts. He was chilled and trembling, and his horse went wearily across the sodden, bubbling heath, its hooves sloshing and slithering on the drenched and swelling turf. There was no sun to guide him, but the faint glow of day that showed between the scudding clouds was fading fast, so he knew that night was upon him. He looked around for shelter. There was none. He rode on, shoulders hunched, peering into the shadowed murk. And then, unbelievably, yes, there in the gloom away to his right, an even darker shadow, and from the shadow a single point of light. He headed for it, cutting off the track and splashing almost withers high through heather and broom. How far it lay he could not tell, but in the storm there was little else to drive him on.

Once or twice he lost sight of the light, but he kept his head and pressed on across the heath until he saw it again. The light at last brightened, flickered, grew and took form as he neared it. And around it the shadow rose until he could see the outline of a roof and a ridge pole.

Gasping with relief, and patting his horse's neck he approached the little cruck. Firelight blazed through the open door.

Cupping his hands, Markward yelled a greeting through the wildness of the wind and rain. He dismounted and waited. Almost immediately, a man appeared in the doorway, stooping low. He held a staff in one hand.

'Who goes there?'

'A traveller, lost in the storm.'

'Your name, traveller?'

'Markward of Eckerheim, seeking shelter.'

The man stared for a moment. 'Well, Markward of Eckerheim, you'd best come in. You'll have to leave your mount behind the cruck. There's a lean-to there, and a manger. It's in the lee of the wind, and dry.'

Markward nodded his thanks.

Inside the cruck it was warm and well-lit. The man was a shepherd, old and grey headed, but with a strong wiry frame, a weather- beaten face, and a sharp look to his eye.

'I'm Cedric,' he said and pointed to a low stool beside the fire. Markward sat down wearily, and let his dripping cloak fall from his shoulders. The heat from the fire warmed his back and shoulders. Outside he could hear the rain lashing down, but although the door was little more than an offset wattle screen the hut seemed dry and snug.

'It's good here,' he said at last.

The shepherd joined him by the fire, two tankards of ale in his hand. He passed one to Markward. 'Aye, it's good enough. And the best place to be on a night like this.'

'I saw your light.'

'That's well.'

'I'm coming from Hochtal, heading for Eckerheim.'

The shepherd nodded slowly. 'Hochtal. I know it. Quiet enough folk, and a fair market.' He put down his tankard and threw another log on the fire. 'Now, Eckerheim,' he said, 'that's a good step from here, and you're a little off your path.'

'I know it. The storm . . .'

'Aye the storm.'

For a time both men were silent, staring into the crackling blaze, and listening to the howling storm outside.

'Perhaps I should check my horse,' said Markward at last.

'No need, laddie. He's as dry as us, and near as warm, but before we turn in for the night, I 'll see to the stable and the fold. You stay here in the dry.'

'I thank you.'

The old shepherd grunted, and nodded but said nothing. After a while he got up, rummaged in the corner and returned with bread, cheese and an apple.

'Here,' he said. 'Supper. In the morning, before I set you on your way, I'll boil a pottage for us both.'

'You're a good man, Cedric.'

'I'm a shepherd, laddie, and it's what shepherds do. We take care of sheep, and we look out for lost folk.'

Markward ducked his head and reddened.

'How lost are ye, then?'

'I know I'm bound for Eckerheim.'

'Aye, but do you want to be going there?'

The fire crackled, the winded howled outside, and the wattle screen shook.

'Do you think the storm will pass by morning?' asked Markward.

'I do. It'll blow itself out soon enough. It's all puff and no teeth. You'll see. The sun'll be on your back before the third hour, and you'll make the Scharfgipfel before you know it.'

Markward grinned with that hard, tight grin that the shepherd read so easily.

He smiled and patted the young man on the shoulder: 'And what would you be leaving behind in Hochtal?'

Markwards shook his head. 'It doesn't matter now. Tomorrow I'll be on my way home.'

The shepherd looked at Markward for a long time, then he stirred the fire again with a stick. 'You left a girl behind, perhaps.'

'How do you know that?'

'Oh, I can see the sorrow. I was married once you know. She was a fine wife, Helga. Bore me three fine children.' He paused and stared at the flames. 'The sickness took two of them before they could run. A lad and a lassie. Golden they were, and everything to us. I think of them every day. Two and twenty winters since they're gone.'

'I'm sorry.'

'Aye, aye. It's how it goes. We had another son, Gunther. It took some of the pain. He's a shepherd like myself and married a lass from Emmsbruch. I scarce see him these days, though. He keeps a flock on the lowlands. It's well south of here.'

'And your wife?'

'Ah, Helga. Dead these ten years past. A fever took her one Summer. I miss her bad. I surely do. She was a good friend, and strong too. Kept me going in the dark days.'

He sighed and then stood up slowly. ' I'll see to your horse. You'd best get some rest.'

Markward nodded, but got up as well. 'I thank you, Cedric, but my horse is my horse. I'll look to him.'

In the morning the storm had passed. It was still overcast, but the breeze was breaking up the clouds, and the sun was already trying to break through.

Markward took breakfast with Cedric, then walked with him to the sheep fold. The shepherd planned to move the flock slowly back towards the valley of Maibach where they could Winter over.

'There's a lot of work for one shepherd', said Markward looking at the sheep as they pushed against the wicket.

'Nay, lad. Not if you know them all by name, and they all know you. Sheep are not like goats, y'know. You call and they answer. You lead and they follow.'

'But the wolves!'

'Aye, wolves that run on two and four legs! But we're alive to them, aint we my beauties!' laughed Cedric as he gazed at flock. 'They're my friends ye see. I've lost just about everything over the years, but I still have this flock. I keep these sheep for the good people of Maibach, but for me they are just like children. Up here on the heathland, we are free and happy and safe – well safe enough.' He laughed again, opened the wicket and began to call to his sheep.

Some he called with a whistle, some a click of the tongue, and some with a name – but each trotted out to him in turn. Soon the flock was all about him.

'Will ye stay awhile, Markward? I'm away to the south, and you are for the West, but we could swing away from the sun with you until you are sure of the way.'

'It's easier going for a flock to the south, Cedric. I'll come with you for a time then turn for Scharfgipfel when it's clear on the skyline.'

'Agreed!' said the shepherd.

By noon they had led the flock across the rain-drenched heathland, and down the long spur of Glabhaberl where it reached out to the distant southern lowlands. They crouched in the lee of a granite boulder and chewed rye bread and cheese, and cursed the wind that whistled through the crevices and found them out. It was a sunny enough day, but there was little warmth in it, and already they could see lines of grey geese heading south from the great grey sea where the Balts and Wend-folk dwelt.

'I'll bid you farewell here, Cedric, and turn west to Schafgipfel. I see it clearly now.'

'Aye, that's fine. But you'll lose sight of it soon enough. If you keep to the goat track, see' – he pointed and Markward nodded – 'You'll come to a little vale they call Hunter's Pass

– don't ask me why. Head up there, and it's easy going all the way to where you want.'

They shook hands, and Markward swung up into the saddle.

'Keep that broad sword loose in its scabbard, laddie', said Cedric, 'there's wolves about.'

Markward waved turned the horse's head and trotted off down the path. He had not gone far when he turned in the saddle, but a fold in the ground hid the shepherd and his flock. 'Come on boy!' he said.

Cedric was right. It was a good path, well drained and firm, and easy to follow. By the ninth hour Markward had reached Hunter's Vale. It was little more than a large open meadow with a large stand of pine at the far end. A ruined cruck, long since abandoned stood on the lee slope. Markward let his horse crop the grass for a time, and then cantered across the meadow, and skirted the woods. He breasted the low rise and gasped. There, not 2 miles distant lay Hochtal.

He stood in the stirrups and gazed open mouthed. There was no doubt about it. The single spire of Hochtal thrust through the mist, and he could just make out the roofs of the houses around the market square. Somehow, Cedric had set him on the wrong path, or he had himself wandered off it. Well, there was nothing for it, he would have to try and cut back to the north and west, and find shelter before nightfall.

He was about to flick the reins, when he took one more look towards Hochtal. The mist was swirling, spreading low and then billowing upwards. It spiralled then gathered, white and grey in a heavy cloud above the town. Just like smoke.

He looked again, staring into the fading light. It was smoke! Too much for hearth fires, and too wet for burning stubble. And there, here and there, the faint flickering of orange and yellow. The village was ablaze.

For a moment he hesitated. He could not go down there. Whatever was happening, he would not be welcome in that place. Never again. If he hadn't left of his own will, he would surely have been thrown out. Or worse. They were as like to meet him with jeers and cuffs, and a dagger thrust if he showed his face again so soon. But perhaps . . . He could not take his eyes off the burning village. Elsa was there. If she was in trouble . . . for all that she said . . . Whatever she wanted . . . She had once been his Elsa . . .

He shook the reins, put spurs to his horse and plunged down the slope.

The horse shook the cobbles as Markward galloped into the village square. All around was smoke and ash and fire. People were running, shouting and screaming, in every direction. There was the smell of blood.

Women and children were huddled in small groups, and there were bodies, some twisted and contorted, lying scattered about the square. From the midst of the smoke came the sound of clashing swords, and the groans and cries of men fighting. A dull, reddish glow filtered through the gloom, and Markward smelt the sickly stench of blood mixed with burning timber and thatch.

He loosed his sword and looked wildly around. What was going on? A figure clutching its shoulder lurched out of the smoke. Markward leaned out of the saddle: 'Tell me! Tell me! A friend! A friend!'

The man, his tunic torn and bloodied, his eyes wide, gazed up at Markward:

'The king's men! They said they were the king's men.' He pushed by and staggered away.

Easing forward towards the sound of the fighting, his eyes stinging with the smoke, and his throat already hot and dry, he was suddenly confronted by two men at arms, swords at hand. They were dragging a young woman between them. Her head was hanging down, and her hair hung about her face. She was sobbing and choking.

'Hold!'

The men stopped and looked up, then grinned.

'Out of the way, dog spittle!' one of them shouted. This one's ours. Go find your own.'

'Let her go, or I'll kill you where you stand.' Markward's voice shook.

'Oho! Will ye now? Big words from such a little man.'

Markward was suddenly aware that he heard and saw nothing except the men in front of him. Even the woman faded before his eyes, and he felt a high ringing in his ears, and his heart pounding in his chest. It was just like before battle when he stood in the shield wall and watched the enemy come on.

The men eyed him cautiously. Then one of them, barrel-chested and brindle-bearded, with a coat of mail and iron cap, shrugged and spat – and took a step forward as if to drag the woman by him.

When it's two on to one, an old soldier from Ghent had once told Markward, never be polite. Leaning quickly out of his saddle, Markward struck down with his sword. The blade bit into the mail where the neck joins the shoulder. The rings of soft iron broke under the edge of the steel blade. The man went down without a sound, almost wrenching the sword from Markward's hand. The other soldier cursed, let the woman fall forward, and lunged at Markward. He had a heavy, broad bladed short sword, ideal for close quarter fighting, but it lacked reach in an encounter such as this. The tip of the blade brushed against the brigandine, but even at full stretch there was no penetration. The man had over reached himself, and his eyes widened as he realised his mistake.

Markward twisted on the reins to bring his horse's head around, and cut low and hard with a back hand sweep. The soldier ducked, but it was not enough, and he was struck with the full force of the blow on his leather neck guard. The blade split leather and spine in one crushing blow, sending the dying soldier sprawling onto the cobbles.

Shaking, sweating, Markward swung out of the saddle and knelt by the woman.

She was face down on the muddy cobbles, still sobbing, her dark hair tangled, her kirtle torn. Gently, Markward took her by the shoulders.

'It's all right,' he said, 'They can't harm you now.' He lifted her, and she sat back, curled up like a child, shaking. 'It's all right,' he said again, trying to sound calm, and looking about him for what to do. The smoke was still swirling about, and there was still the sound of fighting across the market square. Suddenly a huddled group of folk appeared out of the smoke. A man, tall and strong armed only with a quarter staff led them. Markward called out: 'Over here!' They saw him and hurried over. The man dropped his staff knelt down and lifted the woman in his arms. He cradled her in his arms and softly called her name over and over again. ' Katrin, Katrin, I'm here Katrin, I'm here.'

The others stood nervously about. One of them, an old man with a wall eye, tugged at the man's cloak. ' Come on Lukas! We can't stay here. They'll be on us. We must go!'

Lukas looked at him, but said nothing. He glanced down at the two dead soldiers and then looked at Markward.

'You did this?'

Markward nodded.

'Then I am forever in your debt. You have given me back my wife. I thought I had lost her forever.'

'I was riding by. I saw the smoke and came.'

'God be praised you came!'

'We'll be seeing God and all His angels soon, if we don't get going!' hissed the old man. 'For pity's sake, Lukas, we must go!'

There was the roaring sound of a thatch roof crashing in somewhere in the gloom ahead, and a shower of sparks leapt above the smoke. Lukas, still cradling his wife, nodded. 'All right old Peter, all right. We'll go now. Someone, here, my staff!'

He turned to Markward: 'Come with us.'

'Thanks, but no. There's someone I must find.'

Lukas's eyes narrowed. 'I know you! You're the stranger. Yesterday! The whole village was talking about it. You and Elsa.'

'Lukas! We must go!' Peter picked up the staff, shook it, and headed away with the others. Lukas nodded again, and grunted. He followed then half turned. 'She's still alive, I can tell you that. Or at least she was when we headed this way. She and her father. Over by the mill. There's a few folk there taking shelter. Good luck!' He smiled, and disappeared into the smoke.

Markward took the reins and led his horse deeper into the village. It was a blazing ruin. He was finding it harder to breathe now, and his eyes stung and watered. He stumbled over scattered goods, and broken furnishings, and here and there a body. There was shouting ahead, even laughter, but it was mingled with the screams of women and children – and still the clash of steel, and the roaring of the fires.

As he neared the mill, he saw lit up against the flames the dark figures of armed men. There were about thirty of them, and they stood and moved as a body. No stragglers here, thought Markward. They know what they are doing. Professionals. Mercenaries. Good at what they do, and bad because they do it.

They were putting the village to the sword: the king's men, with a king's warrant, out of control, and full of blood lust and cheap beer.

He sidled into the shadows, and stroked his horse's nose. 'Easy, lad, easy. We don't want to draw attention to ourselves, just yet.'

He knew, hoped, that Elsa was somewhere out there in the darkness. And he knew that though he had lost her forever, he had to find her. He could not leave her to die like this.

There was a sudden shout, and a roar of approval and the men surged towards a building, half-hidden in the flickering shadows.

He left his horse and followed, crouching, trotting along behind, sword held low and his buckler across his chest.

The building was already on fire – the thatch had taken despite the recent rain. It was a mill with high narrow windows and a big wooden door, all set with iron studs and hinges, and it was clear that some of the villagers had taken refuge there.

'Stay in there and burn you dogs!' one of the soldiers called out and threw a blazing brand up at the windows. It bounced away harmlessly, but others followed and soon flames appeared from inside.

'They'll burn!' Markward muttered. 'And if they come out they'll be cut down.'

The door burst open, and a villager staggered out of the smoke. He was swinging a spade and yelling. Three crossbow bolts hissed out of the dark and struck him, two in the chest, one in the knee. He crumpled backwards and lay still. A younger man dashed out and tried to lift the body. A soldier laughed, and a crossbow sang, and the man was flung back into the doorway by the force of the bolt striking him in the neck.

'Enough!' Markward gritted his teeth, raised his sword, and hurled himself among the soldiers.

He knocked down three of them before they realised what was happening, but then the rest turned on him with cries and curses. He was too close for them to use their crossbows, and in the confusion many of them could hardly tell what was happening. Whirling his sword in scything arcs, he splintered shields and smashed blades aside. Twice he cut clean through spear hafts, and once he severed a man's hand at the wrist before opening his shoulder on the back-cut. He knew he must not thrust with the point. He might kill once, but never again. 'When outnumbered', the old Goslar knight used to tell him, ' clear a space with the edge of your sword, not the point – then keep it clear.'

He kept moving, shouting with each stroke, and gasping at the return. Blow after blow fell against his buckler until his arm and shoulder shook with pain and shock. He ducked and rocked back as the spears drove at his groin and throat, and once missed the savage downstroke of an axe only by leaping back, crashing against another man's shield, and then rolling away.

But it could not last. The men he fought were not village oafs or a shire levy. These were soldiers, trained in battle and easy about shedding blood.

Once they had recovered from their initial surprise, they settled calmly for the kill.

Their leader was a tall, blond haired Thuringian with bronzed conical helm, kite shield and knee length hauberk. He carried a falchion – a heavy-backed sword with a curved blade. A short-handled war-hammer hung from a belt at his waist. He smiled at Markward, spat at his feet, and then with a quick nod to left and right he shuffled forward, blade extended.

There was a clash of steel, as Markward met the attack. He swept the Thuringian's sword up, hoping to cut under the swing, but as he did so he saw two soldiers closing in from the side. He knew, too, that he was about to be struck from behind. There were just too many of them. Abandoning the cut, more by instinct than skill, he dropped to his knee and felt the breath of the axe as it swept over his head. Someone cursed, and then they were on him. His sword was torn from his hand, and he reeled as a blow from the pommel of a sword caught him high on the cheek bone. A kick to the stomach, a thrust from the butt of a lance and he was down.

The Thuringian put his boot on Markward's chest, and the tip of his sword to his throat.

'Well who do we have here?' he said, and Markward clenched his eyes, as he felt the falchion begin to bite into his neck. He thought of home, of Mutti, of little Brunni, and the October sky over the long meadow. But most of all in that blinding flash of time he thought of a girl with flame red hair.

The sword jerked against his throat, and then was gone. There were shouts, roars and screams, and the thud of feet and the ring of iron. He opened his eyes. Wherever he looked men were fighting. Some had fallen already, some were being wrestled to the ground. Some seemed surrounded by villagers, both men and women, hacking out and down at them, pounding and slashing and screaming. Flails, staves, spades and axes. A ragged Hochtaler hauled him to his feet and put his sword in his hand. 'Come on!' he said.

He blinked and staggered forward. A soldier broke free, his great sword bloodied, and a gash down his cheek. He ran wildly forward as Markward met him, swinging his own sword low and then upwards, taking the soldier where the thigh meets the groin. It was the Thuringian. His blond hair streamed back as the bronzed helmet fell, and he collapsed amidst his pursuers. There was a shout of triumph, the staves and axes rose and fell, and suddenly it was all over.

Markward, hunching over, leaned on his sword, breathing deeply, shaking.

He could feel the blood trickling down his neck, and sweat stung the wound.

All around him now was an excited babble. People were picking over the bodies for anything of value. A child poked nervously with a stick at a dead soldier, and giggled. Someone was giving some orders, but Markward couldn't make out what was being said. Slowly he straightened up and blinked as some ash got into the corner of his eye. He was tired, very tired, but he wanted to find Elsa. All the villagers had come out of the burning mill by now, and it suddenly fell in with a crash. The flames and sparks swept across the cobbles driving the people back into the shadows.

Chattering, calling out, even laughing, they emerged once more. A woman knelt by the two blackened bodies that lay near what was left of the doorway to the mill. She was keening softly, rocking back and forth, her hands stretched out over her husband and son. It was as though she could not bear to touch them, but wanted to take them in her arms.

Another woman, cloaked in a shawl, came and knelt down beside her, resting her head against her shoulder. As the fires burned themselves out the village grew quiet.

'Thank you.' A man was speaking to him.

Markward looked around.

It was Bernhardt the Blacksmith. He had a cut over one eye, and he was covered with ash and mud. In one hand he held a hammer. With the other he held Elsa. She was leaning against him, her hair all tangled, and her face stained with tears. She clung to the blacksmith.

'Thank you for what you did here,' said Bernhardt again.

Markward nodded. His throat felt dry. He could do with a drink.

'Why did you come, Markward?' Elsa smiled, and Markward felt the warmth of her voice.

'I saw the smoke. I had to.'

She paused, still smiling. 'You're shaking. Are you hurt? Your neck.'

'It's nothing.' He reached up and felt the wound. 'I'm glad I came.'

Elsa nodded and looked up at Bernhardt. 'I'm sorry, Marki.'

For a time Markward stood uneasily, then suddenly spoke; 'My horse! I left him on the other side of the square.'

'He'll be fine!' said Bernhardt. 'I'll send a lad to bring him over to our place, or what's left of it. You're welcome to lodge with my family tonight. There's not much. Those jackals burnt the barn and ransacked the house, but they've left us enough to keep warm and dry. Elsa's folks were burnt out completely. They'll be lodging in the smithy tonight.'

'I don't know,' replied Markward. 'I should be going. Elsa is safe. That's all I need to know . . . God bless you both. I mean that.' He looked at Elsa, and then turned to Bernhardt. 'You're a good man. I can see that. Take care of her.'

Suddenly he just wanted to be away and gone. Out of the burnt village and away into the night. It seemed good to be gone.

But Elsa reached forward, and put a hand on his arm. 'Stay Markward. For the night at least. Have pity on your horse, if you have none for yourself.'

He stood uncertainly, and then shrugged. 'I'll stay the night, then.' The air was full of the smell of blood, of burning, of mud and ash. The woman somewhere in the darkness was still moaning softly over her dead ones. But soon the night would be quiet, and they would bury the dead in the morning.

Markward hardly slept that night, though the family made him welcome, and he had a warm dry place by the hearth. He stared into the flames and thought of everything and nothing. His body hurt, but his mind would not let him rest. The embers had burned to a pale glow, and the early dawn light was filtering in through the rough sacking curtain across the window when he got to his feet and went outside.

It was still, peaceful with a dull grey mist lying across the sleeping village. There was that same reek that hung in the air, but it was less now, and there was a freshness to the day.

He breathed deeply, felt a muscle in his shoulder twinge, and walked towards the sound of a stream. He would wash by this stream, find his horse, saddle it, and take his leave. It would be better that way.

It was good water, clear water, fresh and sweet. It flowed from the hills, and through the village by the remains of the burnt-out mill. Markward drank and washed, and let the water run through his hands. He was tired, very tired, but it was good to be awake, to be alive, and going home.

He heard the sound of a foot on river gravel and turned. It was Elsa.

She stopped, looked down and folded her hands together in that nervous way he knew so well. 'I thought I might find you here', she said looking up quickly with an awkward smile. I was afraid you might go without saying goodbye.'

Markward grinned despite himself, 'Hah! Caught me out! Well, I'm away soon. It seems better this way.'

'You don't have to go so soon, Markward. We owe you so much, Bernhardt and I. If you hadn't have come, those soldiers, they'd have killed us all. We'd have died in the mill along with everyone else.'

'Elsa, I can't stay – you know that. You knew that two days ago when I first came and you . . .'

'I know, I know! I know I shouted. I was, I was . . .'

'You were angry . . .'

'I was afraid.'

'Afraid?'

'Yes, afraid. Oh, I don't know. Upset. Yes, upset *and* afraid.'

'Why?'

For a long time Elsa was silent. At last she spoke:

'Because, Markward! Because!' Elsa spread her hands and let them fall by her sides. 'It's hopeless, that's all, just hopeless.'

'I don't understand.'

She frowned and bit her lip. When she spoke again, her voice was calm and level, with a slight tremble. 'Marki, you never did. You never understood.'

Markward was silent, looking up at the hills, so she went on: 'We loved each other, Marki, I know we did, and I guess you still do. And the good Lord knows I still feel affection for you.' (Markward lowered his gaze.) 'But we . . . I . . . couldn't ever marry you.'

'You told your father this?'

Elsa nodded: 'Yes, yes. And he said I was right to think the way I did, and he would never force a daughter of his to marry a man, any man, against her will.'

'He's a rare man then.'

'He's a good man, and not weak, neither.'

'I've always known that, but you still haven't told me why.'

'For pity's sake, Marki! Can't you see? If I married you, you'd be off to the wars before the spring ploughing, and I'd be a widow inside a twelve month.'

'You mean . . .'

'I mean you're drawn to that king and his mad dreams like a moth to a candle.'

They stared at each other. The stream chattered away, and there were the faint sounds of the village stirring: dogs barking, a cow calling to her calf, and men trudging through the mist towards the fields. Today they would bury the dead, dampen the fires and clear the rubble – but first the cattle must be seen to, and the sheep that were scattered on the hills must be brought in.

Markward stooped and tossed a pebble into the stream. 'The king's men came. They had a warrant, so I went – even though not all went. And when I left for home, I left with a promise that I would return to the king in the spring.'

'So I was right then. You would go. You would leave me.'

'But I would love you no less.'

'But the king, more.'

'It's not like that, Elsa.'

Elsa sighed and tossed her head so that her long hair swirled across her face. 'So you say, Marki, so you say. But it is like that, and what good would all your love do me if you're lying dead somewhere in a Friesian swamp?'

'God will keep me.'

'Hah! How many lips have spoken those words so warmly, and yet are now chilled by death? God will keep you Markward of Eckerheim when you learn to keep yourself, and those who love you.'

'Elsa, listen! I see you cannot marry me, and I know you are promised to another . . .'

'I am.'

'But then, we can at least part as friends with no bitterness or anger between us.'

Elsa smiled. ' That's easily given! You will always be my friend, and I am sorry for my . . .'

'No, no', Markward waved his hand. 'No more. It's all I want – that we part as friends. You are precious to me Elsa, and always will be. A sister.'

A drover's whistle made them look round. A group of cattle appeared from beyond the barn.

'I must go Elsa. The village is safe now, and you are safe and if I ride now I can make the Scharfgipfel by nightfall.'

'If you go tomorrow you can go with the market folk. They are away to Maibach, but will travel by the Scharfgipfel, and then down the Susstal. It's safer I think.'

Markward grinned, and stood aside as the cattle splashed across the stream.

'All right. Perhaps I can help a bit here. Some of your folk may still be in the hills. As I came in last night there were people leaving.'

'Running.'

'Aye, running, but well led. A man called Lukas.'

'Lukas! My uncle's cousin. A good man. He'll be back.' Elsa smiled again, and took Markward by the hand. 'Come. There's breakfast, and then work to do.'

By the afternoon, most of the villagers who had fled – Lukas and his wife among them – had returned. There were tears, and laughter and kisses as though they had been gone for a year, instead of a single night. Everybody set to work with a will to clear and clean the village. Some of the houses would have to be completely rebuilt, others could be repaired. The dead soldiers were buried in a pit on the wasteland. The dead villagers were buried in the churchyard while the priest said Latin over them and waved a cross. A grim sky gathered overhead and a chill wind blew among across the village whipping up the ashes, and driving clouds of leaves among the ruined buildings and across the muddy streets.

To keep their spirits up the elders and the bailiff suggested that all the villagers meet in the church where it was warm and dry and relatively safe. Everyone brought something for a communal feast that evening, and reluctantly the priest agreed that a fire be set and lit in the nave, and a few of the roof tiles be lifted out to allow the smoke out. The tanner gave a bullock out of his own herd, and the beast was slowly roasted on a great spit over the blazing fire. Huddled in their cloaks and hoods and tattered kirtles the families of the ruined village crowded around the fire, drank rough maize beer, chewed on barley bread and sang old songs as they waited for the meat to cook.

Markward sat in one corner, knees drawn up to his chin and watched the shadows dancing on the walls, and beams and plastered ceiling. It was a handsome church, and difficult to burn down. Some of the villagers had fled here at the outset of the trouble, and armed with bows and staves had managed to turn the soldiers away. The priest himself had picked up a bow, and it was noted that he drew it to his ear and kissed the fletchings like a true archer. He had felled two soldiers and skewered the arm of another before the rest made off into the night.

'You'll stay with us a while, then.' Someone spoke.

Markward looked around. It was Lukas. He had come into the church by the south porch, and noticing Markward, had come straight up to him. 'I cannot thank you enough', he went on.

'You've thanked me too much this day already,' said Markward.

Lukas sat down beside him. He was streaked with sweat and grime, and his clothes were torn and scorched but he grinned cheerfully. ' You, my friend, can be a stranger to all other men, but you are a brother to me. Nothing will change that.'

'Two days ago, or was it three, I was the running dog of Eckerheim.'

'And one brave moment changed all of that – forever!' Lukas slapped Markward on the back. 'Listen my friend, my brother! I know all about you and that lass Elsa. I know your troubles, and I know the man who has cut the hope from your heart, and there's nought I can say or do about that, but . . .now hear me out, hear me out . . .You will always have a welcome in this village now, and you will always have a place to rest your head. Isn't that so, Katrin?'

Lukas' wife appeared from out of the shadows. She nodded and smiled, gave a brief curtsey, and then with a glance at Lukas bent forward and kissed Markward on both cheeks. 'For my life, for my honour', she said simply, and then was gone once more, back into the shadows.

'It was good you came, Markward of Eckerheim,' said Lukas.

'Aye, but I'm a king's man too, and it was the King's men that brought all this upon your heads.'

Lukas spat. 'King's men! King's dogs more like! No, less than that! The devil's whelps. No king of this land would ever own them, unless to hang them from the nearest gibbet!'

'Oh, aye, he'll do that right enough if he catches any of those that escaped your picks and flails, but it was his coin you found in their wallets this morning when you stripped the dead. They fought for him in the Friesian War, and bravely too I'll warrant, but once he set them loose . . .' He paused and flicked some rushes with the tip of his boot. 'It was no matter that you were his own people in his own land.'

Lukas shook his head. 'War!' he said. 'War and the King's Peace! It's all the same. Death, burning, hunger and shame. There's no end to it.'

They paused to listen to the people singing. It was a lament about a failed harvest, a harsh winter and wolves in the woods. The sound rose into the rafters, spiralling upwards with the smoke into the darkness, and then fading away as the song came to an end. Someone threw another log onto the fire, and the priest cursed as the sparks leapt toward the beams. Soon the meat would be cut and the people would be fed. Then they would sing of Springtime and green fields and the hopes of fair maidens.

'I believe in this king,' said Markward.

'Oh, hoh! Do ye now, and does he believe in you?'

Markward smiled: 'I met him once. On the road. He was every inch a king, and yet he treated us as equals.'

Lukas looked up: 'How so?'

Markward told him, and as he spoke, Lukas nodded slowly: 'Aye, aye it would fit what I have heard tell about this dark Henry. The bishops and monks love him, the barons for the most part fear him, a few ignore him, and one or two would have his head if it were within their power.'

'You know this?'

'I hear it. Shepherds' talk and pedlars' tattle I know, but it drifts in on the wind every Spring, and hangs around the hearth fires till the Fall. It's not idle rumour. He's different. Not like his father. Not a straight prince somehow. There's a twist in there. All this talk of truce and peace and no more fighting: just wild dreams, the chatter of priests and hermits. It doesn't make sense.'

'It makes sense, but not common sense.'

Lukas laughed, and stood up. 'Come now, my friend! They're beginning to eat. If we don't move soon there'll be nought but bones and gristle for us.'

The following day there was much to do, clearing up the village, repairing the damaged houses, and getting ready for the onset of Winter. Though he was ready to move on, Markward stayed to help. The people who had rejected him, now urged him to stay, though they knew that Elsa was no longer his. And so he stayed on, and worked the days away, and found good lodgings in the tanner's house which overlooked the market square.

But then as the daylight hours drew in, and Christmastide approached he made ready to leave, and chose St. Thorbald's eve to pack his gear and say his farewells.

Markward would have left the following day, but a storm broke in from the north, so he rested up for two more days. The days became a week, and the week ten days and then at last he rode out of Hochtal when the weather cleared with the dawn. He went with the market folk, and Elsa and Bernhardt watched him go. They waved as he cleared the high ridge. He turned in the saddle, raised his arm and then was gone.

'A full moon, Elsa,' said Bernhardt. 'A full moon tonight. If he doesn't reach Scharfgipfel by nightfall, he can travel the trackway by moonlight.'

'Then, moon stand still,' said Elsa, and she turned away, surprised by the tears in her eyes.

For a time Markward rode quietly with the market folk, but his horse caught a stone under its shoe, and he stopped to free it. That took some time, and when he looked up, the folk had gone, and he was alone on the heath. He looked back the way he had come, and felt the chill breeze against his face. There was no sign of Hochtal, only oak trees, black against the sky and the first rough stretches of heathland running down to the pastureland. But then he saw a movement, a figure, hurrying along the track towards him. He paused, his hand going instinctively to his sword, but he was not afraid. The man seemed unarmed, a villager – perhaps one of the market folk trying to catch up.

Markward waited and watched. At last he saw – it was Oswald, Elsa's father. He carried nothing but a staff, and there was not even a wallet at his belt. He came up to Markward and stopped, breathing heavily, his jowled face puffed out and sweating.

'Glad I caught up with you,' he said at last, and he looked about anxiously.

'My horse pulled up lame. I stopped awhile,' said Markward.

'I see.' Oswald sat down on beside the track, and laid his staff beside him. He stared at his feet, and rubbed his hands together. He spoke:

'I . . .er. . . I wanted to say something before you left . . .wanted to tell you something, no to ask you. Yes, that's right – to ask you . . . to ask something of you.'

'Yes?'

Oswald stood up, and tugged nervously at his belt. ' It's just that . . .'

'Yes?' Markward was keen to be going. He wanted to catch up with the market folk.

'I want you to stay away from Hochtal. To leave and never come back.'

Markward frowned, but didn't reply.

'Never come back, that's what I say mind you. That's never.'

'I know what never means, Oswald, and I know what you mean – you mean not before they are wed, and not after, and never again.'

Oswald grimaced and ruffled his balding hair. 'Aye, that's a fair way to put it. But I mean no insult young Markward. I owe you a debt, as more than a few of us down in Hochtal do, so it's hard for me to ask this. There seems no friendship in what I say, and precious little gratitude.'

'Ah, be at peace with that. I'll not be coming back to your village. There's nothing here for me now, not since . . .'

'Aye, I know, I know.' Oswald waved his hands about. 'Well, it all works out in the end. These things can seem hard, but they're usually for the best.'

Markward reddened, nodded and offered his hand.

Oswald took it. 'Just one more thing: promise me this.' He looked hard and clear into Markward's eyes. 'Promise me that no matter what, you'll never seek my Elsa as your woman.'

'No matter what?'

'No matter what.'

'Even as a widow?'

'Even as that, God forbid.'

Markward was silent. He stared away up the track. The sun was already pushing its way through the mist, and the cattle were in the autumn pastures above the village. He could see the cowherds, and hear them calling. They were children.

'I loved her.'

'And she you. But you can't go hammering away at a girl's affections and expect her not to crack. It's like leaving good boots out in the rain.'

'The war you mean.'

'Aye, the war. War and marriage don't go together. Never have, and never will. Even in the Bible it says a man newly wed must not go to war for a twelve month. The priest told me that.'

'Priests!' muttered Markward, and he stared at the track again.

'I know what I'm asking.' Oswald tightened his grip on Markward's hand, just a fraction. 'You're a good man, Markward – I can see that – but you're not the one for my daughter, nor will you ever be. That much I know. So it's best you know that too. For sure you should. That way we won't be muddying the waters.'

They released hands, and Markward swung up into the saddle. 'It's a clean cut, Oswald, but a deep one. Does Elsa know you came after me?'

'No, and neither Bernhardt. I told them I was off to check the hoar apple bothy, and so I am. God speed you, Markward.'

'And God keep you, Oswald! We'll not meet again.' He spurred his horse and galloped as fast as he dared up the narrow track. He didn't rein back until he caught sight of the market folk, and by then even the high pastures of Hochtal were long since lost from view.

He left the market folk by Scharfgipfel where the road forks away beneath the steep crags. They headed down towards Susstal and beyond to Maibach.

Pausing for a moment to glance back towards Hochtal, Markward turned his horse's head to the North and West and set off along the rocky path that leads across the 'Gipfel.

The moon came out as he reached the summit. It seemed as the whole world were stretched out before him in a glittering silver glow. A few twinkling lights showed where there were villages and hamlets and lonely crofts, but otherwise it was all painted in silver and shadow. He knew he should rest for the night and ride on with the dawn, but he was impatient to see home. Besides, the Scharfipfel was a grim place full of legends and dark stories.

He gave his horse some water, and let it crop the grass awhile. It was quiet up there on the rugged heights above the heathland, so still, so deserted. The stars came out, bright and clear. He felt he could reach out and touch them, perhaps pick one and put it in his wallet and take it home to Brunni. He stared upwards. They were beautiful, and cold and far away even though they seemed so close.

There was a ring around the moon. 'A frost tonight,' he said to himself, 'And this is no place to be when it comes.' An owl hooted from somewhere below among the twisted trees that clung to the slopes, and his horse looked up and whinnied.

'Come on lad,' Markward said, 'We'll ride tonight with the full moon, and be on the road to Eckerheim by the morning.'

Far away, in Hochtal, the villagers were all abed, and the dogs kept watch in the doorways and the barns. Elsa lay on her bed and stared up at the rafters lit by the flickering firelight. She thought of Markward and she thought of

Bernhard. She thought of sorrow and joy, and she thought of the moon standing over the Scharfgipfel. At last she slept.

Winter came early that year to the Harz and its Northern reaches. Snow clouds drove in from the Baltic, and with them came the sudden raids of the Liutizen. Out of the forests they came, lean and bright eyed, riding on shaggy little ponies, or marching with a weird rolling gait in fur boots bound with leather. They burnt, they destroyed, they looted. They left the snow stained with the blood of their victims and slew without pity men, women and children. They took slaves as they needed, roping them together, and driving them back across the ruined fields and into the endless forests and marshes from whence they had come. They were the Liutizen, and they were feared as men fear wolves and children fear the night.

They were the Liutizen, and they were hated as all men hate the plague and beg God that it might not touch them. The priests taught that they dwelt in darkness and made war against the light, that they were the scourge of Christendom, and that they drank the blood of chosen prisoners sacrificed to pagan gods when the moon was full. The warlords taught that much of what the priests said was nonsense, and that the Liutizen were mighty warriors, skilled with sword and bow, fearsome in battle and masters of the sudden ambush.

The king taught that the Liutizen threatened the king's peace, and that the king's sword was against them as the cliffs of the Neuburg stood against the sea.

FIRE AND SNOW

The good people of Maibach knew all of this, and much more when the Liutizen came upon them that morning. They suffered. And the news of all they suffered was carried by a shepherd who was driving his flock to market along the Susstal when he saw the shattered town, blackened and smoking in the snowy fields.

Cedric the shepherd stood on the edge of the woods and looked down on what was left of Maibach. He shook his head slowly and gave a low whistle. Then he turned and spoke to his sheep: 'There's nothing for us here, my little ones', he said. 'We'll be back to the tops, and away to the heather. There's nought here but death and madness.' He led the flock back into the shelter of the woods and searched until he found a clearing hidden from all but the most careful eyes. The day was full but it was chill, and heavy with the dull warning of snow to come. The flock settled around him. He wrapped himself in his old grey cloak, took a flint from his wallet and some shavings from the folds of his tunic and made a little fire.

And that's where the market folk of Hochtal found him. They too had come down the Susstal, and seen the ruins of Maibach, and had headed into the woods. They came silently, cautiously out of the shadows, and Cedric knowing that he was a dead man to an enemy, but safe to a friendly stranger raised his hand in greeting.

They gathered about him, men and women, fearful, clutching their market goods. They trembled with the cold and the thought of that burnt out village.

'Are we welcome?' said one at last, an older man with an awkward stoop, and a quarter staff across his shoulder.'

'Aye, aye. Ye are welcome. Come to the fire, though it's a poor one I confess. Warm yourselves, and rest now, but I have precious little in the way of food or drink. I was hoping to . . .'

'We, too. But we have food enough, and drink enough to share. Maibach has gone. It has gone to the Liutizen.'

'I know it. I have seen it myself. And the king must hear of it, too. That's why you find me hiding in these woods, with snow on the way and trees alone for shelter.'

The man of Hochtal who had spoken was Rainald. He spoke for the others. They were too weary, or too shocked to speak for themselves, and as they crouched around the fire and spread their hands to its warmth the first flakes of snow drifted quietly down. So Rainald spoke. He rubbed his hands together and blew into them, and then his voice came in that soft, gravel lilt that the men of Hochtal have.

'We are from Hochtal, over the west ridges. On our way to market. Trying to do some trade before the winter snows set in. Furs mainly. Rabbit, stoat and polecat – but a few more things besides.'

Cedric nodded and put some bracken on the fire. They watched it crackle and blaze. Rainald went on. 'This is not all of us. The others have turned back. Back along the main path. But I wouldn't go that way. I told them. Those devils from the East will sniff it out and run them down before the morning.'

'Aye, or follow them all the way back to your village.'

Rainald grimaced. 'What's left of it. We had a visit from the king's men.'

He told Cedric of all that had happened, and mentioned what Markward had done.

Cedric raised his eyebrows and smiled. 'Ah! True love makes lions out of sheep, and madmen out of wise.'

'You know him, then.'

'Aye, I do. In passing. He took shelter with me. There was a storm on the heath, and it blew him in like a half-drowned swallow. He was on his way back from Hochtal. He had been to see his girl.'

'His girl no more. She's to be wed to another.'

'Aye, so it would seem.'

The snow was falling more thickly now. They built up the fire as best they could, and huddled together. One of the womenfolk passed round some bread. Another had a round of cheese. There was some dried fruit, and vinegar wine that made the shepherd cough, but warmed him to his bones.

It was dark. A wolf called somewhere away off in the woods, and its mate answered with a high-pitched yelp.

Cedric put his head on one side and listened. There was silence, just the crackling and hissing of the fire.

'Wolves?' asked Rainald.

'Maybe,' said Cedric, 'but they're wolves that go on two legs and not on four.'

'How so?'

Cedric stood up. 'Just one call, and just one answer. And see, the flock didn't stir. They know the difference between man and beast.'

Rainald stood too, and stared into the darkness: 'Liutizen?'

Cedric nodded. 'And not far away neither. They're tracking someone.'

'Us?'

'Could be. We're well sheltered here, so they shouldn't be able to see the fire quite yet, but I guess we should put it out.'

' Now?'

'Aye, now. Better cold than dead and cold.' He scattered the fire with his boot, and the others quickly trod out the embers. It was suddenly freezing and very dark. A boy among the market folk began to cry. His mother held him close and whispered to him. The sheep stirred but were silent. Rainald noticed that they kept in a tight circle, each one looking towards Cedric. He had heard of such flocks, that were so loyal to their shepherds, and that could keep silent when danger threatened.

They waited, and the time crept by, and the snow fell. Their breath came in steaming clouds, and they shook with the cold. Soon the snow had all but covered them in a cloak of freezing whiteness. Unless the Liutizen came straight upon them, they might yet escape.

The wolf called again. The answer came, this time more guttural. It was much closer now, off to the right. Cedric slid his saex blade out of the leather sheath he wore at his hip. Rainald took hold of his staff in both hands and nodded to the other men among the market folk. Slowly they freed their arms: here and there the glint of a dagger; one man had a hammer, but most had staves, each one long since tempered over a fire and rubbed with grease to keep it from cracking.

The snow was slackening now, and it whirled down in fierce little flurries, as the clouds moved away. Cedric licked his lips, and tasted the cracked and dry saltiness of the skin. He kept looking to the right, and signalled for Rainald to watch their front and left. Nothing moved about them, save the last wild flakes of snow. How long could they last?

And then a branch snapped about thirty paces ahead of them. One of the market folk gave a short gasp, but no one moved. The sheep stirred again, but Cedric raised his hand slightly and they settled instantly.

After a time, there was the faint sound of footfalls crunching through the snow. And they could hear the branches of a furze bush rattle as someone pushed their way carefully towards them.

For the third time the 'wolf' called, now well to the left and behind them. When the Liutizen scout answered he seemed almost upon them. There was a shadow moving out there in the dark scarcely twenty paces distant. It paused, turned, waited and then at last drifted slowly by, fading into the gloom with a last few crunching steps. – And then it was gone.

They waited in the cold and dark. The snow stopped, the skies cleared, and the trees began to creak and crack as the early frost settled over the forest.

It was Cedric who finally lifted his head, paused and then shook the snow from his shoulders. He looked out into the shadows, waited again, and then slowly stood up. Carefully, uncertainly, the others followed, brushing the snow from their cloaks and caps, and stamping their feet to get the blood moving once more.

'They're gone?' asked Rainald.

'They're gone. Headed back East, which is good. Means they've given up.'

'We can light a fire then.'

Cedric shook his head. 'Not just yet. Just in case they circle round for one last look to the north. You can spot the glow from a fire under clear skies, forest or not.'

The sheep stood up from where they had been buried in the snow. They looked at Cedric who whistled softly to them. They bleated, just once, and then sat down again.

'Never seen that before,' said Rainald beating his arms across his chest, and stamping up and down.

'Then you need better shepherds in Hochtal,' replied Cedric and smiled, and hit him gently on the shoulders.

The market folk gathered about, glad to be on their feet, but still fighting against the cold, and looking around anxiously into the dark. The womenfolk – there were three of them – were worried about one of the children, a boy of about ten years. He was coughing badly, shaking, and deathly pale. They wrapped him in a shawl, and rubbed his back and chest as best they could.

At last one of them turned to Cedric: 'We must light a fire, or move on. He'll die if we just do nothing.'

'And there's a chance we'll all die if we light a fire, or move too soon.'

'Then so be it! I'll not stand here and watch the lad freeze to death. He's my sister's son, and I said we'd look after him.' For the first time she raised her voice, and Cedric saw her eyes begin to water.

He turned away, took two steps and then turned back. 'Well, all right. I'm not your leader anyway, but you seem to want me to help. I guess I know the lands around here a little better than yourselves.' He stopped, then looked about uncertainly. Rainald nodded encouragingly, and the others gathered about him.

'There's a few hours till dawn. No good blundering about in the dark at this time. If we don't attract the Liutizen, we'll probably draw in the bears and wolves. Bears won't settle for the Winter yet, and the wolves are hungry all the time.'

'But if we light a fire . . .'

'If we light a fire . . .Who knows? Still, at least we'll be warm, and the lad here will probably survive.'

Rainald frowned: 'But the Liutizen! You said . . .'

'I know, I know what I said, but if we put a watch out beyond the fire, say thirty paces, we can at least get warning if someone approaches.'

'That's cold work, Cedric.'

'Aye, I know that too, but we'll spell on the hour – I've got a length of candle here with the hours marked – and we'll only use the menfolk.'

Rainald thought, and rubbed his chin and looked across at the sick boy. 'Well, start with me then,' he said.

Markward peered cautiously out of the cave. It was dark, but the ground shimmered white with snow under a frosty moon. He shivered, and looked again. All was still. He took a short breath, and his chest hurt with the icy air. The trees stood out black against the snow. They were silent, motionless. Not a sound.

He ducked back into the cave, where his horse was standing, its head almost brushing the roof.

'Well, lad, no chance of Eckerheim in the morning.' He gave it a gentle slap and went and sat down next to the little fire he had lit in the middle of the cave on a small circle of stones. He had found dry wood and furze branches in the cave – it was clear someone used it, perhaps a shepherd, so it was easy for him to get a cheerful blaze going. The smoke seemed to filter away as it swirled along the roof – there was a natural chimney somewhere above his head - and the bitter cold stayed outside.

Markward kept his sword by his side, and out of its scabbard. There was always a danger of intruders, perhaps even of a bear who had claimed the cave for the Winter. Scharfgipfel was a lonely and fell place, but the weather had trapped him here this night, so there was little he could do but wait for the morning. The snow had stopped, but it was too cold and too dark to ride in safety. Despite the moonlight, the trees and rocks cast deep shadows which meant he could easily lose his way, and perhaps ride over a precipice.

As he sat and stared at the flames his mind kept drifting back to Elsa.

He could not forget her, though she was gone, lost to him forever, and betrothed to another man, and a good man too – confound him!

Well, he would return to Eckerheim in the morning, and leave Scharfgipfel and Hochtal and all its people behind him. And then, it would be back to his king, and back to the wars. He had promised, and it would be so.

His father had told him that a man's word was his honour, and that no matter how sharp a sword it could only strike true in the hands of an honourable man. His father had been a farmer, but he had served in the royal muster for twenty years, and his great iron sword had hung over the fire place ever since Markward could remember. That sword and his father were one. The royal warrant that the provost-marshal had signed over to Markward was his bond, but his word was his honour and it was bound to the memory of his father: that more than anything was dragging him back to the king, and the king's peace. It could break his life, he knew it, and could break the hopes of others he loved, but it must be so.

Still, he feared to go, but not for what lay ahead. Since he had lost Elsa, death seemed of far less account to him. But what he feared was what he would be leaving behind. He had fought the King's men at Hochtal, but they were only a few among many of their kind. It was not over.

At any time others like them might swoop down on the villages and hamlets of this province, on Eckerheim itself – and he, away to the wars, would be powerless to help. If only the lord of the manor, the Markgraf himself were there, all would be well. No one would dare to cause trouble among his people while he was there in the Burg. But he had not been in Eckerheim or in any of his villages for nearly a year – he was fighting at Henry's side. He and his little force of knights were valued as much as any in the king's army, and the Salian prince was loth to let them return home before the campaigning was over.

The fire began to die down. Markward searched around for more fuel, bracken and twigs, and threw them on. The blaze sent shadows dancing up the walls of the cave, but it soon died down once more. He drew his cloak around him, and lay down as close to the ashes as he dared. 'God keep me', he said, and slept.

He awoke with a start. For a moment he did not know where he was, but the faint glow of dawn creeping in through the pitch dark told him. He got up, stretched and staggered to the entrance of the cave. It was a morning of heavy frost. Through the branches of the trees he could see the first tinges of a steel blue sky. It still hurt to breathe. He thumped his chest and turned away. It was time to saddle his horse and make the icy ride down the slopes of Scharfgipfel.

As Markward took the first careful steps away from the cave, leading his horse to open ground, he noticed that the moon still hung shimmering above the forest. It was a false dawn, but there seemed little point in turning back now. There was light enough to travel by, and though the frost was heavy, the snow was firm under foot, and there was plenty of grip for both man and horse.

As they came out into a clearing, the ground fell way in a steep slope high above the valley floor. The fields and copses far below glistened in the moonlight. It was silent, beautiful and still. If he could clear the Scharfgipfel by sunrise, then by noon he might yet make the high road to Eckerheim.

He clicked his tongue, shook the reins and began the descent. It was cold, and icy, and the path was rocky and treacherous, but the moon shone full and clear so that his horse was able to pick its way without stumbling.

He felt and saw his own breath in painful clouds of steam which froze against the stubble of his beard. The cold struck across his forehead, and tore at his fingers through the leather of his gauntlets. His heavy woollen cloak seemed to do little against the steely air, and he was soon so chilled he felt that if the sun didn't rise soon he would have to turn back. It was safer travelling in the early hours before dawn in these parts, but he did not know if he could endure

the biting of the frost. He tried whistling to himself through his
cracked lips to keep up his spirits, but the burning sensation was too
much and he had to stop. Even when he sang an old hunting song
almost under his breath, it was as though he was gulping in handfuls
of glass, so he wrapped his scarf about his face, and rammed his
arming cap hard down, almost over his eyes – and rode on.

His horse's hooves rang against the ice-covered stones, sending
sharp little echoes scudding away amidst the trees. But otherwise all
was silent, except for the gasping breath of man and beast.

Down and down, in a slow, painful, cramping spiral he descended
the Scharfgipfel. On and on through the bitter stillness, beneath the
moon. When at last he felt he must cry out with pain and cold, he
saw away to the East the skyline suddenly brighten. The ghostly
shadow-whiteness of the night fell back before the rising sun. All at
once – or so it seemed – there was red, and gold and a soft, soft
yellow all atop the far ridges where they flowed away to the Liutizen
lands.

It was no warmer, but it was brighter, and Markward knew that
soon the warmth would come. It came little by little, creeping in
across the tree tops till he felt it reach out and touch his face. He had
come through the worst. There was no more point in turning back,
and no more profit in stopping. He had to go on. Down and down
he went, his horse snorting steam, impatient for gentle meadows and
easier going. Down, and down, sometimes through frozen thickets,
sometimes through crouching heather, sometimes among groves of
pale and twisted mountain beech. And as he went down, so the sun
rose – brighter than warmer. It was a comfort to him, and his spirits
lifted as it rose. At last as the sun crested a ridge of poplars he
reached the foot of the last spur of Scharfgipfel where it looked away
to the North and East.

He almost sang with relief, but he merely slapped his horse's flank,
and whispered in its ear: 'Well done, boy –well done!'

There was a frosty pasture ahead, trapped between two stands of
birchwood. He trotted across to it, and looked around. Yes, it would
do. There was shelter here, and wood to make a fire, and water
nearby in a little stream half hidden among ferns and bracken.

Swinging painfully out of the saddle, he beat his arms across his chest. A fire, yes, he would build a fire and take a meal and rest his horse awhile. He had tinder and kindling in his saddle bags, and the dead branches in the lee of those rocks looked dry enough. He would build a fire. Then they could set off to the north until they struck the road to Eckerheim.

It was a good fire. It warmed him — or at least his chest and face and hands. He squatted down by it, as he ate a breakfast of coarse bread, cheese and bacon. There was water from the stream, but it was too cold to drink yet, and he stood it in a little wooden cup near the fire. That little cup! How he loved it, and how his friends had laughed to see him with it, as they sat around King Henry's camp fires on the great marches to the west. That little cup! Brunni had made it for him three summers ago, and hid it under blankets in the cruck, and gave it to him at Stephenstide. A small, brown wooden cup — he took it with him wherever he went. It was his keepsake, against he knew not what. Some men wore crucifixes, or old pagan charms. A few men even had copper rings they wore high on their arms as if they themselves were ring-bearers. Many had monkish relics picked up from wayside pedlars or wandering friars: nails from the Holy Cross, tears from the Virgin Mary, a feather from the Archangel Gabriel and all manner of trifles and trinkets that soldiers kissed and rubbed against their brows before a battle.

But Markward had the little brown cup. It always made him smile no matter what. It made him think of little Brunni, and Mutti and all the family, and all the folks of Eckerheim, good, honest and not so honest. And it made him think of the long meadow, and the land he might have one day when he came back from the wars for the last time. He would build a cruck on the edge of that meadow if his lord the Markgraf gave consent. And he would make a home there, of some sort. And he would stand at the door of the cruck when the sun set fair on a clear summer's day and look down, all the way down, the long, bright meadow.

His horse whinnied and he looked up. A rook screeched somewhere among the high trees to his right. And then he saw it. It flapped lazily into the air, circled and then settled again. Then nothing.   Markward waited, listened, and slowly stood up. Still nothing. He looked around. It was an empty place, and cold, almost quivering in the morning frost – a white world of white ice clinging to the branches and covering the rocks and grass. So peaceful. So cold. Too quiet. He counted slowly as he listened and looked – listening for the faintest of sounds: a twig breaking beneath a footfall, bracken being moved carefully aside – and looking for the merest movement from behind the rocks or among the trees. He counted to twenty under his breath – his fingers and his toes – twenty. That was how he was taught by the old hunter from Ruhhaus: at the least sign of alarm, stand stock still and slowly count to that number. No more, no less. Then wait, then count again.

There was nothing. Just the burble of the stream. He squatted down again, and continued his breakfast, but he couldn't help glancing nervously about him. This place no longer seemed safe. It would be best to leave it. He kicked the fire out, drank quickly from the little cup, and got ready to leave.

He swung back into the saddle, tensing himself for the sound of a bow string, and the zifft of a black barbed shaft. His spine tingled and his hands trembled just a little, as he shook the reins and moved out across the clearing, over the stream and into the broken heath land. He no longer felt the cold, but he knew it was still freezing. This was not a good place, and he was keen to be gone. He galloped hard when he reached some open ground, and leant forward in the saddle the icy air cutting into his face and hands.

The snow and ice splashed up around him, and across his horse's flanks. He slowed as the snow deepened, and finally came to a walk.

'Good lad!' He patted the throbbing brown shoulder and neck, and looked across the whitened vastness of the heath.

Cedric paused. He stopped and raised his hand, and the market folk halted behind him. The flock straggled about them. They had come out of the forest some time ago, and now were struggling across the open ground toward the road to Eckerheim.

The snow was deep, but still frozen, and they crunched across it, sometimes sinking to their knees between the clumps of heather and broom, sometimes hauling the sheep bodily through the narrow drifts. The sun was up, the mist was clearing and at last they could see.

Cedric looked again. There it was: a figure, a figure on a horse, not more than half a mile away, and moving across their path.

Rainald came up beside the shepherd. 'Liutizen?'

'No. They go mostly on foot, and when they ride they come at you on those shaggy little ponies the Lapps and Balts use.'

. 'A king's man then.'

'Aye, could be, but I'll warrant he's bound for Eckerheim and I think I know him, by the way he sits that horse.'

Rainald looked at Cedric in surprise. 'You must have eyes like an eagle.'

'Hah! Not like an eagle, but like an old shepherd, perhaps. I know that lad, and you know him too.'

They hurried on, and sent one of the younger men ahead, across the snowy heath towards an outcrop of rock about three hundred paces away. He scrambled up it. As he reached the top and waved, they saw the horseman hesitate, then turn towards them.

'He's seen us!'

'Aye he has,' said Cedric. 'I just hope he's the only one. If the Liutizen catch us out here in the open, we're dead men, all of us.'

A short while later Markward leant down from the saddle and shook Cedric warmly by the hand.

'Well met! Well met! I see you still have your flock, and another one besides.' Markward looked at the market folk, and acknowledged their nods and smiles.

Cedric grinned. 'This is Rainald – but you know him of course, by sight if not by name. These folk are all from Hochtal and were bound for . . .'

'For Maibach.'

'Aye, and Maibach is no more.'

Markward cursed under his breath: 'No more!. Not the king's . . .'

'Ach, no. Not this time. This time is was the Liutizen.'

'Wolves from the East!'

'Aye, wolves — and enough of them to burn Maibach and more besides. We could not hunt them down, and so they hunted us. Nearly took us too, but the snowy night wrapped about us, and they passed by like shadows.'

Markward shook his head in dismay. 'They'll head for Hochtal then.'

'Mayhaps.' Cedric shrugged. 'What think you, Rainald?'

'I think we'll freeze if we stand here much longer, and whether or not they head for Hochtal is not my care. Hochtal is my home, and that's where I'm bound no matter what — all of us.'

For a time Markward stared, his brow furrowed. If the Liutizen having razed Maibach, turned to the West — which they would do - , then Hochtal lay in their path, and after that Eckerheim. He saw now that these market folk and Cedric had swung wide out of the forest to avoid the Hochtal Road. It would surely now be too late to give a warning to the village. Elsa!

Rainald seemed to read his thoughts. 'I know it. They'll reach the village before us, if they're not already there. It's hopeless, but we have to go. It's our home, and our folks . . .'

Markward nodded and held up his hand wearily. Elsa! He must go back to Hochtal, but he could never get there in time and there could be nothing there but death. There was no pity in the Liutizen, and there would be nothing left of the village except what was fit to bury. Hopeless.

And then a single crushing thought came upon him: he could warn Eckerheim. If he left now, turned his back on Hochtal and rode hard across the heath and through the snow there was a chance he could get to Eckerheim in time enough to warn the folk there and clear the village. But it would have to be now.

He swung his horse's head as if to go, and Cedric caught the bridle: 'Whoa! Where to, young Markward?'

The horse stamped and snorted, but Markward reined it in. 'I'm away to Eckerheim, to warn the folks.' He could feel the tears starting in his eyes, and brushed them away with his arm.

Cedric let go the bridle and stepped back. 'It's a hard choice you have there — where these folks have none at all.'

'I must go, Cedric, I must.'

'And where's your heart, good lad – tell me that.'

'In two places, and in two pieces. Wherever I go there will be sorrow.'

'And regret.'

'You don't make it easy, old friend.'

The shepherd laughed. 'I thank you for remembering my friendship, but I'll not thank you for remembering my age.'

Markward smiled, and bent low from the saddle. 'God be with you, Cedric.'

'And God speed you.' He slapped the horse on the flank, and Markward spurred away as best he could across the snow covered heath.'

They watched him go, and then took their own path which would lead them towards Hochtal. It was slow going. They were tired, desperately tired, and the sick child, though able to walk a little, had to be half carried by two of the menfolk.

'If there's nothing for us in Hochtal,' said Cedric as they crunched through the snow, 'What then?'

Rainald sighed and shortened the strap on his pack. 'Well, it's pity for us, and the road to nowhere, but I'm hoping there'll be enough of something left in the village for us to scratch a living. The Markgraf will surely hear of this and come back from the wars. He'll see us right. He's a good lord.'

'Aye, but he's not here, is he? He's deaf and blind to all that goes on here. He's away with the king's army. They will be at Goslar by now.'

'At Goslar!'

'Aye, and in no mood to come out of winter quarters because of some rumour about a winter raiding party.'

For a time they tramped on across the heath, encouraging the others, and shepherding the flock. It seemed a little warmer and the snow wasn't so deep. They could feel the firmness of the track beneath their tired feet. The clouds hung low and grey over the horizon, but the breeze was slight, and the gripping chill of last night had gone.

'What do you think of our king, then?' asked Rainald as they came upon a scrub covered ridge, and looked down the broad sweep of grassland that would take them home.

'He's a king like any other.' Cedric spat, then touched his forelock to show no insult was meant. 'But he's not the measure of his father'.

'Say, how so?' Rainald looked across at the shepherd.

'His father had iron in his soul, and iron in his fist. He left the praying to the priests. This Henry is too precious for my liking.'

'And that's why you think . . .'

'And that's why I think he'll huddle up in Goslar for the Winter and send us nothing but prayers and good wishes to keep myself and folks like you alive.'

'If he knew what was going on.'

'If he knew.'

Rainald grunted and held his peace. Whether the king knew or not, or whether he came or not seemed to matter little now. All he knew was that Hochtal was probably in flames, and all or most of the villagers put to the sword. He shook his head, as the folk began to clamber and slither down the slope. So much had happened in so few days. He had known hard winters and lean times, but nothing to match this, and it wasn't even Christmastide.

They reached the base of the slope, rested up for a time and then pushed on. The clouds began to break and a keen wind soughed up the valley cutting into their faces. They crouched and pulled hoods and scarves about them and staggered on. The sheep that had come so far, and so silently, began to fall behind and drift apart, bleating as they struggled in the snow. Cedric paused, looking anxiously left and right. He cursed and bit his lip, and drove his staff into the ground.

'Enough!' he muttered.

Rainald stopped and turned around, and saw the shepherd standing in the midst of his exhausted flock. 'We'll camp with you here, Cedric.'

'Nay, but you won't', replied Cedric. 'You've a home to go to, and things to see to. My home is here. These sheep are my people. We'll meet the darkness as it comes along this little valley, and rest in the meanwhile.'

'Out here? In this?'

'Aye, aye. In this! Now get you gone. The way is clear enough, and if you bend your backs you'll make it before nightfall. No torches mind – you'll attract nothing but trouble if you light your path.'

Rainald hesitated. 'It doesn't seem right.'

'No matter how it seems. Look to your own folk, I'll come on in the morning.'

There was a silence. Both men faced each other. The market folk stood wretchedly waiting. At last Rainald nodded, and took Cedric by the hand: 'In the morning, then', he said and turned away.

Cedric watched them go, and called his sheep. 'Huddle close my beauties. There's warmth between us, and grass beneath this snow. You've come far this day. You've done well, and see! - we are all still here.' He clicked his tongue, and whistled, as he moved among them rubbing their backs and necks and ears. They called back to him, and he smiled and spoke to them again.

'Such times, my little ones – such times, but we will see this winter out, and we will taste the fresh spring grass. What say you?'

Markward rode as if in a dream. It was as if the countryside rolled away – no melted – beneath the hooves of his gasping horse, and unseen hands lifted them both up and carried him towards Eckerheim. His eyes smarted from the cold and the brightness of the snow, and his head felt light, and once or twice he swayed and nearly fell from the saddle. But there was no sense of pain or even weariness. He was simply there, being drawn towards Eckerheim, and away from Hochtal, and there was nothing he could ever do to change it. Elsa was in Hochtal, Mutti and Brunni and the folks were in Eckerheim. He loved them all, but there was no more he could do for Elsa now, and there was everything he could do for the others.

His horse stumbled, and nearly fell. He was thrown hard against the pommel of the saddle, and reeled back, both hands on the reins. The blow to his midriff was cushioned by the brigandine, but the pain and nausea jolted him wide awake. As the pain cleared, and the horse steadied to a trot he looked about him. He knew this land. He had not come this way for years, but he knew it well enough. It was harsh, open, wild land, good for hunting, but little else.

The low scrub, and rocky outcrops looked strangely beautiful beneath the thin crust of snow, and as the light faded over the far horizon a soft crimson spread across the sky.

The breeze was up again, but it was at his back, and if it held would drive him home by evening tomorrow. He rode on, eager to find shelter before the night swept in across the moorland heath. The Liutizen, men said, prowled like wolves at night, and it was 'best to hide, not ride' if you wanted to see the dawn.

At last, as the snowy drifts stiffened beneath the evening chill he spotted a fold in the ground protected by a ragged spinney of birch, and a low tumble of grey boulders. He could build a fire here, and his horse could graze. It would be cold, but it would do.

Some miles away to the east and south, Cedric and his flock sheltered in the little valley that led to Hochtal. And further on, at the head of that valley, Rainald and the Market folk crested the narrow pass, and looked down upon their village.

It looked quiet, almost peaceful beneath the moon. It was still, etched out by ice and moonlight against the broken forest that ringed the common land. The jumble of rooftops was still there, but here and there they could see the wooden skeletons of roof beams once covered by tiles or thatch, and even in the frosty chill they smelt a sickly burning carried by the dying breeze.

For a long time they stood and stared down at the village, hoping, praying for a single flickering light – just one – or the sound of voices that they knew, or even just the bark of a lone dog. But nothing came, nothing but silence and the faint smell of burning.

Slowly, carefully they came down the long lea towards the village. And as they came they began to make out scattered patches in the snow between the blackened buildings: sprawling patches, broken twisted shapes – people.

There were children, men, women – lying in the snow: dead, bloody, torn.

The closer the market folk came, the more they saw, and their groans and sighs grew louder until finally they broke down in shouting, sobbing howls of rage and grief. They rushed forward and fell about the bodies, kneeling, crouching, lifting up loved ones and cradling them to their chests.

For Rainald the blow fell again and again: his children, his wife – he could scarcely breathe. There in the bloody snow – and all his half-held desperate hopes that somehow, somewhere, someone might have escaped were dashed in a moment. He knelt, shaking, wide eyed, transfixed by the sight of his slaughtered family. They had died together, the children about their mother – clinging to her, and she to them as the weapons rose and fell. Dead, all dead. The anguish took hold of him from deep inside, welling up, flooding his chest and throat, and roaring in his skull till he thought his heart would burst. He threw back his head and cried out, a single drawn out cry and his cry echoed through the village. And he was alone. They were all alone with those they had lost, and the darkness came, and crept over them, yet they did not move. Even in the bitter cold they stayed with the dead, keening, and weeping and holding them close.

At last it was Rainald, his eyes sunken, his jaw slack with grief, who lurched to his feet and ordered the folk to take shelter.

'We bury them tomorrow,' he said, and wondered that his voice sounded so hollow, so different, as though it was not him that spoke, but some quiet friend who stood beside him and took on the task he could not bear.

The others hesitated, looking up at him.

'Come', he called gently. 'We can do nothing for them. They are at rest, God rest them.' He put his hand to his brow and clenched his eyes, and the tears coursed down his cheeks. 'We'll find shelter – see, in Matti's house. The roof is good. We'll light a fire, and maybe find some food.'

They got to their feet. It was Elspeth, wife of Oskar the tanner who then spoke: 'We cannot leave them here. We cannot leave them in the snow for the wolves and foxes to find. If we took them in, we could bury them tomorrow, priest or no priest.'

Rainald nodded. 'Aye, let's do that. There's room enough in barn by there.'

He stooped and gently picked up his wife, his own dear Ada whom he had kissed for the first time so many years before in the grove by the mill race. So cold, so lifeless she hung in his arms like a broken doll, but her hair still shone as it had when he had kissed her farewell the day he left for Maibach. He carried her to the barn, and laid her down. Then back for his two sons Ralf and Simon, so little, so shrunken in the snow – and then at last for his daughter, his Hetti, his bright eyed one, not yet three years old.

As he took her up, her cheek brushed his, and for a moment he felt warmth.

He stopped. She looked so cold, so pale, so still. Surely it could not be. Again he lifted her close. A faint warmth. There was no mistaking it. He gasped.

'Hetti!'

Someone put their hand on his shoulder. He turned. It was Elspeth. 'She lives? Your little one lives?'

'I . . . I don't know. She's warm. See! She's warm on the cheek.'

'If she's warm she lives, but mayhaps she's dying. Give the lass here.'

They hurried her indoors, and laid her in among some blankets and rubbed her feet and hands.

There was blood about her head – lots of blood, her hair was matted with it, but the cut was not deep. She was bruised about the face, and swollen, but she was warm – just.

Elspeth knelt down and put her own face to the little girl's mouth. She waited. She waited, and then gave a faint smile. 'She breathes. It's precious shallow, but she breathes. It was the cold was killing her, not the blow.'

'She breathes! She breathes!' Rainald stepped forward, then back, then waved his arms and crouched down. ' Hetti breathes!'

'Aye, ye loon, but not for long unless you get a fire built. Quick, get you gone and find some tinder.'

He turned and looked wildly about, the aching sorrow of his loss, now mingled with excitement and joy.

He had lost all and then found much, but his grief still burned fiercely. If his little one might live, then he might live, and have someone to live for. He scrambled about in the corner of the barn and found some old hurdles of dried wattle. They broke easily, and he soon had a fire going on the hard earth floor of the barn. Elspeth and another of the women moved little Hetti close to the blaze and bathed her wounds. She was still pale, almost blue and grey, but at length she began to breathe more easily, and once or twice her eye lids flickered.

'Such a bonny wee thing,' said Elspeth as she wrapped the girl more closely in a blanket.

'Aye', sighed Rainald. 'She takes after her mother, right enough.'

Elspeth looked up, but said nothing and Rainald turned away. 'I'll be getting some more wattle', he said.

The darkness deepened over Hochtal, and the wolves came down from the wooded hills, drawn by the smell of death. Some of the men lit a fire in front of what was left of the tanner's house and kept watch. Two of them had just brought in the body of the priest. He had been nailed to the church door – and killed with an arrow to the throat. 'Strange shrift for a priest', muttered one man. 'The Liutizen like better to let the holy men die slow.' His companion, a tall spare farmer with a crooked nose, grunted. 'True, but if a man fights well, they let him die well. They crucified our priest as a priest, they killed him as a warrior.'

Out in the darkness a wolf howled, and another answered, and another, just beyond the stream.

The men piled more wood on the fire and watched the sparks whirl upwards.

And as men do, they talked of what the day had brought, and what the morrow would bring. There was no shortage of fuel in the shattered village and few folk to argue over it. In the morning – if the Liutizen didn't come back – they would see if there was enough left of Hochtal to build once more, and to start again. The grain was gone, or scattered and spoilt. The village well was blocked, and all the houses around the market square looted: that much they knew. Someone said that the king would surely hear and bring help. Another laughed and said that would be a fine thing if the king arrived before Summer. One of the lads had found three clay bottles of maize beer in the corner of a burnt-out cruck. They sat and drank – not enough to forget their sorrow, but enough to feel some warmth. Few would sleep tonight, and the day ahead would be long and harsh – but they were home, and they would bury their dead, and sing a psalm over them, and pile rocks over the graves. That much they could do.

In the barn, by the fire, Rainald sat and cradled little Hetti.

His Ada, his Ralf, his Simon – all, all gone, and with them near all his heart. But he had his little Hetti: if only she would wake, and he could see her eyes and know that she would live. He prayed as he had never prayed before, with words he could not understand, and his sorrow spilled over into hope and filled his eyes with tears again. No priest, no wise woman, no green man – but he had his God, and he called to Him from the harvest, and in the Spring and from the midst of what his Ada used to called ' the fields of blessings'. This God was never trapped in a church or on a crucifix or in a box of relics. This God, his God would hear him on a dark night and answer his cry. He must.

The flames from the burning wattle threw dancing shadows against the walls. People shuffled aimlessly about in the shadows. Someone was sobbing quietly on the other side of the fire. Rainald held Hetti close and dozed, and at last as the deepest hour of the night stole in, he slept.

Cedric too, slept. Among his flock, his staff at his side, and his rough wool coat pulled about him, he sat propped against a rock and slept. It was a shepherd's sleep – a wakeful, alert, yet dreaming sleep, more of a rest than a slumber. Every time the flock stirred or a sheep bleated his eyes opened and he looked up – but there was always nothing to see save the Winter darkness, and nothing to hear but the wind in the heather, and nothing to feel but the sharp cold. The wind would keep the frost at bay, and the flock together would take the bite from the wind. And if the wolves on four feet and the wolves on two kept their distance all would be well.

Tomorrow, he would go on to Hochtal, and perhaps find a fold for the sheep: who knows?

He saw in his dozings good pastures, sunlit fields and peaceful grazing; he saw family and   friends from long ago; but most of all, he saw the ruins of Maibach.

When the dawn came to Hochtal the survivors of the village roused themselves and stomped wearily into the chill, grey day.

The ruins of one or two houses still smouldered, and smoke still drifted like mist among the buildings, but the worst was over, and the Liutizen had not returned.

They buried the dead.

That morning Rainald's daughter opened her eyes. By evening she was sitting up, though still very weak. The women of the village fussed over her, with bowls of soup and clean blankets and much tut-tutting. But Rainald never left her side, even when the surviving elders called him to a moot to talk of the village and what was left.

'Let them come to me', said Rainald. 'I can talk and listen here as well as any other place, and we have no secrets from the womenfolk. We all know that the winter is upon us, the granaries are bare and the cattle gone.'

The elders when they heard, just shrugged, and came to the barn. And there they talked while the children played and the women listened, and Rainald sat with his daughter.

When evening came, they were resolved: they would leave Hochtal and return in the Spring. Eckerheim was the nearest friendly village: that's where they would go. Two days to rest and find what provisions they could – two days for Rainald's daughter, and the son of Ashlar the woodcutter who was also sick, to have time to recover. But no longer. The heart of winter was upon them, and delay could be fatal.

If the Eckerheimers turned them away they would push on towards Magdeburg, and take their chances along the King's Highway. It seemed good: it was not good, but it was the best they could do, and they were resolved, and of one mind. They sang an old folksong to close the moot, and the oldest villager raised his staff and said the prayer that the priest used to say before people set out on a journey. That was all.

Two days later the weather cleared and by mid morning the sun was up and bright. It was a day for walking a twelve mile at least. The spirits of the villagers lifted, they bustled about and soon were on the road. No one looked back – that was thought a bad omen – and they crested the high ridge within an hour. There were not many of them, maybe thirty all told. The men marched at the front and rear, carrying what weapons they could find – mostly sharpened sticks, bill hooks and staves. A few carried the long ash spears their fathers or grandfathers had once proudly owned. One man, Weingar, had a shield, with a leather facing and an iron boss, but it was split through the outer rim. Still, he grinned through broken teeth, and joked that one old shield made him the House-Knight of Hochtal.

Rainald carried his daughter on his back, while Ashlar's son, leaning on a stick, hobbled along beside his mother. The womenfolk kept to the centre, bowed down by packs and knapsacks. They were cheerful enough, but spoke little, saving their strength for the long slow climb out of the valley and up onto the heathland. What talk there was, was about coming back to the village in the Spring. No one dared mention what they might find at Eckerheim, or who they might encounter along the way.

The sun had little warmth, but much of the snow had gone, even high up on the heath, and with the air so clear, they realised that though an enemy might spot them more easily, at least they could see the attack when it came.

The Liutizen struck fear most because of the suddenness and swiftness of their attacks: they appeared out of nowhere and melted away in the same way. 'Like ghosts,' Weingar had once said to Rainald. 'Like Liutizen,' Rainald had replied.

But up on the tops where it was fresh, and clear and bright they felt they could see forever, and not even the devil himself could take them by surprise.

They made good progress, and after a day's march made camp near the Heissmer, a high pool which never froze in Winter, and was always covered in a thin veil of steam. It was there that they found Cedric and his flock. He had turned aside on his drive to Hochtal, anxious to find shelter and good pasture for his weary flock. And so they found him and his sheep sitting quietly among the rocks and scrub beside the steaming pool. Nor was he alone. As he stood to greet them, two other figures rose from the hill bracken nearby.

'Bernhardt! Elsa!' Elspeth shouted, waved and ran, half-stumbling, towards them. Soon they were surrounded by all the folk, laughing, chattering and weeping for joy. Elsa, her hair loose and in wisps across her face hugged and kissed them all one by one, while Bernhardt, always the shy one, stood by awkwardly. But he was smiling broadly, and shook Rainald's hand as the other stepped forward.

'Well met, Bernhardt! We thought you were surely dead, or at least slaves by now.'

'Aye, and so it should have been, had not the good Lord been with us.'

'What happened?'

Bernhardt looked at the ground. 'They came – without warning – as we hear they always do. They came in with a squall of snow at eventide. There was nothing we could do.' He clenched his fists.

'It was bad then.'

'Aye, bad. You saw then what they left behind? Cedric said you had gone ahead. So you would have seen.'

Rainald nodded.

The others had fallen silent now, and were standing breathless, with fading smiles, listening to Rainald and Bernhardt.

'We buried the dead', said Rainald. 'There was nothing more we could do.'

'No corn, no cattle?'

'Nothing, except what a squirrel might find.'

'That would be so.' Bernhardt looked up, and squared his shoulders. 'Lukas and I and several of the others fought – the priest too – but it was hopeless. Lukas went down, and then the priest, but he was only wounded and they dragged him off. They kill like wolves: everything, anything.'

Rainald put a hand on his shoulder. 'But you've escaped, and Elsa too. This is good. And not just for yourselves. For us, too. You know that, Bernhardt?'

The blacksmith nodded, but there were tears starting down his cheeks. 'The children, Rainald, the children – you must have seen them.' His voice shook, and he turned to look for Elsa who came and hugged him, and buried her head against his chest. 'Not all the children', she said at last,' Look, Bernhardt. See! It's Hetti. Rainald's little one. She's alive!'

Bernhardt turned and looked at the little girl who smiled up at him. 'God be praised,' he said. 'Not all the sparrows fell.'

They all rested by the Heissmer, sharing food and chatting quietly about the day, and the days to come. Elsa described how she and Bernhardt had escaped, fleeing to a barn, hiding amid the straw, and then as the barn was set ablaze, slipping away in the midst of the smoke and heat and confusion.

'You were blessed,' grunted Cedric as he tore a hunk of rye bread and chewed it. 'The Liutizen have eyes like owls, especially in the night.'

'"Tis true' replied Elsa, 'but bright flames make deep shadows. Once a raider stared right at us, but seemed to see nothing. He was no more than a spear cast away, and we were in the open, a full thirty paces from the woods.'

'You kept still.'

'As death.'

'Then that is what saved you. That and the good grace of Christ.'

Elsa nodded, and looked at Bernhardt who smiled as he sat beside her. She went on: 'If our wits allowed us to escape Hochtal, it was surely an angel who led us to find you here. We were lost, and badly so – no idea where we were, or where to find help.'

'Hah! The perils of a blacksmith and his girl. You spend all your time in the village, then take one step into the wasteland and lose yourself completely.'

They all laughed, and someone slapped Bernhardt on the back, and muttered the old Saxon proverb: 'Wise in the village, but a fool in the forest'.

A crow called, and swung in a lazy circle above their heads.

'Snow coming,' said Cedric. 'We'd best camp here, and push on to Eckerheim in the morning.'

There was a silence. 'Do you think they'll give us food and shelter?' asked Rainald.

'They don't have to. Perhaps they'd be wiser to turn us away, but I don't think they will.'

'Why's that?'

'Because they're Eckerheimers, that's why. They'll not flee before the Liutizen, and they'll look to you to make a stand with them.'

Again the folk were silent. They knew that nothing was certain, that the Liutizen might have already overwhelmed Eckerheim, that the village might already be in ruins, and that they themselves could even at this moment be cut off from any hope of retreat. Besides they were not soldiers, not warriors, not men used to warfare and fighting. The menfolk might turn out for the annual military muster, and their forty days service under arms for their king, but that hardly made them confident that they could face a Liutizen raiding party. The musters they attended by feudal obligation were simply reluctant gatherings and most of the time they amounted to little more than a few days aimless marching and a series of tiresome military reviews.

The Hochtalers were farmers and tradesmen, peasants and labourers – just like the good people of Eckerheim. The greater part of them of them had never raised a pitchfork in anger, let alone stood in a shield wall and heard the sounds of battle. They looked to the Markgraf and his men at arms to defend them when raiders came in from the east, or bandits slunk across the heathland to their village. Certainly, they would play their part when called upon, but they knew they could do little without the support of seasoned veterans and professional infantry.

And so they were silent, and sat and listened to the crackling of the fires they had lit by the pool at Heissmer. They listened too to the bleating of Cedric's sheep, and knew that nowhere were they safe – not here upon the heath, not in Eckerheim, nor back in Hochtal.

'Now, if the Markgraf were here . . .' said Simeon the Potter suddenly.

'If the Markgraf were here, we'd all of us be cardinals and dining with the pope', Rainald cut in bitterly. 'He's with the king, and with the king he will remain until the Springtime. That's what the bailiff said – God rest him – and that's where he will be. Until the Spring.'

'When like as much we'll all be dead – with bones picked clean by yon crows', said one of the other men, and he tossed a branch on the fire.

Cedric stood up and stretched: 'Enough of this gloomy talk. We're alive are we not, and most of us hale and hearty. Take the days as they come, and don't wish yourself into the grave. Tomorrow we'll make for Eckerheim, and if our spirit is good, and the weather is fair we could put 20 miles behind us by nightfall.'

There was a low mutter and a nodding of heads. As the twilight drew in they settled for the night. By custom the womenfolk and children slept together by the fires, while the men kept a shared watch beyond and around them in a protecting circle. Bernhardt and Cedric kept watch over the sheep. The two men sat side by side, hands spread out over a glowing fire.

The night was clear, though Cedric said he smelt snow coming at dawn, a hard frost was promised by the moon. For a long time they said nothing, and just stirred occasionally to put more fuel on the fire. At length Cedric spoke, just a single word, whispered into the darkness: 'Eckerheim,' he said.

'Aye,' said Bernhardt, pausing briefly, 'And where else would we be going, I wonder?'

'It's a village like any other.'

Bernhardt shrugged, and gazed into the flames. 'I half expected to see him, you know.'

'See who.'

'Markward.'

'Oh, aye.'

'I half expected to see him come over that ridge with Rainald and the rest of the folk.'

Cedric smiled. ' Well, laddie, he half expected to be with them, himself.'

'But he's gone to Eckerheim.'

'He has, he has,' said Cedric quietly. 'But he went cursing that he had to.'

'I guess he did. You saw him then?'

'Aye, up on the tops. He crossed our path. We talked, and then he went on.'

For a time they did not speak.

Bernhardt stood up. 'I'll check the flock,' he said.

'Sit down, sit down,' replied Cedric, 'They are fine, and besides we can keep a good eye on them from here.'

Bernhardt grunted and slapped his chest. 'She called out for him, you know – just once. Called out. She did. In the fighting.'

'Sit down. You're worrying the flock. Sit down and speak your mind in a whisper.'

'Aye. . . aye . .' Bernhardt squatted down and tossed some more bracken onto the blaze. The fire flared and crackled, and sent sparks up into the winter sky.

'It was in the fighting. We knew we were done for. We had fought but it was hopeless. I saw my folks go down, one by one. Hacked down they were, or spitted like wild boar. Then Elsa's father fell, and Lukas too. We – Elsa and I – fell back against a wall. It was Elder Jarl's house, and it was on fire. There was smoke and flames all around, and I could see the Liutizen working their way forward, killing the wounded and hunting for the last of us.' Bernhardt stopped and looked at the shepherd.

'Go on.'

'It was then Elsa cried out. She cried out his name: Markward! – just like that; only she screamed it, just once, dropped the staff she was holding and stood there shaking, and the tears coming down. It was . . .'

'What'd ye do?'

'What'd I do? I scarce remember. For a moment I just stood there, but then as a Liutizen came out of the smoke I swung at him with my quarter staff. He ducked, but not enough, and the tip of the staff hit him right under the ear. Lucky, really. He went straight down and didn't move. I grabbed Elsa and we made a dash for it. That's all.'

Cedric reached into his pouch and took out his pipe. 'That's enough, and that's well. Ye got her out. She'll never forget that.' He offered the pouch to Bernhardt, who shook his head. 'A pipe at the forge, but nay at night',' he muttered, but smiled his thanks.

The old shepherd lit his pipe, and blew a stream of smoke.

'He'll be there ye know,' he said.

'Who, Markward? Aye, I know. You said so – but there's precious little we can do about that. Besides, we won't stay any longer than we have to. Elsa and I are to be wed, and I hardly think the priest at Eckerheim will say the vows over us.'

'Tis true enough. The priest will know Markward well and it'd be salt in the wound to marry his girl in his own village before his own folks.'

Bernhardt broke a branch and threw the pieces on the fire. 'She's mine now. Elsa's mine. And I'm hers, and there's nought of Markward between us. She cried out for him, but he wasn't there. It was me who got her out. It's me she loves now, and me she'll wed. I know it.'

Cedric looked thoughtfully into the fire and wrinkled his brow, but said nothing. The sheep on the far side of the flock shuffled about, and a tremor ran through them all. The shepherd got to his feet and whistled into the dark. There came a coughing sound, and then a kind of snort and a scrambling in the furze.

'Hill badger,' he said, sitting down again. 'What is he doing way up here at this time of year?'

'Strange times,' said Bernhardt.

'Aye, and wild times, too. Enough to scatter the badgers and . . .'

'Scatter us . . .'

Cedric smiled. 'You love her, then,' he said.

'I do. More than anything. Why do you ask?'

Cedric picked up a small stone and turned it over in his hand: 'Because I'm a foolish old shepherd with nothing to do, but to watch sheep graze and folk go by.' He glanced up at Bernhardt. 'But don't worry, young friend, don't worry. The girl will be yours, I see that right enough. It's just that . . .'

'It's just what?'

'Oh, I don't know, really. Just to say that a lass like Elsa is not your lass until she's wed – and then she'll be yours forever without one backward look over her shoulder.'

'You mean . . . ?'

'I mean she sent Markward away because she had to, not because she wanted to. Oh, aye, she loves you right enough – and there's the mystery of it – but she'll not hate him to please you, nor will she make a balance in her heart. She's not that kind of lass.'

Bernhardt frowned. 'You know her that well, then?'

'I know her well enough, and I know Markward better, even though the both of them were strangers to me before these days.'

The blacksmith sighed and shook his head. 'You're too deep for me, old shepherd.'

'I'm a simpleton, my friend, and that's what makes me seem wise.'

'There you go again! Talking like a Magdeburg clerk.'

They both laughed. An eagle owl, drawn to the fire, swept low over their heads and disappeared into the night. The moon shimmered in the pool, and slowly the frost drifted down upon the heath. It was a still night, and soon all but the huddled watchers slept.

Markward rode into Eckerheim as the sun was dipping behind the clouded hills. Men coming in from the fields raised hands in greeting, and the children called out to him from between the crucks and byres.

Brunni and Albrecht appeared from nowhere and danced around his horse.

'Oh, Mark! Oh Marki, Mark!' they shouted, and their cries brought Mutti to the door of their house.

He swung off his horse and hugged the children, and kissed them, and then took his mother in his arms and held her.

'I'm home, Mutti.'

'Home it is, and here you are!' She stood back tears in her eyes, and then glanced over his shoulder. 'The lassie?'

Markward shook his head. ''Twas not to be.'

Mutti looked at her son for a long time, and smiled through her tears. 'It's never over till the church bells ring,' she said.

'It's over mother, and there's another man she'll wed. That's all. But see! I've come home again!'

'So you have, my son. So you have! Come into the house. There's a pottage on the boil and fresh bread and bacon for the table. We'll have a family feast tonight.'

They all moved towards the house, but Markward suddenly stopped, and put his hand to his head. 'I forget! How could I! Wulfstan! Where is Wulfstan? And the bailiff! Where is the bailiff?'

'Hush now! They're coming in from the fields with everyone else. What's wrong?'

'I must see them at once.'

'What now? Can it not wait till morning?'

'No, it must be now. No time to lose!'

Mutti laughed: 'Oh, Marki, you ever were this boy! Always forgetting, and always running about afterwards because you had forgotten.'

Markward smiled ruefully: 'Aye, Mutti, aye. But I must see them. There are raiders headed this way. From the east. Liutizen!'

Albrecht and Brunni stopped dancing about: 'Liutizen!' they chorused, and Markward noticed that while his little sister was wide-eyed with fear, Albrecht's eyes were bright with excitement.

He knelt down, and took them in his arms: 'Listen little brother! Listen little sister! There are raiders coming, and they are coming this way. They come from the East, not out of story books and fairy tales. They are cruel and wicked men. They have burnt Maibach, and probably Hochtal as well.' Mutti gasped, and Markward went on: 'Now they are headed for Eckerheim, and that is why I am here.'

The children were both silent now, and they began to tremble.

'But don't you worry! I have come to look after you. When Wulfstan and the bailiff hear what I have to say they will rouse the village and send for help from our Markgraf. All will be well.'

'Do you think so, Marki?' asked Brunni, her voice thin and piping.'

'I know so, little Brunni, I know so – as sure as you gave to me that little brown cup, I know so.' He stood up. 'Now get you both into the cruck, and fix a meal for a king and queen. I'll be back before you know it.'

They ran in, no longer afraid, giggling and laughing once more. Mutti hesitated. 'The village,' she said. 'How can it stand against Liutizen if Maibach fell, and Hochtal too?'

'I'm not sure it can, but I know we won't be taken by surprise. Not like Maibach. I met some Hochtalers who had news of Maibach. They were bound for their own village, but perhaps they will come our way . . .' He trailed off as he looked down the street and saw Wulfstan trudging towards him.

'Away Mutti. Inside, now. I must see Wulfstan while there's still time!'

Cedric, and his little flock, along with Rainald and the surviving Hochtalers came to Eckerheim two days later. There were awkward greetings, but they knew they were welcome, and Eric the bailiff led them down to the great barn where they would make shelter, and shift for themselves as best they could.

The winter hay was stored there, and the roof was newly thatched, so it was warm and dry. The cow byre was down one end, along with the pens for pigs and goats, but there was plenty of room, and some broad, beaten earth to set a fire on.

Cedric left his flock in the sheep fold, as good a fold as ever he had seen. It was solid built of drystone, with a wattle and thatch roof, and a wooden door to turn any wolf. He had just come away from the fold and was chatting to one of the shepherds when he noticed Markward walking across to where the Hochtalers were gathering, by the doors to the barn. As he approached them Elsa stepped forward, her hands on her hips. Even from where he stood Cedric could hear what she said:

'So you leave me again! Markward! You leave me again, and this time you left me to die. How many times does your word mean nothing? How many times do I have to call for you, and you are not there?'

There was a silence. Markward turned and walked away. He walked out of the village and down towards the river bank. No one followed him.

THE FIGHT

The Eckerheimers called a moot in the long meadow and invited the newcomers to join them. There was feasting, and singing and speeches of welcome and then, with logs blazing and crackling on the moot-fire, they settled down to the business in hand.

The bailiff spoke first: he said the Markgraf was away in Goslar, but a rider had been sent and, God willing, help would come within a fourteen night. Another rider, Ulf the ploughboy on a village pony, had been sent to the Weissburg, the Markgraf's castle, which lay over a day's journey to the North and East. There was little prospect of help from this quarter – the castle would only have a guard of about twenty men – but at least they would be alerted. In the meantime they had to look to their own defence. Already watch beacons had been set on the high hill and river crossing. The scrub and brush had been cleared away from the out buildings and yards. The blacksmith was busy hammering farm tools into rough and ready weapons – mostly pole mounted axes, glaives and pikes - , and the shepherds had abandoned the higher folds and driven their flocks into the heart of the village itself. The grain stores were now constantly guarded, and no one was to leave the village for more than a bowshot in distance without the permission of an elder.

Smoke from burning thatch or crops had been spotted on the horizon to the South and East, and it was thought that the Liutizen were moving towards them from that direction. Every man between the age of sixteen and forty years was to help keep watch on all points both day and night.

The people listened in silence, except for the occasional muttered assent or grunt of approval.

At last the bailiff finished, nodded to Wulfstan the moot elder, and sat down.

There was a pause, then Rainald slowly got to his feet:

'People of Eckerheim, we of Hochtal are here as your guests, and for that we thank you. It is a debt we will not easily forget and will find difficult to repay. In the meantime, we will stand alongside you, and share your burdens here, as we share your salt. Our shields are yours, our spears are yours, our hearts are yours.'

A few of the Eckerheimers smiled quietly, but nodded. They appreciated the words once handed down by old warriors, but they knew that there was scarcely a spear or shield among them. When the Liutizen came there would be no shield wall to face them, no warcry of 'Ut! Ut!' and no thunderous stamping of boots on earth. Instead, a pitifully small group of ragged, ill-equipped villagers for the most part trembling with the fear that grips a man in his first battle.

Rainald sat down, and the priest rose to speak, but Wulfstan waved him down. This was a moot of the old times, and they would not be looking for a Latin blessing and a cloud of incense.

The miller, Edvart, now stood up. He carried a flail in one hand and held a fist full of grain in the other. 'Our seed, our soil, our children,' he said. 'This is how we stand. This is how we fall. There is no other way.'

'Then we stand together,' said the bailiff, and the people all said 'Aye'. But it was not a shout, it was not a cheer, it was a quiet telling.

There was little more to do or say, save that the folk voted Markward as the captain because he was so soon back from the wars, and had proved himself against the king's men at Hochtal. He was silent, but raised an arm to give his assent. Elsa, standing with the womenfolk in the shadows saw that he did not even raise his head. She was still watching him as the moot broke up and the people drifted away. He was almost the last to leave, and glancing to one side got slowly to his feet as Cedric came up and put a hand on his shoulder. He smiled weakly as the shepherd spoke to him, and shook his head wearily.

Elsa took a step forward, but suddenly Bernhardt was at her side and the moment was gone.

'Come,' said Bernhardt. 'I've found a family for you to stay with. They're good folk, with a good cruck house and a bed to boot! It'll be better for you there than the barn.'

'I should stay with everyone else!'

'You should look after yourself,' Bernhardt answered quietly, and gave her a peck on the cheek. 'Now come, they're waiting for you. It's Johan the carpenter and his wife Helga. They've three children, two cows and a goat. It's a fine cruck.'

Elsa sat down and burst into tears.

Bernhardt knelt beside her and hugged her. 'I know,' he said, ' I know.'

'No you don't know! You can't know. You can't!'

'But I do. I do. Listen! It's everything isn't it? I know it is. It's Hochtal, and your father. It's all your family – and all those who died in the fighting. All gone. Even the little ones. All of them gone. . . . And buried, God rest them. It's the coming here. And having to be here. And waiting. And for what?'

Elsa stopped sobbing and looked up. 'I will marry you Bernhardt.'

He smiled and gave her a squeeze. 'In the spring.'

'The spring?'

'When this is all over, and the green leaves come.'

He helped her to her feet and brushed the hair back from her eyes, and dried her tears.

Elsa smiled and smoothed her kirtle. 'When the green leaves come,' she said, and took his hand.

The Liutizen came on Christmas Eve. The snow had all but gone, but there was a hard frost that night. Two shepherd boys crouched by a beacon on the South side of the village heard the sound of soft leather boots crunching through the ice, and raised the alarm.

They put a torch to the beacon and sounded a horn. The villagers came running, tumbling out of cruck and barn, and running down towards the long meadow. They came wide-eyed and breathless to the beacon and found the boys gasping out the news of the attack. Liutizen scouts had appeared out of the blackness of the tree-line, circled the beacon and then melted away.

'I think we must have frightened them off,' said one of the lads.

Wulfstan grunted: 'Aye, as like a beetle frightens a bull.' He stared at the trees, their trunks etched out by the frosted field. 'They came to see if we were awake, that's all. They'll be back before morning, and this time they won't stop for the sounding of a shepherd's horn.'

The villagers pulled back from the beacon, though they left it blazing, and waited. They posted a few guards to the North and West, but most of the men stood in a ragged line between the last of the crucks on the south and eastern side of the village, and a broken down sheep-pen.

Ronan of the Wood stood by Markward. He was a charcoal burner, and he and his family had left their cottage in the forest and come to the village as news of the Liutizen spread. He gripped the long ash spear his father had once carried in the Bohemia War, and wrapped his great wolf-skin cloak more tightly about him:

'Why do they come so?'

'At night, you mean?'

'Aye, at night when goblins and trolls and fell things stalk the woods.'

Markward gave a short laugh. 'Some folk say they have no fear of trolls because they once mated with hobgoblins.'

'And you say?'

' I say, the Liutizen come because they find men and women easier to kill if they find them asleep.'

'And now we are awake.'

'But we will be drowsy by dawn, and frozen to the bone, and scarce able to hold a spear let alone strike with one.'

Ronan was silent, but he tensed his tall, gaunt frame and peered into the dark. All along the line of waiting men Markward could hear muffled whispers and low mutterings. Edvart the Miller was there, with flail and buckler. Next to him the bailiff, Eric of the Lea, in quilted jerkin, and holding a shield of linden wood. Johan the carpenter was there too, trembling at the thought of battle, but with a firm grip on the long hafted adze his father once used. Among the shadowy figures Markward heard the deep chuckle of Weingard whose broken grin and broken shield seemed to comfort those around him. And then there was Rainald, his head hooded against the cold, and his arms tensed to hold the old war spear his uncle had taken from a Magyar. They were afraid, but they were steady, and he felt that they stood with as good a will as many of the kings men he had fought alongside.

He thought back to his first battle, his first shield wall, and the terrible rising of his stomach to his throat as he heard on that day so long ago the unearthly guttural roar of a thousand heathen voices somewhere out in the mist in front of him. That had been years past but the fear had never left him. He had learnt to swallow such fear at the first shock of shield on shield, and spit it out as blade and spear point crashed and splintered against the ranks of linden wood - but always and everafter it was there with him: ever again when there came a time to fight. It never failed to find him, and always his sword hand shook before a battle, and his bowels rumbled, and beads of sweat stood out on his brow, no matter how cold the day. It was always and ever the same.

And so it was this night, but he smiled at the old enemy that had found him yet again, and told himself that for the first time in his life he, Markward, was a leader in battle, a chosen man – and that if he did not stand the whole village would run, and if they ran they would be slaughtered in the frost like hobbled goats. And Eckerheim would burn, and when the Markgraf came in the Spring there would be nothing left to find but blackened ruins and whitening bones. He touched his hand against the little wooden cup tucked inside the wallet at his belt.

'Puts steel in your soul!'

Markward turned. Wulfstan had appeared beside him. He tapped Markward on his sword arm and chuckled. 'It puts steel in your soul, lad. Fighting does. You've stood in worse than this and come through with blood and honour to your name – or so I've heard.'

'Then you've been listening to the chatter round the well!' said Markward, 'I shake like a girl before a fight, and throw up like a drunkard after it.'

'As all good warriors do,' muttered Wulstan, and rested the haft of his axe across his shoulder. 'You know,' he said, 'If these wild men come at us three score strong and all at once we'll never hold.'

'I know it,' replied Markward, 'But we'll mix their blood with ours before we're done.'

'Aye, and they'll sing about that I'm sure in the halls of this Salian king when they've done their drinking on a winter's night and there's nothing else left to sing about.'

Markward grimaced but held his peace.

They stood all night. The women of the village came with mulled wine and oat cakes in the early hours of the morning, and the men took turns to crouch down and eat while others kept watch. It was bitterly cold, but no one seemed to notice, and they even laughed and joked when someone tried to sing a Saxon carol.

There was a boy, Branulf, who had a bow, and he kept pacing up and down and asking Markward if he could run out and put more wood on the beacon fire. At last, in the hour before dawn, Markward said he could go, and slapped him on the back and told him to run like a hare and keep his fool head down.

With his bow and quiver slung across his back, Branulf picked up a bundle of twigs and branches and set off towards the beacon. He ran straight out for about twenty paces, ducked down behind a low hedge and then after a short wait, made a dash for the beacon.

'He's a brave lad', said Wulfstan, rubbing his beard.

'He is that, but if his mother hears what I've done, she'll skin me alive, Liutizen or no.'

They watched as Branulf reached the beacon and slithered down beside it. In a moment he had thrown the wood on the fire which immediately blazed into life.

'Back now!' shouted Markward, and his voice echoed across the frosty meadow. Branulf glanced over his shoulder, unslung his bow, nocked an arrow and fired it into the darkness.

'Young fool!' hissed Wulfstan. He had barely spoken when a dozen or so shafts flickered out of the dark and fell about the beacon.

Branulf staggered as though he had been hit, but regained his balance and sprinted back towards the village. As he did so more arrows ziffed and hummed about him, as he swerved wildly and put one hand to his head. He fell in a heap at Markward's feet, and sprang up grinning.

'I did it!' he said.

'And here they come!' said Wulfstan. As he spoke his words seemed to be swallowed up by the deep, pulsing sound of beating drums, sounding from across the meadow.

One by one, or in twos and threes the men of the village knelt down scooped up a handful of icy soil and pressed it to their lips. A few crossed themselves.

As the arrows fell closer, men crouched behind their shields: and then came the thud and thwack of arrow heads biting into leather and wood. Those without shields crowded behind those who carried them, and so the line was broken up, and then forced closer together, drawing in between the houses, and shortening the perimeter that Markward was trying to defend.

The beat of drums was now mixed with howls and whoops as the Liutizen warriors appeared from among the trees and began to trot across the meadow.

'Steady lads!' roared Wulfstan.

'Aye, steady!' shouted Markward. 'Keep down till I tell you. Don't look up! Don't look up!'

There was a cry from somewhere along the line as an arrow found its mark, and then just to the right of him Markward saw a villager pitch forward with an arrow in his chest: two men down already, and not a blow struck in return.

The Liutizen were now some sixty or seventy paces away, grey shadows against the tree line, and as they neared the arrow fire slackened. Branulf, darting back and forth behind the villagers was picking up Liutizen arrows and firing them back as best he could. Another boy, with a short-bow, joined in but he was struck through the calf almost immediately and fell to the ground clutching at the barbed arrow head.

'Brace! Brace!' yelled Markward, his voice cracking with rising fear. The villagers steadied, took one pace forward, locked their shields and thrust forward with spears and staves and sharpened sticks.

'This is it!' Wulfstan called to Markward as he stood, shield strapped to his back, and axe held in both hands. 'We must stand here, and kill as many as we can. Here!'

Wulfstan's words were again all but lost in the rising din of drums and war cries, but Markward nodded, and took guard behind his shield. The Liutizen, all with sword and spear and shield, and most with helmets, and some with faces weirdly painted swept towards the waiting villagers. Markward picked his man: a warlord of some sort with gilded helmet and face mask. He had a bronze dragon as a crest, with the motif repeated on his shield. In his hand he held a heavy-bladed single edged sword with a curving point, and he wore a hauberk of fine ring mail. But most of all Markward noticed the set of the teeth beneath the mask, and the blond moustaches which swept back along the jaw line. The man seemed to see him at the same time, because he checked momentarily, and then veered towards him, sword held high.

'Eckerheim!' someone cried – it sounded like the miller, and the lines crashed together. The single shuddering, gasping wrench that hurled along the writhing ranks seemed to rush with blinding pain up Markward's shield arm and across his shoulder. He twisted wildly to stay on his feet, and threw his sword up to meet the scything blow from the Liutzen blade. Sparks flew from the ringing steel, and he shook his head to clear his vision. Again the blades clashed, again he twisted, and this time almost slipped. He ducked as the pommel of the Liutzen sword flashed by, scoring his cheek.

With a cry he drove forward with his shield, and felt the boss grind against the painted dragon. All about him men were hewing, hacking, screaming, and gulping in the frosty air – but nothing mattered save the grinning Liutizen in front of him.

They were shield to shield now, snarling at each other over the iron rims, and struggling to force a gap big enough to slip through the point of a sword.

Already sweat stung Markward's eyes, and he could smell his enemy's breath – he stank of fish.

Something struck him hard in the shin, and he thought for a moment that his leg bone had been cut through, but it was only a kick, trying to knock him off his feet. He lunged forward, trapped an ankle, hooked his own boot around it, and stepped back. The Liutizen swayed off balance, just for a moment. Markward found the gap he was looking for and thrust his sword hard for stomach and groin. He felt the point of the blade enter the ring mail, and snapped his wrist round hoping to burst the rivets.

The line heaved and surged. Someone crashed against his shoulder, the sword point slipped free, and the Liutizen warlord was gone. Another grinning warrior faced Markward, and another sword bit against his shield.

Further down the swaying ranks, and just where the Saxon line came up against an old oak tree, Bernhardt the blacksmith stood. His arm was bloodied above the elbow, and there was a swelling bruise on his jaw where the pommel of a sword had found its mark – but he was still standing, and the owner of the sword had fallen, skull crushed by the great hammer Bernhardt carried. The villagers had withstood the first mad rush, but only just, and a good many were now lying in the reddening frost. There were too few shields and too few swords, and too few men skilled in how to use them. The men of Eckerheim were strong and determined but they were set against an enemy that knew its trade, and was not about to be denied by a handful of tattered peasants.

And so the Liutizen locked shields and screamed and stamped their feet and drove hard against the trembling line. That the line held was a wonder, that it pushed back was a miracle. But then above the shouting, clashing din came the reason: the great war-cry of the miller and the power of the weapon he held. Bernhardt turned and saw the whirling flail rise and fall some few paces to his right. It was there that the Liutizen raiders buckled and gave way – just a step, but just enough to open the shield wall by an arm's length. Shouting and cursing with excitement and rage some four or five villagers tore into the gap hacking and thrusting with what weapons they had. The men about Bernhardt roared like bears and charged forward. Some were cut down as they charged, but most stayed on their feet and knocked their startled opponents backwards.

Bernhardt was no warrior, but like the miller he had strength, and he used it to smash the shields and stove the helmets of those in front of him. His strength, born from the anvil, was mingled with fear that wrapped itself about his heart, and brought his hammer whistling down with awful weight and speed. It was the fear that comes to men who fight not to die, but because they have so much to live for, and it was tested against the battle-madness and pitiless skill of the pagans from the East.

For a time it looked as though the Liutizen might be thrown back to the woods and scrubland beyond the long meadow, but they withstood the villagers' charge, and steadied their line within half a bowshot. There they stood gasping and snarling and gathering themselves for another assault.

Markward, Bernhardt, the miller and all the other surviving villagers retreated slowly, dragging their wounded with them. Their shields were splintered, their weapons all hacked about, their tunics and jerkins torn and bloodied – but they were still wide-eyed for the fight. A pale, limpid sunlight crept across the valley, so that at last they could see the true strength of the enemy.

'Well, it's not a host,' grunted Wulfstan, 'but it's more than a raiding party.' He turned and looked at Cedric who was limping along beside him. 'You did well, old shepherd.'

Cedric shook his head. 'I'm too old for this anymore. I'd rather be on my own and facing a forest full of wolves.'

They reached the place where they had first made their stand, and looked towards the Liutizen.

'They'll come again before long,' said Wulfstan. 'We've given them pause for thought, but not much else.'

Cedric studied his staff where a sword blade had bitten deep. 'Aye, and if they have the wit to come upon us from two sides at once, then we're done for, that's for sure.'

A horn sounded from somewhere among the Liutizen. They roared that heavy guttural roar the Saxons called the devil's cry, and began to trudge forward again, slapping their shields with sword and spear and axe haft as they came.

Back in the heart of the village, the women had gathered up the children and retreated to the church. The old priest, kneeling at the altar and babbling out prayers, scrambled to his feet and opened the great wooden doors to let them in. It was cold and gloomy in the grey stone building, but it was safer than the tithe barn, and not so easy to set alight.

Elsa found herself with Mutti, Albrecht and Brunni as they put their few possessions down, and sat on the rush-strewn floor. They nodded greetings and smiled at one another. Through the high narrow windows they could hear the sound of the Liutizen as they attacked once more across the meadow. The priest was back on his knees again, and the women spoke quietly. They soothed and shushed the children, and drew them to themselves.

The staccato slap of iron on wood grew louder, and with that came the rising war chant and the stamp of feet. And all the while, the drums.

Elsa looked up. Shafts of morning sunlight were streaming through the windows, and lighting up the walls in golden bands. It looked as fine a light as she had ever seen. She fixed her eyes on the top of a rounded pillar which seemed to glow with the deep soft yellow of ripened wheat. Her ears throbbed with the beat of her heart, her mouth felt dry, and her teeth chattered with the cold, but she knew she must never take her eyes off the pillar. As long as the sunlight played on it, all would be well she told herself.

Suddenly, there was a hand on her hand. She started. It was Mutti.

'If they come,' she said, and her voice shook slightly though she smiled, 'we must fight.'

'If they come, then our menfolk are dead, and all is lost. What do we fight for, then?'

'Each other,' said Mutti, and turned to hold the children more closely as outside the war chant turned to a single shaking yell and the Liutizen broke into a charge.

'Eckerheim!' shouted Markward, and the villagers replied, and locked together what shields they had and rushed forward.

Some good leagues distant from Eckerheim, in a gentle valley, there is a stream called Daan – and where it bends away by a stand of birches it forms a pool deep and clear. A rider had stopped there to give his horse water, but now he turned and looked to the ridge which marked the southern way. He listened. There it was again – a sound – a throbbing rolling sound, rising and fading then lifting once more. Grasping the reins the rider eased himself into the saddle with the smooth easy rhythm of a knight, though he was still a squire, and bore the simple blazon of the Markgraf of Weissburg on his shield. He turned his horse's head towards the sound, and it flicked its ears and snorted.

'Come, lass! We'll see what's to be done!'

He spurred away to the top of the ridge, paused and then galloped across a fold in the ground, and then on up to a grassy crest some thousand paces beyond. He could hear more than he could see, but off in the distance he could just make out the roof tops of a village.

He looked long and hard, and all the while the sound like broken thunder drifted across the heathland.

'Liutizen!' he said, under his breath, and snatching his horse around, hurled back down the slope.

Somehow the villagers had held the second charge, but they had been driven back among the buildings of the village and were now desperately fighting to hold their ground. Edvart the Miller had been badly wounded, his arm gashed from shoulder to elbow. Ronan of the Wood had been staggered by a glancing blow to his head, and was barely able to fight. And Weingar of the broken grin lay lifeless in the frost, his broken shield beside him.

Markward was now fighting alongside Eric the Bailiff, with Wulfstan on his other shoulder. The gripping fear had gone, but there was no battle-joy, only exhaustion, and a growing heaviness in his arms and legs. He brought down a Liutizen spearman with a lucky stroke, and stamped down hard to break the neck. At the same time an axe came as if from nowhere and bit into his shield above the boss. His arm and shoulder shook with the force of the blow, but the shield held, and Eric's saex killed the axe man where he stood.

'Hard work!' yelled Wulfstan as he hacked against the Liutizen line. Markward grunted, and then tensed as a bronzed spear point drove at him from the Liutizen shield wall. He took the blow at the boss, and twisted to deflect its force, but the pain still leapt up his arm. He swung his sword and felt it skid against the iron rim of a shield. Someone cried out above the din of battle, another dying man fell beneath the shield wall, and the ground was suddenly slippery with blood.

'We cannot hold them,' gasped Markward. 'We must fall back towards the church.'

'No!' yelled the bailiff. 'If we break now they will kill us all for sure.'

Markward swung twice more with his sword, then stepped back out of the battle line. A villager, it was Johan, rushed into the gap, while Ashlar of Hochtal took the bailiff's place.

For a time both Eric and Markward lent on sword and shield, breathing heavily and saying nothing. Then Markward straightened up, and put his hand on the bailiff's shoulder:

'You fight well, Eric – you and all these men. We have held.'

Eric stared back but said nothing. Markward went on, raising his voice above the din.

'But now is the time to fall back. See the line is buckling already, and the Liutizen will soon set fire to the houses. If they bring their archers forward we are lost.'

'So we run like dogs!'

'No, we go back like men – a step at a time, the shield wall locked.'

'We have no shield wall! Look at us!'

'It is enough. It has held this long, but now we must go back. To the church, while there is still time.'

'And then?'

Markward smiled sadly. 'And then . . . then we are all in God's hands.'

The bailiff looked at the fighting, a sword's length from where he stood.

'Well, all right, but we'll want a charge to throw them back a pace or two first.'

Markward slapped him on the shoulder. 'Just so.' He slipped his shield to his back, took his sword in both hands, and whirled it high above his head. 'Eckerheim!' he shouted, and charged. The bailiff dragged Johan out of the way and Markward was through, splitting a Liutizen through his leather cap with a single blow. The villagers roared and pushed forward. They snatched up shields and axes as the Liutizen fell back, and chased them across the meadow. But soon barbed arrows began to hiss and zip among them and three men had fallen before Markward called a halt. They made a stand about him, overlapped what shields they held and began a retreat back into the village.

This time the Liutizen did not follow, being content to send one more flight of arrows and then shout a few challenges and insults before regrouping in the middle of the meadow.

Markward and the bailiff kept the men moving past the houses and up the street towards the church. He knew that once the Liutizen realised that the villagers were abandoning their line they would advance once more. However, it was still early morning, so there was a chance the enemy would pause to take a meal and rest before the final assault. Although the raiders had been surprised by the determined defence of the villagers, both Markward and the bailiff were in little doubt that the Liutizen would hold all of Eckerheim by noon at the latest: the wolves had time to rest and look upon their prey.

As the sun climbed through the mist, the Liutizen lit cooking fires just beyond the tree line, and sat down in groups to eat and drink and laugh about the fight.

The drums stopped and a strange silence settled over Eckerheim. Markward, the bailiff and all the men who had survived the fighting retreated to the church. The priest, the old men and the womenfolk welcomed them in. There was weeping and moaning, for the living and the dead. The wounded were taken care of as best they could: the badly injured were stretched out on the straw covered benches which were set into the walls of the church. They were given wine mixed with herbs, and their wounds were dressed with what cloths and rags could be found. The walking wounded were patched up, and set to guard the windows and doors, while the rest of the men readied the church for the attack that they knew must come. Doors were braced with what timbers could be found, and buckets of water were hurried in from the priest's well which lay just beyond the West porch. The women had already lit a fire in the nave, and hung a cauldron over it for cooking. They bustled around it, chattering and sighing, and scolding the children who got too near, and the ones who didn't come when called.

Markward, Wulfstan and Eric the Bailiff climbed the narrow stair that wound up to the top of the squat stone tower of the church. A trap door led onto the roof, which was flat, lined with lead and defended by a low stone parapet. Jan the priest was already up there, keeping watch.

'Well met,' he said. 'Are ye well Eric – and you, Markward, Wulfstan?'

The bailiff nodded and looked around. 'Two bowmen,' he said,' could hold this awhile'. Markward didn't answer. He was looking towards the Liutizen camp. It was wreathed in smoke and there seemed little sign of movement.

'Well, bless you sir priest for making such a tower!' said Wulfstan.

'Bless the Markgraf for telling him to,' replied the bailiff. 'There's a good part of five year's tithes in this tower, and the bishop was not happy to see them spent.' Jan smiled and ducked his head.

'I remember,' said Wulfstan as he leant on the parapet and looked out over the village. 'And it was just as well that yon bishop and our good King Henry are friends and not foes. Henry may be a confessor king, but he likes towers on his churches when they stand guard on the Eastern borders. What say you, Markward?'

The young soldier turned. 'I want two men with bows, and three sheaves of arrows apiece. I want them up here, along with Bernhardt the blacksmith from Hochtal. And bring Grimwald too. He's got a limp, but he's as strong as an ox.'

'You mean . . .?'

'I mean we loosen the stones on the parapet, and when the time comes . . .' Markward paused.

'I understand,' Wulfstan said, and looked at the bailiff, who nodded:

'Well, let's be going then. Those wolves over there won't rest for much longer, but I'm thinking they're not likely to attack again afore the forenoon. Until then they'll be happy enough to burn the houses and steal what they can. They know they've got us trapped, and they think they can gobble us up at any time.'

'And when they come,' said Wulfstan, 'They'll come straight for the tower.

He headed for the trap door and the others, with a last glance towards the long meadow, followed, leaving Jan the priest to keep watch.

Down below, in the church, the villagers were gathering to eat and talk. The mood was low. All were bracing themselves for the next attack. Even the children were quiet now, and were happy looking after the village dogs which had come scratching and snuffling at the door, now that the village was deserted.

Two men were sent up onto the tower with bows, and Grimwald went ahead of Bernhardt to begin loosening the parapet stones.

Markward sat down against the wall by one of the Eastern windows. He chewed on a piece of bread, and looked up at the heavy beamed ceiling.

Bernhardt sat down beside him. 'A good roof,' he said.

Markward didn't reply, and seemed lost in thought.

'It won't burn easily,' Bernhardt went on. 'You don't often see a roof like that, not on a village church, leastways.'

Markward nodded, but said nothing. He finished his bread, got slowly to his feet and moved towards the fire. For a time Bernhardt watched him go, then smiled and shrugged. Elsa came and sat beside him. 'It's not a good day for talking', she said and touched his arm.

Bernhardt grinned. 'And we seem to have forgotten that it's Christmastide!'

'Aye!' said Rainald who was standing nearby. 'Even the priest forgot to ring the bell, and I haven't heard a carol all day.'

'And no roast chestnuts for the children!'

'Forget the children,' chuckled Wulfstan. 'What about me?'

The laughter faded quickly, Bernhardt went up to the tower, someone went to find more wood, and those that were not guarding the door and windows gathered closer to the fire and stared into the flames. The smoke hung above their heads as it filtered through the windows and the chinks in the tiling. It smelt of heather and oak and laurel and birch. It smelt good. Markward breathed it in. Mutti was suddenly there at his shoulder.

'Are we to die?' she whispered.

'Mutti . . .'

'Are we to die this day?'

Markward swallowed hard. 'God only knows that, Mutti. I thought this morning, early in the frost, we were set to die before the sun crossed the trees — and here we are.'

'Most of us.'

'Aye. Still standing, still breathing, and willing to fight.'

Mutti took her son by the sleeve. 'Look at me.'

He looked into those clear, pale eyes, and felt her hand trembling on his arm. He was aware that everyone was now silent and listening.

'What do you want of me, Mutti ?'

'I want you to make your peace.'

'With whom?'

'Ach! Tshush, now! With young Elsa of course. Whether we live or die this day, you can't leave things as they are. You know that.'

'If we die, it hardly matters.'

Mutti frowned: 'You know as well as I, because it's how I taught you. It's not when we die, it's how we die that counts.'

'Mutti . . . you say too much.'

'I say not enough. Now away with you, and think as you go. There may not be much time.'

Markward gave his mother a hug, and moved away towards the tower steps. Cedric picked up his staff and followed him. The women of the village tutted and frowned, and turned again to the fire. Outside, in the stillness of the village, a calf called for its mother from the byre, and called again. Branulf looked up, and made a step towards the door, but his uncle motioned him down. He came and sat on a shelf in the wall by a window, cradling his bow and staring into nowhere.

Back up on the tower roof, Markward breathed deeply. The cold air felt good, and cleared his head. The Liutizen were still not on the move, but he knew they would come soon, and burn the houses. Bernhardt and Grimwald were working on the parapet, chipping the mortar away and loosening the stones. They lifted several stones down and placed them along the wall-walk. They scarcely spoke as they worked, and when at last they had finished, Bernhardt straightened up with a sigh, slapped Grimwald on the back and turned towards the steps. He glanced at Markward, and nodded and smiled, but his greeting wasn't returned – the young Eckerheimer was still staring at the Liutzen encampment.

Grimwald pushed past him with his usual grunt, and followed Bernhardt down the steps. Then the priest left. The two bowmen acknowledged Markward and Cedric, and then turned again to their watch.

'They'll spit us like rabbits when they come,' said Cedric. 'You know that, don't you?'

'Aye, I know it, but we'll make more of a fight of it from inside this church.'

'Maybe so, but when the end comes, I pity any prisoners they take.'

'Then they musn't find any.'

Cedric looked hard at Markward, then walked to the other side of the tower and gazed at the far ridges. 'No chance of slipping away, then?'

'No, not once we decided to make a stand. Besides, even if we had two days on them, they would run us down before we reached Magdeburg.'

'And the Weissburg?'

'No chance. north and east is all their territory now. We're cut off.'

Markward came and stood by Cedric. The sun shone bright and crisp against the frosted landscape. It looked strangely beautiful, and the wreathing smoke from the Liutizen campfires only added to that beauty.

'I'm sorry for your flock, old friend.'

'And I'm sorry for your girl – but sorrow on sorrow won't change a thing in these hills. Not by the morrow, and not ever.'

The drums started again from the edge of the trees and small groups of men armed with torches began to make their way across the meadow.

'So they come to set fire to us,' muttered Markward. 'Tell the priest to ring the bell.' One of the bowmen scrambled down the steps, and moments later the old brass bell began to toll.

'If they fire the fold,' shouted Cedric suddenly, 'I can't stay here!'

'They'll kill you for sure, and you'd die for nothing.'

. 'Aye, but I'd die well.'

Markward took the shepherd by the shoulders: 'Stay here! We need you!'

Cedric shook his head: 'I couldn't stay — not if they fire the fold.'

'Then, pray God they don't,' said Markward, and loosened his sword in the scabbard.

Both men were now watching as the Liutizen worked their way cautiously into the village. The other bowman came breathlessly back up the steps, and took his place on the wall walk. Bernhardt and Grimwald appeared soon after. 'You need us now?' asked Grimwald.

'Not yet, not just yet, but you can tell Jan to stop ringing the bell — he'll wake the dead.'

'Not so bad, if they'd fight for us,' replied Grimwald with a short laugh as he ducked back down through the trapway.

Down below, in the church, Elsa sat down against the wall, smoothed her kirtle and called to the children: 'Come now, and I'll tell you all a story.'

'A real one?' chirped Brunni as she ran towards Elsa, dragging Albrecht with her.

'Why all stories are real, Brunni, but this one is magic as well.'

'Magic enough to drive the bad people away?' asked Hetti, all wide-eyed.

Elsa took a deep breath: 'Aye, magic enough for that. You'll see. And all you have to do is close your eyes when I tell you to, and wish for whatever you like.'

The children clustered around Elsa, and as the deep throbbing note of the drums surged across the meadow and through the streets of the village, she began her story.

'Once upon time, in a country far, far away lived a king, and his only daughter, a beautiful princess. Although it was a beautiful and peaceful land, and they lived in a beautiful palace, the king was very sad.'

'Why was he sad, Elsa?' asked Hetti.

'He was sad because . . .' Elsa looked up. Bernhardt was standing watching her. He smiled, and she smiled back. She went on: 'because in all the kingdom he could find no one to marry his daughter.'

'But everyone must have wanted to marry his daughter!' shouted Albrecht.

'Of course,' replied Elsa, 'But no one was quite good enough for the king. You see, he wanted someone very special to marry the princess, someone who was not only wise, and brave and handsome, but someone who could prove beyond doubt their love for his daughter.'

Some of the other men and women had stopped to listen to the story, and drew near. Others moved around quietly, as if not to disturb the story.

The beating of the drums grew louder, and some of the children trembled and looked around. Elsa wrapped her arms around the two closest ones, and went on. 'You see, the king knew that the most important thing in the world was love, true love – and that was the greatest gift his daughter could receive.'

'But did she deserve this gift?' Branulf asked quietly, his bow still nestled in the crook of his arm.

Elsa nodded. 'She did – for you see she loved her father very much even though . . .'

There was a harsh cry from somewhere in the village, and the sound of a war chant. Everyone started. Branulf leapt to his feet and ran to a window, as others headed for the embrasures and the barricaded doors.

Brushing her hair back from her face, Elsa bit her bottom lip and then went on: ' Even though...'

Up on the tower Markward was pointing towards a column of smoke rising over the furthest of the houses. 'There, you see! They'll fire the houses one by one, and with the breeze just blowing this way, it'll send the smoke drifting towards us.'

'They'll come at us through the smoke, while we're still coughing and choking and half blind.'

'Just so.'

'So what do we do?'

'We fight.'

One of the bowmen nocked an arrow, drew his bow back and fired high into the air. The arrow buried itself in a rooftop. He swore and shook his head.

'Too far yet Aylrick. Wait a bit, and they'll come.'

The bowman glanced at Markward and grunted. Just then, the bailiff appeared. 'We're ready below', he said, and walked across to the parapet. He leant on it with his elbows and gazed across the rooftops: 'Not long now. They must be getting hungry.'

'And no sign of help, neither,' said Cedric nodding towards the ridge.

'And none likely,' replied Eric. 'It would be a miracle if the Markgraf came before a six week, and only slightly less if anyone showed from the Weissburg.'

'Aye', Markward cut in, 'Those folk who spot smoke from these parts will give us a wide berth that's for sure.' He was about to check the fastenings on his sword belt when a change in the drum beat made him look up.

'You're right, Eric! Here they come! See! Up the main street. And running too. Eager for their supper.'

Out of the smoke of the burning houses and barns came the Liutizen, yelping, whooping and leaping as they attacked. It was though they knew, or sensed, that all the villagers were in the church. They headed straight towards it, and then fanned out as they approached, and began to close in from all sides. It was not long before they caught sight of Markward, Cedric and the others on the tower, and soon flurries of arrows began to fly over the parapet, and rattle against the stonework.

The two villagers with bows did the best they could to return fire, and one of them claimed a hit, but there was little they could do to weaken the attack, and soon a mass of Liutizen had gathered beneath the tower.

Grimwald and Bernhardt appeared yet again, and without hesitating began to hurl stones down onto the heads of the Liutizen.

There were cries of rage from below, and the storm of arrows increased. Soon Grimwald was hit, and fell backwards with an arrow through his shoulder. The bailiff helped him below, and came back with the news that Liutizen were now attacking the church door, hammering against it with axes, and the pommels of their swords.

Cedric and Markward helped Bernhardt throw down the last of the loosened stones. For a time this scattered the Liutizen from the base of the tower, but they soon regrouped and came surging back.

'If they find a ladder, we're done for!' said Eric.

'We're done for anyway!' replied Markward, and ducked as an arrow skidded off the parapet and whistled past his ear.

Cedric grinned. 'Aye, but you're still more quick than dead young Markward. We've fight in us yet, and those dogs have left the fold alone, God be thanked.'

Markward crouched down, and grinned back: 'Then pray to God that those sheep of yours still have a shepherd at the end of this day, old friend. It won't be long till the dogs are at our throats, and then we'll see who rules the heavens.'

Aylrick and the other bowman fired off the last of their shafts. Smoke was now swirling around the tower as the nearby buildings were set alight. It was difficult to see clearly, and clouds of sparks and embers swept over the parapet.

'There's little more we can do here,' said Markward at last. ' Let's go below.'

They fled down the spiral stairway and into the church. The air was heavy with smoke and ash, and dust and sweat. People were running to and fro, uncertain what to do – or cowering in corners trying desperately to protect their children and old folk. There was moaning, and sobbing, and a few shouted commands which nobody seemed to hear.

Markward called to Mutti and Elsa: 'The women and children, you must get them into the middle – there! There by the fire. They must be at our backs. We need to know where you are if they break through the door. Quick now!'

He turned away: 'Ho! Harald, and Morcar, and Ronan! Yes! The barricades. Put your shoulders to them – the door will never hold otherwise. Lads! You lads! Keep to the windows and loose whenever you can, but keep your bow well back – they'll grab you at the wrist if they get half a chance!'

He scanned the church. 'Ho! Jan, take Tomas with you and block the stairs, and stand guard there – take that hammer! Aye, that's good, swing it hard if anything comes down the steps.'

Someone took him by the shoulder. He turned. It was Eric: 'We'll still need someone on the tower, in case they get up onto the roof. I'll go.'

'No, Eric! You're needed here. Send Geyorg and two of the other lads. They're safer up there, and they might get in a few lucky shots.'

Eric nodded, and turned and yelled to Geyorg who was waiting by one of the windows.

The pounding of weapons against the door seemed to fill the church now, and Markward could hear the yells and jeers of the Liutizen as they gathered for the kill. The pounding suddenly increased, until it became a series of shuddering thuds.

He rubbed his eyes against the stinging smoke, and drew his sword. It would be over soon, very soon. Not much longer and they would break down the door and come pouring through. Outside, through the narrow windows came the sound of crackling thatch and timber burning. It mingled with the shouts of the fighting. Smoke and sparks were gusting into the church, and the great door shook to the blows of a wooden beam the Liutizen were using as a ram. The men of the village stood to the barricade, bracing their shoulders against it. The boys with bows, Branulf among them, were firing arrows as best they could from the windows. The women had gathered all the children in the centre of the church and Rainald stood beside them with his quarter staff.

'Will the soldiers come soon?' asked Hilda Who-keeps-the-Geese, her voice shaking.

Elspeth looked up. 'Soldiers? What good to us are soldiers, lass? King's men or Liutizen, they're all the same.' She reached out and touched Hilda on the shoulder. 'They come, they take, they go away – that's all, and if we're lucky they leave us alive.'

'But the king, our king!' said Hilda.

Rainald motioned for Elspeth to say no more, but she seemed not to notice.

'Our king? We have a king who gives us laws and takes our taxes, but still the soldiers come.'

'Hush, now Elspeth.'

'We have a king who sends us priests who take our tithes and steal our corn, and gabble prayers in Latin, but still the soldiers come.'

'Be quiet woman! Be still now!' The door shook to a massive blow, and the hollow boom filled the church, but the hinges held.

Elspeth went on, her voice rising: 'And when these soldiers come, we run and hide, or stand and fight – but still they come and burn and kill and go away gain. And who buries the dead? And who rebuilds the barns and crucks, and who scratches in the fields and woods for roots and berries – and who plants again, and sows again, and digs and hopes and prays to God and all his angels for half a happy harvest? Who, then? Our king? Our noble king? Our dark and muttering Henry? I think not! I know not!

Elspeth was standing now, hands on hips, her voice rising above the noise of the flames and fighting

The beam crashed against the door yet again, there was a sound of splintering wood, and some of the children began to scream.

'Ready!' yelled Markward. The villagers around him gave a roar of defiance. Some of the women went down on their knees and began to pray. Others took up sticks, and lumps of burning wood and anything they could find. Bernhardt, Ronan, Rainald and Johan charged forward and threw their weight behind the toppling barricade as the splintered door began to give way. Edvart the miller, one arm strapped to his side stood holding his flail in one hand. 'Give me space! Give me space!' he roared.

They could see the tip of the ram now as it smashed its way through the timbers and metal fixings of the door. The hinges were bowed back and ready to give way.

'Up shields!' growled Wulfstan, and he turned and winked at Cedric who stood beside him three paces back from the barricade. 'A good day to die, old shepherd!' he said.

Cedric smiled and spat. 'No day's good to die, if you've a day to live for', he replied, and swung his staff off his shoulder and levelled it at the door.

'Hah!' shouted Wulfstan. 'A Viking among us, a Viking!'

The ram burst through the centre timbers with a crack, and the top hinge snapped from its mounting. Helmets, hauberks, spearpoints and swords glittered through the shadows from the other side. Markward took one last glance back over his shoulder. Elsa was there. Standing in the middle of the church, by the fire, her arm wrapped around Brunni. She was staring at him.

He nodded, and she gave a kind of half wave with the fingers of one hand.

As he turned back to the breaking door, shards of tile crashed at his feet, and shouts were heard from above.

'They're on the roof!' said Eric. 'Small matter, now. Perhaps young Geyorg can tickle them with his bow.'

Markward looked up. ' Well, if they come through on our heads, we'll die quicker, that's all. Up, men! Here they come!'

With a final tearing groan the door gave way, twisted sideways, and then crashed inwards to the floor. The barricade scattered, and the ragged line of shields flinched but held. Roaring and screaming the Liutizen hurled themselves into the church.

Up on the tower, Geyorg gave a gasp of amazement, and half-smiled. One of his arrows had struck a Liutizen warrior in the neck sending him spinning over the edge of the roof. He nocked another arrow, and called out to the other two lads: 'Keep firing! They're breaking through the roof!'

This time his arrow struck a Liutizen in the small of the back as he was hammering at the tiles. He lurched sideways, clutching at his back and slithered down the roof. There was a cry of rage and a throwing axe appeared as if from nowhere, struck the edge of the parapet, and skimmed Geyorg's shoulder. He dropped his bow and fell on one knee, shaking with fear and shock.

'It's all right!' called one of the lads, and then slumped back with an arrow in his chest.

Geyorg, the tears starting, fought to control his breathing. He took hold of his bow, and still kneeling, nocked another arrow. More Liutizen shafts, black and barbed, hissed over the parapet. The sound of fighting welled up from inside the church, and he knew that the raiders had broken in. With a shout he sprang to his feet, the remaining boy with him, and they fired one last time at the figures on the roof.

Markward felt his sword bite through leather, flesh and bone, twisting it as the blade went home. An iron-masked warrior grunted and went down among the stamping feet. Shields clashed and thudded, and screams filled the air as the villagers fought to protect wives and children huddled at their backs. It was all over now. Only a matter of time. Only a little while before the blood-crazed mob overwhelmed the fading circle, and killed all that lay before them. But the villagers fought on, cornered, desperate, filled with rage and fear and driven by the kind of madness that men feel when death reaches out to take them and their loved ones by the throat.

Edvart the miller fell to a spear thrust. He brought his flail down hard upon the head of the man who slew him, then sank to his knees, cried his wife's name once and died. Morcar fell, and Aylrick too, as they stood in the shield wall and shouted defiance at their killers. Johan had his jaw broken, but stayed on his feet and used his splintered shield to cover Bernhardt as he hammered at the Liutizen line.

Slowly they were forced back across the church towards the fire where the women and children, the old men and the wounded were gathered. Tiles and chunks of rough plaster crashed about their heads as the Liutizen broke more holes in the roof. Soon the attackers would be able to fire on them from above or even drop down onto the shoulders of the villagers. Gusts of icy wind cut through the shattered doorway and blew smoke and ashes and sparks in stinging clouds of grey and black.

Markward fought, and cried out loud, and prayed that the end would come swiftly for them all, and that there would be no prisoners for the Liutizen to sacrifice.

Jan the priest suddenly appeared with a great wooden crucifix raised above his head as though it was a club. He shouted, pushed through the shield wall and rushed at a Liutizen axeman who cut him down with scarcely half a glance and kicked the crucifix away. A groan ran through the villagers, but they fought on, gasping and sobbing, and clenching their teeth against the rain of blows that fell upon shields and weapons and unprotected limbs.

Elspeth, wife of Oskar the tanner who fell at Hochtal, lifted Mutti up from where she was crouched, holding Brunni and Albrecht.

'Come, mother,' she said, 'Time to do our work here.' She handed Mutti a sharpened stick. 'Make them feel our pain and sorrow – then no more.'

Elsa stood too, but this time she kept one arm firmly around little Hetti, and whispered in her ear, and told her all would yet be well. Rainald, torn and bleeding in the battle line, just a pace or two from his daughter, risked a fleeting look, then flinched as a sword point darted at his throat.

On the tower roof, all seemed quiet. Geyorg lay panting, fingers gingerly holding the shaft of the arrow that had driven through his arm. He was listening to the sounds of the fighting far below, wanting to move, yet not daring to. The pain from his arm throbbed through his shoulder and neck, and his back felt bruised and sore where he had fallen against the stonework.

Soon he must move, but not yet. He would wait till the pain lessened a bit, then perhaps he could sit up. The cold seemed to eat at him now, and he could hear screams and shouts above the crackling of the flames and the din of iron on iron.

And then there came a sound, a soft sound from afar off. It came to him like a dream, like a breeze, like a soughing wind among the trees beyond the meadow. It was almost as though he had not heard, only imagined such a sound, as if he were drifting off to sleep and soon nothing more would matter: a sound of angels. There it was again: far, and far beyond. A rising sound like no other he had ever heard. It was not a dream. He lifted his head. For a moment the sound was lost in the noise of fighting, and then there it was again – this time clear, and sharp and ringing, and as close as the crest of the far ridge: the sound of a horn.

In the church the Liutizen had gone back a pace to snatch their breath before they went in for the kill. Their quarry had shown sharp teeth, and had fought back, but it was weakened now, and on its knees and ready to die. These Saxon villagers had fought well, too well, but of course the end had come, and there was a time to take breath, and lean on sword and shield, and taunt them before they were finally struck down.So the Liutizen called out in their own tongue to the villagers telling them to beg for mercy and a quick death. The villagers did not reply, and Markward, standing in the middle of their exhausted, broken ranks had simply pointed his sword at the chieftain warrior with the bronzed helmet and horsehair plume, then spat on the blade and pointed again.

It was a challenge. It was a call to personal combat that all men on the Eastern Marches understood: a fight to the death. There was more despair in it than honour, but it was part of a rough code that passed between the tribes and clans and villages of these lands. It had to be answered.

The Liutizen ranks fell silent. The chieftain warrior paused, glanced at his men, and then smiled. He opened his mouth to speak, but before he could utter a word, the call of a horn sounded through the windows. It sounded long and clear, and had the deep, harsh note of a battle-horn. It was still far off, but not too far off, and when it sounded again, they all knew it was coming this way.

'The Weissburg!' shouted Wulfstan, and all the villagers cheered, and rattled their shields.

The Liutizen warriors looked to their chieftain. He screamed with rage, raised his battle axe and rushed at Markward.

Geyorg got painfully to his knees and risked a look over the parapet. There up on the ridge was a single horseman, almost silhouetted against the pale sky, but even at that distance he could tell that he was carrying a banner.

As Geyorg watched another horseman appeared. The horn sounded once more, and as if it were a signal the length of the ridge seemed suddenly covered with riders. For a moment they held their ground, the fading light glinting off ringmail and helmets and spearpoints. Then they surged down the slope. The deep greens and washed browns of the sloping heathland seemed to flow around them, as they galloped downwards, following the shadowed folds of the northern ridge. For a moment they disappeared behind and beyond a straggling grove of laurel and birch, and then as Geyorg watched, his eyes shining with excitement and relief, they burst into view at the end of the long meadow. With spears dipped, and shields held from shoulder to knee, they thundered towards the village.

The attack of the Liutizen chieftain sent Markward sprawling, but he rolled to one side and avoided the swinging axe blade which rang against the stone floor. He was scrambling to his feet when the Liutizen struck again, this time with a scything back cut aimed at the ribs. He caught the blow, on the hilt of his sword, where the quillon joins the blade. It jarred his wrist and elbow, but he drove with his shield, and caught the chieftain under the chin, making his teeth crackle. With a cry, Markward closed on his opponent, shortening his stroke, and striking with the pommel at the face. The Liutizen swayed to one side, and then stepped forward and butted him hard with the rim of his helmet, just above the nose. For a moment the room spun, and a thousand pinpoints of light filled Markward's eyes. He staggered back, and waited for the axe to strike.

There was a thud, and the screech of steel against iron. From behind his left shoulder a hand grabbed him and tugged him back. He felt the cool wind of the axe blade as it swept by his cheek, and he shook his head to clear his vision. Wulfstan had stepped in front of him, yelling defiance, shield held out at arms length, and his short-hafted axe held at the low guard.

It was now that Markward, still stunned by the blow, realised that the whole Liutizen line had charged forward. They were desperate to finish off the villagers before help arrived, and enraged that somehow their prey might escape them. Cursing and bellowing they tore and battered at the ragged line of shields. But the villagers shouted back, lifting their voices above the din, and urging each other on. The shouts of 'Eckerheim!' and 'Saxon!' mingled with the Liutizen cries, and shields were split and bloodied as men fought and struggled to keep on their footing.

Markward found himself back by the fire, where Ronan had dragged him. He tried to stand, but the floor seemed to sway, and suddenly there were arms about him and he saw Elsa's steady gaze.

'You're hurt,' she said. He could hardly hear her above the roar of the fighting, and the ringing in his ears.

'I'm fine,' he replied, and pushed her away. 'It's nothing.' The floor was still swaying, but not as much as before. 'I must help.'

'Then help by staying here!' Elsa was shouting now. 'If they break through, we'll need you!'

Markward gazed at her blankly, then nodded slowly. 'I'll be here.'

She swallowed hard, sat back and looked away for a moment. Markward caught her glance. 'He fights well', he said. 'He's a good man.'

'Bernhardt?'

'Aye, Bernhardt. He fights for you this day, Elsa. You know that, don't you? He's like a lion, a warrior, a ring bearer. There's no blacksmith in him today!' He gave a short laugh, and got unsteadily to his feet. Elsa reached out to steady him, but he waved her away. 'It's for you, Elsie, all for you – and there's no way I'll blame him.'

'Nor me?'

Markward tensed, his eyes fixed on the fighting men, not much more than a sword's length away. He frowned, then stood his own sword point down and leant on the pommel. 'Nor you, Elsie, nor you.'

The shield wall buckled, Ulrich the swineherd staggered back with a gash across his neck, and Markward swung his sword to guard. 'The children!' he called. 'Keep them close with you, and stay down!' His head was pounding, but he felt steady on his feet, and he knew that help must be close by. A Liutizen spearman broke through the shield wall with a snarl of triumph and rushed towards the fire. Markward stood his ground for just a moment, then fell on one knee so that the spear-point passed over his shoulder, grazing his neck. He drove his sword out, and upward, grasping the hilt with two hands and grimacing as he braced for the shock. The point of the blade caught the spearman in the midriff, just below his ring mail shirt, and transfixed him. The blow knocked Markward backwards, almost into the fire, and the dying man toppled onto him. He wriggled free, and snatched up the spear, as pain and nausea swept across his chest.

The horn sounded again, this time from inside the village itself. As if bent to its call, the Liutizen fell back. They dragged their wounded with them, spitting and hissing as they went.

The villagers gave a gasping, croaking cheer but too exhausted to follow, leant on their spears and staves and watched as the Liutizen crowded back through the doorway. Women wept with relief, hugging the children and rocking back and forth.

Now all they could hear was the thunder of the approaching horsemen, heading up the street towards the church, drawn by a single small figure on the tower waving a piece of bloody rag through the drifting smoke.

There were cries of command as the Liutizen formed themselves into a battle line across the street. Almost immediately the rising sound of hooves and harness was swept away in a single crushing torrent as the squadron of horsemen charged home against the Liutizen. The sound of men and horses and the clash of weapons was almost lost in the drumming thud of the collision.

Slowly the fighting faded: a last clash of steel, a few groans, a call for water – nothing more. Here and there a horse snorted and reared, jangling its harness, while others skittered, wheeled and stood to the command of their riders. Someone called out in a heavy Saxon curse, and there was weary laughter in reply.

Markward, scarcely standing now, and supported by Wulfstan made his way out into the street followed by Eric, and Rainald, Johan and Ronan, and all the other men who were still able to walk. They looked up at men who seemed like giants – giant men on giant horses, men in gleaming coats of mail and conical helms, with great kite shields and pennoned lances. They in turn looked down on the ragged, bloodied villagers.

'I see we are in time', said the leading knight. He pushed back his mail coif and ran his fingers through his raw black hair. 'Liutizen?'

'Aye, my lord!' said Markward. 'They came at us last night.'

The knight nodded and smiled his dark eyes flickering over the bodies of the dead and dying. 'I am Robard, a captain of the Weissburg, and knight to our lord the Markgraf. Our scout brought word. You're lucky he has sharp sight and a good wit.'

'And a good horse!' called out one of the other knights, and someone laughed.

Eric the Bailiff stepped forward: 'God's blessing on you sire!' he said, touching his forelock. We were all dead men here, if you had not come.'

Robard waved his hand. 'Tis our due,' he said. 'We are of the Weissburg and Eckerheim lies within our lord Markgraf's estates. You are his people, and we heard your cry.' He looked around at the smoking, burning houses and the church. 'You took your stand in there?'

'Aye, my lord. With the women and children. It seemed the thing to do.'

The knight nodded. 'But there are bodies in the meadow. You tried to meet them in the open, with a shield wall.'

Eric looked at Markward who was about to speak, but Wulfstan cut in: 'We did, my lord. We could not tell how many there were at first. They came at us from the dark . . .'

'Just so, just so.' The knight swung down from the saddle. 'Anyway, 'twas bravely done. Bravely done. Someone here knows of soldiering, I'll warrant.'

'Aye, lord,' replied Wulfstan. 'But we are for the most part farming folk. It was Markward here who held us together.'

The women and children came cautiously out of the church. Someone went up to the tower and helped Geyorg down. The Wise Woman and Gustav the tanner looked to his wound. Cedric hurried to his flock. Bernhardt and Johan, his jaw all swollen, were helping Elsa, Mutti and the last of the womenfolk to carry the wounded from the church to the glebe barn. It was still standing, and it would be warm there, stocked as it was with hay and good straw.

The knights, under instruction from Robard, ordered the men at arms and squires to help with the wounded, to put out the fires, and to strip and bury the Liutizen dead. The dead villagers, Jan the priest among them, would be buried on the morrow with as much ceremony as they could muster.

The day was drawing in now. The skies had cleared and a biting cold was sinking in across the village. Eric and Wulfstan led a group of villagers down to the meadow to bring in the dead of Eckerheim who had fallen in the first fight. Rainald and Rohan helped clear the church. There was no crypt, but there was a storeroom off the South wall and they used it to lay out the bodies and prepare them for burial. They had lost a good many men, but there was still work to do, and a village to be rebuilt, and the heavy grip of Winter was upon them.

First they would rekindle the fire in the church, and re-set the cauldron, and prepare for an evening meal – from such food as they could find among the ruins of their broken village. Robard and his men had brought supplies enough for themselves on a two day ride, so there was little left over for them to share. Besides, the villagers insisted that it was they who should feed the Weissburg knights. Men, women, and children – all who could walk and were not busy elsewhere on other tasks, scoured the village looking for food. Singly, and in twos and threes they came hurrying back to the church with whatever they could find. Mostly it was very little – at best a loaf or two, or a handful of grain, or some dried fruit – but someone found two sides of salted pork, and someone else a rack of half-baked bread from the back of the baker's oven, and still another came across a barrel of mead which the Liutizen had not found and drunk.

As the sun set, the fire blazed in the church and the weary villagers feasted as best they could with their rescuers. They sorrowed for their kinfolk who had died. They rejoiced that they and their children still lived. They sang the old songs of the Eastern plains, and slapped each other on the back and kissed, and then saluted the night and the days ahead with wooden cups of rough maize mead. Joy and sorrow, old and young, on Christmas night in Eckerheim.

Bernhardt sat with Elsa near the fire, and stared into the flames. The madness and the fear of the day had passed, and he felt a deep tiredness. He put his arm around Elsa and drew her close: 'When the green leaves come', he said. Elsa looked up at him and smiled. Death had seemed so close today, and yet somehow they had cheated it. Perhaps after all they would see the Spring. Perhaps, despite all the killing and burning and sorrow, they would see safe days and peace in this valley. There was always that hope.

'A penny for your thoughts?'

Elsa started as Bernhardt spoke to her. 'I was just thinking that we may yet have all we wish for.' She drew her cloak about her and stared at Hetti snuggled up against her father on the other side of the fire.

Bernhardt nodded. 'I pray I never again take my hammer from the smithy.'

'You fought well. Markward said so.'

Bernhardt shrugged. 'Look you, Elsie, I was mad today, just mad. I fought full of madness and anger because . . .because . . .'

'We might never see the spring.'

'Aye . . . aye, just so. You have it. There was no warrior in me, Elsie, just anger.'

'Well, it kept us both alive.' She reached out, and took his hand and squeezed it.

Robard found Markward down in the glebe barn among the wounded. His head was still sore, and he needed rest, and felt that there he could find it.

But he looked up and smiled when he saw the knight come in.

'Well met', said Robard, and placing his torch in the holder on the wall he sat down on a wooden bench.

'I'm grateful my lord . . .' Markward began.

'Enough of that!' laughed Robard. '*I* was grateful to find you folks still alive. The old Markgraf would've boxed my ears if he came back from Goslar to find that I'd let all his villages be razed to the ground.'

'There's precious little left of Eckerheim.'

Robard rubbed his short-cropped beard thoughtfully: 'The buildings are burnt – well most of them – but the people are here, and that's what counts. Still, we've got to make sure you don't freeze to death or starve now that the Liutizen have gone.'

'They've all gone then?'

'Aye! Those we didn't kill. I rode their chieftain down myself. A few scuttled away between the crucks as we came up the street, but I've sent scouts after them. They'll ride them down or drive them deep into the forest. Either way, they won't be troubling you anymore – or not for a good while yet.' He sighed and looked around. 'And by then the Markgraf will be back, and all should be well.'

'In the spring.'

'Aye, in the spring. My lord Henry the king will send the Markgraf back to the Weissburg in the spring. Rumours are that mayhaps the king will come himself, but I'll expect it when I see it.'

Markward suddenly realised that he was lying down in the presence of a constable and started to get to his feet, but Robard waved him down:

'Rest up! Markward is it? Aye, well you led these people well. Without a leader they'd be like marsh rabbits, and prey to any Liutizen blade – but you kept them together – with a shield wall no less.'

'More hedge than shield wall I fear, my lord.'

'But good enough. It held, didn't it? Come on, man, take the credit where it's due – and tell me now, where did you learn your soldiering?'

A woman appeared out of the shadows with a steaming bowl. It was the wise woman. She nodded to Robard and then knelt beside Markward: 'Here! Drink this. Good herbs. From the forest. They'll help your head.'

Markward thanked her, drank, and she was gone again. He felt the warmth flowing through his body, and soothing his head.

'My soldiering? Three seasons ago now, I mustered with others from the village, and marched to Fulda. The bishop had summoned us, but it was a royal warrant, and we were to fight in the king's wars.'

'Friesia?'

'Aye, my lord. Friesia. A place I'd never seen before, and hope never to see again.'

Robard laughed. 'Aye. I know it well enough myself: where the marshes touch the sky, and the sun is lost in the sea.'

'And full of pirates.'

'And king's men full of Rhenish wine.' He stood up. 'Well, Markward of Eckerheim, rest up now and take your ease. You've earnt it. Tomorrow, or maybe the day after, once we're sure the Liutizen have gone, we'll be returning to the Weissburg. But do not forget me. If in the spring you tire of this village, and you would do more soldiering then come to the Weissburg. My lord the Markgraf will welcome you into his hall, that I know.'

'My lord is generous.'

'My lord Dietmar is a soldier and he would defend this Mark. That's all.' He acknowledged Markward's awkward bow, then turned and left.

Markward leant back, and gazed up at the rafters. Yes, maybe that was it: he would be a retainer in the service of the Markgraf. Perhaps one day a squire. Perhaps one day . . . His shoulder ached, his head hurt . . . He could still visit Mutti, and Albrecht and Brunni, he could still do that. . . .And no more talk of marriage. Yes, he would be as a priest, a warrior monk . . .He smiled at this . . .but without his Elsa, without her, what was there? He may as well go a soldiering . . .after all, yes he would be a soldier. And no need to go to Fulda.

The drink the wise woman had given him was strengthening now. He felt warm and somehow light, and the pain was fading. There were people stirring in the shadows, like shadows themselves, and groans and mutterings and someone crying in their sleep, but he scarce heard them. He kept his eyes fixed on the rafters, hanging in the gloom, and wondered if there were still a roof and rafters above his own hearth.

His father used to sit by that hearth on winter nights and tell them stories of far-off lands and strange folk, though he had never left the valley himself. He used to say that a man is born to carry a spear or push a plough, and it's foolish to make him do both . . .

Someone had lit a fire on a make-shift gathering of bricks in the centre of the barn, and smoke was drifting across the rafters.

His mother used to sing them a rhyme whenever they had a fever, or it was a stormy night and they could not sleep:

'The boy will be a farmer
The girl will know the loom
To gather wood
Or draw the well
Its known from the womb.
But one will be a soldier
And one will thresh the wheat
And one will die in foreign lands
And they should never meet. . .'

How she sang. So soft, so clear. And she had long fingers and slender hands, like a princess, but all calloused and rough from a peasant's life.

'And they should never meet . . .' His Elsa, she would marry a farmer, but he would be a soldier, and they should never meet.

Still, he could picture himself, three times a twelve month, on a fine horse, cresting the ridge to the north of the village, come from the Weissburg to see the family. He could see that . . . But he could not see his Elsa. She was lost to him, and he would not marry . . .and so the rafters faded, and so he slept.

Three days later, at the height of the morning, the men of the Weissburg left the village. They had helped to bury the dead, to clear the village, to put out the smouldering fires, and even to start some of the rebuilding work. They left with a promise to return in the spring, in time for the Barley planting. Robard took Eric and Markward aside and told them to send word at the least sign of trouble. 'I will come myself', he said, 'And I will come in the same way.'

The village folk watched them go, and then turned to the work of repairing the village, and getting in what food they could before winter found them out. The harvest was in, but there was work to be done tending the fields and looking to the newly sown crops of rye, and corn and winter wheat. The weather had cleared, but the frosts were sharp, and a gentle breeze from the east promised snow again before long.

Cedric was hard at work raking out feed for his flock when Markward found him. 'Well met, old shepherd.'

Cedric paused and straightened up. 'And well met to you, old friend.'

'I thought I'd find you here.'

'Where else?'

'Just so.' Markward scratched the back of his head, and stared thoughtfully at the fold.

'You've a question for me, or you've come to help', said Cedric bending to his task again.

'Both if you like.'

'I like that well enough. Here, there's another hay fork by that bothy.'

For a time they worked together, and neither said a word.

At length, Markward stopped, and leant on his hay fork.

'In the spring, I shall be a soldier.'

'For my lord the Markgraf.'

'You knew?'

'I guessed. It was not a clever guess, but a guess all the same.'

Markward raked out the last of the feed and sat down by the fold.

'If I serve at the Weissburg . . .'

Cedric held up one hand. 'No need to explain. I understand.'

'And you approve?'

'Approve? Am I your father that I should approve what you do?'

'I would that you were my father, and even if not, I respect your opinion.'

'Respect or no, you may not like the telling of my opinion.'

'Let me be the judge of that.'

'You would judge me then?'

Markward shot Cedric a fiery glance, but saw that his friend was smiling. He shook his head and stood up. 'I would just know what you think, that's all.'

'My young friend . . .' Cedric knelt down beside one of his sheep that was munching away at the straw. He ran his fingers through the fleece on its back. 'See this sheep. It's content. It's happy. And why is that? It's because it takes one day at a time. It deals with what's in front of it. It does not worry about tomorrow.'

'Aye, it has you to do the worrying for it.'

'And we have the Good Lord to do the worrying for us.'

'You're preaching, old friend.'

'I'm trying to tell you something.'

'And what is that?'

Cedric sighed, and stood up again. 'You cannot serve at the Weissburg until the spring. That's many days from now. Weeks, even. Things change. People change – their minds, leastways. Rest here, now. There's work to do, your family to look after, the village to see to. Eric needs everyone.'

'She means to marry Bernhardt. There's little for me here now – save . . .'

'Save everything else! Your words are full of dust, Markward: old words, dry words, words with nothing in them except wounded pride.'

Markward reddened, but held his peace. At last he spoke: 'I love her.'

'Hah! Love! Such an easy word to say!' The shepherd shook his head wearily. 'If you really love her, then let her go, and she'll love you, but as a sister loves a brother and not as her man.'

'That's not enough.'

'Aye, aye – I suppose it's not, and I suppose it never will be, but it's best you have, and it's a good sight better than rotting away in the castle guard at the Weissburg.' With a shrug, Cedric tossed the rake to one side, and stared up at the hills.

Markward got slowly to his feet. 'If it's not Elsa, then it's no one. I'll marry no one else. I'll . . .'

'Be a monk and a priest, and without the habit. Aye you will – just to spite yourself you will, and when the right young lass comes along you won't have the wit to spot her – you'll be so buried deep in your wounded pride.'

'Sharp words, old friend.'

'Faithful ones. Mark them well. If Elsa's not yours, then take it like a man, and look to what each day brings, and don't go whimpering off on some crusade to nowhere.'

Markward was silent. He looked away down the long meadow, and scuffed a stone with his boot. 'I'll be away then', he said. He waved, and was gone, heading back towards the village.

When Spring comes to Eckerheim, the first sign is a blue haze on the high tops as the heather flowers bloom. And then, the birds long gone to the South come wheeling about in little clusters and settle in the trees beyond the meadow, chattering and calling as they come. And the leaves: suddenly they are there, as a mist of softest green, shining against the frost blackened branches of the oaks and birches, and broad-limbed elms. And the people lift their heads – and sweep clear the hearths, and kick out the straw, and stand in doorways to let the sunlight fall against their faces.

At last, in the spring, the land was at peace. For over three months now there had been no sign of raiders, nor bandits, nor wandering King's men. In late January the snows had come, deep snows that blew in from the East, piling up drifts against the hedges and spinneys, and covering the valley in a shimmering white blanket that all but hid the little village. But there was enough food – just – and enough wood, and the people did not starve. The wolves had gathered on the tops, and howled when the moon was frosted, but they would not come down while fires burnt on the hearths, and watchdogs slept on the threshold of every cruck.

The folk gathered around the house fires and ate their rough rye bread dipped in lentil pottage, and blessed their fortune and remembered the fight. It was already called the 'Christmas Fight', though folks from the hams and hamlets to the West of the village simply called it the 'Fight at Eckerheim'. Already someone had made a song of the fight, but they were slow to sing it. It reminded them of their dead, and all that they had lost.

And so as the snows melted and the days grew longer, Eric the Bailiff called the people to the fields. There was ploughing and sowing to be done, and when the Markgraf came, as surely he must, he would look to see it all in hand.

Nearly all the houses had been rebuilt, though on some the thatching was incomplete, and they had been forced to use winter rushes instead of the summer ones they favoured. The miller's house still lay in ruins, and his widow now lived with the tanner's family. Gustav had agreed to take over the mill, though he himself had lost a son in the fight, and he would need help to quarry stone, and bring down timber from the low ridge forest.

Most of the folk from Hochtal were still living in the village, and they were welcomed. With the grave yard full of those who had fallen at Christmas, the families of Eckerheim were glad for anyone who would stay and help. For the most part they had built their own crucks on land given to them by Eric, and they worked alongside the Eckerheimers in the fields and in the woodland. A pedlar who happened by, looking to sell trinkets and ribbons, said that Hochtal still lay in ruins, as did Maibach. There was talk that the Markgraf might call the people back to Hochtal by Whitsuntide, but as yet there was no need and little desire. There was no sign of any survivors from Maibach, and unless the King brought in colonists from Magdeburg it seemed that the village would be lost forever.

Cedric now called Eckerheim his home. He had built a fold of stone and wattle and thatch, and his sheep grazed among the others on the spring meadows that lay beyond the stream. Bernhardt was living with the blacksmith's family, down by the old barn. He worked happily alongside Jakob and his son, Hec. The family all called him Brother Bernhardt, and it was said that he was thinking of settling down in Eckerheim. Rainald and Hetti were living with Johan the Carpenter and his wife in the house by the sheep pond. And there, too, in a little cruck Johan had built with Rainald's help, lived Elsa and Elspeth. The talk of the women at the village well was that Elsa would marry Bernhardt before the spring was full, and that Rainald would marry Elspeth, now her Oskar had gone.

Some folks said that they would have to wait until the good bishop of Fulda sent a priest to say the vows, but others said that a country wedding would do just as well until the priest came – as long as the bailiff said the prayers, and as long as the bride price was paid.

Some folk talked of Markward, but he had gone. He had ridden out of Eckerheim with the first breath of spring, promising to return within the three-month. He had stayed to repair the cruck for Mutti, and to make sure that all was well for the family – and then he had gone. There were tears: Mutti cried, and Brunni cried, but little Albrecht just held his breath and said he would never cry. Instead he stood for ages staring up at the high ridge long after Markward had waved for the last the time and disappeared. It took Wulfstan, and a hunting trip for rabbits to make him smile again, and chase the chickens round the yard.

THE MUSTER

As the warmer Spring days softened the land and brought colour back to woods and fields, news came drifting in that the King himself was on the march - and coming this way. At first the folk shook their heads and said that such talk was chaff on the wind, but there came a day when a rider from the Weissburg galloped into the village. He handed a letter to Wulfstan who could not read, and so handed it to Eric who could. The bailiff read it out loud to the villagers all gathered at the well. It said that the Markgraf was coming. It said that he was coming within ten days, and that he wanted to see the headmen of Eckerheim: the King would speak with them, and so they must needs know what they should say.

The king! Eckerheim! The word fled round the village like an excited thrush. No king had ever come to Eckerheim before. It was rare enough to see the Markgraf, though he was lord of this village, and few men or women had ever seen the bishop in these parts.

The king! Once his father's seneschal had passed by on the high road that led to Maibach, but that was years ago and only the old folk could remember it.

And so Lord Dietmar, the markgraf came, and twenty men with him, and one of these was Markward – riding a deep chested black stallion and dressed in a fine coat of mail, with a red leather scabbard for his sword. The children scuttled back into the crucks as the horsemen thundered into the village. They peeped nervously out from the doorways, pushing each other and giggling as their mothers and cousins and aunts bustled about making ready the meal Eric had promised to welcome his lord.

The barn had been cleared and set with trestles and boards. There the villager elders gathered and there they waited for their master. The Markgraf, tall, bluff, with greying beard and deep dark eyes, took his time. First he wanted to look at the village he had not seen for so long, the village that had stood against the Liutizen, and survived, but barely.

Sir Robard, with Eric three paces behind, showed him around. The other soldiers looked to the horses and exchanged a few awkward greetings with the young men and girls of the village.

Markward and another man at arms were told to take three of the horses down to the blacksmiths. Albrecht trotted along behind them. They found Jakob and Bernhardt, working together at the anvil and forge.

Bernhardt looked up, paused, then smiled and waved a greeting. Markward nodded, but barely. 'These horses,' he said. 'They have thrown shoes.'

Jakob grunted and shrugged, and brought his hammer down hard on the hinge plate he was forging. There was a silence.

'The Markgraf would be obliged if you could shoe them,' said Markward.

'At the Markgraf's price no doubt.'

'We will pay you. Two silver pennies for each horse.'

Jakob looked up, and placed his hammer to one side. ' It'll be bronze shoes you're wanting then?'

'Aye, bronze.'

'Well' — he scratched his head — 'I'll see what I can do. No promises, mind. We don't get much call for horseshoes in Eckerheim. You'd know that, my lad.'

'I know it, Jakob.' He glanced at Bernhardt who had turned back to the forge. ' But we . . .'

'Aye, aye. Just so. Leave your horses here. Hec will take care of them. But remember, no promises now. I can't go spiriting bronze up from nowhere.'

'I'll thank you then, and leave you to your work.'

Jakob watched Markward and the other soldier, and Albrecht, their little shadow, head back towards the other end of the village. He sighed, and picked up his hammer again.

'Come on, young Bernhardt! We'll finish this hinge then see what we can find that'll please their lordships.'

Bernhardt laughed. ' He's not so bad, Jakob.'

'Not so bad? He's a whelped bear with a sore head, because you've got his girl – that's what he is.'

'Well, I can't help that,' Bernhardt smiled, and stirred the charcoal fire, and watched the embers glow.

Jakob stared after Markward and shook his head. He steadied the hinge, spat on it to see if it had enough heat, and then gave it three hits with the hammer.

'There! That's it. Old Peter can get that barn door up again. Now come on, help me find some bronze scrap from the box out back. Either that or some good quality iron should do well enough.'

'We'll need a strong fire if we're going to cast those shoes.'

'Too right we will, but Hec won't let me down there. He's a good lad with the bellows . . . Come on! Stop dreaming about your girl. If we don't get this done by the morrow we'll have the Markgraf dancing on our backs.'

Markward headed towards the barn. There were women, Brunni and Mutti among them, bringing food down for the feast. They were laughing, chatting but turned and smiled and waved when they saw him. He waved back, and looked down as he felt a tug at his sword belt. It was Albrecht.

'Ho there, little man! Are you going to follow me all day?' He stopped and lifted Albrecht up in his arms. The boy beamed and gave his brother a hug.

'What's it like at the castle, Marki? Tell me!'

'Oh, it's nothing much. Just high white towers, and shining battlements, and deep dungeons, golden halls and beautiful princesses – that sort of thing.'

'Really?'

'Really! Well almost. But listen, you'll have to ask Mutti if you can visit me one day. It's not far you know. Just a couple of days away.'

Albrecht dropped to the ground and danced about his brother: 'Oh can I, oh can I? When? When?'

Markward laughed and held up his hands. 'Slow down! I'll speak to Mutti.'

'Will you? Promise?'

'I promise. Now come along. There's work to be done.'

Albrecht ran in front, then suddenly stopped and turned about. 'Can Bernhardt come, and Elsa too? I know they'd like to.'

Markward halted in mid stride, his eyes flashed and he frowned – but just for a moment. 'Ach, no. No. It wouldn't be right. I mean . . .'

'But why, Marki? Why?'

'Because little Albrecht . . .' There was a soft voice almost out of nowhere. Man and boy spun round, and there was Elsa. 'Because little Albrecht' she went on, 'It would not be right. Is that not so, Marki?'

Markward blushed, not sure whether to be angry or happy that Elsa had used his familiar name. He stared at the girl he had lost. She smiled back at him, and gave a little curtsey – just a bob – then brushed her hair back under the scarf. 'I'm away down to see the men at the forge. They'll be wanted at the moot now.'

'They're seeing to new shoes for our horses.'

Elsa hesitated, uncertain whether to continue or not: 'The folk are gathering. The Markgraf is there, and his knights too. And I see you are set that way yourselves.'

Markward turned away. 'Do whatever you please', he said. 'Come on Albrecht!'

Elsa watched him go. Her head dropped a little and for a moment she clasped her hands. Then she made as if to brush her hair once more and hurried on down towards the forge.

Albrecht trotted along beside Markward. 'You're not angry are you Marki?'

'I'm not angry.'

'But you look angry.'

'Soldiers often look angry.'

'Even when they're not?'

'Even when they're not.'

'Well that's all right then.' Albrecht laughed and took his brother's hand, and led him to the moot.

The trestle tables were weighed down with every type of food and drink the villagers of Eckerheim could provide. They stood around in stooped and anxious groups, while the men of the Weissburg took their places at the feast. Then the Markgraf stood and waved the people forward. He cleared his throat. He was not used to this sort of thing. Announcements and pronouncements he usually left to his chaplain but the poor nervous fellow was not with him. He had begged to be allowed to stay in the shelter of the castle. As a chaplain who never left the bounds of the Weissburg, he was terrified of riding across the moors while there were still Liutizen about. Reluctantly the Markgraf had agreed to leave him behind, and so now he had to speak for himself.

'Come forward!' he said. 'There is food enough for all – thanks to your generosity. But before we eat you must listen.' He waited while the villagers shuffled forward. 'Now, the King – whom many call the emperor, and you will address him as such – the King has set out from his palace at Goslar to march to the Eastern borders. He is coming at the head of a great army, and he is coming here.' He waited again till the murmuring stopped. 'And why does he want to come here? Why? Well, I'll tell you. It's because you're the only village between here and Leipzig that put up anything like a halfway decent defence. And what's more, you have survived.'

'God bless you for that, my lord!' someone called out.

The Markgraf nodded. 'Well, you've got my men to thank for that. I was busy filling my belly at the King's table at Goslar, while you were fighting for your lives.' He paused. 'Anyway, enough! You survived where others did not, and the King has come to hear of it, and he has decided to begin his Spring campaign against the Liutizen from this very spot.'

There were gasps, and anxious looks.

'Oh, don't worry, you won't have to feed the imperial army. The provenders will see to that. Nor will you have to billet them. They will camp beyond the meadows in the waste land. They'll be no trouble to you. They may be king's men – and I know your opinion of king's men – but they are under the forfeit of their lives to treat you as they would treat their closest kinsmen – and to be ready to pay for any service they may seek.'

'But my lord! The Liutizen have gone.'

The Markgraf grunted and stuck his thumbs in his belt. 'Gone have they? Gone? No my friend, they have not gone – well not as you might hope they would go. They have just gone back apace, to Dresdany by the Elbe, and beyond the Neisse to Lusatia. They have gone to their tribal villages to lick their wounds and rest their bones. But they will be back, all of them: Zirzipanen and Redarier, Tollenser and Kessiner. And this time they will come in a great host.'

'We have stood against them once my lord,' said Rainald quietly.

'Aye, you have and well. We scattered them like crows. But this time they will come down as wolves, because they left the blood of their chieftain in the mud of this village. It is blood for blood. He was of the Kessiner – Sir Robard tells me – and his death here is an insult that they will not let rest.'

There was a long silence. Some of the villagers glanced anxiously at one another. Many stood with bowed heads. The soldiers looked restless, eager to begin the meal.

'Will the king march from here, then my lord?' asked Wulfstan.

'Aye, he will', replied the Markgraf, grateful to carry on with what he had to say. 'Maibach has been destroyed, and Hochtal is good for little until next Spring. Kamienca was burnt to the ground, even though there were Slavs living there, and several farmsteads between Leipzig and Magdeburg are now no more.'

'Not all the work of Liutizen, I'll warrant', muttered Johan under his breath but the Markgraf did not seem to hear him.

'The king – and you will call him emperor whatever you feel about Salians – he will led the army from here, track along the Mulde river, and then head for the Elbe, crossing at Dresdany. If he fails to find the Liutizen he will head for the Neisse, cross it and strike East. That should draw them out.'

'We need to know this?' whispered Wulfstan to Eric from behind his hand.

This time the Markgraf did hear: 'Aye you do, because a good number of you Eckerheimers will be coming along.'

A groaning sigh ran among the villagers.

'Enough!' He held up his mailed glove. 'You will fight for the King as you have fought for me.'

'We fight for our homes and families!' someone called out.

'You fight for your king, because without him you would have no homes and no families!' roared the Markgraf and he brought his fist crashing down upon the table.

There was a terrible silence.

Then at last, with a slight shake in his voice, Markward spoke: 'My Lord, how many of us will the Emperor need?'

'He'll ask for a score, but we'll give him less: fit men, armed as a levy, no more than a dozen – but I would not count you among them. You are my liege man now.'

'I would be honoured to lead them in your name, my lord.'

The Markgraf smiled: 'Clever. But no – you will ride with me. Still, you can choose who will lead them, and the bailiff can choose who will stay.'

Markward thought for a moment. 'Then, I choose Wulfstan, First Man to the bailiff, my lord.'

'Done!' The Markgraf clapped his hands, and then sat down. 'Let the feasting begin!' he said.

Two days later, under an overcast sky and a gentle west wind, the men of the Weissburg prepared to leave. But before they did, as was customary, the Markgraf held a manor court.

A stone which stood in front of the village oak tree was where the people met, and here the Markgraf heard petitions and pleas.

There were the usual complaints about stolen eggs, missing boundary stones, and someone's cow wandering into someone else's crops. Several villagers applied to go to market at Leipzig, and two brothers agreed to divide their inheritance equally because their father had been killed in the fight against the Liutizen.

And then Eric the Bailiff brought forward Bernhardt and Elsa. The Markgraf looked up. 'Ah, Hochtalers! You have a petition!'

'Aye my lord,' said Bernhardt, glancing at Elsa, 'We are Elsa and Bernhardt of Hochtal and we would be married.'

'Marriage? Where are the parents?'

'Dead my lord.'

'What all of them? Both sides of the family?'

'Aye, my lord. When the Liutizen came to Hochtal. After the King's men came and burnt . . .'

'No more! I understand. Who speaks for you then?'

'I do my lord', said Eric.'They would be wed this spring but the priest is dead, and the bishop of Magdeburg is not like to come before Michelmas, nor the bishop of Fulda.'

'Nor any else of his brood', grunted the Markgraf. 'Well, what do you want of me? I can't say the vows. You know that. And I won't be having any of these pagan weddings, not with the King and his confessors due to descend upon us.'

'We thought perhaps your chaplain might . . .'

'At the Weissburg?' The Markgraf rubbed his chin. 'Aye, I suppose that's a possibility – the more so since that rascal is never likely to come here.' And he gave a short laugh. 'Now before we think any more of that, are there any objections here to these two becoming man and wife?' He raised his voice and looked around. 'Come on now! I'm a busy man, and off back to my castle by the forenoon hour. If any one has anything to say, let him speak now or hold his peace from this day.'

The rooks stirred in the tree tops behind the moot stone, but no one spoke. Elsa and Bernhardt looked straight ahead, heads slightly bowed. A thin misty rain began to fall.

'My lord!' It was Markward.

'Yes?'

'I . . . My lord . . .I . . .'

'Come on man! Get on with it. I haven't got all day. Do you have anything to say or not?'

'Well no, my lord – I mean yes. I mean . . . It's just that the horses won't be shod until gone the sixth hour.'

'So? So? What's this got to do with this couple wanting to get married?'

'Nothing my lord.' Markward bowed. 'I just thought you should know, seeing as you were going to leave earlier.'

The Markgraf stared: 'Man's a fool!' he said to Robard who stood grinning broadly at Markward's embarrassment.

'Anyone else?' roared the Markgraf. 'Any other bright suggestions? Right then.' He motioned towards Bernhardt. 'If you, Bernhardt of Hochtal, can come up with the bride price, I'll get my chaplain to do the rest. All right?'

'I am grateful my lord.'

'I hope you will be still saying that in a twelve month! Eh?'

'My lord, I will be saying it till the day I die.'

The Markgraf smiled. 'Spoken like a troubadour. Which you are not, I trust.'

'I am a blacksmith, sire.'

'A blacksmith. Well, you'll be responsible for shoeing my horses then. Away with you now, and come to the Weissburg with your lass when you have the bride price . . .' (Robard lent over and whispered in the Markgraf's ear.) '. . . which I set at 5 imperial shillings.'

Wearily, the Markgraf got to his feet. 'If that be all, then I close this manor court.' He clapped his hands together, all the villagers said 'aye', and bowed, and slowly moved away, except Eric who stayed behind to talk with Sir Robard.

Bernhardt hugged Elsa: 'I told you Elsie! When the green leaves come!' She laughed and kissed him on the cheek. 'To the Weissburg, then.'

'Aye, to the Weissburg. I have the bride price – well, I'm a shilling short, but Jakob will lend me that, I know it. He said he could help me out if needs must.'

'He likes you. You're a good worker, and he would have you stay.'

Bernhardt nodded. 'Perhaps, perhaps so. He's strong and he's honest, and he bears me no ill will.'

'Ill will? How could he?' She looked puzzled.

'He's Markward's uncle, Elsie.'

'I never knew.' Her face fell.

'Aye, well –he told me, but it was a passing remark, and not meant to hurt. There's no hurt in the man. He just wanted me to know.'

They walked arm in arm back down towards the forge. The rain grew steadier and little droplets covered their grey woollen cloaks, but the breeze had no chill, and all about them were the soft green leaves of spring.

Markward watched them go, and felt the same breeze against his back. It seemed to cut him to the bone, and the rain felt heavy against his cloak, and trickled down his neck beneath his tunic. He leant against the tree and watched them go, and was only half aware that Eric, Robard and the Markgraf were deep in conversation about the coming campaign.

Another campaign, another march, another wet and bloody summer tramping the roads of this ragged Empire. What a king they had, and what a task this king had set his people! To set God's Peace over good men and bad, over priest and pagan, peasant and lord: hopeless! What God could doubtless do, this sad, dark King could surely not – despite all his prayers and strivings. March, march, march! From Friesia to Bohemia, from the Harz to Saxony, from the Baltic to the Alps. And beyond. March, march, march! And for what?

To Markward it had seemed once so good, and pure and honourable – so full of adventure and valour and fire. But now what was it, but a broken dream, and broken hopes on a road to nowhere. And it had cost a boy from Eckerheim his girl. It had. If only he had not rushed off to join this Salian king in his mad crusade, all would have been well: Elsa and him. All would have been as it should have been. He and Elsa, together, but instead . . .'

'Markward!'

He straightened up. Robard was talking to him: 'Markward, you are needed.'

'Sire?'

'Eric says that the shepherds will be wanting to take the flocks up onto the tops before long, and there's still the Spring planting to finish. Can you pick ten good men to be at the service of the King when he arrives? They will be away until Mid-Summer's day at least.'

'They are to bear arms for the king?'

'Aye, for the king and emperor himself.'

'Free men or bond?'

'It matters little, except they be strong of wind and limb, with good teeth and a steady eye.'

Markward laughed: 'As are all Eckerheimers, sire!'

'Aye, aye, perhaps so – but one more thing – it would be best to levy the single men first, before the married. Less grumbling, less complaint.'

'Agreed, sire, but cannot Eric do this? He is the bailiff.'

Robard nodded. 'In truth he is, but my Lord Dietmar picked him for his wit, not his swordplay. So it was Eric here himself who chose you to choose the men for the Levy.'

'Because I can fight.'

'Because you can lead when there is fighting to be done.'

Markward frowned. 'I will do this, sire, because it has to be done.'

'And because the king would have it so', muttered the Markgraf. 'By rights we should be sending at least twenty men, but they can't be spared – not now at least.'

'Very good, my lord.'

'Hummph! Not good at all, but it's the best we can do, and the least expected of us.' He signed to Eric and Sir Robard. 'Come, I wish to see the fields and flocks before we leave.' They strode away leaving Markward alone by the oak. He stood there for another hour. The rain pattered down through the branches, but the breeze had dropped, and already the wind was beginning to shift. Above the high ridges scattered lines of birds were drifting in from the South, and lambs were bleating in the fields. Soon he would tell ten men that they were to follow him out of this valley.

Two days later news blew in with the east wind that the king had left Magdeburg and would arrive within the week. The Markgraf had returned to his castle leaving Sir Robard and Markward along with two sergeants to welcome the imperial column. They were to organise the Levy and march with the king along the intended route which would go via the Weissburg.

As the villagers went about their tasks the clouds overhead thickened and flurries of small icy snowflakes (the folk called it 'grabel') swept along the valley. The sheep huddled against the dry stone walls, and crept in among the low hedges but the goats stood unconcerned chewing on the thorns and brambles that ringed the lower meadow. Cedric, now very much part of village life, kept watch over his flock from a high rocky spur that jutted out over the main pasture to the West of Eckerheim. Markward had sought him out, and they had spoken again as friends, but they talked of the weather and the crops and the fatness of spring lambs and little more besides.

At the village well, life was pretty much back to normal with chatter and banter and the gossip about the coming weddings. It was said that Rainald and Elspeth would follow Elsa and Bernhardt to the Weissburg, but when they all returned there would be a great feast in Eckerheim to welcome them.

The women of Hochtal fussed over who would clothe and bedeck the brides — but it was universally agreed that the Eckerheimers would carry the feast. The Wisewoman threw her stones and clicked her tongue and said the runes favoured the couples, but Mutti said quietly to Katrin that she had never said anything else and they both chuckled.

By evening the weather had cleared and a long, pale sunset warmed the valley and eased the backs of the menfolk as they trudged in from the fields.

Eric had called for yet another moot, but this time the women were to stay away. He and Markward waited at the oak tree and watched as the men came slowly up the slope towards them. Soon they would hear who had been chosen to go with the king.

'They'll take it hard,' said Markward.

'Ach, no!' The bailiff shook his head. 'They may mutter and curse apiece, but they'd be fools not to have guessed what we're about. They know the king is upon us, and they know he's planning a campaign to the East. And most of all, they know he cannot do it without their heads and hands.'

'And hearts.'

'Aye, and hearts. We're all of us peasants in Eckerheim, but proud peasants for all of that. We've no problem in fighting for our King, but we like to be asked and not told.'

Markward nodded. 'He's a gentle enough King, but his liegemen are as hard as iron, and in the end it's them we serve, and them we run to obey.' He yawned and stretched. 'And here come some weary servants, now.'

In the morning the men returned to the fields. Elsa came with them. She caught up with Markward and Albrecht as they began the ploughing of the old glebe field. With a whisper in his ear, and a gentle pat on the shoulder, she sent Albrecht back to the house for a jug of milk and half a loaf of bread.

Then she turned to Markward who was busy with yoking the oxen. He seemed not to notice her.

'*You* chose the men,' she said, her voice shaking slightly. 'You chose them, and Bernhardt among them.'

Markward tightened the yoke, but didn't reply.

'It was not Wulfstan, nor even Eric. It was you, wasn't it? You chose them!'

He sighed and turned towards Elsa. 'Aye, it was me. I chose them.'

'Why?'

'Because I had to.'

'But Bernhardt . . .'

'I know, Bernhardt. I chose him, and I chose him because I had to.'

Elsa stepped forward and put her hand on the yoke. 'But why? Bernhardt and I, we . . .!' She was shouting now, and her eyes flashed. Some men clearing a ditch nearby stopped working and looked up. 'It's spite, Marki! It's spite and you know it! You couldn't bear to see us wed. You couldn't stand to see it, so you drag him off to the wars with you!'

'It's not that way, Elsa.'

'It is, and you know it is. I hate you, Marki! Hate you!' She aimed a blow which caught him on the jaw. He turned away, and then back again. 'Elsa!'

'No!' She headed away, brushing the tears from her eyes, and stumbling over the broken ground.

He watched her go until she disappeared behind the line of laurel and birch that flanks the way back to the village. And then he returned to the plough. Suddenly there was a hand on his shoulder. It was Wulfstan.

'Trouble, lad?'

'Aye, aye. But it's nothing.'

'Doesn't look like nothing. The lassie's upset.'

'Aye, she is. And I can't blame her. I've sent her man to the Levy.'

'That was a brave move.'

Markward smiled. 'It would only have been brave if I didn't have to do it. But ye see, he had to go: he can fight, ye see, and he's a smith, and he's still single.'

'Even if he's to be wed.'

'Even that.' Markward ruffled his hair and stared at his boots. 'Did I do the right thing, Wulfstan?'

Wulfstan slapped him on the back and laughed: 'The right thing? The right thing, ye say? Well, you say ye had to do it, so I guess that makes it right.'

'And yet I could be wrong. He is to be wed, and if it wasn't for the king's levy . . .'

'Just so: the king's levy. There's the thing, and there you have it. It was not you who decided, it was my lord the king, God bless him! The lad was single, so the lad had to go!'

'You think so?'

'Hah! It's your conscience, lad, not mine, but at the very least I'd say you did the wrong thing for the right reasons, and that's maybe in this case a tat better than doing the right thing for the wrong reasons.'

'You make me dizzy, old man.' Markward shook his hand, and turned to the ploughing.

'Seems you were dizzy already from that clip across the jaw she gave ye!' Wulfstan called over his shoulder as he trudged away.

As he approached the cruck that evening, Markward could smell the mutton stew Mutti had made. It smelt good. It reminded him of when he was a boy. He sat down wearily at the table, and the family gathered about him. They ate in silence, but happily.

Finally, Mutti spoke: 'You knew she'd come after you, Marki?'

'Aye, I knew, and I see it's got round the village in good time.'

'Did she really hit you, Marki?', said Brunni.

'She did', grinned Markward, 'But that's no excuse for any other of you lassies to have a go at me.'

Albrecht looked up from his bowl: 'She hit you because she's angry, that's all. It doesn't mean she doesn't love you.'

'Hush now! Hush!' said Mutti.

'It's all right' said Markward. 'Yes, little Albrecht, Elsa is angry with me, but it's nothing to worry about. It will pass.'

'The winter will pass! The winter will pass! No matter how deep the snow!' sang Albrecht, and they all laughed to hear the proverb.

Down at the forge Bernhardt and Elsa sat talking. Jakob was sitting quietly in one corner, his grandson on his knee, whispering to him stories of the ancient forests and hills.

'I must go if I am called,' said Bernhardt. 'It's the custom, and besides I could not bear to hear that some one else had to go in my place.'

'But it's just not fair.'

Bernhardt shrugged. 'It's the way it is.'

Elsa stared into the flames. 'We could run away.'

'Where to?'

'To Magdeburg,' she said hopefully.

'No, Elsie, no. There's nothing for us there, and every reason for us to stay here in Eckerheim. How could I live with myself if I ran away now? It's only right that I go with the King. I am bound to him by the Markgraf. There's an oath. You know it.'

'I know, I know. You don't have to tell me, Berni! It's just so hard, so unfair. It could ruin everything. It could ruin us. It's . . so difficult!'

'Nihil difficilis amanti'.

Elsa looked up: 'Latin?'

'Nothing is difficult for those who are in love.'

'That's beautiful Berni. I never knew you were a scholar.'

'The priest taught me to read. I wasn't always at the forge, not when I was a youngster anyway. Old Werner – remember him – he was priest at Hochtal when my father was a lad: he taught me. I guess he hoped one day I might take holy orders, and help him keep the church.'

'Nothing is difficult for those who are in love,' repeated Elsa.

'It's Cicero. He was a Roman nobleman.'

'He knew a lot.'

'Well, he said a lot, or leastways that's what old Werner used to say.'

Bernhardt hugged Elsa and drew her close. 'It'll be all right – you'll see. The king will come, we'll march off with him into the hills for a few days, chase a few shadows, set a few fires and then come marching back.'

'You think so?'

'I know so.' He kissed her on the brow.

'But the Liutizen.'

'They've gone. Beyond the Elbe and beyond the Neisse. I doubt that our King will follow them across those rivers, not even in the spring.'

'So you are a soldier as well as a clerk?'

Bernhardt smiled: ' No, my love, but I heard the soldiers talking when I was shoeing the horses.'

There was a pause. Jakob kissed his grandson goodnight, and wandered over to the fire. He stirred the charcoal, and held out his hands over the glowing embers. 'Ye should wrap up warm tonight. There's a sharp old breeze out there.'

Elsa seemed not to hear him. 'I'm scared', she said. 'So scared. I'm scared you'll go and we'll never see each other again.'

'You'll see me,' replied Bernhardt. 'I'm thinking Markward will bring us all home.'

Elsa sighed. 'I hit him, Berni. I hit Markward as hard as I could. In the face.'

'I heard you did.'

'I thought he was trying to stop us from being wed: trying to get you killed.'

Bernhardt shook his head: ' No, Elsa. Markward may be many things, but he's not a killer – not like that. He may hate me, and I guess he has every reason to, but I know he'd never lift a hand against me. It's not in his bones.'

Elsa sighed. 'I don't understand you sometimes, Berni.'

'And I you, but that's how the Good Lord made us.' He squeezed her tight, gave her a little peck on the cheek and stood up: 'Now away with you to your bed. It's getting late and Johan and his wife will be wondering where you've got to. Is that right, Jakob?'

The blacksmith looked up. 'Aye, young Bernhardt. That's right enough. But you walk the lass back to her cruck. There's time enough to tidy up in the morning, and ye are not needed here this evening.'

The king came to Eckerheim on a Sunday. He took mass in the little church. His personal chaplain, Wipo was there, along with an acolyte or two, but there was no sign of the bishops of Magdeburg or Fulda. They were busy seeing to the repair of their own city walls and gates, now it seemed certain that there would be a campaign on the eastern borders.

The village folk kept to their crucks, and the imperial army camped on high ground to the West as promised.

In the afternoon, the king – as the markgraf had done before him – held court beneath the oak tree. But this time he sat on a small wooden throne, and two imperial guardsmen, each bearing a royal banner stood either side of him. Wipo crouched on a nearby bench, and balanced a writing board on his knees.

Someone blew a trumpet – not very well – and the seneschal read out a series of prepared greetings and decrees. It was what the villagers feared and what they knew must come: their Lord King was to hurl himself against the Liutizen, and they were to be the weapons in his fist. But there was not a murmur of dissent, not even a shuffling of feet. Everyone stood stock still, and gazed with curiosity and awe at the Salian prince some men called their emperor.

He was tall, and wiry, slightly stooped with piercing black eyes and jet black hair and beard. He looked weary, perhaps unwell, and he coughed every so often into his sleeve. A golden circlet, studded with garnets sat slightly askew on his head, and a rich cloak of black velvet trimmed with gold was wrapped about his shoulders and chest. As the seneschal spoke the king looked out upon his people. It was not an arrogant gaze, there was even a trace of affection there, and the way he searched the crowd with those dark eyes suggested interest not boredom. His hands, gripping the arms of the throne, were fine and slender, but seemed to have purpose and strength in them.

The folk afterwards said that they knew they were in the presence of a king, even without the banners and trumpets and golden crown. He did not have the fiery manner and bull-like frame of a Saxon lord, but nonetheless he was a king, and every inch a king.

And when he spoke he stood, and when he stood the people instinctively knelt. He told them to lift themselves up, and then spoke on. His Salian accent seemed strange to their ears. It sounded soft. It had a curious lilt, and a lightness they were not used to. Still, what he said came from a king, and had the measure and dignity of kingly speech. Or so the people said.

'Eckerheimers! You have heard from my seneschal, and now you must hear from me. I will not keep you long. I will not hold you from your tasks, or even your rest. But know this: I am determined to keep these borders, and keep them well. I am your king, and it is my duty under God to protect and uphold you against all attacks, whether from bandits, or from raiders, or from armies of another nation. That is why I am here. Your villages have been attacked and burned, and so I have come. Those who have attacked you will learn that there is a heavy price to pay for such a crime. Some, I hear, have already paid with their lives, but you too have also suffered much, and fear that you may suffer more. God willing your sufferings are over, and after this campaign you will be able to till your fields and keep your flocks and raise your families in peace.' He coughed, and then went on: 'In peace and prosperity.'

There was a pause. Willibrord was scratching away on his writing board. At last he looked up and the king went on:

'I am your servant by imperial oath, but above all I am God's servant and liegeman. Therefore I keep the laws: God's Law and imperial law. You are Saxons, I am Salian, but we all live under these laws, and are duty bound to uphold them." He coughed again, this time for longer. 'Your permission and patience.' He held up one hand and then sat down wearily on his throne. An acolyte brought him a cup. He drank, and then went on, but this time more slowly:

'And so I have called you to this Levy. But not you alone. Even as I speak the levies march from Kamienca and beyond the Stony Brook to Zwickauer Mulde. They come from Meissen and they come from Magdeburg. They come from Dresdany, and Leipzig and from all the villages in between.

'They even come from Konigsberg – yes, Konigsberg, a town so far to the North that people scarce believe it is still in the Empire. And yet they come. Why? Because I have called them, and because they know their duty. Soon they will gather at the Weissburg, and men of this brave village will meet them there.'

The folk nodded, a few said 'amen'. A thin gust of wind flapped the banners and Henry drew his cloak around him.

'But this you have to know: I as your King and Emperor will march with you and my army to the Weissburg. After that, I must farewell you and return to Goslar. I keep all the borders of this kingdom, and there are enemies to the West, as well as to the East. Your lord the Markgraf will lead you against the Liutizen.

The villagers were silent, save for Ronan, who whispered to Johan and Helga: 'There's death in this King, fine words or no!'

Helga put a finger to her lips as the King appeared to stare in their direction. He was waiting again for Wipo to finish writing, and as he waited he stared, and as he stared his fingers tapped on the armrests. And then when the little monk nodded, he signalled to his trumpeter, who stepped forward and placed the trumpet to his lips. But Henry suddenly frowned, and raised his hand. The trumpeter stepped back.

'I came,' said the king, 'because you fought to defend your homes. I came to honour that. And now I ask of you a higher duty: to fight for others, and perhaps to suffer loss helping other folk. This is worthy of more honour still.'

'And so . . .' He breathed deeply . 'And so you are relieved of tithes for a space of twelve months.'

Wipo gasped, and dropped his pen, and scrabbled around for it muttering apologies. The villagers stood gaping, and then all at once broke into a ragged cheer.

'Never heard the like!' laughed Rainald, giving Elspeth a hug and lifting her off her feet.

'Put me down, you great ox!' she said, but smiled at little Hetti who was capering about, but scarcely understood why.

'The bishops will dance when they hear of this', Rainald went on as he set his Elspeth down, amid the excited chatter.

'Aye, but not like the little ones', replied Elspeth. 'This King loves God and justice more than he loves these market priests. He'll make them hop all right!'

At last the crowd fell silent once more. The trumpet was sounded, Henry stood, the people bowed and the imperial entourage straggled away towards its encampment on the high ridge. Wulfstan, Eric of the Lea and Markward stood together and watched them go. The villagers, too were dispersing.

'Well, that's that,' said Eric, slapping his thigh, and turning to look over towards the fields.

'It wasn't a pretty speech,' said Wulfstan, 'But there was power behind it. I'd hate to cross our good King Henry.'

'You mean, not show up with the Levy at the Weissburg?'

'Aye. He's a just king and fair, but if we tried to scuttle away and hide in our crucks he'd bring them crashing down about our ears.'

'Then you know him better than I do, Wulfstan. It seemed to me he was tired and sick.'

'But still dangerous. Like a wounded boar', said Markward quietly as though talking to himself. He walked off down the hill alone. They watched him go.

'That young man thinks too much.'

'Because he's young, Eric, and because he too is wounded.'

'Maybe, maybe so, but he's got work to do: the Levy's to be mustered by the second quarter on Wednesday, and is to march five leagues by sunset.'

'Ten men.'

'Ten men we can scarce afford to lose. We've suffered much this Winter. If we don't have enough folk to get the autumn harvest in we'll starve by next 'Three Kings', and that's the truth of it.'

They set off down the slope following Markward. Across on the far lea, they could see Cedric and two other shepherds shifting their flocks to fresh pasture. The clouds parted and the whole valley seemed suddenly bathed in sunshine.

'That's a fine sight', whispered Eric.

'Could be warmer', said Wulfstan, and I'll be happier when the rains lengthen. It's too dry for my liking.'

Eric didn't reply, but he breathed deeply, and looked across the valley again, and smiled.

Several days later the levy left Eckerheim and marched slowly up the long heather slope to the East Spur of the village. They paused on the ridge top. Each man stooped, picked up a handful of earth, and ran it through his fingers. Then turning, they waved for the last time to Eric and the villagers far below, and disappeared from view.

The imperial army had already left the day before. An uneasy quiet fell across the village. The day was clear and bright, but the shadows were chill, and a steady wind made the trees roar and sigh.

Elsa was down by the stream helping Katrin and Helga with a basket of washing. She stood up to watch the Levy cross the crest of the ridge, and then knelt down again, and began to pound the water-soaked smocks against the washing stone. The water splashed against her face and hid the tears, but Katrin and Helga knew, and all the women, and all the village knew. Still, she determined to say nothing, and as she pounded the washing stone she promised herself over and over again that no one would know her heart till Bernhardt came home again.

And over the ridge, some five leagues distant, Bernhardt marched steadily along, and thought of his Elsa. He looked up, and saw the back of the man who had once called Elsa his own, but had given her up at Hochtal.

Markward had dismounted, and was leading his horse at the head of the levy. He tried not to think of Elsa, but turned his mind to

Mutti, and Brunni and little Albrecht. How often could he leave this village before he said 'No more!' Perhaps the day would come when he would leave this village for the last time, and end his days face down in a Liutizen bog somewhere in Poland. And then there would be no coming back, no return home, no welcome at the door of the cruck.

He put his hand into his wallet and felt for the little brown cup. Today they would march towards the Weissburg. On the morrow they would arrive. After that, who knows?

He glanced over his shoulder at the Levy. They were all there, Rainald, Gustav and Bernhardt among them. Most of them wore leather jerkins and scale armour they had scavenged off the Liutizen dead. They all now carried weapons worthy of soldiers, though whether or not they could use them remained to be seen. Wulfstan had told the levy not to wear the masked helmets of the Liutizen warriors.' 'It drives their kinfolk to a fury', he had said, ' One glimpse of you wearing a trophy like that, and they'll tear your heart out – and more besides.'

The youngest of them was Branulf. – Markward had chosen him, despite his mother's tears, because he could handle a bow. He trotted along beside his father, a new quiver full of Liutizen darts bouncing on his hip, and a great black bow slung over his shoulder.

The oldest was Wulfstan himself. He knew he had been the first chosen, and had laughed to see Eric's worried frown and shaking of the head: 'I've less years to lose than most, and more year's swinging an axe than any of ye', he had said and slapped the bailiff on the back. And now he walked just half apace behind Markward humming softly to himself, and occasionally calling to the others to keep up, or keep an eye on the path.

Gustav had brought his dog with him, a big boned, ragged grey mastiff with a keen nose and a sharp eye. It bounded ahead of them, ranging to right and left through the heather, but always coming dashing back to its master's low whistle.

As the afternoon shadows lengthened the wind slackened to a gentle breeze, and the men felt the warmth of a Spring sun. They found a good place for the night, and made camp. Soon there was a bright fire crackling and the smell of heath-smoke. They sat around talking of the day, and chewing on rye bread, salted mutton and stiff cheese. As the sun set, they set a guard and lay down to sleep. They would be up before dawn the next day, and there was a long way to go before they reached the Weissburg.

They awoke to grey skies and steady drizzle. Grumbling and moaning they took a hasty breakfast, kicked over the fire, and set off for the Weissburg.

It wasn't long before the skies cleared and the drizzle lifted. Their way took them across heathland, and then it dipped down into a long, sweeping valley filled with trees. They entered the woodland cautiously. It was cool and still. The morning sunlight filtered down through the fresh green foliage, and their feet passed soft over the forest floor. All about them were the flowers of an ancient wood: Veronica, Bluebell, Dog's Mercury, Bugle and Sedge.

The trees stood massive and silent all about them: not an animal stirred, not a bird sang, and no breeze moved the branches.

'I don't like it,' muttered Rainald.

'Well, it has no opinion about ye,' laughed Wulfstan. 'This is my lord of Weissburg's forest. There are no folk here, save a charcoal burner or two, and perhaps a mad monk turned hermit because the abbot cast him out.'

'Good hunting then,' said Gustav.

'No hunting at all, unless you happen to be the Markgraf himself. This is a forest for deer and wild boar, but there's none here will fall, but they'll end up on the dining tables of the Weissburg.'

'And who should see me if I winged a stag and put it in a pot?' laughed Branulf's father.

'Who indeed? Who indeed but the Green Men, and all their faithful servants. You spill blood in this forest and the news of it will fly to the Markgraf's ear before you've skinned your prize.'

'You're mad, old man!'

'I'm alive, that's what — and you'd be wise to listen to the madness of an old man if you want to keep life and limb in these parts.'

'Peace, now!' said Markward. 'There's enough chatter here to wake the dead. We've a good hour's march before we clear this neck of the woods, then it's on across the 'Fair fields' before we stop to rest. On now!'

The men fell silent, and quickened their pace.

In Eckerheim, the village had been awake for some time. There was plenty of work to be done in the fields, and now that ten men had left with the levy, some of the women had to help with the planting and sowing. Usually, the women kept to the village until harvest time and haymaking. Then everyone helped with bringing in the crops and getting in feed for the Winter. Later they would do the winnowing. It was a time of singing, and dancing and celebration, as well as hard work. That was the Autumn, but now it was the Spring, and this year there were wives and sisters and daughters working in the long meadow and beyond.

Johan the Carpenter was still busy repairing houses that had been damaged in the fight at Christmas, and Eric had asked Jakob to help him with hinge plates and nails. They had agreed to work all day on the tanner's house, but they had both of them promised their wives that they would help cut rushes the following day. That meant a good half hour's walk to where the river bank broadened and the best rushes grew. But it never felt safe for the womenfolk at the best of times, and now more than ever they felt the need for the men to be with them, and a watch to be kept. Still, fresh thatch was needed as never before, and the earlier repairs would not see them through the heavy Autumn rains, let alone the first snow of Winter.

The church roof had been made good, and the debris of battle had been long since cleared from inside. Reluctantly Eric agreed that the church could be used to dry the rushes. There was no sign of a priest yet to replace Jan, and although they gathered every Sunday in the church and said a few muttered prayers and sang a psalm, the little stone building seemed more of a barn to them than anything else.

When the noon sun stood over the South pass, the women in the fields stopped working, sat on a grassy headland, and ate a simple lunch.

Elsa took out a shepherd's talley stick and cut a single notch with a small dagger. She looked up and smiled at Katrin's enquiring glance:

'Forty four days,' she said. 'That's two days to the Weissburg, forty days as a king's man, and two days to get home.'

'Your man?'

'God willing.'

Katrin nodded and broke a piece of bread and handed it to Elsa: 'He'll be home before you know it.'

As Markward, still leading his horse at the head of the levy, neared the edge of the woods he saw a figure approaching them from across the Fair Fields.

It was a young priest, lean and wiry in a plain brown habit. He was stooped under a rough leather pack which crashed and clattered against his back as he strode along.

They stopped and watched him as he made his way towards them. He came on, head down as though unseeing, and then at the last moment straightened up, and shambled to a halt with a broad grin:

'Greetings, my friends! From Eckerheim?'

'We are', replied Markward. 'A levy for the King at the Weissburg. And you?'

'And me? No more than a poor priest from the Weissburg, sent to your village by my lord the Markgraf, and my lord the King.'

Markward raised his eyebrows but Wulfstan stepped forward and shook the priest by the hand: 'Well met! Well met! Our priest was killed . . .'

'Aye, I know, – the fight at Christmastide. And no communion since.'

'We were expecting a priest from Magdeburg.'

The priest grunted, and swung down his pack of plates and communion cups. ' Well, my lord the King – or should I say, my lord the emperor – says that if my lord the Bishop of Magdeburg will not look to his flock, then he my lord the Emperor, will have to do so. And so, I Ulrich son of Asgar am here.' He put his hands on hips, stretched his back, then breathed out with a long, drawn out sigh. 'That's better! It's a fair step from the Weissburg, and that pewter weighs a bit more than my brother the chaplain said it would.'

'Well, my friend,' said Rainald, 'If you had managed to carry it to Eckerheim two days before now, I could have been wed, and at home, and not standing here with these fellows in the middle of nowhere.'

Ulrich smiled at the awkward silence. 'Ah, now there's a thing, and I'll not say it's any easier for you to bear than this heavy load I've been sweating across the valley. Still, what is, is – and what is not, is not, as someone once said, but I can't tell you who. But I'll see thee in Eckerheim, God willing, and there I'll wed thee to your love, and there you'll find your slice of heaven.' He took a drink from a leather bottle at his hip, and then offered it to Rainald.

The Hochtaler drank and handed the bottle back. 'God speed thee then, sir priest.'

'And the Lord keep thee!' He hoisted his pack onto his shoulders, waved, and was gone, striding off along the path into the woods. They could hear the pewter ringing, and fading, and then no more.

'I like that priest!' said Wulfstan, slapping Bernhardt on the back.

'I'd have liked him better were he two days earlier', replied Bernhardt.

'You and Rainald, too! Wed you'd be, and wed you will! Cheer up, lad. A little wander in these little hills, and then we'll be back home.'

'You think so?'

'I know it!'

Bernhardt frowned, and shrugged, and slung his shield strap over his shoulder. 'Let's go,' he said.

The Weissburg stands on a rocky outcrop high above a valley called Schontal. It is massive, grey and turreted. A great central keep rises darkly above the outer walls, themselves guarded by battlements and corner towers that seem to grow out of the hard grey ridge. The white plaster that once gave this castle its name has long since gone, save for a few patches and flecks around the gateway, and along the walls of the inner ward. Still, it is a formidable sight, and the men of Eckerheim came to a halt when they first caught sight of it.

'Will ye look at it!' whispered Gustav. 'Have ye ever seen the like?'

'No,' said Wulfstan. 'Nor am I likely to. They say there's nothing to compare it with, between here and Aachen. What say you Markward? You're a man who's been to the wars.'

Markward put his foot in the stirrup and swung into the saddle, patting his horse on the neck as it skittered. 'I've seen finer,' he said, 'but not better built. Come! We'll present ourselves at the outer gate, and they'll tell us where we can make camp.'

The guards standing at the gate waved to Markward as they approached, and called his name. He waved back, and rode forward to talk with them. Soon he returned to the Levy. 'We are to make camp in the meadow there, by that stand of trees. The imperial camp is beyond the village, and the other levies when they arrive will camp near us. No one is to go inside the castle walls.'

'No one?' asked Wulfstan.

'Well, not the likes of us, leastways. The Markgraf doesn't want any tomfoolery and petty theft inside the Weissburg, and King's men have a reputation as bad as any.'

'That we know. But you are one of the Markgraf's men.'

'I'm a King's man, and so are you until this campaign is over. Once we've been signed onto the official rolls tomorrow there's no going back until the King's provost dismisses us in forty day's time.'

'Well', said Rainald to Bernhardt as they trudged off down to the meadow in the fading light, 'At least they give us food and beer until they send us home.'

'Aye, but when and how?' I see no sutler's wagons, and there's no sign of a cooking pot.'

Rainald sniffed. 'You're right. Now there's a pity, and a poor start. I think I'll be off down to the imperial camp to ask there for a hot meal and a fire to crouch by.'

'You'll do no such thing', said Markward, who had been listening. 'The King is no more keen to see us than the Markgraf is. Tomorrow his clerks will get us to sign our names or make our mark, and perhaps he will make a speech of some sort before he leaves, but that will be all. We've come to march with him, not feast with him.'

'And a pretty poor march it will be I'm thinking', Wulfstan cut in. 'While we're headed east over the Elbe and into the jaws of the Liutizen, our brave king is hurrying back home to Goslar.'

'As a good king would do!' replied Markward. 'There's trouble in Lorraine again, and the Friesians seem to be stirring. We've men enough here to teach the Liutizen a lesson, and still time get back home to help with the start of the haymaking.'

'I can smell it!' said Gustav.

'Smell what?'

'The hay. I can smell the hay – down in the long meadow, all fresh cut under a bright warm sun, and waiting to be stooked.' He closed his eyes and breathed in, and then out again. For a time everyone was silent, staring and thinking. At last Branulf's father, Ralf, gave a short laugh: 'Well, here's us, two days out of Eckerheim and homesick already. Like young girls chasing stray geese and lost in the woods. Hah!'

They all laughed now, except Markward who spurred his horse down the slope, and gestured for them to follow on. Slowly they followed. Already as the dusk deepened they could make out the twinkling lights of the imperial camp at the end of the valley, and if they had turned they would have seen that the torches and watch-fires of the castle-guard had been lit all along the ramparts of the Weissburg. It was going to be a clear night, with a nearly full moon and the chance of a frost. Skeins of chill white mist hung among the pine trees that crowded the lower slopes, and the stream that bubbled and chattered across the valley floor was hidden by a dark and jagged line of willows. It was a good place to camp, but cold at this time of year. They would need their heavy woollen cloaks, and some would sleep half curled up in their shields.

Each man carried tinder in his pouch, and a few had picked up dried sticks and bracken on the march. It would not be long before there was another fire or two to light the darkness.

The young priest yawned and eased himself carefully out of his truckle bed.

He could hear the sounds of the household awake, just beyond the curtain of rough sacking. He drew it back.

'Good morning, father!' said Mutti as she bustled about, with a jug of milk and a trencher of bread. 'It's a bright day, and breakfast is almost ready.'

'I thank you good lady, but please don't call me 'Father'. Call no man father, but your Father who is in Heaven.' He yawned again.

Mutti, paused, shot him a puzzled look, then set about getting some cheese for the table. 'Brunni!' she called. 'Have we eggs enough for our guest? Go see in the barn.'

Brunni who had just appeared in the doorway with two pails of water, sighed and put them down. 'Yes, Mutti, yes – but what is all this fuss?'

'Fuss? Fuss? You're the fuss, that's what. Now get you gone, and find us some eggs before I paddle you with my broom.'

Brunni grinned and ducked away, little Albrecht hard on her heels.

It was a good breakfast, a better one than Ulrich had tasted in a long while, even at the Weissburg. But, he said, as he nodded his thanks to Mutti, he had to admit that his chaplain was too saintly a fellow ('more monk than priest') and therefore insisted on a very sparse table whenever possible.

'Except for the high days and holy days', said Ulrich, ' And it's a blessing we have so many, because then we have cakes and ale and rich meat pudding and apple pie, and fine cheeses reaching to the rafters. Yes we do. No word of a lie – and all because my lord the Markgraf would have it that way.' Ulrich leant forward, elbows on the table, hands clasped, and looked this way and that, as though he were about to utter some great secret: 'You know, my good lady, the Markgraf cannot abide all this 'half-starved religion' as he calls it. He says folks have enough trouble getting food in their bellies anyway without their masters deliberately robbing them.'

'He sounds a good man.'

Ulrich leant back. 'Aye a good man. He means well, leastways, and that's a rare enough virtue among our masters these days.'

Mutti gave a little bow, and stood back from the table. ' Well, Father we're grateful that he sent you here to say the mass and keep the church.'

Ulrich yawned, patted his stomach and got up; ' Aye, good mother – you'll find I teach the Bible and nought else. The Gospel doesn't come with incense, and robes of gold and purple. It's a simple truth, and Holy too, and it should cost a man nothing.'

Mutti glared and put her head to one side: 'Are ye a druid or are ye a heretic priest?'

'I'm your priest, but no heretic.'

'You're a mad priest then.'

'A fool for Christ? In truth, I am.'

'Huh!' She flicked her cloth at some harmless crumbs. ' You play with words, Father!' Her voice was rising.

Ulrich held up one hand. 'Peace, mother, peace! I meant no harm. It was the brash tongue of youth. I meant no harm. I will keep the communion, and say the prayers, and do the baptisms – you see if I don't.'

Mutti relaxed and smiled. 'Well, there's an end of it, then.' She looked up as Eric appeared in the doorway. The bailiff was carrying a staff and spade. He was on his way to the fields: it was high time to finish the Barley planting.

'Ah, Sir Bailiff! It's good you've come. Here's our new priest, come in late last night. Cedric brought him down with the flock.'

'So I hear Mutti! Welcome, Father.'

Ulrich opened his mouth to reply, glanced at Mutti and smiled. 'I am welcomed indeed. My name is . . .'

'Ulrich, son of Asgar. Aye, Cedric told me. And I am Eric of the Lea, bailiff to this village, and first servant to my lord the Markgraf.' He offered his hand and the young priest took it.

'So, Eric of the Lea – if you could be showing me the church and my cruck I could perhaps prepare to serve the good folk of Eckerheim.'

Eric nodded. 'We'll be away then. I'm bound for the lower meadow, but we can turn aside to show you the church, and your cruck, or what's left of it. We've repaired the church, but your house is in a sorry state. Still, no matter we can put that right soon enough. Now, away! See thee at the dusk, Mutti!'

'Mayhaps, mayhaps. I'm away to cut rushes at the noontide, and we won't be back till the moon is high.'

The two men walked slowly through the village, greeting the last of the folk who were headed for the fields. The sun was pushing up over the Eastern ridge, but the frost was slow to melt. It crunched under their feet, and made the thatch and hedging sparkle. It would be a warm day, but their breath still steamed in the morning air.

'We are simple folk here,' said Eric, as they reached the top of the village, and standing by the church looked down across the valley.

'All folk are simple. It's just that some don't see themselves as such.'

Eric grunted, took off his boot, and shook out a stone. Ulrich walked to the door of the church, and ran his hand over the heavy-grained wood, hinge plates, and rivets. 'Good timber, good frame', he said and looked up at the weathered stone arch. 'It's been here awhile.'

'Aye, and seen lots,' replied Eric. 'Did you want to see inside?'

Ulrich paused and looked around slowly. 'Maybe later. Let's go to the fields, and see my flock.'

'And your cruck-house?'

'It can wait. I'll lodge with the good mother and her family if that's all right.'

'Aye, I daresay it will be. We can sort the cruck on the morrow.'

They reached the fields by way of the stream, wading across where it was only ankle deep, and then cutting across the patch of water meadow and wasteland by the mill. There were kites circling above.

Edvart's widow was standing at the door to the mill. She looked weary and drawn. They waved, she stared and turned and went inside.

The low meadow lay just beyond a line of furze and bramble bordering the wasteland. They pushed their way through, and looked across the pasture. A pheasant screeched and darted away into the scrub. There were sheep grazing, and some cattle too with a couple of young lads with sticks looking after them.

'Calm enough,' said Eric.

'Wonderful,' said Ulrich.

'Wonderful? Father, it's a field!'

Ulrich sat down on a marker stone and gazed across the meadow. 'At the Weissburg you know, there's a fox.'

'Oh, aye.'

'Aye, a fox, an old dog fox, with a dull old coat and worn teeth and a straggly tail. I see him, most every morning, just as the sun is rising. He appears from somewhere beyond the little chapel-without-the-walls, on the down slope away from the castle gate. Every morning, it's always the same. Same place, same time, same fox. Trots across the meadow, head down, tongue out, and disappears into the woods.'

'A fox you say.' Eric risked a yawn.

'I do. Only, he's like a little old man. So steady, so head down, so sad – doing what he's always done, and doing it till the day he dies.'

'And so?'

'Well, it's wonderful ye see. Like this field and the things in it. So simple, so cunning, so wonderfully made.'

'You're a philosopher then.'

'I'm schooled. I can read. I can write, I can recite psalms and follow Greek. But I'm no better a man than you Eric of the Lea, so I'd be obliged if you'd call me no more than Ulrich the priest, and leave any other titles to those who crave them.'

Eric stood beside Ulrich and looked across the meadow. He looked for a long time. At last he spoke: 'We've a blacksmith here can read. Only, he's away with the levy'.

'I would that every blacksmith could read. And all the ploughboys too!'

'Ah, you'd turn the world upside down, Sir Priest!'

'And the bishop would have me hanging from a gibbet on the castle walls. Aye I know it.'

Again, for a time Eric said nothing. He scratched his head, rubbed his chin, and stared at some villagers who were digging a ditch on the far side of the meadow. ' You're a strange one, all right, young Ulrich.'

'I am, but that's my way. I'll keep the church, and I'll serve thee well.'

The bailiff swung spade and staff onto his shoulder in one easy movement and strode away across the meadow. He had covered no more than ten paces when he stopped and half-turned:

'If ye, Ulrich son of Asgar, can bring the Lord's blessing on this village, I'll ask no more of ye, and I will call you whatever ye wish.'

Ulrich stood smiling: 'You're a good man, Eric!'

'Call no man good, but your Father who is in Heaven!' laughed the bailiff, and he turned away, leaving the young priest gaping.

On the last day of April, under a bright Spring sky, the king bade farewell to the imperial levy and took the long road that leads from Weissburg to Goslar. For seven days the levies of Saxony, Thuringia and the Harz had been trailing in to the valley where the men of Eckerheim had made camp. The tents, and bivouacs and bothies crowded up to the walls of the great castle. All day long the encampments bustled with activity. At night, it seemed as if the whole valley was lit up with myriads of torch lights, rushlights and blazing fires. The banners and blazons of a hundred dukes and warlords flapped over proud and gaudy pavilions, and everywhere came the sound of iron on iron as armourers and blacksmiths, farriers and squires repaired, tested and polished the weapons and harness of war.

Provosts and imperial guardsmen strode about the camp checking supplies and muster rolls, as well as seeing to good order and discipline. Here and there a pedlar or wandering merchant moved easily among the lines of tents calling out their wares and offering trinkets to the scattering of womenfolk who had chosen to follow their husbands into battle.

The imperial encampment where Henry's household guard had pitched their tents was now taken over by the local forces of the Markgraf of the Weissburg. His great eagle banner of black and gold and white stood outside the pavilion of Count Hubert, castellan to the Markgraf. Hubert himself was a warrior of renown, big and barrel chested with a greying beard, and eyes of brightest blue. Men called him 'the eagle', and it was said that his battleaxe had felled two men at a single stroke.

The Eckerheimers were content to keep their distance from such a warrior, but there came a day when Sir Hubert himself appeared at their camp fire, without escort, and sat beside them as though he was a common soldier, and talked with them as though they were his brothers. He ate their meat and drank their wine, but left them with more and better than he had eaten.

They found out later that he visited many of the scattered camps, and talked, and listened and won the hearts of men he never knew.

He had recognised Wulfstan from an earlier muster, and slapped him on the back, and called him comrade, and asked after his village and his folk. Hubert listened and nodded as Wulfstan told the story.

'Aye, Wulfstan, I heard as much. King Henry spoke of it. He was much taken by your mettle. You Eckerheimers stood when most would have run.'

'Too cold to run, sire. The snows were upon us.'

'How many Liutizen came against you?'

'A good size raiding party, my lord. More than I could count and hold my breath.'

'Hah! Well, God willing, you'll be seeing a few more before the Summer Harvest.' He stirred the fire with a stick and looked into the flames.

'And how many do we have to bring against them, sire?' someone asked.

Hubert looked up. ' Ah, Markward! Well met! How many? As many as the hosts of Israel, or near enough. We've at least three thousand lances from the imperial household, though that includes squires of course. And then there are all the levies with their warlords and retainers: good fyrdsmen all.' (He used 'fydsmen', the old Saxon word for the levy.) 'I'd say in all there'd be over six thousand men here in this valley: Six thousand men, and a good measure over three thousand horses. And that's why we have to be moving and moving soon. They've already torn the pasture up, stripped the woods and begged, borrowed and stolen anything they could from our people here.'

Bernhardt leaned forward and cut a piece of mutton off the spit. 'If we march tomorrow, my Lord, it cannot be soon enough.'

'Well, my lad, I'm thinking you may get your wish. Our good King Henry left word that we should leave when we heard news from the Bohemians: today I saw a rider come in from the South bearing Spethinew's pennon.'

'The son of Duke Bretislav himself!'

'Aye, well leastways his messenger, and bearing glad tidings I trust. Henry will never move against the Liutizen until he knows that Bohemia will guard his flank.' Hubert stood up. 'Must be going. Things to do ye know. Keep watch! Stay ready! I've a feeling we march on the morrow.' He faded into the gloom, and the men turned back to the fire, drawing their cloaks about them.

It rained in the morning, a soft, gentle drenching rain that fell in drifting curtains over the valley and filled the encampment with muddy pools and sodden turf. Everywhere, men crouched in dripping bivouacs and shelters and cursed the skies and drank bad wine, and played irritable, noisy games of dice.

Slowly the news spread: they would strike camp post noon and march south and east towards Dresdany and the Elbe. The smouldering camp fires were put out, the tents came down, horses were saddled and harnessed. The shouts of captains and sergeants rang through the muddy valley, and men splashed back and forth loading equipment and provisions onto the wagons and pack-horses. By noon the rain had eased, and the camp was all but struck. Some of the wagons had mired in the churned mud, and wouldn't move despite the efforts of the oxen under the whip. Teams of cursing soldiers were set to push and drag them out, and they were finally freed just as the Markgraf himself came galloping down from the Weissburg at the head of a company of horsemen.

They were all in gleaming mail, and conical helms, and carried kite shields faced with riveted leather. Each man bore a lance, and across his shoulders, a riding cloak of blue emblazoned with a gold lion. The men of the levies paused in their work to watch their arrival and returned the salute of the Markgraf with a low cheer. He smiled grimly, then driving his lance into the mud, he stood in the saddle and shouted: 'You will follow this lance as if your lives depended on it, because your lives do depend on it. I am the Law now. I, and no other man. I alone carry the imperial seal across my chest. My word is your command. Do it and you may live. Fail to do it, and you will surely die.'

An uneasy shudder, almost a groan, ran through the levies who were within earshot. The others, running forward, called out that they could not hear, and were beaten back by the provosts and sergeants with the flats of their swords.

'What I have said,' roared the Markgraf, reining in his horse as it skittered about, 'I have said! It will be posted about the camp before I leave, and will be hung around the neck of the first man who offends against it. Then all will see. Then all will know. Am I your lord?'

'Aye!' thundered the levies, the warlords, and the imperial guards.

'Then follow me, and may God be with us all!' He wheeled his horse about, galloped up to a grassy knoll beyond the camp, and pointed with his lance towards the South and East. The men cheered again, but this time in better heart, and some even threw their caps into the air.

Again the shouting of the captains and the calling of the sergeants. The army stirred itself, and began to unwind in a lazy, ragged coil of men and horses, carts and wagons that slowly moved up the rain-soaked valley towards the Southern pass. A few folk working in the fields watched them go, and some children ran ahead, but there were no shouts, no waving of scarves, no words of farewell – just the heavy sounds of a marching army: iron on leather, and leather on earth, and the deep rasping breath of thousands of men and horses under arms. The clouds rolled on above their stooped heads, and slowly, slowly the jangling of harness and the tramp of feet faded from the valley.

'Well, that's it, then,' said a guard at the main gate to the Weissburg, as he watched the last spear point disappear over the crest of the Southern Pass. He leant against the stonework of the gateway, and crossed his arms. 'There's a few of them won't make it back, and we won't be seeing any at all for a good few months I'll warrant.'

The other guard rested his spear over one shoulder, and loosened a shield strap. 'Aye, but they carry the relics of St Adolphus and St Bran: one for fortune in battle, and one for a swift homecoming.'

'Pah! Relics! Pedlars' trinkets, and old wives tales, that's what. Anyone who trusts in dead men's bones is a fool, and like to be dead

himself before too long. No saint, buried or burnt, ever held me up
in battle: it was e'er my sword arm and my shield that saw me home.'
He took a drink from the clay jar at his feet, rinsed his mouth and
spat. 'I've never seen an arrow yet that swerved because a man had
some charm or keepsake hung about his neck, and I've heard enough
wounded men cry out to Mary and all the saints before they coughed
their last and died.'

A trumpet sounded high on the walls above their heads and the
men straightened to attention. It was the eleventh hour, and soon the
watch would be changed.

Markward was leading his horse and marching beside Rainald.
Wulfstan had gone back to check on Branulf who was struggling to
keep up in the heavy, muddy conditions. They were going across a
broad, slippery slope, made uneven and treacherous by the men and
horses and wagons that had just passed over it. The greasy, rutted
surface squelched beneath their boots, and the last of the rain
pattered down soaking cloaks and gambesons, brigandine and jerkin.
Ahead was a forest, flanked by high, rocky outcrops. It loomed
darkly, and there was no way of telling how far it stretched. The army
disappeared into it, as though into the mouth of some fantastical
monster. It seemed to Markward a fearful thing that so many men
could disappear so easily into such a place. It was like a black gate in
a great wooden wall. Who knew what lay beyond it?

They trudged across the open ground, closer and closer to the
forest which seemed to lie in wait for them. The sun was setting now.
Surely they would not make camp in this forest. That would be
madness! Markward glanced uneasily about him, but no one else
seemed to hesitate. Heads down, silent, they marched stolidly on.
Now they were almost upon the forest. The trees rose up in front of
them, and spread their branches and boughs, out and over their
heads. The last of the daylight faltered and dimmed, and all at once
they were through the gate, and inside the jaws of the great creature.

Markward's horse snorted, and he put his hand up and stroked its muzzle. 'Easy, boy! Easy!' A deep and softening silence settled over the army as it moved steadily forward into the darkness.

The rich smell of pine needles rose about them, and the further they marched the darker it became till the army itself was little more than groups of lurching shadows filtering through the trees. The outriders began to call, and trumpets answered, warning every man to keep to the line of march. On and on they went, now almost blind in the depths of the forest. At last torches were lit, flaring against the blackness and showing the way ahead as a bobbing chain of flickering lights. When it seemed as if they would wander forever in this silent world, there was an almost imperceptible lightening of the dark, and a cool breeze brushed against them. Markward looked up and saw the moon. It was on its back, a floating crescent of silver against a star-filled sky. They had crossed the forest.

A broad plain stretched before them, and there, a thousand paces to the south, the Markgraf was making camp. Already tents were up, and fires were lit, but most men had simply flung themselves down on the ground, wrapped themselves in their cloaks and gone to sleep. The cavalry looked to their horses, and the imperial guard set pickets, but few of the fyrdsmen kept watch that night. Exhausted, hungry and damp they thought little of what dangers might close in beyond the watch fires and the sentries' torches.

Markward lay on his back in the curve of his shield and stared up at the shining moon. He thought, as he had so often thought, of Eckerheim and Mutti, and Brunni, and Albrecht – but most of all he thought of Elsa, and wondered how far he would have to march, and how old he would have to grow before he forgot her at last. He knew to his dying breath that above all things he would have to forget that shining hair, and those clear, bright eyes. He knew, and sorrowed for the cold, damp shadows that clung to him now.

A few paces away, wrapped in his cloak, Bernhardt fixed his tired and slowly closing eyes on the same drifting moon. And all his mind and all his heart were filled with Elsa. But all the days that lay ahead of him were empty, until this army turned for home. The moon drifted on, and at last he slept.

At Eckerheim the days crept by. The village seemed quiet since the ten fyrdsmen and Markward had left. The daily round came and went, and slowly day by day the talk was less of the levy and more of the weather, the crops and the wandering stock.

Elsa, still lodging with Johan the carpenter and Helga kept herself busy. She had brought her father's skill as a baker to Eckerheim, and more and more she spent her time down at the mill with Edvart's widow and family. She sifted the flour, checked it, and using the great ovens that Edvart had once built, baked bread to order as the villagers claimed their portion of the harvest. She worked hard, long and cheerfully, and the folks said that Bernhardt was blessed beyond measure if only he could get back from the wars.

No one at the village well spoke of Markward. The talk was of Elsa and Bernhardt. Once or twice there were awkward silences, especially when Mutti or Brunni were at the well, but for the most part the people held their peace and were content to wish the young couple good fortune, and leave it at that.

There came a day, weeks later, when Elsa went alone to gather from the tops. She took a pruning hook, and a kit, and as always her tally stick, and climbed the worn path that led out of the village and up to the Great West Ridge. It was a clear day, and warm, and she knew she could see for miles in all directions when she reached the highest point. The heather up there grew thick and strong with bright white flowers, and was good for bedding, and even for fuel.

As she made her way up the last reach before the ridge top she saw a man coming towards her from the North. He was a way off, and silhouetted against the sky. She could see that he carried a staff over his shoulder, and he walked upright with a relaxed stride, almost a swagger. Elsa paused, uncertain, and looked around. Perhaps he was a stranger, perhaps unfriendly, and here she was alone and far from the village. For a moment she thought of turning and running — that was what her mother had always told her to do — but it seemed foolish when perhaps there was no harm at all in the man.

He came nearer, quickening his stride, but still she could not make out who he might be, save to say he was lean and broad shouldered, with a sense of power about him, despite a slight stoop. A sudden surge of terror gripped her. She stepped back, and caught her foot on a root, and fell back into the heather. Her hand tightened on the pruning hook as she scrambled gasping to her feet. But he was upon her. She cried out and swung wildly about her, eyes clenched shut.

'Elsa!'

There was a hand on her wrist, and one on her shoulder. She opened her eyes. It was Cedric.

She sobbed with relief, and clung to him. 'Cedric!'

'Aye, couldn't you see me?'

'The light was at your back. I couldn't tell . . .'

He stood back, his hands resting gently on her shoulders. 'I'm sorry. If I'd known . . .'

She laughed, but was still shaking, and brushed her hair back from her face. 'It's all right. It's all right. You gave me a fright, that's all. I didn't recognise you without your flock.'

He smiled. 'I was up here looking for a young ewe that's gone astray.'

Elsa returned the smile, sniffed and quickly wiped a tear away: 'And you found me instead.'

There was a silence. Cedric looked away and down the ridge. 'Cutting the heather, then?'

'I am. I love it up here. You can see for miles. Almost . . .'

'To the Weissburg?'

She blushed. 'Yes, to the Weissburg. I count the days, you know. It seems to help . . . Not long now.'

'Aye.'

'Four and forty days they said.'

'Aye, they would. Four days to travel, and forty days muster for the fyrd.' Cedric frowned and studied the folds in the ridge. 'No sign of that ewe', he said. 'She's a stubborn one. Always wandering off since she lost her little one at lambing.'

'That's hard.'

'That's life, but you're right, it is hard. Still, no sense worrying about it. There'll always be lambs in the Spring, and there'll always be wolves and snowstorms waiting to take them.'

'You're a good shepherd, Cedric.'

'I'm a shepherd, that's all. No more, no less. Now lass, do you need a hand with that heather? Otherwise I'll be away along this ridge, and then back down to the flock.'

Elsa shook her head. 'I'm fine. But it was good you came.'

'For what?' He smiled. 'To give you a fright?'

With a little shrug, Elsa sat down in the heather and drew her knees up to her chin. 'Cedric,' she asked, 'Do you believe in fate?'

The old shepherd grunted and leant on his staff. 'I believe in God, and that's enough for me. Too much talk of fate can get a man down. It smacks of sorrow.'

'What do you mean?'

'I mean, you don't go worrying about what might happen on the morrow – you deal with the day the Good Lord has given you.'

Elsa laughed. 'You should have been a priest, Cedric!'

'Hah! Keep me from these priests. They're bishops' men, most of them, with more Latin in their souls than common pity. Tithe gatherers, burying the dead, that's all.' He looked across at Elsa who seemed confused. 'Sorry, lass! Don't heed that. I've been too long a shepherd. No patience with folk, that's all.' Elsa said nothing, but pulled at a sprig of heather.

'You're afraid, lassie, afraid that your man will never come home – that ye'll never be wed.'

Elsa nodded and tears started to roll down her cheeks.

Kneeling down beside her, Cedric put his hand on her shoulder: 'If love could bring him home, then there's nothing can stop him.'

'As strong as death,' whispered Elsa.

'Aye, as strong as death. Now, up with you, and away to your heather. It's a terrible thing to see a fair lassie weeping. Come now!'

Elsa stood up slowly, her head down. 'I'm tired, Cedric. So tired. I'm tired of waiting, tired of hoping, tired of being afraid.'

'And so you work like a thrall.'

'I do my due, no more.'

'You work too hard, lassie – all the folk say so.'

'All the folk?'

'All the folk.' He breathed deeply and looked out over the hills. There were clouds rolling in from the West, but they were full and white; there was no prospect of rain. 'I'd best be going,' he said.

'Take care now, and try not to worry. Your man'll be home before you know it, and the priest will ring the bells.'

Elsa waved him goodbye and turned to the heather. It fell easily before the pruning hook, and its scent filled the air. When she had filled the kit, she hoisted it on her shoulder and set off back down the slope. Just once she stopped to glance back towards the Weissburg. The hills were quiet, with only the shadows of the clouds moving over them. A lark, startled by her approach, rose out of the meadow with a thin piping cry, and began its slow and circling ascent. Up and up it went, and by the time Elsa had reached the stream near the bottom of the West Ridge, the lark had disappeared against the sky.

The army had marched for three days towards Dresdany. The weather was good, but the going was slow because of the earlier rains. Twice, the Markgraf had called a halt, and sent out scouts to see if they could find a better way around the rutted road they were trying to march along. Twice the scouts returned to say that there was no better valley than the one they were presently floundering through.

At the end of the third day they had covered only eleven miles. Exhausted, they sank into their tents and bivouacs of branch and brush. Everyone grumbled, even the veterans. The firewood was damp, the ground was sodden, and mosquitos were flocking about the encampment. The imperial wagons carrying provisions were mired some distance further back, and the levies were told that they would have to look to their own meagre supplies. News also filtered down the column that a cart filled with wine and beer had tipped over, shortly after leaving the Kamnitz plain, and all the contents had crashed down into a rocky defile. The men muttered and groaned, and crouched around the smouldering fires, talking of home, counting the days and wondering when the Markgraf would end this madness.

Few slept well that night, and dawn broke drearily over a bedraggled army its senses dulled by low cloud and early morning drizzle. They ate a cold breakfast with the prospect of another day staggering and slithering through the mud. The trumpets called, the fires were doused, and the soldiers shuffled into line. Many of them were now bent under the burden of extra equipment and supplies. The Markgraf had ordered that most of the wagons be abandoned and that the pack animals and common soldiers be required to carry what was needed. Those who objected were beaten and given more to carry. This soon stifled any further protest, but the levies and their fyrdsmen soon sank into a kind of sullen resignation which the sergeants and captains eyed anxiously. They knew, as did Sir Hubert and Sir Robard and the other knights, that if things did not improve soon there would be a steady trickle of desertions. With at least four more days to go before they reached Dresdany, the army could be severely weakened and reduced even before it struck a blow at the Liutizen.

They marched on. The skies slowly cleared, the sun shone, and at last they felt the warmth on their backs. Someone started to sing, there were a few ironic cheers, but in half a league whole lengths of the column had joined in. It was an old Saxon drinking song, and as the army lifted its weary voice the muddy valley rang to the sound of marching men. For three hours they marched without pause, clearing the valley by way of a narrow, forested pass. The lead patrols came out onto a gentle sweep of lowland hills: there in the distance they could see the sunlight glinting off the Elbe.

By nightfall the army had made camp nine miles beyond the Valley of Mud as the men now called it. Sir Hubert strolled about the campfires, sometimes standing in the shadows, sometimes squatting down and joining in the conversations. What he heard and saw heartened him. There were still grumbles and petty quarrels, but for the most part the men had forgotten the cold, damp and discomfort of the previous days. On his advice, extra rations were handed out from the Markgraf's own personal supplies, and men who had carried equipment from the carts were relieved of that duty for the following day.

And it was on that evening that the men of Meissen arrived, trailing in behind the Markgraf Ludwig and his standard bearer. There were fifty of them, all mounted on fine black horses, and all with burnished hauberks and helms. They came from the great castle which stood on a towering crag high above the Elbe, twelve miles from Dresdany. And they came reluctantly. The Markgraf Ludwig made no secret of his annoyance that his lord and Emperor, Henry, had summoned the Marches to this expedition. 'Madness!' he had barked, even before he swung down from his saddle, and made his way to the tent of the Markgraf of Weissburg. Those of the levy who were within earshot stared in surprise, while the nearby sergeants and knights merely shrugged and shook their heads. But while the guards outside the tent heard voices raised for a time, by the second watch there was nothing but the sounds of laughter and rough good humour: Meissen and Weissburg were as one.

Two days later the army stood on the banks of the Elbe. On the evening of the third day it marched into Dresdany, and camped in the marshy meadow beyond the town. They were welcomed by the townsfolk, most of whom were Saxon, but some of whom were Easterlings or 'Sorben' as the Meisseners called them.. The soldiers eyed them suspiciously, even though they were offered cakes and wine. It seemed strange that such a town, with so little protection, could survive here so close to the dark lands of the Liutizen that lay just beyond the river.

The following day was the Market, and soldiers crowded in among the narrow streets and muddy alleyways looking for fresh food and cheap wine.

The main square, little more than an open field surrounded by houses, was set up with stalls and tents, barrows and carts. Market traders shouted their wares, while country folk pushed through the jostling crowd, and children, laughing and squealing darted in and out among the buyers and sellers.The sounds of oxen, calves, sheep, goats, chicken and geese filled the air, as did the rich smells of baking bread, roasting chestnuts, sweetmeats, smoked bacon, fresh herbs, and green cabbage soup.

The brown, grey and huddled black roofs and tippling walls of Dresdany were wreathed in smoke from a hundred fires, and only the bright banners of the Markgraf set up in the centre of the square added colour to the scene. Still, it was peaceable, and by mid-afternoon, when the best was sold, and the most was drunk the good folk of the little town were on better terms with the levies and their captains. A few of the fyrdsmen had retired to a hostel to trade drinks and play dice with some Dresdaners. Mostly, however, they milled about in laughing, chatting groups as the market slowly melted around them. Markward, along with others, had bought some trinkets for loved ones back home: a comb for Mutti, a headscarf for Brunni, and a small dagger for Albrecht.

Towards dusk, the trumpets sounded and called them back to the camp. The smoke from the evening watch fires was drifting over the field to the tree-lined banks of the river. As Markward walked towards the pickets, he noticed a group of men standing down by a fishing jetty. They were staring out across the river and talking quietly. All were dressed in coats of mail. None carried shields, but one was leaning on a great sword. As he headed away, Markward heard someone call his name. He turned. The swordsman was waving him across. As he walked towards them through the long grass, Markward recognised the Markgraf Dietmar and Sir Robard. They stood silently, waiting for him.

'My lord?' He bowed to the Markgraf and acknowledged the other knights who nodded in return.

'Well met, young Markward of Eckerheim' said the Markgraf, puffing out his moustache, and putting one hand to his belt. 'Are your men happy?'

'Passing happy, sire.'

'Aye, aye, still dreaming of home and family I expect. Well, no matter. Now listen! We've a job for ye.'

'My lord?'

'A simple job, but important. Sir Robard here will explain it.'

Sir Robard coughed and stepped forward. 'Just so. It's when we cross the Elbe in two days time. You will cross at the head of the army, and scout forward. You and two others. We need to know what – and who – lies ahead. We cannot march blind.'

'I see.'

'Good! We don't want the imperial cavalry wandering off on their own. They need to be here covering that lot.' He gestured vaguely in the direction of the levies' encampment.

Markward swallowed hard: 'I ride until I see something, sire.'

Sir Robard gave a short laugh, but scarcely smiled: 'Or until something sees you.'

'Pray God, not so, my lord.'

'Pray God. Now will ye do it?'

'I am your liege man, sire. If someone will show me the best crossing place for man and horse . . .'

'Easily done! Easily done!' broke in the Markgraf. ' That's settled then. Away to your men now, and report to the Provost's tent at first light the day after tomorrow.'

Markward bowed, and headed back to the camp. As he walked, almost stumbling, his hands trembled and his shoulders felt tight. Breathing hard, he reached into his wallet, and grasped the little brown cup.

At first light on St. Rog's Day, Markward led his horse down to the river bank. The Provost-Marshal was with him, and also a company of knights and men-at-arms, as well as the two other scouts chosen by the Markgraf. The early morning mist lifted in grey-white skeins across the face of the steadily flowing waters. 'Black Elbe' the locals called it, and black it was in the first hour of the day. Willows and Alders crowded the banks, but near the fishing jetty the bank was clear, and sloped gently to the river. There was a man there, waiting. He was dressed as a townsman, but carried a staff of office: the mayor. He grunted a greeting, gave a tight smile and signalled Markward and the other horsemen forward.

As Markward eased himself into the river it felt chill, and heavy, almost oily. The waters dragged and pulled as he sank up to his hips making him gasp out loud. Quickly he found his balance as his feet moved from mud to sand and then gravel. He led his horse forward until it too found its footing, then he swung himself up into the saddle, struggling with the weight of water streaming off his tunic and leggings. Carefully he nudged his horse's flanks with his knees and it began to walk forward. The other riders followed. When they were in about centre stream, Markward turned and signalled to the bank. The men-at-arms, spears held in both hands above their heads, began to cross behind them. Away back in the camp, trumpets sounded for the 'stand-to' and the heavy sounds of an army shaking itself awake rippled across the meadow.

Keeping his eyes firmly fixed on a single oak on the far bank, Markward urged his horse forward. It flicked its ears and tossed its head, snorting and shaking the bridle. 'Easy, boy! Easy, now! Just a short step, and we're at the other side. Come on now!'

The horse settled and carried on. Ahead a bird whistled and called, and a heron started out of some rushes and flew away low, skimming the river.

The dark green world of trees and bushes seemed to climb slowly out of the gloomy waters which swirled ahead of Markward. His breath steamed and merged with the lifting mist. It was quiet, too quiet – and he was afraid. He tensed. He waited, waiting with every nerve and sinew for the flickering hiss of a Liutizen arrow. Through the water, on through the water – hoofstep by hoofstep: here a half slip, there a hesitation, but mostly firmly and without pause. He could see the opposite bank clearly now: branches, leaves, tree trunks and shadows. Too many shadows – all still, all quiet, but dark, mysterious and waiting.

BEYOND THE ELBE

He urged his horse forward, gently now, its flanks quivering against the eddies of the dark flowing waters. Ahead the old grey oak leaned out to meet him, its branches hanging low over the water as though to catch him, and sweep him from the saddle. A greybeard, surely a greybeard!

Behind him, the other two scouts splashed heavily forward. Without turning, he threw up one arm. The splashing stopped. He waited again, listening, looking, straining every sense to see into the world that lay ahead of him. Nothing. The shallows were upon him now, thick and greasy beneath the struggling hooves. The horse staggered clear, head tossing with the effort, and he sprang from the saddle, almost falling in his haste to gain the bank. Reins gripped and sword drawn he half led, half dragged his slithering mount up the well worn slope. At last! One of the scouts, a good natured sergeant from Kamnitz muttered something under his breath, flicked his reins and began to follow. Another bird called, this time somewhere off to the right and high up. Then silence once more.

The warm, musty darkness of the forest flowed about him. A pagan forest. A forest of druid and greenman. Deep, dark and menacing, with the smell of another world mingling with the heady scent of pine and bracken. The great wood east of the Weissburg had gripped his heart, but this fell forest chilled his soul.

He peered into its depths. There was a path: dull yellow, clay, worn smooth by years of cautious feet. It wound uncertainly between the massive trees, and drifted away on a woodland mist. Back in the saddle he eased his way forward, sword still drawn, and his shield tight across his back. He did not look back. Pride stopped him. No man must see his fear, though his horse could sense it, and snorted uneasily. Behind he could hear the soft thud of hoof on clay, and the faint jangle of harness. And even more distant the faint curses of the spearmen as they clambered to the shore.

And so he rode on, as though drawn into the shadows of this strange land beyond the Elbe. But as he rode so his senses were slowly softened. The fear which had set his heart beating wildly, and had made him clench and unclench the reins with almost every stride began to fade. And as it faded so the trees themselves seemed to retreat: the forest thinned and the woodland giants grew bigger and less numerous. Daylight now filtered down through the interlacing branches in great columns of golden light thronged with mayflies and lacewings. Patches of furze and bramble grew all around the path, and sometimes across it, but his horse pushed through them easily. At last he could see a good fifty paces, but even with the sunlight breaking through, deep shadows clustered all along the line of march within a spear cast of the path. He began at last to loosen his grip on the reins, and relax his shoulders, and to look around him with a more relaxed gaze, but he was always aware that with every passing moment he was going deeper and deeper into Liutizen territory.

He had ridden in this way for perhaps an hour when something made him pull up: he was out of earshot and sight of the other two scouts and all of the advance column. He wasn't surprised that the scouts had disappeared – they were probably riding out somewhere on the flanks – but he was alarmed that he had lost touch with the spearmen and archers. There was neither sight nor sound of them. He turned and began to trot back along the path, cursing himself for losing contact so early, and in such a place.

When it came, he neither heard, nor saw the arrow. It struck him high on the shoulder, wrenching him round, and throwing him back against the saddle. He gasped as the heavy, dull thud against his chest exploded into a flash of searing pain. Barely managing to keep a grip on his sword, he ducked low over his horse's head and dug his spurs into its flanks. It leapt forward as another two arrows zipped and whined about him. Dizzy with pain and shock, Markward almost toppled from the saddle, but somehow clung on and galloped clear of the ambush.

He came upon the advance guard some five hundred paces further back. They stopped when they saw him hurling back down the path, and formed up quickly into a defensive line. He skidded to a halt, half falling to the ground, and stumbling awkwardly before the staring captain.

'Liutizen!' he said, wondering himself why he had not yet collapsed.

'How far?' asked the captain, unsheathing his sword.

'Around the bend up ahead. Right on top of us.'

The captain was staring at the arrow. 'Are you all right?'

Markward could feel the warm trickle of blood inside his gambeson. He waited for it to come frothing up inside his mouth, but there was nothing.

He looked at the arrow and smiled with relief. It had struck his baldric, driven through the thick leather and embossing, and then smashed through the chain mail links protecting his chest and shoulder. But then, slowed by the impact it had only had sufficient force to penetrate the woollen padding of his gambeson and then finally stopped less than an arrow head's length in his shoulder. He was alive! Hurting but alive!

Three hours later he was sitting on the trunk of a fallen tree, his shoulder wound dressed and his head still spinning from the herbal potion the barber surgeon had given him before he drew the arrow. He reached up and touched the poultice of moss and mutton fat held in place by clean rags and strips of leather. It still hurt, and throbbed badly, but the surgeon had said that it was a clean wound, and not likely to fester. 'You're lucky!' he said. 'Those savages mostly rub their arrow barbs in the dirt or worse before they let loose. Even a flesh wound is often fatal.'

The other two scouts had failed to return, and they had been given up for dead by their captain. But a good part of the advance guard was now encamped among the trees all around Markward, and the smell of cooking fires was spreading across the clearing where he sat.

Sir Hubert had sent two squadrons of cavalry in pursuit of the Liutizen who had ambushed the scouts, and had warned everyone else to stay within the area of the pickets. 'No hunting!' he had warned. 'We'll not forage until we've sent the first Liutizen village up in flames.'

By evening most of the main body of the army had crossed the Elbe, and a rider brought word that the rearguard under the command of the Markgraf of Meissen would camp that night on the western bank of the Elbe.

When Sir Hubert heard the news he sucked his teeth and spat thoughtfully into his camp fire. 'Our Markgraf of the Weissburg will not be overjoyed by that', he said. 'Still there's little he can do about it today. If the Lord of Meissen choses to dilly and dally, we'll just have to wait until he summons up the enthusiasm to get his feet wet.'

'We can go on without him,' said Sir Robard.

'Aye we could, and it would relieve us of his mutterings and moanings about ill starred expeditions and unknown forests. The problem is we need him. He's a fine soldier – a brave one – and he probably has more experience fighting against these Liutizen than all of us put together.'

Sir Robard squatted down by the fire and stared into the crackling flames. 'Should we have come here to this place my lord? Should we have crossed the Elbe?' Sir Hubert did not reply. Sir Robard went on: 'We lost two good scouts today, and nearly a third to boot. They didn't stand a chance. It's too closely wooded, and the path is too narrow. We haven't time to clear it, and our cavalry isn't used to covering areas like this. As for the infantry . . .'

'I know, I know.' Sir Hubert held up his hand wearily. 'You're right of course. It's bad territory. You know it, I know it, and so does the Lord of Meissen. But we're stuck with it. As long as our good King Henry wants those pagan fellows taught a lesson, we're stuck with it. And that's why the Markgraf will not be backing off. We will march through this forest losing men every day until we find a village to burn. We will burn it and kill as many of the locals that we can run down. Then we will turn around and get back to the Elbe with as much dignity as we can muster.'

'No battle then.'

'In this? By St Aylward's teeth, Robard, how can we fight a battle on ground like this? We will have our hands full just trying to keep our line of march together.' He spat again, and half turned away. 'I'm off to check the pickets. If you could see to the Weissburgers . . .'

'Aye, my lord.' Sir Robard stood up. As he did so a trumpet sounded to the East of the camp. 'The cavalry are back,' he said simply, and with a brief salute began to walk towards the horse lines.

The next day the army did not move. It lay on its back in the dappled sunshine of the clearing and waited for the rearguard to cross the Elbe. All day long the army waited, but by evening there was still no sign of the Markgraf of Meissen and the rearguard.

As the night pickets were being set out, a horseman cantered into the camp. He carried the banner of Meissen, and a sword, mace and kite shield bounced at his hip. His horse was flecked with foam and blood. It had been ridden hard, and looked at the point of collapse. The Markgraf of Weissburg himself, caught hold of the bridle, and helped the rider from the saddle.

'What news?' he asked.

The Meissener nodded his thanks to the sergeants who were leading his horse away, and then turned to the Markgraf: 'My Lord, I thank you. That's a fierce ride. Narrow, dangerous. There were times . . .'

'Yes, yes! Now tell me, man, what news?'

'The rearguard is still at Dresdany.'

'What!' Dietmar stood back, hands on hips, glaring.

'Yes, sire. My Lord of Meissen sent me to tell you that he cannot move this day, nor perhaps tomorrow.'

'Cannot or will not? Confound it! He knows we are stuck here unless he comes. We cannot move without him.' The Markgraf smacked his fist into his open palm, strode away a few paces turned and strode back, eyes blazing. 'Why is he not here?'

The Meissener, still breathing heavily from the ride, lowered his head but spoke clearly and steadily: 'Because my Lord we have received word that Liutizen raiding parties may be about to cross the Elbe at Meissen.'

A murmur of alarm ran among the men who were now crowding in to hear what the messenger had to say.

The Markgraf frowned, paused and then shook his head. 'Enough! Come to my tent, we will talk some more. Sir Hubert, scatter these vagrants if you will, then report to my tent. You can leave Sir Robard and Sir Ulrich to set the watch.' He took the weary messenger by the shoulder and led him across the clearing to his pavilion. Sir Hubert followed soon after, and the rest of the army settled down for the night around the camp fires.

By morning, before breakfast had been taken, the news had reached everyone in the camp from baggage boy to priest, from fyrdsman to captain: the rearguard was still at Dresdany, and would not cross the Elbe until it knew that there was no threat to Meissen. Some men said that war skiffs had been seen ten miles downstream, crossing to the West Bank. Others claimed that the Markgraf of Meissen had sent word to the son of Bretislav of Bohemia to come with all speed to his aid before raiding parties razed the Saxon Marches. Even though no one could say that they had seen or heard of burning farms and villages that Spring, rumours kept drifting down the Elbe that the Liutizen were massing for an attack.

Dietmar of Weissburg fumed and protested, but there was little he could do. He did not even bother to send his own messenger back to Dresdany, but entrusted the Meissener with a simple but urgent reply: 'For pity's sake, make haste! Every day lost weakens our cause. Every delay strengthens the enemy!'

They waited five more days. In that time they cleared an area to half a bow shot around the camp, dug a ditch and threw up a rough pallisaded fence in the Roman style. The middens hard against it soon stank, but it offered a good measure of protection against Liutizen attacks. These attacks took the form of sudden arrows which flew in out of nowhere and struck sentries and even tethered horses. After several attempts the Markgraf abandoned sending out cavalry patrols. He had lost too many men already, and the patrols rarely accomplished anything but to scatter a few isolated tribesmen, or run down a stag or two.

The weather held, but the army's patience was rapidly weakening: the levies were counting the days when their service would be ended, and they could return to their homes. The sergeants and captains were eager to be on the march once again before idleness and boredom led to disorder, quarrelling and desertions. The knights drank too much wine and yearned for the chance to prove their valour and skill at arms. And Sir Hubert and Sir Robard feared the outbreak of disease and plague in the camp: that above all things could cripple the army and send it crawling home.

At last on the morning of the 6th day, excited cheering broke out along the Western ramparts of the camp. Banners had been sighted: black lions on a gold field, the lions of Meissen. At last the rear guard had come: a thousand strong, knights, men at arms and levies – and all led by the Meissener horsemen in their gleaming armour and blazoned shields.

They were led by their Markgraf Ludwig, who looked grim and determined, but seemed moved by the warmth of the welcome he and his men received.

He dismounted by the makeshift gate of the camp, and waited as his men marched in ahead of him. It was there that the Markgraf of Weissburg greeted him:

'Well met Sir Ludwig! We scarcely hoped to see you this day, but our prayers were answered.'

'Hummph! You know as well as I do my Lord, that I'm only here because our noble Salian prince requires it of me. But I would be damned if I crossed the Elbe while my own Mark was under threat.'

The Markgraf of Weissburg managed to hold his smile – just – but his tone was suddenly clipped and more formal: 'You need to remember, Sir Ludwig, that your right to call Meissen a Mark and your determination to entitle yourself 'Markgraf' has not yet been recognised by his majesty the emperor. However, you are right in this one thing: you are here by direct command of that same emperor who, as it happens, placed me in command of you, - and your men.'

There was a steely silence. Both men looked at each other, unflinching. The last of the rearguard tramped into the camp, and the sentries stood by nervously waiting to close the gates. Still, the two warlords stood. When it seemed as though one of them might tear off his gauntlet and throw down a challenge, Ludwig gave a slight cough, brushed back his long black moustache and said, slowly and carefully:

'We came with all speed once we got word that Meissen and all the villages between there and Dresdany were safe from attack.'

The Markgraf Dietmar nodded, paused and then replied: 'You have done well, my Lord. I would that you were here sooner, but there is nothing now would make me send you away: your sword is feared Sir Ludwig, on both sides of this river!'

And so the moment passed. The Meissener relaxed his shoulders, and gave a brief smile. The Weissburger roared with laughter clapped the other on his back and led him into the camp. With a sigh of relief the sentries hurried the gates closed, and brought down the bars. Word spread through the camp that all was well: the rearguard had arrived, Sir Ludwig had arrived, and tomorrow the army would march.

Bernhardt, Rainald, Wulfstan, and the other Eckerheimers crouched around their fire and watched the meagre pottage bubbling in the little pot. The supply of lentils and rye flour was getting low. Soon they would have to forage, Liutizen or not. Right throughout the camp, rumours spread and gathered, and grew where ever men lit fires and cooked. The rumours as always said many different things: that they would have to march tomorrow; that the Liutizen had been joined by Wends from the North; that Sir Ludwig had only crossed the Elbe when the son of Bretislav and his Bohemians had arrived to defend the West Bank; and that the forest they were attempting to cross was fifty miles wide and one hundred miles deep.

'Smoke in the wind! Smoke in the wind!' chuckled Wulfstan as he stirred the little pot with his dagger.

'But it's true, Wulfstan! Every one is saying it,' said Branulf. 'We march tomorrow, but the forest is too big to cross, and the Wends have come from the North and Sir Ludwig . . .'

'And Sir Ludwig is here at last, and all will yet be well. Aye, I know, I hear the talk, but I don't think much of it. Soldiers were ever dreamers and liars. All you'll ever hear around campfires like these is one wild story after another. Mark my words young Branulf, there's not one of these rumours has any spine in it, any real backbone. It's all gossip, campfire gossip. That's all. You'll see!' He leant over the pottage and sniffed. 'Now, here's something you can rely on: a good bean and lentil pottage – good for the spirits and good for the bowels. Just what we need when our bellies are set to flap against our ribs. What say you, Branulf?'

But before the young lad could reply, Wulfstan had stood up: 'Ah, now! Here comes our young wounded warrior. Make a welcome now! Look to, lads – it's Markward.'

They all turned. Markward was coming towards them. His shoulder was still bandaged, but he was walking freely, his shield on his good arm, and his sword at his side.

'Well met, Markward! What news?'

Markward smiled as he came up to them. 'News enough, my friends. We move out in two days time, and push East until we breach this forest.'

'Two days?' said Rainald. 'I thought it was tomorrow.'

Markward shook his head. 'No. It's two days all right. I heard it from the Markgraf himself.'

'The Markgraf!'

'Aye, Sir Hubert brought me to him. He wanted me to scout ahead once more when the army marches out of here.'

'You'd be mad!' laughed Wulfstan.

'Aye, I would', nodded Markward. 'Mad enough to do it, but not mad enough to tell the Markgraf I wouldn't.'

'You're doing it then?'

'I am - and look! See here!' He reached behind his shield and took out a couple of cheeses and a leg of bacon. 'For you fine fellows, courtesy of the Markgraf himself – for agreeing to do without me for a few more days.'

'Now, I know you're mad,' said Wulfstan. 'That old fox wouldn't have given you more than a clip over the ear if he knew you had any chance of coming back alive. He's given two days rations to a dying man.'

Markward sat down by the fire. 'Maybe so,' he said. 'But it's better than sitting around here in this giant pig pen we've built for ourselves. We need to get moving.'

There was a murmur of agreement, as the men fell on the cheeses and bacon and began to eat them. Only Bernhardt stayed back, nodding his thanks to Markward, but passing his portion to another. Rainald looked quizzically at Markward, but he only shrugged and turned to talk to Branulf.

A troop of horse galloped by heading for the gates and the outer pickets. It would be a clear night with no mist. The moon was up and full making it easier to spot the Liutizen as they crept in towards the pallisade. But, the priest was there to bless the men as they rode out, and there would be doubtless fewer riding back in the morning.

Two days later, with the early morning sun on his face, and a gentle breeze at his back, Markward trotted his horse through the Eastern gates and across the clearing towards the woodland path. He didn't look back, but he knew that the Markgraf, Sir Ludwig and Sir Hubert were watching him. Behind them, the camp was bustling into life, as trumpets called men to the march.

As he reached the tree line he reined in, and stared at the way ahead. It was the same path he had galloped wildly along several days before. His shoulder was still a little stiff, but the pain had gone, and the wound had healed. Instinctively, he reached up and touched it, and then eased his horse into a gentle walk. The trees folded around him once more. The sounds of the trumpets and the shouting of the captains faded. That familiar, heavy silence flowed out of the shadows and swirled about him. He moved on, following the path, deeper and deeper into the woods. He passed the point where he had been ambushed. He paused and then moved on again. Deeper and deeper he went, the narrow clay path winding lazily ahead of him as the pine-woods slowly gave way to the great forest oaks and dark-trunked elms. It was so quiet. So quiet. Surely they were watching him. Just as before. Watching and waiting. Drawing back on the bowstring even now. Sighting along the shaft of the barbed arrow, and waiting until they couldn't miss. He was not a scout. He was a sacrifice. Already fallen. Already missing. Not expected to return.

A branch cracked somewhere away to his right. He whipped up his shield and ducked his head, his horse shy-ing as he did so.

'Whoa, boy! Steady, now!' Slowly he eased his sword out of the scabbard, and was, as ever, strangely comforted by the sharp and steely hiss it made as it glided free of the leather. Another branch, this time rustling and moving as though being pushed aside. Closer, much closer.

He tensed for the charge, teeth clenched and his hand biting into the wire and leather hilt of his sword. A bead of sweat trickled down from under the brow of his helmet and his heart pounded as though it would break his ribs. Let them come! Let them come!

All at once there was a crashing of leaves and branches - and a stag, antlers tossing, leapt across the path in front of him. A moment later it was gone, the sound of its hooves thudding away into the distance.

He breathed out heavily. His hands were shaking, and he felt sick at his stomach. He rubbed away the sweat from his brow with the back of one hand. His mouth felt dry, and his whole body seemed to tingle.

It was quiet again. The path stretched away before him, and the trees stood still.

'Too much!' he muttered to himself. Almost without thinking, he turned his horse off the path and into the undergrowth from where the stag had first appeared. He found that without too much difficulty he could ride away from, and then parallel to the path, his way now screened by low hanging branches, forest scrub and furze bushes. With care he was able to move with little more sound than a subdued rustling as the leaves brushed by him and his horse. He was certainly less visible, and far more likely now to surprise the Liutizen or at least goad them into a hasty shot.

He pushed on, angling away from the path for a time, and then circling back towards it. Every so often he would stop and listen, letting his horse crop the thin grasses that grew here and there among the massive trunks. Slowly, he began to feel more part of the forest, and less an intruder, though there was always at the forefront of his

mind that this great woodland was the realm of the Liutizen. The
silence of these woods, in the end, meant nothing. What he could not
see was what he most feared. What he could not hear, could almost
certainly hear him. It was a world of silent watchers, waiting to strike.

Towards noon he decided to take a rest and wait for the vanguard
of the army to come up with him. He rejoined the path where it
crossed a sunlit clearing, dismounted, and tethered his horse to a
laurel. After a glance around he sat with his back against a twisted old
elm, thrust his sword and dagger into the turf in front of him, and
began a simple lunch of bread and cheese. There were birds singing:
song thrushes and forest finches. It seemed cheerful after the deep
quiet of the hours which lay behind him. Ahead, beyond the clearing,
the tall trees grew straight and strong, but they seemed to be more
spaced, giving way to low brushwood and slender birches. Perhaps
this forest was not so vast after all. Perhaps he would soon be leading
the army out onto grassland and open fields.

For a moment he thought of closing his eyes and letting the
warmth of the sun play across his face, but he knew that it could be
fatal to doze even for a short time. So he kept awake, humming an
old folk tune to himself, and thinking of Eckerheim, and all the folks
and Elsa.

As she knelt by the stream, rubbing the washing against the flat
river stone, Elsa heard someone walking down by the bank. She
turned and looked up. It was the young priest.

'Good day, Father,' she said, and turned again to her work.

'And a good day to you, mistress,' replied Ulrich. 'I'm not
disturbing you, I hope.'

'No, Father. Not at all. As you can see, I can work and talk as well
as not.'

She slapped a tunic hard against the rock, and set to scrubbing it.

Ulrich sat down on the bank, not far away. 'Such fine weather
we're having,' he said, almost as if to himself, and lobbed a pebble
into the stream.

Elsa nodded but did not reply. Ulrich leaned back on one arm and watched the stream as it bubbled and swirled between the banks. For a time he seemed lost in his own thoughts, then he suddenly said:

'The Levy's been gone a good few days now.'

Still she did not reply, but kept on scrubbing the tunic. He noticed how strands of her flame red hair, from under her headscarf, hung across her face.

'We should get word soon enough,' he went on. 'But I expect that all is well.'

Elsa stood up. 'And how should you expect that, Father?'

'I - well, I . . .' he was suddenly at a loss for words, reddened, and stood up himself. 'I'm sorry,' he said.

'It's all right, Father.' She wrung out her washing, gathered it up, and set off back towards the village.

'They have my prayers!' the young priest suddenly called out.

Elsa walked on a few paces, paused, then turned and came back. 'Your prayers, Sir Priest? Your prayers! The graveyards, the woods and the hard hills are full of the bones of folk who had the prayers of priests to keep them safe!' She almost spat the words out, and her eyes filled with tears.

He stood awkwardly, trembling with indecision, and almost reached out to touch her on the shoulder, but pulled his hand away.

She turned again to walk away.

'Wait!'

'Yes?'

He swallowed hard. 'I cannot know of love,' he said slowly. 'Not the love that goes between a man and a woman. We are taught to crush it you see – to drive it out of our souls – to flee before it like a stag before a forest fire.' He smiled. 'You understand?'

She nodded.

'Well then, I cannot know what you know – what you feel. I cannot know that. But I do see in your eyes loneliness and sorrow, and I do see fear. These things I know, these things I can pray about. I . . .'

'Thank you Father.'

'Oh, it's . . .' He waved his hand. 'It's part of my trade. It's what we priests do, and I know it can work. It can, you know.'

Elsa put her washing down, and tucked her hair under her scarf. 'But then, why so much prayer, and yet so much sorrow?' Her voice was level, flat.

Ulrich sighed and nodded. 'Because so often our faith is mixed with doubt, our prayers are mixed with ignorance. Like clay in iron. We are born to be shattered at the first hard shock.'

'You read that in a book?'

'No, no.'

'Someone told you that?'

He laughed, but gently, and shook his head. 'It's just something I've come to know.'

'Father Ulrich?'

'I wish you folk would stop calling me that.'

'Well, all right, then: Ulrich?'

'Yes?'

'He will come home, safely then? He will come home?'

'I pray to God they all do, but I've a feeling there's a passion in that man of yours will carry him through blood and fire no matter what.'

'You sound like the old shepherd.'

'Cedric? Aye, well – that's not such a bad thing. He's a wiser man than me.' He looked into her eyes, so clear and blue and shining with tears.   Quickly she ducked her head, bobbed a curtsey and hurried away.

It was late afternoon and Ulrich stayed by the stream until the sun had almost set. No one else came near. Most of the women were in the fields or sitting outside their houses spinning wool and churning goats milk. The menfolk were away hunting and gathering food in the high woods, and the shepherds and shepherd boys had long since led the flocks down to the long meadow on the far side of the village.

At last when the warmth had been drawn out of the day, and the hazy shadows of twilight fell across the valley Ulrich got stiffly to his feet and began to walk back towards the church. He was anxious, almost afraid, and he could hardly explain it. There was a girl, much the same age as him, - a girl who was head over in heels in love with a young peasant lad, and worried half to death that she would never see him again. And she was so beautiful, and so strong, and yet so terribly alone: she frightened Ulrich. Well, moved him – worried him really. Worried him so that he could no longer think like a priest. All he seemed able to do was sit by the stream and lob pebbles into the water. Was he a priest or was he a man? Well, he was both, no matter what that shrivelled old bishop back at Magdeburg had said. Elsa! She was beautiful and full of life, and were he not a priest, he would marry one as her, and build a cruck, and keep a farm and raise a family.

. He stopped by the stream again, lobbed another pebble, and watched the ripples swirl away. Tomorrow he had promised Eric that he would help him build his barn in return for three ducklings and a round of cheese. Now that was work for a priest: rough on the hands and good for the stomach. He smiled, and hitched his cassock in his belt. If he ran now, and cut across the fields he would be in time to ring the bell for eventide, and old mother Helga would not be telling him off for being an idler. 'God bless her for a sharp tongue,' he said to himself, and set off.

The army came up with Markward as the sun set. It came with good news. There had been no attacks on the column all day. Not one. They had marched nervously, but unopposed. Even the outriders and flanking patrols had neither seen nor heard anything unusual. It was as though the Liutizen had faded away into nothingness. 'I believe,' pronounced the chaplain, 'That the good Lord has sent his archangels down, and spirited all those pagans away.'

'If you believe that,' muttered Sir Hubert under his breath, ' then you're either a simpleton, or a chaplain and little else besides.'

The knights around him guffawed, and the chaplain looked around, gave a little sniff, and disappeared into his tent.

'Well,' said Sir Hubert, taking off his helmet and sweeping back his mail coif, 'What did you see, young Markward? As little as us.'

'Little more than you, sire. A stray stag, that's all. But that is not what worried me.'

'Say on.'

'It was not what I saw sire, it was what I could not hear.'

Sir Hubert raised his eyebrows, so Markward went on: 'Until I reached this clearing my lord, there was no birdsong. None at all.'

'None?'

'Aye, my Lord, none.'

'Hmmm!' Sir Hubert rubbed his chin. 'Well there was certainly birdsong when we came through. So that can only mean one thing . . .'

'They're pulling back in front of us.'

'Aye. They saw you by, and then fell back as we came towards them.'

Some of the other knights nodded, but no one spoke. The old warlord signalled to Sir Robard and together they walked towards the edge of the clearing and stared into the woods. They stayed there for some time, deep in discussion, and then wandered slowly back. 'Join us for supper', said Sir Hubert to Markward, and then went off to find the provost.

They dined well that night. Several stags had fallen to the imperial archers, and the campfires blazed and crackled as the venison fat dripped from makeshift spits. The Markgraf had ordered the provost to break open extra skins of wine to celebrate the day's march, and the clearing soon rang with the shouts and songs of weary but cheerful men.

'Tell me,' said Sir Hubert to Markward as he sucked on a greasy bone, 'Do you think the Liutizen have gone?'

Markward paused before he answered. He frowned slightly. 'I think, sire, that they are waiting for us.'

'An ambush, you mean?'

'Perhaps.'

'But why not ambush us here, in the forest?'

'Where we would expect to be ambushed, sire?'

'Yes, precisely. Ah, I see what you mean. They prefer to catch us off guard.'

'It's possible.'

'It makes sense.' He threw the bone into the fire. ' Sir Robard here thinks they will attack tonight.'

'Sir Robard is a very experienced soldier.'

'But he did not see the ground today as you have seen it. You are my eyes and ears. What do you say?'

Again, Markward paused. 'I think, sire that they will not attack tonight, nor with the dawn. The trees are thinning here. Cavalry can charge through them. Our archers can pick their targets. If they wanted to take us in this forest, they lost their chance further back.'

'So, then! You have scouted further ahead of this clearing?'

'Aye my Lord. Just two bowshots. The trees are thinning all the time. We'll be out of this within an hour tomorrow.'

Sir Hubert grunted and looked at Sir Robard who gave a faint smile and a brief nod, but held his peace.

'Well, I hope you are right, Markward. Still, we'll post double pickets tonight, and build up the watch fires. No sentries to stand guard for more than an hour before being relieved, and I want the sergeants to rouse the camp an hour before dawn.' There was the usual growl of assent, and the men went back to their venison and wine.

Dawn came slowly with a low, damp mist that drifted through the trees, and made the forest hang in glistening web of filtered light. The camp woke groaning, but stood to arms in shambling haste as the sergeants strode among the tents and bivouacs swearing, and cursing, and beating anyone they caught half-asleep. The pickets reported a quiet night, although the guards of the third watch had seen shadows moving among the trees some fifty paces beyond the fires on the northern bounds.

The army snatched a cold breakfast, and then set off eastwards on the narrow trail that led through the fading forest.

Markward was sent on ahead, but this time with a detachment of heavy cavalry which included Sir Robard and Ludwig of Meissen.

They trotted easily through the open woods, hoofbeats muffled by moss and fallen leaves. The mist melted before the morning sun, and their armour shone. With spirits lifting they at last cleared the forest and came upon a patch of open, marshy ground flanked by low scrub and gorse covered hills.

'Faith, you were right!' said Sir Robard reining in his horse. 'Scarcely an hour, and we are rid of that death trap.'

Markward frowned. 'My lord,' he said, pointing at the way ahead, 'that ground is not safe. Too boggy for my liking. Infantry may cross it at a pinch, but the cavalry will flounder.'

'You think so? Then we'll skirt it.'

'Skirt it!' broke in Ludwig of Meissen. 'Have you gone mad? Those hills are miles away, and like to be swarming with pagan devils. We've found open ground, let's stick to it. We're bound to come upon a Liutizen village soon, or at least we'll catch some of them out in the open.'

'But if the ground is to soft, Sir Ludwig . . .'

'Too soft! Too soft! It's you who are too soft, Sir Robard! I've ridden horses since I was knee high to a cockroach, and I can tell you that ground is fine!'

He spurred his horse forward and plunged into the marsh. For a time the horse held its own. It was a tall, well built warhorse, and Ludwig was a superb rider. But he had gone no more than half a bowshot, when his horse began to struggle. It sank to its fetlocks, reared up, and then sank even deeper. Cursing, Ludwig leapt from the saddle, freed his mount, and led it panting back.

'My Lord?' asked Sir Robard with a barely concealed smile.

Sir Ludwig shrugged. 'Well, halfway across is no way across, I'll give you that. Still, we can send the infantry that way, and scout to left and right until we find better ground for the cavalry.'

And so it was agreed. Word was sent back to the main column, and by noon the army had cleared the forest, and crossed the marshland. The cavalry worked their way cautiously around the edges of the open ground and rejoined the footsoldiers about a mile further on towards the East.

By that time Markward, along with Sir Robard and Sir Ludwig had found a rough and worn track that led over some rolling, open fields and ragged meadowland. At last they could see for miles in all directions. Sir Ludwig laughed out loud. 'What a fine place for a battle. We could make a harvest fit for a king on a field such as this, eh, Sir Robard?'

The other knight nodded. 'Which is why they'll never attack us here,' he said. 'We must push on.' He clicked his tongue, flicked the reins and spurred away across the field with his squire and sergeant in pursuit. Sir Ludwig waved his own men on, and set off after him. Markward stayed where he was. He had caught a glint of sun on steel out of the corner of his eye, up there on the hills to the North. It was a good distance away, too far for imperial outriders, but it had to come from a weapon, a helmet, a shield or a coat of mail. There it was again! And again! Not one man, but two, maybe more and moving along the line of march.

He looked back over his shoulder. The imperial army was just visible coming slowly over a long, low crest about a mile to the West. Its flapping banners and pennons were black against the blue sky, and the spear points glittered like dew above the haze of dust. Surely the Liutizen would not attack here. Not in the open where the imperial cavalry could wheel and charge in an extended line, and the footsoldiers could shelter behind a hedge of steel and leather. He gazed again at the northern hills. There was another flash of light, but then no more. He waited and watched, but the hills stared blankly back. There was no more to be seen, except the dull shimmering green of the far horizon. He galloped his horse back to the head of the advancing column and reined in, raising his arm in salute as he recognised the Markgraf riding before the banner of the Weissburg.

'Well met, Markward! What news!'

Markward told of what he had seen, noticing as he did so that the Markgraf was sweating freely, and looking red and flushed. But he listened patiently, and when Markward had finished the warlord grunted his thanks, and then ordered the sergeants to bring the army on with all possible speed.

'If they are massing for an attack here', he said, 'they must know something about this ground which we do not. So we press on, and make sure that we choose the ground for battle, and not them. Besides, every step we take is a step deeper into their territory, and a step closer to their villages. The sooner we can make their thatch burn, and their crops blaze the sooner we can go home and forget we ever came to such a place.'

Markward took his leave, and trotted back down the line until he met up with the men from Eckerheim.

They greeted him with loud and ironic cheers. Leaping off his horse he replied with an exaggerated bow. 'My lords!'

'My liege!' they replied, and crowded round him, slapping him on the back, and eager for any news.

Eric was worried. The Summer harvest was almost ready, the air was heavy with the threat of thunderstorms and there were not enough folk to bring the crops in. They would have to start reaping early, and that was that. There would be grumbles, that he knew, but it could not be helped. Better a harvest not quite ripened than no harvest at all.

He stood by the marker stone on the Great South field and looked over the gently waving crop. It was good. It was full and fat, but it needed just a few more days. If only the levy were here. How many days had they been gone? A while, a long while – that was all he could say, but he knew it would be a miracle if they showed up before the harvest, and some folks said it would be a miracle if they showed up at all. A cow lowed and moved from the meadow towards the crop. Where is that lad of mine? he thought. 'Aelric!' he called.

'Yes, papa!' A head popped up from behind a bush some thirty paces away.

'Ah, there you are! Come on now. Do your job! There's a beast headed for the crop.'

Aelric leapt to his feet, and ran towards the cow, waving a stick and whistling. The bailiff watched his son, smiled and then headed back towards the village. There was to be a feast tonight: St Bran's Day, or was it St Ada's? He wasn't sure, and didn't care. At least it was a feast, and at least it kept the folk happy and dancing for a few short hours. Perhaps that would be the time to tell them about the harvest . . .

Elsa got up the following morning, and headed for the tops. It was the four and fortieth day since the levy had left Eckerheim. She walked to the crest of the ridge, sat down on the old cairn stone and took out her tally stick: forty four days, forty four tally marks. She counted them: once, twice, and then leaned back and looked towards the North and East.

They would come from that way, they had to, and she would see them as they came. It was a clear day, and she had a clear view all the way to the hills that shielded the Weissburg.

Below, the village was quiet. Eric had given the villagers the day off before the harvesting began. There were a few sore heads from the night before and a few mutterings about bailiffs who thought they were barons, but for the most part the folk were grateful for the brief respite.

Elsa felt at peace high above the valley. She had waited for this day and now it had come. A warm breeze blew from the South rippling the fields below, and chasing the shadows of light, white clouds across the ridges. It fanned her cheek and tossed her hair as she leant against it. Soon the Levy would be home.

Ulrich the priest swung the mallet and drove the wooden peg hard into place against the beam. 'There!' he said, 'That ought to do it.'

Eric paused at the saw bench and came across, and ran his hand over the joint. 'That's good. Now, I'll just finish this cross beam and we can lift it into place.' He returned to the bench and with a few more strokes the beam was cut. He dressed it, and rubbed it down while Ulrich shifted the ladder and tied it firmly to the scaffold. Then the beam was carefully lifted into place and fixed with wooden pegs. Twice they had to lift the beam back down and re-bore the holes for the pegs, but in the end all was done, and the frame for the roof was complete.

They sat together at the corner of the barn and ate their bread and cheese.

'A job well done, Ulrich. If you were not a priest, you would have made a carpenter.'

'Aye, and been the happier for it,' replied Ulrich quietly.

Eric glanced at the young priest. 'What's happier than a priest? One foot in heaven, and two hands in the tithes.'

Ulrich laughed and shook his head. 'I'm a man to be married, Eric, and all the tithes in Christendom won't change that.'

There was a silence while Eric poured out two cups of maize beer from the clay jug, and handed one to Ulrich.

'I see. And who would you marry — supposing you were not a priest?'

'Were I not a priest, Sir Bailiff, I would marry a lass like Elsa — flame red hair and bright blue eyes and a voice to strike the heart.'

'She's promised.'

'And so am I. And so am I. And there's the pity of it.' He drank the beer, and wiped his mouth, then stood up. 'But there's no use in sitting here moaning about it. I'm a priest, and that's all there is to it: a priest, sworn, blessed and tonsured — and like as not to go to the devil if I don't get lasses out of my mind.'

Eric sighed, got up and walked over to the ladder. 'You're a good priest Ulrich. Many of your kind, vows or not, would take a lass or two just to slake their thirst.'

'Aye, don't I know it. Well, they may have consciences seared with a red hot iron, but not me! I'll stay a faithful priest or none at all.'

'Well said! Now come and help me check these trusses before we put the poles and wands in place.'

Elsa waited all day up on the tops. Three times she thought she saw someone coming and started to her feet, but each time it was only a passing shadow, or a distant tree moving in the wind.

As the sun set and the shepherds led their flocks back to the folds, Elsa looked for the last time towards the Weissburg. Then turning, she headed back down into the valley. The breeze had cooled, and there was a threat of rain in the air. She pulled her shawl close around her. If the rain held off Eric would call them to the fields before dawn, and they would work all day and even through the night to get the harvest in. But she could not think of that. The levy had not come. Her man had not come home, and her heart was fit to burst. As she neared the high field she ducked her head, not wanting to see little Albrecht as he ran up the slope towards her. There was no dream any more. No coming down the hillside arm in arm with her man. No kisses. No warm embrace. No tears of joy. Just a cold breeze sweeping in over the tops and an empty path all the way to the Weissburg. Forty four days and nothing. A tally stick with forty four grooves. And nothing.

She pushed through a wicket gate, crossed a ditch, and there was Albrecht.

Three days after they crossed the marshland, the army began to grumble. It was not unusual to hear a mutter of discontent around the campfires, but this time all the army spoke: it was time to turn for home – it was time to get the harvest in. They were getting short of water, the days were long and hot, and the harvest was due. They marched each day in a cloud of dust and flies through a seamless wasteland. The horses were suffering, the levies were dragging their feet, and it was no good burning Liutizen crops if their own were rotting in the fields.

And so the army spoke. It spoke to the sergeants, and the sergeants to the captains. The captains brought word to the warlords, and the warlords gathered uneasily at the tent of the Markgraf.

He listened to them in silence with furrowed brow, and coughed, and shrugged and looked hard at the men who stood about him. What they said he already knew. He would not have been in charge of such an army if he did not know its heart. He was the Markgraf, and they were his children so long as they marched under his banner and called him lord.

'Leave me,' was all he said, and they bowed and quietly left.

An hour later his trumpeter blew the assembly. The men stood to arms, then all the knights and all the captains of all the levies came to listen to their Lord of Weissburg.

He had dressed in full armour – hauberk, helm and shield – despite the heat, and now stood under the Black Eagle banner of his fathers. His sword was in his hand, and his great ash spear was carried by Sir Robard.

For a time he stood and gazed at the men before him, and then he spoke:

'Men of Saxony! Soldiers of the king! We have come far. We have crossed the Elbe. We have marched through a mighty forest, and across an open land. We have come bearing defiance to our enemies – and yet they will not fight. They run and hide, and fall back before us . . .'

He stopped, and put his hand to his brow, as though in thought. For a moment his shoulders seemed to sag, but then he straightened up.

'Men of Saxony – we cannot fight against men who will not be fought.

'We are not here to chase rabbits!' There was a murmur of approval, and even faint laughter.

'And so, this I decree, and let no man play me false.' He breathed in deeply and gave a heavy sigh. 'This I decree, as commander of the imperial army: We march for another two days.Full marches mind you, fifteen miles per day, no less. Deserters and slackers will be hung. Then if we still have not brought the heathen to battle, if we still have not found a village to torch, then – then my friends – we turn for home.'

There was a silence. Then a shuffling, a whispering, and brief and hurried bows as the captains took their leave. Moments later the sound of distant cheering came from the far side of the camp where the levies were waiting, drawn up in order of the march. The cheering grew, and became a roar, and crows flew up from a grove of larches nearby.

The Markgraf stood motionless, grim, his face set, and beads of sweat on his forehead. 'Well, that's that!' he said after a while, and turned and went back into the tent followed by his captain and castellans.

Within a day the advance guard of the army had come upon a Liutizen village. It was small, rundown and deserted, but they set fire to it nonetheless. The well was blocked, but there was a stream, and they watered the horses before pushing on to open ground where they made camp for the night.

The following day scouts brought in a Liutizen family they had found wandering in the woods. They looked so wretched, frightened and bedraggled the Markgraf didn't have the heart to hang them. But he cut the man's bowstring fingers and sent them away. By evening it was clear that the campaign was over. In the morning they would turn for home.

Down by the mill at Eckerheim, where the stream curves and channels, and rushes over the smooth, round rocks, the women had come to sharpen the sickles and billhooks for the harvest. They brought their washing too, and spread it out on the hot, dry banks of stone. And then they sat in the sun and talked to the sound of whetstones on iron. Katrin was there, and Elspeth, Mutti too, and Hetti along with some of the other children. They had not long been there when Edvart's widow came out of the mill with a platter of scones. She didn't speak, but walked quietly up to them, and smiled and put the platter down. The women thanked her warmly, and she smiled again, but didn't reply. They watched as she disappeared back into the mill.

'Poor lass,' said Elspeth.

'Aye, she's scarce said a word since her Edvart fell, but young Elsa keeps her company, and can even make her laugh.'

The smell and sight of the scones drew the children like wasps to honey, but when Albrecht came running up and said a bear had been spotted in the woods they all yelped and screamed and ran to get sticks and stones. Moments later they were scampering away across the fields heedless of their mothers' shrill warnings. The womenfolk set to work once more, and soon the talk had turned to the levy, and to the men coming home, and to Elsa.

Elspeth held her peace, though she knew she missed her Rainald as much as Elsa seemed to miss Bernhardt, and she too had counted the days and known the disappointment. Katrin had just opened her mouth to say something when Mutti put a hand on her arm. Elsa was coming across the fields towards them.

She waved, a slight uncertain movement of the hand, and they called a greeting in return. As she neared them, stooping under the bough of the old oak by the mill, they could see that she had been crying. Her hair was unbrushed, and her shawl hung loose across one shoulder. She sat down, took up a billhook and began to sharpen it. The others glanced at one another and returned to their whetstones.

No one spoke. At last Mutti came and sat beside Elsa and put an arm round her shoulder.

'You're afraid, lassie?'

Elsa sniffed and nodded and kept sharpening the billhook.

'They'll be home soon.'

'You can't know that Mutti.'

'That's true, but I know that Fear is the lock, but Love is the key. In the end, love brings them home.'

'Words, Mutti. Just words.'

'Aye, aye. Maybe you're right, but at the moment, words is all we have to play with. Words and these billhooks. Whatever happens the harvest has to come in.'

'That's why I'm here.'

'So you are, lassie – so you are, and your man'll be beside you in the fields before you know it.'

Elsa looked up and brushed away the tears. 'You think so, Mutti, you really think so?'

'I told you so when they left, and I tell you so now. I feel it in these old bones of mine. Your man is coming home.'

Elsa dropped her billhook and hugged Mutti. 'Oh, Mutti, if only it were today!'

Mutti smiled and looked up at the sky. 'Today would not be too soon. Eric keeps smelling rain, and I'm not so sure he's wrong.'

'Hah!' said Elspeth putting down her whetstone and snatching a drink from the jug beside her, ' About all a man can ever smell is his dinner in the pot!'

They all laughed, and Elsa kissed Mutti on the cheek. 'Never leave me, Mutti!' she whispered.

'Leave you?' chuckled Mutti. 'I'll be throwing you out the door the moment those men get back!'

THE STORM BREAKS

It was a still, grey morning the day the army turned for home. Men sang cheerfully, joked and shouted as they broke camp and made ready for the march. The womenfolk bustled about excitedly, gathering up belongings and chattering all the while. The last of the camp fires were put out, the horses were saddled, trumpets sounded and the Saxon host slowly headed West towards the Elbe.

Markward did not go with them. Nor Rainald, his chosen man. Today, they were to scout behind the army, working together on foot and on horseback to cover the retreat of the Rear Guard. The Lord of Meissen had been curt in his commands: 'Head east when we head west. After an hour turn and make your way back to us.' He glanced at Rainald. 'You'll have to be quick on your feet today,' he muttered and turned to mount his horse. Rainald nodded and winked at Markward. They both knew that one horse would carry two men back to the rearguard.

As the rest of the Eckerheim levy marched away, they had time to do no more than wave briefly, and shout farewells. Bernhardt ran back as if he wanted to say something, or give something to one of them, but a Meissener captain roared at him, and he returned to the line. The two men watched the army tramp away across the meadow until it disappeared over a low ridge. When the Black Lion of Meissen had dipped below the crest they turned and began to walk east. Markward led his horse, and Rainald strode along beside him, spear over his shoulder, and a leather shield on his arm. The sky was lifting, the birds were singing in the larches, and the world was theirs. For a time they chatted as they walked, but as the open woodland began to close about them once more, so they fell silent and became more wary. Markward judged that when the sun had cleared its first quarter they would turn around. He hoped that they would catch up with the army by mid-afternoon.

It was not long before they came upon a series of rocky outcrops with pine trees growing all about them. Rainald quickly scaled the nearest one, stared in all directions and signalled that all was clear. He came puffing down again, and picked up his spear and shield.

'Not bad,' he said. 'You can see a good distance from up there, and all seems quiet. But away to the north and east there's a row of willows. It goes for a fair way, and I'm thinking it's a riverbank.'

'We should scout it?'

'I'll check it out. If you ride on for a bit, and then circle back to meet me somewhere here, that should be fine.'

Markward thought for a bit, then nodded. 'Well, all right, then, but be careful. We couldn't be more alone out here, if we tried.'

Rainald laughed, slapped him on the back and set off at a loping run towards the willows.

With a frown, Markward swung up into the saddle, and began to ride eastwards, making his way carefully among the outcrops, and then urging his horse into a canter when he found himself at the head of a long grassy slope. The sky had long since brightened now and the sun felt hot against the side of his face and head. He reined in, took a drink of water, splashed some across his face and neck, and then rode on. He squinted into the shimmering haze but could see little. His way seemed to lead across a plain with low hills in the distance, but it was hard to make out any more than that. As the sun climbed the heat grew more intense. His mail hauberk became uncomfortably hot, but he dare not take it off, or even loosen the lacings. Even out here in the open he could be caught out by a sudden charge, or clever ambush.

On he went, dust gathering about the horse's flanks, and across his boots and leggings. The grass, burnt brown and dull yellow, sang as he pushed through it, while here and there high-necked field daisies bobbed wearily in the dryness of the day. He longed to lower his head against the glare, but he knew that a moment's carelessness could be fatal. As the sun crawled towards the crest of the first quarter his head began to pound, and sweat began to sting his eyes. His skin itched and chaffed against the gambeson.

Not much longer, he promised himself. Taking one hand off the reins, he reached for the little brown cup inside his wallet: 'Home!' he said.

Nearly two hours march away the Eckerheim levy trudged along, amid the great, sprawling length of the imperial army. They were tired and they were hot, but they were happy. With each step they were closer to the Elbe, closer to Dresdany and closer to home. Some of the men to the front and rear of them were singing as they marched, but mostly they just watched their boots and talked in brief and half-heard snatches. They were on their way back home, and that was all that mattered. It filled their heads with a thousand thoughts, and made them wish the hours and days away.

Bernhardt felt a quiet joy and strength rise through the rhythm of his shambling stride. The hammer and haversack felt light across his shoulder, and though the sweat ran freely down his brow from under his leather cap he hardly felt it. Elsa filled his thoughts. Soon he would see her again. Soon they would be together, and they would talk, and he would tell her how much he had missed her, and she would tell him . . .

The sound of trumpets rippled along the line, and the army lurched to a halt. A horseman galloped by. And then another, this time from the opposite direction.

'The usual confusion,' said Wulfstan as he sat down by the side of the track. They were in open woodland now, and the trees gave some welcome shelter from the increasing sun. The birds were singing, the army waited, and the sound of crickets and cicadas rose above the quiet talk of weary men.

Branulf took his bow and wandered over to an old ash tree about twenty paces away. It was cool and well shaded beneath its spreading boughs. His father, Ralf, came and sat beside him.

'We'll be home soon, son.'

'I know father, but we have not yet fought. I've done nothing.'

'You've stayed alive. I promised your mother I'd bring you home safe, and that's what's I'm doing.'

Branulf scratched at the ground with the tip of his bow. 'Do you think they'll attack us, father? Will they come for us now?'

Ralf tousled his son's hair. 'Ah! This love of fighting! Where do you youngsters get it from? Listen, son, I don't know if the Liutizen will come or not, but if they do, stay close by me and keep your head down.'

Branulf nodded, 'But I'll shoot my bow as well!'

'Aye, I daresay you will – but remember this; they'll like as not shoot straight back at ye.'

A butterfly settled on a leaf in front of them. Branulf reached out for it, and it floated away among the trees. They watched it go. 'I'll shoot my bow', said Branulf. 'I will.'

A short time later the trumpets sounded again, and they got to their feet and made their way back to the column.'

'Four more hours,' called Wulfstan. 'Then we make camp. That's what the captains say.'

Gustav, his dog by his side, grinned. 'Then let us march like eagles!' he said. He swung his shield over his shoulder, pulled the baldric tight and set off, whistling as he went.

Wulfstan shook his head and smiled. 'Such men make me weary', he said. 'Give me an honest idler any day!' They all laughed, and began to follow.

When Markward returned to the rocky outcrops there was no sign of Rainald. He waited for a bit, and then headed in the direction his friend had taken. He soon caught sight of the willows and the river bank, but Rainald was nowhere to be seen. Cautiously he approached, and scouted along the bank, peering among the willows and ducking under the low sweeping branches. It was quiet, save for the hum of insects and the sound of flowing water as it pushed along the bank among roots and reeds and hanging branches.

He called once, softly, but his voice was swallowed up in the still air, and there was no reply. He told himself that Rainald must have gone further along the riverbank – he could not have crossed – and was now probably on his way back. He would wait here in the shade of the willows until the sun dipped and touched the far hills, and then he would return to the rocky outcrops. There was no need to worry: Rainald would soon return.

He climbed down from the saddle, tethered his horse by the bank, and waited. All day long he waited, at first watchful and expectant, but then increasingly tired. Soon he found himself dozing to the sounds of the riverbank, and finally he slept.

He woke with a start. Twilight swept around him in cool shadows and a glowing sky. The river burbled on, and his horse champed at the grass along the bank. Standing up, he noticed that he was stiff, almost cold. He loosened his shoulders and rubbed his arms as he looked around. There was no sign of Rainald. Where could he be? With a frown and a shake of the head he swung into the saddle and galloped back to the outcrops, arriving to find the place dark and still. There was no one. He called. Loudly this time. His cry echoed around the rocks. He called again. And then once more. But no one answered and no one came. He looked about him. It was silent and still. What could he do? Where would he go? Rainald had gone. Was he dead – and if he was dead, where were those who had killed him?

So he sat and waited and thought hard. The sun had set. It was dark. There was no use trying to find his way anywhere when he could not see. There was nothing for it but to wait, and to wait all night. In the morning, if there were still no sign of Rainald he would head back the way the army had gone. Yes, that was it. If there were Liutizen about, he was a dead man anyway, whether or not he moved from this place. At least if Rainald had somehow just got lost . . . No, that didn't make sense, not unless Rainald had also given him up for dead, and decided to return to the army. But that was not Rainald. That did not make sense. Rainald would never desert a friend so easily, and neither must he.

He found a sheltered spot at the foot of a rough, brush covered slope and settled down for the night. The clouds moved slowly across the face of a new moon, and a cool breeze wandered in among the rocks, sighing as it came and went. His horse flicked its ears and snorted as an owl ghosted by, but that was all. By the third watch he was asleep.

The rooks came with the first flush of dawn, cawing and flapping among the larch and linden woods that faced the slope where Markward lay.

He woke, with a faint splinter of hope that Rainald might appear even now. He looked, shrugged, and saddled his horse. There was no time for breakfast. He had far to go, and a hard ride before him if he were to catch up with the army before it reached the great forest.

Three days later a Saxon horseman cantered across a grassy meadow, skirted a grove of birches and reined in just short of the marshland. It was a hot day with thunder clouds gathering on the far hills, and he pushed his mail coif back from his head. Sighing with relief, he reached for his water bottle. He was just about to drink when a sudden movement among the trees caught his eye. He looked up in time to see a fallow deer break cover and begin to pick its way across the marsh. But there was little else to see. He waited for a bit, then turned his horse and cantered back toward the vanguard of the Saxon Host which was just emerging from the open forest half a mile to the East.

The Markgraf with Sir Robard and Sir Hubert in attendance, trotted out to meet him.

'What news?'

'It's clear sire, but we'll still have to send the cavalry away to our flanks as we cross. That marsh is too soft underfoot.'

'Are you sure?'

'I am, sire. I watched a young deer cross and it went with more care than a monk in a tithing field.'

The Markgraf chuckled. 'Is that so? Well that's careful indeed!' He turned to Sir Hubert: 'Ride back if you would, Sir Hubert, and tell the cavalry to split into two squadrons and ride to the North and South apiece, and skirt this swamp.'

'Aye my Lord!' Sir Hubert saluted and was gone.

Sir Robard leaned forward in the saddle and studied the marshland, and the great forest beyond. He frowned and rubbed the side of his nose.

'It's the heat of the day, my Lord', he said. 'We would do well to cross into the shade of those trees and make camp for the night.'

'Aye, and if those thunder storms hit us, they'll turn this marsh into a quagmire – no one will get across.' He turned and grunted his approval as he heard the trumpets sound three shrill blasts and the cavalry started forward and began to fan out to right and left across the open ground. They would soon reach their flanking positions, so there was no time to lose. The trumpets sounded again, the captains shouted, and the army advanced, sweating and groaning under the noonday sun.

Within in an hour the vanguard had made the shelter of the trees, and the first of the cavalry were making their way carefully around the edges of the marshland and along the shaded banks of the forest. Pickets were posted and a camp site was scouted a bow shot's length into the woodlands. Men were sent to clear the ground for tents and bivouacs, and a heavily armed foraging party marched away in search of water and firewood.

By mid afternoon the main body, the Eckerheimers in among them, was beginning to cross the marshland. It was heavy going. The feet of those who had gone before them had softened the ground and stirred up the marsh. Mud-brown water oozed and bubbled thickly about their feet, and the lank, green sedge grass sagged and gulped at every step. Some men sank to their knees, and had to be pulled free by their comrades. Others stumbled and fell under the weight of their equipment, and struggled to their feet drenched with an oily mud. And suddenly, everywhere in the stifling heat there were mosquitoes and midges, swarming around their heads, and biting them wherever they could find flesh. Men swore and made a hundred vows to God that He should bring them safely home.

They were no more than half the distance across the marsh when the first flickerings of the storm lit up the far ridges, and low rumbles of thunder drummed across the plain. The air grew heavy, taut – and a few drops of rain from a clear sky spattered briefly across the tortured levies.

Wearily, they looked to the North. As if from nowhere the dark clouds were rising up like giant castles on giant hills and surging towards them. Again the lightning flashed, this time much closer, and the thunder crackled. They fought to quicken their pace, floundering and gasping in the heat, desperate to reach the safety of the trees. A few men, wild eyed and sweating left the line of march, looking for firmer ground. They were roundly cursed by the sergeants, but ignored the shouts and threats and staggered away into the swamp.

It was then that a freshening wind swept down and slapped against the struggling column, making the pennons and battle standards snap and flutter against the staves. The men bent their backs as they pressed forward, hardly daring to look at the black, boiling wall of cloud that bore down on them. The first sharp, wind-driven shower lashed across their backs. They held back their heads and opened their mouths to catch the cooling drops, and then as if some monstrous curtain had been drawn closed, the sun was gone.

Almost at once, there was a crash of thunder and a single piercing flash of light as the storm broke over them. The ground shook, men cried out, and the smell of brimstone swept through the howling sky. The Eckerheimer levy, caught in the middle of the marshland, fell sprawling, as if knocked down by a single giant hand. All around them soldiers were calling out, and scattering. Some had thrown their weapons to the ground and were staggering forward, hands clawing in front of them, or held to their face and ears. Others had turned back for fallen friends, or were trying to keep order in the broken ranks.

Another thunder clap seemed to split the sky above their heads, and a bolt of lightning, as though cast by some avenging angel, struck the very centre of the army, hurling men and equipment into the air and for a time blinding many of the soldiers nearby.

'Run!' yelled Wulfstan, 'We're dead men if we stay here! Run for your lives!' He grabbed Branulf, shoved him forward, and frantically waved the others on.

Now the rain beat down in savage whirling clouds, roaring against the heaving ground and setting it awash. Bernhardt, Ralf and the others struggled through the sedge and swamp grass, sinking up to their knees, and using the butts of their spears to haul themselves towards the safety of the forest. It was almost impossible to see through the torrential rain, but they knew that the forest lay little more than a bowshot ahead.

'Come on!' Wulstan yelled again, but his voice was lost in the fury of the downpour. As he leant forward, Bernhardt glimpsed the body of a man face down in the quagmire. He stopped and reached out, but someone knocked into him from behind, cursed, and then screamed in his ear. He stumbled on and the man was gone.

The levy, or what remained of it, had gone no more than half a dozen paces, when once again the world turned dazzling white, and they reeled beneath the concussive blast. To Bernhardt it seemed as if the whole marsh leapt skywards. The swamp grass rushed up at him, smashing against his chest and winding him. He lay gasping, face turned to one side, hands and feet tingling with the force of the blow.

'Up Bernhardt! Up!' It was Gustav. He grabbed hold of Bernhardt and hauled him to his feet. 'We're almost there!'

Still dazed, Bernhardt lurched unsteadily. He felt something press against his side and looked down. Gustav's hound, bright-eyed, gazed up at him. Somehow, the blacksmith smiled, patted the grizzled head and went on.

At last there was bracken in among the sedge grass. It meant firmer ground, though the rain still hammered down, and the wind tore at their faces and backs. The was one more shattering clap of thunder, one more flash of lightning, but this time it struck some hundred paces to the south.

The ground still shook beneath the blast, and the swamp still heaved, but the men sensed that the worst had passed. Moments later the rain began to ease, and they could see the outline of the forest ahead of them through curtains of mist and showers. They renewed their efforts, called to one another and pressed forward.

It was then that the Liutizen attacked. The arrows came hissing out of the forest, dipping and floating in the rain-heavy air – and then thudding into shield and jerkin, tunic and bare flesh. There were screams, and shouts of alarm. Men ducked wildly, or scattered and then flung themselves down in the marsh.

A few of the archers started to hastily string their bows, but the arrows began to arc and whistle in among them, knocking most of them down before they could fire a single shot.

Wulfstan grabbed Branulf before he could get to his feet. 'Stay down, you young fool! They'll spit you before you can blink.'

An arrow whined over their heads and disappeared into the marsh.

'Where are they?' said Gustav, holding his hound close.

'Everywhere!'

'Where's our cavalry?' ·

'Hiding up ahead somewhere, most like – or drowned in this marsh.'

This time an arrow skimmed the tussock and buried itself in the turf just in front of them. And then another.

Working his way back to the rest of the men, Wulfstan gathered them around him as best he could. They propped up their shields as a make-shift wall, and crouched down behind them. The rain had all but stopped now, and the storm was rumbling southwards. An arrow smacked into a shield with a dull thud.

Wulfstan grimaced and shook his head: 'We can't move, but we can't stay out here, neither. They must have thanked their pagan gods when this storm struck, and us all strung out across the marsh. Wonderful! With their bowstrings all greased and tucked under their caps, they were ready to hit us the moment the storm slackened.'

'So we charge?'

'So we run like the very devil's at our heels, that's what. And don't you head for the arrows, head for the trees in front of us.'

Suddenly the air was thick with shafts. They came at them like a flock of starlings. The men hugged the sodden turf and waited for the fall of shot.

There were cries, groans, a sudden silence – and then the sound of drums.

'Where's the cavalry?'

Wulfstan raised his head warily and looked about him.

'Sweet Saint Hilda's bones!' he said.

Markward heard the sound of thunder away to the West. He reined in, and wiped his brow. The sun was beating down, and he was still a good day's journey away from the army. All around him the brown and dusty green grasslands stretched away to the horizon. He had crossed low hills, forded streams, and ridden through woodlands and fields of bracken. And always he followed the tracks left by the Saxon Host as it marched back to the Elbe. Here and there he found a rag or two discarded by some weary soldier. Sometimes a leather cap, swept off by a low hanging branch and never retrieved. Sometimes an empty water bottle, dropped by chance, or simply thrown down. Once or twice he came upon the body of a horse which had gone lame and been slaughtered by its master. But the army seemed to be retreating in good order, with no sign of panic or distress.

He had hoped that perhaps the Lord of Meissen might have sent back rear-guard patrols to look for himself and Rainald, but he knew that was a faint hope. A missing scout was a dead scout as far as the army was concerned. When a scout disappeared, all that was needed was to keep a sharper lookout, and draw the patrols in closer.

The thunder rolled again and the dark shadows above the far hills pulsed with light. Perhaps it would rain soon. That would be good. His face was caked with dust, and his throat was hot and dry. He thought of cool raindrops splashing across his face, and licked his cracked lips. But the breeze, what there was of it, was southerly, and the storm would have long gone by the time he arrived. Still, there was no point in loitering. He gently kicked his horse forward and began to gallop out and across the plain.

Above Eckerheim there is a rocky cairn that marks the way to the Weissburg. By the time that Cedric reached it, the sun was already in its third quarter.

He stopped and looked back down at the village. All was quiet and peaceful on this warm and sunny day. His own flock, placed in the care of Hec Haraldsson, was grazing on a lee slope just above the mill stream woods.

He watched it for a moment, and waved when he saw Hec turn and look up towards the ridge where he was standing. Then he set off towards the Weissburg. With the wind and sun at his back, he reckoned to make Hermit's Gate by nightfall. He would rest there awhile, and then push on under a rising moon. He knew the lands there well, and since the Liutizen had gone, there was little to fear in those woodland paths and moorland tracks. If it clouded over, or the weather closed in, he could always find shelter, and then go on again in the morning.

He quickened his step, and lengthened his stride so that his arms swung with a smooth powerful rhythm. The 'shepherd', men called such a way of walking, and the older folks had nodded and smiled with approval when Eric announced that he was sending Cedric to the

Weissburg for news of the Army. It would take him two days to walk there and two days to return. Perhaps there would be nothing to report – no news at all – but, and they hardly dared hope for this, perhaps the first of the great host would be straggling in already. And even if this were not to be, there was a good chance there would be rumours drifting in on the winds from the East: rumours of a homecoming, rumours of men returning, rumours of victory, and pillage and treasures for all. Tears of joy, and families together again.

And so the elders sat around the evening fires and talked, and muttered and hoped. And in the morning they sent Cedric up and over the Tops and on the way to the Weissburg.

By nightfall, as he had reckoned, he reached the Hermit Gate, a large cave dug into a sandstone bank in the middle of an oak forest. Here he slept for several hours, woke, ate a meal of bannock and cheese, then set off again.

Even though there was a full moon, it was dark, and he had to pick his way carefully among the trees. But as the moon rose and the forest thinned so the way grew lighter, and soon he was able to see his path clearly. A few of the forest animals were out and about, but they gave him a wide berth and he made good progress. He stopped once more before dawn, and then as the sun rose he found himself striding down a long heather-covered scarp, and into a gently rolling valley. There were crofts and hay ricks and shepherd's bothies scattered about, and away in the distance the squared tower of a church.

'Ah', he said to himself. ' Not far to the Weissburg.'

He stopped by at a croft where a grey-haired old farmer was fixing a goat pen. He asked for some water, and was given fresh, warm milk. Cedric gave him the news from Eckerheim.

The old farmer nodded and grinned, bare-toothed. 'Aye, well it's quiet enough here, too. You're the first through this way since they raised the host for the Weissburg.'

'There's no one returned then?'

'Nay, not a breath of 'em. Nor tale nor tattle neither. Quiet as the grave it is.' He sat down on a bench, and gestured for Cedric to sit beside him. Pulling out a hawthorn pipe, he filled and lit it, then began to smoke. 'We sent men from here y'know. Good men, too – and young. Too young, some of them. Boys they was, and their mothers all crying and telling 'em to be careful.'

Cedric grunted. 'Aye, and the same with us, – and no sign of them since.'

'Nor like to be!' came a woman's voice.

Cedric turned and stood up. A young woman carrying firewood was coming round the corner of the croft.

'Ah, Eadyth!' said the old farmer. 'Come and meet Cedric. He's from Eckerheim.'

'Aye, I heard as much', said the woman. Unsmiling, she stacked the firewood, and tucked her hair back under her scarf. 'I'll be away now. There's more wood to bring up from the spinney.'

'You'll not sit with us then?' asked Cedric.

Eadyth's eyes narrowed. 'Do I need to?'

'Your father gave me a welcome, but I'll stay no longer if the welcome is not shared.'

There was a silence. The young woman glanced toward the spinney, then shrugged and sighed. 'I'll get ye something to eat.'

'No, don't trouble yourself. I've eaten well already, and your father has given me fine milk from one your goats. Come sit with us. I'm bound for the Weissburg, seeking news of the levies.'

With a quick nod of the head and a look towards her father, Eadyth picked up a milking stool and sat down. She folded her hands in her lap – strong hands, but roughened and reddened by work on the land. 'It's been well gone the forty days since the levies left this place', she said, her voice still level and clipped.

'And so?'

'And so I've heard it said that when an army marches good news travels fast, and bad news sometimes not at all.'

'You mean they fear to tell us?'

'I mean, I fear they'll never more speak of anything at all. I fear they are all lost.' She lowered her head, as the tears started, and tugged at the corner of her scarf.

Cedric reached out and touched her gently on the arm. 'Your man? He's with them?'

She nodded without looking up. 'Not my man. My uncle and my brother.'

'Good men, then.'

'I love them as my life.'

The shepherd stood up and looked around. 'This is a fine valley', he said. 'Warm and sheltered. Good grass.'

'Aye', replied the old farmer. 'It keeps us well. Our village has been here since the days of the Great Karl.'

'And many a time the muster has gone out, and the men have always come home again,' said Cedric.

Eadyth looked up: 'Then why are you here? If the levy always comes home? Why? I'll tell you why. It is because this time the men have been gone too long. And there is still no news. And the priests keep praying and the wise women make their chants, and the Greenmen toss their knucklebones – but still no one comes, and the Weissburg is silent. Why?'

Cedric slowly shook his head. 'I don't know lass, I don't know, but I'm away to find out.' He took up his staff, and slung his knapsack across his shoulder.

'God keep you', he said.

'And you, also', replied the farmer.

Eadyth managed a faint smile. 'Bring word', she said. 'Good or bad. Anything. We need to know.' Her voice had softened to the strange lilt of the East Saxon women.

'Within three days', said Cedric. 'Three days, or the Lord has left this valley.'

Dusk was gathering beneath a windswept, broken-clouded day, when Markward came to the marshland. His horse snorted, tossed its head and pawed the ground, as the smell of death filled its nostrils.

He muttered a prayer under his breath, dismounted and with sword drawn began to cross the swampy ground.

There were bodies everywhere. Some were half-clothed, some stripped bare, some still in tunics or jerkins. But all were hacked and torn and bloody. All were stiff, huddled, contorted, blue-white and grey in the evening light. Here and there a hand or arm showed above the surface of the swamp, fingers clenched in death, or clawing at the sky.

Part-buried horses lay among the sedge grass where they had fallen, struggled, bled and drowned. Broken shields and splintered shields were scattered among and across the fallen soldiers. Everywhere the carrion crows hopped and flapped about, or perched feeding on the bodies.

Markward worked his way across the marsh, sinking up to his ankles in the mud, and dragging his nervous horse towards the forest.

All the dead were Saxon. A good many had been killed by arrows long since ripped from their wounds. Others had fallen to terrible blows from axes and swords. Still others had died from the thrust of the broad-leafed spears the Liutizen favoured. There were no pagan dead to be seen. Those that had been killed were doubtless carried away to the honour of a warrior's funeral somewhere afar off from the place of slaughter.

When at last Markward reached the forest he could see that here more Saxons lay in heaps. And there, above a bank of trampled bracken, was a head set on a spear. It was Ludwig of Meissen. For the first time, Markward shook. His whole body shook, and his breath came in short, halting gasps as he stared at the battered face of the warlord. Then he groaned, as he stumbled forward and with shaking hands took hold of the spear and set the grisly trophy free. He covered the head with a remnant of cloak and moved on.

It was nearly dark when he entered the heart of the forest. The dead lay among the trees, piled up, strewn, and tangled like fallen branches. Imperial soldiers, castle-guards and retainers lay in among the men of the fyrd. Here and there, he could see the bodies of women who had died beside their husbands, rather than being dragged away to slavery. A deepening gloom wrapped around him, and the stillness was only broken by the occasional calling of the crows, and the sound of the wind high above in the tops of the trees. He found that he could breath now without gasping, and his hands were steadier on reins and sword.

Surely they were not all dead. Surely some had escaped. He went on, edging around the piles of bodies, and stepping carefully over the scattered dead. Their ranks had all been broken. There was no form, no line. No sign of a shield wall. Yet many, in the panic, had died shoulder to shoulder, companions and shield-brothers swept away in the fury of the attack.

He began to look for any sign of the Eckerheim levy, daring to hope that some might yet be alive. The Rear-Guard, he knew now, had been destroyed along with its commander, and he could see that much of the Middle Guard had also been slaughtered. Deeper and deeper into the forest he went, following the trail of the dead. Soon, it would be too dark to carry on. He told himself he would have find somewhere to camp for the night, and trust his soul to prayers and charms to keep him from goblins and the restless spirits of the fallen.

All at once, as if the wind had driven the clouds away, the forest was dappled with a soft and golden light. The evening sun streamed down through the leaves and branches lighting the way ahead. And there in a clearing he came across a group of fyrdsmen who had made a stand and fought until they too all were slain. They must have fought well, for the Liutizen, as a mark of honour, had left them with their armour and their weapons. They lay three deep in a ragged circle, some staring at the sky, some glazed with terror and surprise, and some just quietly asleep as if at the end of a long day in the fields.

Markward looked at them, still struggling to understand all that he had seen in the marshland and this forest. He knelt down and took hold of a silver charm that hung about the neck of a young fyrdsman. It was intricately carved, a bird in the branches of a tree bearing fruit. He had seen such charms in the market place at Fulda. Mothers bought them for their sons, and sweethearts for their true loves. It kept them safe in battle.

The Liutizen had left this one, hanging around the neck of its dead owner – a young man who would never be going back to his village, never again seeing his mother or his sweetheart.

As he stood up, Markward saw a movement. It was there, in among the bodies. The faintest stirring. A hand slowly unclenching and then going limp. He reached forward, and began clear the bodies away. They were heavy, unyielding in death, and he had to work hard to free them.

At last it was done. Panting with the effort he looked down, and his eyes widened.

'Branulf!'

The boy lay at his feet, staring up at him, lips moving but soundless.

'Branulf!' Markward went down on both knees and took the young boy by the shoulders. 'It's you! It's you! Are you all right?'

The boy nodded weakly. 'Some water', he said.

'Water, yes!' Markward ran to his horse and came back with the leather bottle. He watched as Branulf drank greedily, and then gently took the bottle back. 'Easy now', he said. 'It's not good to drink too much too soon. Rest up for a bit, and you can have some more later.'

He waited till Branulf seemed to have recovered a little, and then helped him to his feet. The boy was covered with dirt and leaves. His tunic was torn and bloody, but it was the blood of others and not his own.

'Come away over here and sit down.'

For a time they sat and said nothing. Markward gave Branulf some bread and he ate. As the last of the light faded, the boy suddenly began to speak: 'I ran. They came at us, so I ran. No time to shoot. Wulfstan, he said run, so I ran.' He looked around distractedly. 'My bow, where is my bow? I had my bow, but ...'

Markward put a hand on his shoulder. 'It's all right. We'll be away from here soon.'

'There were arrows everywhere. You couldn't even look up. They were killing us. All the time. Even in the forest. They were everywhere.'

'The soldiers fought?'

'Us, you mean. Aye, some of us, but they were everywhere. I couldn't use my bow ...Where's my bow?' Branulf put his head in his hands and began to sob. He didn't seem to notice when Markward got him to his feet and walked him over to the horse. Carefully, he lifted him onto the saddle.

'Now hold tight there.' He turned. There was a bow and quiver lying on the ground, almost hidden by a low bush. He picked them up, and slung them from the saddle.

'Is this your bow?' said Markward.

Branulf looked dully at him. 'No.'

'Well it is now. I'll lead. You just hold tight. We'll have you out of here and home before you know it.' Branulf swayed a little, but steadied himself and took hold of the horse's mane, as Markward began to lead them away from the clearing.

It soon became too dark to find their way, so they made camp a little distance off the trail between two big elms, and Markward lit a fire. He was trusting that the Liutizen were miles away by now, celebrating in their great oak-beam halls, and unlikely to return to the battlefield until the Spring. Then they would dance over the whitened bones of their enemies, and make a great mound of all the skulls. But until then, they would stay clear, believing what their shamans said: that the souls of dead warriors kept a curse on the ground until after their flesh had returned to the earth. 'Fool's babble, and the spittle of simpletons', Markward's father used to call it, but it might keep them safe enough this night at least.

Branulf began to moan, rocking back and forth in front of the fire and calling for his father. There was little Markward could do. He wrapped the boy in his cloak, and held him and told him over and over again that his father had died as a warrior and would sleep as a saint.

At last the boy slept. Markward kept watch, and put wood on the fire, and stared into the flames. The wind had dropped now, and the trees no longer stirred, but other shadows moved in the blackness of the night. Wolves had come, slipping in among the trunks of oak and elm, drawn to the dead, with coal bright eyes and the harsh slavering rattle of the hunter that scents the prey. They stood in the dark around the flames, gazing at the living flesh that they would rather tear and feast upon, but not daring to challenge the hot bright enemy man calls fire. One by one they disappeared back into the blackness, and by the morning they were gone.

When the first faint tinges of misty blue and grey came seeping down through the high branches, Markward got to his feet. There was a good distance to travel before they reached the Elbe, and he was keen to escape the forest and all its dead. His horse stood patiently while he put on saddle and harness. It showed no sign of yesterday's nervousness despite the wolves. Branulf slept on. Two or three times he had stirred in the night, and cried out, but towards dawn he had finally settled into a deeper sleep. Markward hesitated to wake him, but knew that it had to be done. He reached down and shook him gently by the shoulder.

Branulf woke with a start, and looked wildly around. 'Run! Run! Hide! Under the bodies!' He leapt to his feet in a half crouch.

'Branulf! It's all right! It's me, Markward. You're safe now.'

With a gasp of relief the boy sank down again beside the fire. He was trembling and rubbing his arms and shoulders. 'They killed Gustav, you know. And his dog. He fought. Gustav fought. Knocked them down.

He was shouting all the time and knocking them down. But there were too many of them. I cried out but Gustav didn't see. It was an axe. And then his dog, they killed his dog.'

'And the others?'

Branulf shook his head. 'All dead. All knocked down. Even Wulfstan. They killed Wulfstan. And my father. They killed my father.' He started to cry, but dashed the tears away, catching his breath in great gulps.

Markward waited for a moment, then gestured towards the horse. 'Come on, lad. Let's be gone. If we push on this morning, we could clear this forest by noon tomorrow.'

'The Elbe?'

'Aye, the Elbe.'

When Cedric reached the Weissburg, it was quiet and peaceful. The guards were dozing in the late morning sunlight that splashed down the face of the Gate Tower and fell across their backs. They greeted the shepherd with an idle nod and a grunt – and waved him through.

When he got into the courtyard, he found it was almost empty. There was none of the usual bustle he expected to see in a castle like the Weissburg. There were no traders, no pedlars, no stalls and no barrows. An old man was repairing a bucket over by the chapel steps, and two small boys were arguing over a stick. Some serving maids were standing by the castle well, chattering away and giggling – and doing their best to ignore the provender clerk who stood glaring at them from the entrance to the inner ward.

But that was all.

For a time he stood in the centre of the bailey, weary and uncertain, then the clerk with an irritable shrug, threw back his cowl and came across to him:

'What brings you here, my son?'

'I am Cedric, shepherd of Eckerheim, and I have come for news of the levy.'

'Ho, have you indeed! Well, Cedric of Eckerheim, you've come to the wrong place, then! There's no sign of them here, nor like to be for a while. We had a rider in five days ago that said they'd crossed the Elbe at Dresdany and were marching East.'

'Five days ago.'

'That's what I said. But I'm sure . . .' and his voice took on a mocking tone, 'If you are unhappy with the word of a man of God, then perhaps you'd better ask to see the castellan.'

Cedric grinned, and looked the clerk in the eye. 'I thank you, Sir Priest. If you would show me where the castellan might be . . .'

The provender clerk reddened, and puffed out his cheeks, but he said nothing. Motioning for Cedric to follow, he turned and headed into the Inner ward and then up the steps of the Guard Tower which loomed over the Western wall.

The castellan was in his solar or private quarters, going over a list of documents that the chaplain had left him with earlier in the day. He was a soldier rather than a courtier, and was irritated by the pinched and convoluted Latin that the court scribes insisted on using. He looked up with a frown as the two men entered, and was surprised to see that one of them seemed to be a peasant or simple shepherd.

'Ah, Wilhelm! What have you brought me here? What trouble have you come to add to the ones you gave me this morning?'

The clerk smiled weakly and wrung his hands together. 'Why, none, my Lord. It is only that this fellow here has come from Eckerheim .seeking news of the levy. And . . .'

'You told him of course that we have no word?'

'Of course, my lord – but he would not take my word for it, and insisted on seeing you himself.'

The castellan beamed, pushed back the parchments and stood up. 'Quite right too. Never take the word of a clerk or a priest, eh Wilhelm? Now don't look so bothered and screw your face up like that, man. You're the Markgraf's chief scribe, and bound to be honest for at least part of the time.'

Laughing to himself, he strode across the solar and poured himself a cup of wine from the clay pitcher.

'Rhenish!' he said, as he drained the cup. 'Good for midday, but hard on the head at night.' He glanced at the old shepherd. 'I'll not offer you such as this', he said. 'But after we have done here, I'll send you to the kitchens where you can sup on mutton, maize beer and whatever else they can find you. And don't you look so hopeful, Wilhelm – I know very well that you and your other monkish friends have enough fine wine to fill the moat and swim about in it.'

The provender clerk bowed. 'If you have no further need of me, my lord . . .'

'You may leave, Wilhelm, but remember to go to the Great Hall. Leofwin and Eadred are there. Tell them they are to meet with me at the eighth hour, here in the solar.'

'My lord.'

When the clerk had left, the castellan turned to Cedric: 'So you are from Eckerheim.'

'I am my lord.'

'Markward: you would know him then.'

'Aye my lord. He is with the levy.'

'He is, indeed. And he is the sort of man we can ill afford to lose.'

Cedric swallowed hard. 'You think they are lost, sire?'

The castellan ran his fingers through his greying hair. 'Lost? Some of them for sure. We always lose some. Mostly the laggards, and blackguards – so that's no great loss. But this time it's different. This time they've been away too long, and that's for sure. We had a messenger in five days ago, but his news was old news. They crossed the Elbe many days ago. Too many days. And no word since.'

'Not even a rumour, my lord.'

'Not even a whisper on the wind, Cedric.' The castellan sat down again at the document strewn table. He clasped his hands in front of him, and studied them. For a long time he did not speak. Cedric could hear the sound of sheep somewhere in the meadows beyond the castle.

At last the castellan lifted his head. 'I am not the real castellan here', he said. 'I am an old knight, who once trained young squires in the courtyard below, and was entrusted with the keeping of the outer guard-house.

'Is that so, my lord.'

The castellan nodded. 'My name is Sir Pietyr of Schonstein, and I have the rule of an empty castle in an empty valley. The true castellans of the Weissburg are Sir Robard and Sir Hubert . . .'

'And they are across the Elbe.'

'Just so.' He turned and stared out the narrow arched window. 'Go back to your folk, Cedric. Go back and tell them that there is no word of the levy as yet, nor like to be till the next full moon. Until then, they are to get the harvest in, and tend the flocks, and keep watch over the village. I will send word when I have it.'

'Good or bad, my lord?'

'For joy or for sorrow, Cedric, I will send word.'

'Then I thank you sire, and I pray that word comes soon.'

'Hmmph! Just pray that the cook has something for ye in the kitchen, and get ye gone, and . . . er, God speed you home to Eckerheim.'

Moments later Cedric found himself in the kitchens of the castle, sitting at a narrow trestle while the servants and serving girls bustled around him. He ate and drank, and thanked the cook who hardly seemed to notice his coming until he was about to leave – then dismissed him with a friendly wave. The guards still dozed as he passed through the great gateway and took the path down to the western woods. It was a bright afternoon, the breeze was soft against his face, and the ground felt easy beneath his boots. Tonight he would lodge with Eadyth and her father.

Faraway, in the fields of Eckerheim the harvest was almost gathered. The corn stood in heaps waiting to be brought to the threshing floor. Overhead rooks circled – the first faint reminders of an early Autumn – but the reapers still stooped and straightened in the dust and the heat, pushing their caps and scarves back from sweating brows, and glancing up at the sun as it slipped towards the Western ridges.

Ulrich the priest was helping too. The old folk muttered their approval as he bent to the task, sleeves rolled back, and bill-hook flashing in the burning air.

It was Elsa who brought him a jug of water that day, and stood and watched as he drank.

'Bless you, daughter', he said, wiping his mouth with the back of his hand, and then splashing water across his head and neck. 'It's hot work.'

'But the harvest is almost done,' she replied, taking the jug.

'And only one storm-shower since we started. It's a good God we have.'

Elsa bobbed and turned to go.

'A moment, daughter!'

She looked back, surprised by the formality. 'Yes, Father?'

'You were praying in the church on your own last week. Three times. I could not help but notice.'

Elsa was silent, so he went on: 'I was wondering . . .couldn't help thinking . . .what you might do if Bernhardt . . .'

'Father?'

Ulrich ducked his head and blushed. 'If Bernhardt, well, if he . . .'

'If Bernhardt didn't come home. Is that what you mean?'

The young priest spread his hands, and for a time didn't seem able to speak, but then finally managed: 'Yes.'

Elsa looked at him with a level stare, but her voice was trembling: 'Father, you and I and all the village have prayed that Bernhardt and all the levy come safely home. Is that not enough?'

'Of course, of course. Forgive me. It was just that it has been so long since there was news, and we have sent the shepherd to the Weissburg and . . .' His voice trailed off uncertainly, and he stood there, his throat tight with embarrassment, and the sun beating down on the back of his neck.

'I must be going, Father.'

'It would please me better if you called me Ulrich.'

'Then pray for me Ulrich, and pray for Bernhardt too. Then all will be well between us.'

Elsa headed off across the field, her hair flowing from beneath the scarf, and tossing to the rhythm of her stride. Ulrich watched her go, and sighed.

'Oh Lord, keep us all safe!' he said, and bent to his task once more.

It was Branulf who noticed first. They had just passed another scattering of bodies half hidden by bracken and low scrub, when he saw a sudden movement from among the trees away to their right.

'Wolves!' he whispered to Markward, and pointed with a shaking hand.

Markward stopped in mid stride, sank down on one knee and peered into the sun dappled gloom. He waited, tensed and motionless, then slowly stood up.

'Could be', he said, 'But there's no sign of them now.'

He was about to move on when he himself saw a shadow stir. With a sharp, instinctive sweep of his arm, he brought his sword up to guard, released his grip on the reins, and swung his shield off the shoulder.

Motioning Branulf to stay where he was he began to walk carefully towards an open thicket of laurel and juniper. It was about twenty paces away and partly obscured by the low-growing boughs of an ancient elm.

The closer he got to the thicket, Markward could see that a good many men had fought and died within its entanglements of roots, and branches and thorn-bushes. The stench of battle hung in the air, and even some of the trees were hacked and blood-spattered. He wrinkled his nose, and stepped in among the mutilated and swelling corpses.

There were no wolves. Just the ever present carrion crows nervously hopping in an out among the bodies. He glanced back towards Branulf, and glimpsed his pale and staring face almost hidden by an overhanging branch. Nodding to reassure the lad, Markward went on, skirting the small stand of trees, and looking all about him for any sign of life. There seemed to be nothing, save crows and myriads of fat black flies. He was about to turn back when he caught sight of a figure slumped against one of the trees. It was half-hidden by shadow, and the curve of the tree trunk, but he could tell that the man, his head bowed and partly covered, was dressed in the heavy woollen tunic worn by the levies. There was no movement in him, except perhaps . . . or was that nothing more than the stirring of sunlight and shadows in the teasing wind.

He crept forward, sword drawn back ready to thrust from the hip, while shield covered throat chest and groin. A bramble dragged against his throat and caught at his boots, but he pushed his way through until he stood over the man.

It was Bernhardt. Even before he knelt down and peered into his face he knew it was Bernhardt. It was the blacksmith and he was dying – slowly bleeding to death from wounds to his arms and head. Flies buzzed thickly around him, settling on his matted hair and crawling across his torn and bloody tunic. His eyes brightened with recognition, and he tried to sit up, but sank back with a gasp of pain. There was a trickle of blood coming from the corner of his mouth.

'I heard you coming', he said, his voice no more than a cracked whisper. 'Tried to wave. Couldn't see. Didn't dare hope it was you.'

Markward put both hands gently on Bernhardt's shoulders. 'You're a mess, old friend.'

'You call me friend. At last.' He struggled to speak, and his voice was fading.

'You were never my enemy Bernhardt. Well, perhaps once, but that's all over and done with now.'

'And now I'm all over and done with.' He tried to smile.

'Don't be daft! Here let me sit you up, and see what's to be done.'

Bernhardt shook his head. 'They've killed me Markward. I'm killed. And all the levy too. Leave me now, leave me. Just give me some water and leave me. I'm a dead man.' His voice choked and faded away completely. Then his eyes closed as he slumped with exhaustion. Markward held him for a moment, then calling out to Branulf to lead the horse across, he began to see to his wounds.

One hand was almost severed, and there was a deep cut on the shoulder of his other arm. The blood from his mouth came from an ugly gash along the jaw line, and some kind of head wound gleamed above his left ear. His tunic was ripped open where a spear thrust had scored along his ribs, covering him with blood from hip to breast. These wounds would need water.

They found it in a nearby stream, beyond a patch of may and shepherd's broom. The summer heat had reduced the flow to a trickle, but there was enough clean water to fill all the leather bottles Branulf had taken from the dead.

They moistened Bernhardt's lips and washed his wounds as best they could, brushing away the flies and cleaning around the cuts and gashes. Using moss from an elm tree, they packed the wounds then bound them with strips of cloth. When they came to the wrist, Branulf blanched and turned away. It was shattered with splinters of bone showing through torn and bleeding flesh. A shred of sinew seemed to be all that was holding the wrist to the forearm.

Markward hesitated, then took his knife and wiped it against a piece of bark. He took a deep breath, held the arm just below the elbow, then sliced through the sinew and broken bone. The hand came free and fell among the leaves at his feet. Bernhardt convulsed in his sleep, shuddered, then finally relaxed with a kind of halting sigh. The stump now bled freely, drawing in the flies, but Markward was able to separate the splintered bone, and pull flaps of flesh and skin across the face of the wound. He had watched an old barber-surgeon do it years before when he first went on campaign to Friesia. It was rough and ready but it seemed to work.

Branulf suddenly darted away, and returned moments later with a leather bottle. It was stamped with the arms of Fulda.

Markward took it, released the stopper and sniffed. He grinned. 'How come those devils missed this? This wine was brewed for bishops.'

Carefully, he poured the wine over the stump while Branulf tore bandages from a cloak he found on a thorn bush. These were then wrapped firmly around and over the stump, and bound to two splints placed either side of Bernhardt's forearm. When Markward was satisfied that the bleeding had stopped, he set about making a stetcher out of laurel and birch branches. Branulf watched fascinated while he trimmed the branches, tied them with leather straps, and then lashed the torn remnants of tunics and cloaks between the poles. As he worked he looked constantly about him, wary for any unusual movement or sound. Once or twice he stopped, stood up and waited, sword in hand. But each time after a long pause he returned to the task. Branulf had meanwhile taken up his bow and a quiver half full of arrows. He slung the quiver across his shoulder, and nocked an arrow. 'I'll do better this time', he said.

'You did no worse the first', said Markward. 'You might not have killed any Liutizen, but you saved a good man, and that is just as good.'

Branulf beamed.

The sun had passed its highest point by the time the stretcher was finished. While his horse waited patiently, Markward fastened it by two of the pole ends to the saddle straps, checked it for strength and stood back.

'There!' he said. 'That should hold until the Elbe at least.'

Eadyth watched Cedric as he came towards her across the field of stubble. He looked weary and hot, but he strode rather than walked, and he had the air of a man much younger than his years. She waited until he was nearly up to her, then put down the pail she was carrying and nervously raised her hand in greeting.

'Well met Cedric.' She paused. 'What news from the Weissburg?'

Cedric stopped and put down his pack, and wiped his brow. 'Well met, mistress. It's a bright day and a long one. Would you have any water in that pail? I've a thirst that talks louder than any news I bear.'

Eadyth smiled, and took a tin cup from her girdle. She dipped it in the pail and held it up to Cedric. He drank, and then splashed a little water across his face before offering her back the cup. Eadyth noticed that he did it with a care and gentleness she had not noticed in other men.

'Thank you, mistress', he said.

She looked at him enquiringly, and he frowned. 'Ah, the Weissburg. No news I fear, mistress Eadyth save that the levy is somewhere beyond the Elbe with the rest of the imperial army, and the castellan has no idea when it will return.'

Eadyth bit her lower lip. 'But the army is not lost.'

For a time the shepherd did not answer, but looked away to the wooded hills that crowded in on the valley to the south. 'There is no word of it for good or ill', he said at last. We know it reached Dresdany, and then crossed the Elbe, but that is all – and many days have passed since.'

'It is lost, then.'

'We don't know that, Eadyth.'

Eadyth picked up her pail, and made as if to turn away, then hesitated: 'Will you lodge with us tonight?' she asked.

'I was not sure . . .'

'You said you would come back, whatever the news, and you came. How could we turn you away?'

Cedric smiled and nodded: 'Well, then I would be obliged for a corner of your barn and some straw . . .'

'Whisht, man! Where do you get such careful courtesy from? If anyone's to sleep in the barn it will be myself. You'll have the palliasse by the hearth and that is that. Come now, my father will have spotted us by now from the croft. He's got eyes like a hawk, and he'll be eager to hear what you have to say.'

'Aye, well it'll be good to get out of this heat. Maybe this evening I can help with some chores, bringing in the animals, or chopping wood or somesuch.' He swung his pack back up onto his shoulder, but as he did so, Eadyth put a hand on his arm.

'Cedric', she said, 'You'd do me and my father a great honour if you did no more than sit by the fire and pass the time with us. We see few enough folk as it is, and I'm fearing that there'll be even less to see in the days ahead.'

'I understand, mistress.' He put his hand on hers, and noticed again how strong and unbent her hand was despite the years of toil. For a brief moment their eyes met, and then she pulled her hand away and lowered her gaze.

'We must be away now', she said blushing, and turned and walked across the field. Cedric waited for a bit, and then set off after her. He caught up, just as they arrived at the bothy. Eadyth's father, Karel, was standing in the doorway, waiting for them.

'I saw ye!' he said. Saw ye clean across that field. Came out of the woodland ye did, just beyond the old mill.' He was grinning broadly.

'Your daughter's right, sir! Eyes like a hawk.'

Karel laughed. 'Is that what she says? Is it? Well she's not far wrong. Forty years of farming in this valley have taught me to be sharp-eyed.'

He pulled back the sacking covering the doorway, and a wave of hot air struck Cedric like a hand. Karel nodded: 'Aye, it's too hot to take our ease in there. But see, under those trees there, we'll find all the cool shade we need, and you can tell me all the news you've doubtless told my daughter.'

In the morning, at the first glow of dawn, Cedric was up, washed and ready to be on his way. He hoped to make the high ground before the heat of the day. If he kept to the ridge path, his way would be much shorter, but he would miss the cooling streams and deep pools of the woodland valleys. With any luck there would be a breeze up there on the heights, and if the Lord was with him the breeze might even be at his back.

Karel had said his goodbyes and was away to milk the cows. Eadyth lingered, not certain what to say, but eager to say something before this shepherd left them once more.

They had talked long into the night, sitting there under the great oak while the valley slept. There was fresh corn bread to eat, and pork from the spit, and the cool maize beer of the early harvest. And they stayed by the dying fire until the last embers sank into the white ash. They talked of the Levy and the return home. They talked of the Elbe and the winter winds that sweep from the East. They talked of the Spring planting and the health of the herds, but Eadyth had secretly wished to talk of other things. There was more to say, but no way to say it, for Eadyth scarcely knew herself what words she wanted to utter. There was within her a deep longing and a deep emptiness that she could not explain to her father, but she might somehow share with this stranger from Eckerheim.

She sensed that Cedric understood what it was to be lonely, and had drunk from its bitter cup for whatever reason. Had he ever been married? Did he have children? How could this gentle shepherd not have close and loyal friends?

As Cedric made ready to leave she stood in an agony. Then: 'I have packed you a cheese and some rye bread.'

He nodded and smiled his thanks.

'Oh, and some parched corn. Something to chew on when the day grows hot.'

Cedric straightened and smiled again: 'You have been good to me, mistress. I won't forget the kindness.' He lifted the pack onto his shoulders and took up his staff.

'Wait!' she said. 'I nearly forgot. Two water bottles filled from the stream this morning. They'll see you home.' She held the bottles out, and Cedric took them so that for a moment their hands touched. 'I'll be back', he said.

'Will it be soon?' Her voice rose, and she felt it tremble.

'Who knows? There's no way of telling. But I will be back.'

'I . . .we'll miss you.'

'And I you . . .both.'

All at once Eadyth wanted to rush forward and take him by the arms and beg him to stay, plead with him never to leave this valley. But instead she brushed her hair back, smoothed her kirtle and looked down for a moment.

'Cedric?'

'Yes?'

'God speed.'

He took her hand. 'And the Lord be with you, Eadyth.'

Then he turned and walked away. She watched him cross the fields. When he reached a boundary marker he turned to wave. She could not wave back, but stood motionless, her heart pounding, tears now streaming down her cheeks.

Soon he was halfway across the great West Meadow. A dog ran after him barking, and he bent down to pat it, then walked on. Smaller and smaller he became, now almost disappeared against the green of the pine woods.

She waved but he did not turn. She waved again and he was gone.

Eadyth stood until her father came up from the milking. He put a hand on her shoulder. 'Are ye well, daughter?'

'I am well father.'

'Are ye well, daughter?' he repeated.

'He's gone, father.'

Karel was silent. He gazed at the pine woods, now lit by the first of the morning sun. 'Aye, he's gone. And he took a piece of your heart with him, did he not?'

'You saw?'

'A blind man would have seen it, lassie! And am I not your father, and you my daughter, eh?'

She reddened and ducked her head. 'You think me a foolish little girl. You must . . .'

'Hah!', said Karel clasping her in his arms, 'You will always be my little girl, but foolish you are not.'

'Will he come back, father?'

'Did he say he would?'

'He did.'

'Then he will, that much you can be sure of, but whether he comes back for you or not is another matter.'

Eadyth stood back and looked up at her father. 'Do you like him, father?'

Karel shrugged:

'He's a good man. Shepherd's mostly are. The hirelings don't last ye see. They're either dead or gone. Aye, he's a good enough man, all right. But listen, lassie! I know what you're thinking, and I know where we're headed in this talk, and that's why we stop right now. The question you're dying to ask is the question that stays inside your head until next time young Cedric comes into this valley. And even then I'd pray that you hold your peace until you've given him time to brush the dust off his boots.'

Eadyth laughed, and dried her tears. 'I love you father.'

'Ah, well, do ye now? Well that just goes to show what a poor wee girl you are! Now away with you, and make me some breakfast. I've promised the headman I'd help with that fallen tree by the glebe cruck, and time is creeping by.'

He kissed his daughter on the cheek and watched her as she hurried into the cottage. 'Just like her mother', he said as he sat down wearily onto the bench.

That same day Markward, Branulf and Bernhardt came to the clearing where the last of the imperial army had made its final stand.

There were none alive.If any had escaped, they had long since fled.The bodies had lain in the forest heat for days. A heavy stench filled the air, and as they approached a black cloud of carrion birds flapped away into the branches cawing with annoyance.

Markward knew that there was little point in staying. They began to edge around the clearing. The stretcher bumped along making Bernhardt moan, and causing the horse to skitter. Branulf steadied it, and they went on slowly.

To their right, and just ahead, there was an imperial standard. It was leaning to one side, and broken near the top, so that its eagle banner draped across the knights lying beneath it. They had fallen shield to shield. Robard was among them, and sir Hubert too, his helm cleaved by a single blow from an axe.

Further on, they found the Markgraf. He was lying on his back beneath a thorn bush, his shield bearer beside him. His sword was in his hand, and he was reaching up as if to grasp the lance that had driven into his chest.

Despite the swollen progress of decay, they could see a faint smile on his lips, and his eyes were closed as if he were asleep. He had died a warrior's death.

'They stink,' said Branulf, holding his nose.

'We should bury them', replied Markward, 'But there is no time. And yet, perhaps . . .' He turned and ran back to the broken standard.

Carefully, he took the ragged banner, folded it and thrust it under the saddle.

'It's a token, I know. Only a token. But in times to come, it may ease the blow.' He checked the bindings on the stretcher, and as he did so Bernhardt stirred and opened his eyes.

'Some water,' he gasped through cracked lips. He drank greedily from the bottle Branulf offered him, the water spilling out of his mouth and down his face and neck. When he had had his fill he sank back on the stretcher and raised his hand in thanks.

Markward came, and stood looking down at him. 'You look a little better' he said.

The blacksmith nodded. 'Soon I will be able to walk.'

'Not this side of the Elbe. We've what's left of this day, and then a day more before we make the river. Then we'll see if you can ride. That way we will all get across.'

'Saxony,' whispered Bernhardt.

'Aye, Saxony and home.' The horse snorted and stamped as though it recognised the sound of the name, and Markward chuckled. 'All right soldier!' he said rubbing its nose. 'You show us the way and we will follow.'

They set off once more, passed by the clearing and entered into the cool of the great forest. The path unwound before them in the uncertain gloom, but slowly, step by step they left the smell of death behind them.

As the evening drew on, they made camp a little way off the path, and built a fire in the hollow left by a fallen tree. Bernhardt felt strong enough to sit up. He sat by the fire with his cloak wrapped about him, and his boots almost touching the embers. Markward had re-dressed his wounds, and pronounced them clean, though more in doubt than certainty. At least the wounds were not livid, and they did not smell.

Fever was the only fear, and so they piled the fire high with hazel twigs, because the wise women of the Border Lands said that the smoke of hazel and the heat would keep away the sickness. As the crackling fire blazed into life they knew they would have to trust in the hollow to keep most of the fire-glow from searching eyes.

At length Bernhardt began to speak. At first he spoke of the attack, away back there at the marshland. His voice was low, hesitating, and at times no more than a whisper. He said that they had been caught unawares. When the cavalry came in from the flanks to help them, they became bogged down in the heavy ground, and were themselves overwhelmed by a second wave of Liutizen who poured out of the woods to the North.

'We fought as best we could. Some of us were like lions. Lions! But nothing could have stood against that attack. In a moment it was every man for himself. There were a few of us still dazed and confused by the thunder storm. They didn't stand a chance. As for the rest of us, well, a fair number made it through to the woods. It was better there. We weren't fighting up to our knees in mud, and the arrows didn't come in clouds.

'But still they came at us like fiends. They were everywhere, shrieking and shouting and hurling those long lances. Clubs too, and throwing axes. They can split a shield and a man's head at the same time. I saw it.

'Soon there was nothing much left of us, though we took a good number of them as well. Branulf here would have told you.'

Bernhardt paused and took a drink from the little brown cup. Then he went on: 'Wulfstan fell. I liked that old man. He died shouting 'Eckerheim', and Ronan stood over him fighting and cursing until they cut him down as well. It was a mess.'

'But you fought your way clear?'

'For a time, yes. We even thought some of us might make it. Maybe some did. I don't know. The Liutizen seemed to fall back – around us, leastways – and we managed to group together and head deeper into the woods. Levy most of us, but there were a few Imperials, and one or two Meisseners.'

Markward stirred the embers with a stick. 'You did well.'

'Aye, maybe so, but not well enough. They caught up with us near where you found me. Came at us again. Like wild animals. We were running and fighting. Two of us stumbled and fell. There was no time to stop and help them up – they were gone.'

He stopped, gathering his strength, and for a while just stared ahead, his eyes wide with the memory of the slaughter. 'No pity', he said at last. 'No pity.'

'And in the end?' asked Markward quietly.

Bernhardt looked across at him. 'In the end there were just four of the levy left. The others had scattered. They could have shot us down like dogs, but instead they threw down their bows and closed with spears and axes and those long knives.'

Branulf shuddered and drew his knees up, and hugged them tight.

With a little nod to show he understood, Bernhardt went on: 'One of them – he was tall and red faced. A bullock of a man. He looked at me, shook his spear and laughed and spat at his feet. I saw a club on the ground. I picked it up and threw it at him. He ducked and laughed again. But he didn't duck my hammer. I hit him clean and down he went. He had a bronze chain around his neck. It caught on a branch as he fell and twisted him all around. I remember that. Then nothing more until you came.'

There was the sound of a twig snapping somewhere out in the forest dark. Markward put his finger to his lips and stood up. Branulf reached for his bow. They waited a long time. The fire burnt low. At last Markward squatted down again by the fire.

'If they're out there, they're getting no closer, and if they come we can never stop them.' He put some more wood on the fire and they watched it crackle into life.

'Arrows in the dark!' muttered Branulf as if to himself.

'The arrow that flies by night,' answered Bernhardt, holding his hand out to the blaze.

No one else spoke until once more the fire burnt low and the shadows crept in close about them.

'Your arm?' asked Markward, 'It pains you?'

'A little,' replied Bernhardt, ' but I think come morning I will be able to walk for a while.'

'See how you go, but take it easy. There's little point in your escaping the Liutizen, only to die of a fever half way to home.'

The blacksmith smiled at Markward. 'I owe you my life.'

'You owe me nothing!' Markward's voice was curt, almost sharp. 'Your life is your own, and you've promised it to another.'

'Markward . . .'

The young soldier held up his hand. 'No. Don't worry yourself. There's no bad blood between us on this matter. And no anger either. A little of sorrow, perhaps: that I grant you. Sorrow, but no anger.' He grinned, and filled the little cup once more for Bernhardt. 'What is, is and what is not, is not. That's all. And by God's good grace we'll all come home to Eckerheim.'

When they set off in the morning, there was birdsong all about them.

Bramlings, sparrows and thrushes darted and swooped back and forth across the path. There were blackbirds too, and once they spotted a jay as it flew among the oaks and elms. Their hearts lifted. Branulf began to chatter, and Markward found himself whistling an old Swabian marching song. Bernhardt tried walking beside the horse, leaning against the saddle, and holding the cantle. He managed to walk in this way for about a mile, before they rested up, tethering the horse and finding a place to shelter between two broad oaks. The warmth of the day streamed down among the leaves and branches of the great forest, and there was a patch of honeysuckle growing amid the hazel where the trees thinned.It drew in the humming bees.

'Not far now', said Markward. He was sitting with his back resting against an oak tree. The sunlight played across his face as the light wind stirred the tree tops above him. He relaxed in the warmth. The birds were still singing. It was peaceful in the forest at last. His eyes began to close. He was tired. Very tired.

'Markward!' Someone was shaking him by the shoulder. He awoke with a start. Mutti's cooking pot was gone, the fields of Eckerheim melted away, and he was back in the forest. Branulf was kneeling beside him.

'Markward! We should be going. You fell asleep.'

He stood up. Bernhardt was there, waiting by the horse. He smiled, and Markward smiled back. 'I'm sorry. I must have dozed off.'

'No matter! We wouldn't leave without you.' They all laughed, and the moment was gone. With a flick of the reins, Bernhardt led the way. Branulf came next, and then Markward, sword still drawn and shield across his back. The birdsong was still with them, but it was wise to keep alert. Not until they crossed the Elbe could they promise themselves a homecoming.

When Cedric came back to Eckerheim the harvest was over. The corn of the inner fields had been reaped, and brought into the barns closely watched by priest and bailiff. For two days the air above the threshing floors had been heavy with dust, and the women sang their high-pitched chants as they winnowed the grain against the Eastern breeze. And now on the evening that the old shepherd made his way down the last gentle slopes to the village, he could hear the sound of merry making. The people were singing and dancing because the harvest was in, and the barns were fat and overflowing. Even on the outer fields where the barley and rye were grown the harvest had been good. And the wheat harvest was yet to come. Next year much of this land would have to lie fallow – it had been worked too hard in recent seasons, but for now at least there was rejoicing. The tithes would be paid, the people would be fed, and there would be surplus enough for market.

If only the levy were home.

A sudden shower pattered across the roofs of the crucks and barns as Cedric wandered down the rutted street. He pulled his cloak about him, and quickened his pace. The rain had the fresh chill of autumn about it, but what drove him on was his need to check the fold. He knew all would be well: Hec was a good man. After that he had seen his sheep he would go to his lodging. Who ever he first met could spread the news. There was not much to say, but he knew that such news as he had would run about the village like a startled fox. In Eckerheim there was a hunger that no harvest could ever fill, and he had precious little to offer that any might find comfort in. Still, he was here now, and happy to be home. Home! He surprised himself to think of this little clutter of dwellings in this little valley as home. And yet it was.

He turned the corner by a tumbledown bothy, and there was Katrin. She was hurrying, head down, with a basket of apples, and they almost collided. 'Cedric!' Her eyes widened. 'You're back. What news?'

He told her. She nodded, thanked him, and headed away. There was no joy in her glance, nor even hope.

'Well, that's that!' he said to himself, and headed on down to the fold.

Elsa had seen Cedric arrive in the village. She was standing by the well, drawing water for the cooking fires. When she looked up and noticed the figure of a man coming down the hillside, she knew at once that it was the shepherd. The sounds of singing, of clapping hands and stamping feet faded into nothingness. All she could see was the shepherd, and all she could hear was the sound of blood pounding in her ears. She did not move, but waited motionless, watching as he passed the last of the boundary markers or balks, and came down into the village itself. Then she saw him stop to talk to Katrin, but try as she might she could not tell if the news was good or bad. When Katrin hurried off, Elsa thought of dashing after her, or even trying to catch up with Cedric, but something made her pause. All of a sudden she did not want to know. Not yet. She was not ready. As long as Cedric was coming home there was always hope, but now he was back in the village and right there before her – it was just a short step to joy or sorrow, and she feared to take it.

With a gasp she took the pail. It was heavy, overfilled, and splashed against her as she walked. Now she could hear the singing again. They were drinking too much, as usual. Strong harvest beer, and some honey mead kept back by the bailiff to celebrate the Autumn reaping: it was the same in Hochtal every year until . . . She shook her head to clear the thoughts that came crowding in, and went on down towards the threshing floor.

When they rounded the bend and glimpsed the way ahead through the overhanging branches of the broad oaks, Markward realised with a start where they were: they had come to the place where so many days ago he had been ambushed and nearly killed. Instinctively, he put his hand to his shoulder and felt the ache of the wound, then turned to look up at Bernhardt who was sitting wearily on the horse.

'I know this place,' he said.

'For good or ill?' asked Bernhardt.

'For good, because I know now that the river lies about an hour ahead of us – for ill because it was here that an arrow nearly took me.'

Bernhardt and Branulf stared uneasily about them but all seemed quiet.

'We move on', said Markward quietly, 'but keep your wits about you. Almost home, is 'not home at all', if we slip up now.'

And so they went on, this time Markward leading, then Branulf, bow at the ready, and finally Bernardt on the horse. After a while, when they had covered perhaps a thousand paces, they came to a place where the way narrowed and forked. Laurel and juniper grew close about the path, so that it was difficult to see on either side for any distance. And the birdsong had stopped. Markward held up his hand. They all stopped. Nothing moved ahead. The forest seemed to hold its breath, and the bright shafts of sunlight only made the shadows darker. The river now seemed so far away, locked behind the dense green walls of oak and elm.

And now the birds had fled. Just as before.

Perhaps they were being watched. It seemed certain now that some of the Liutizen had been sent back this way to guard the approaches to the Elbe, and cut off any stragglers that might have escaped the slaughter.

Looking back over his shoulder, Markward put his finger to his lips, and signalled for them to move off the path. They pushed into the huckleberry and furze bushes that grew all about the laurel, and began to skirt the tangled grove. It was slow, nervous work, and twice Markward had to take the horse firmly by the reins, and drag it forward when it baulked. At length they came to a clearing due north of the path, and then swung west again, heading through more thickets of juniper that grew between the bigger trees. At length they came to a small sheltered clearing.

Here they stopped. Bernhardt's wounds were paining him, and Branulf was tired and thirsty. They rested up for a while, then Markward decided to scout ahead on his own. He left the others, and headed off to the west and south, slowly arcing back towards the path. It was more of the same: juniper thickets, clumps of hazel and furze bushes, scattered stands of oaks and elms, and sometimes birchwoods. He was aware that there was little wind, and that therefore any movement of the branches and foliage would immediately alert an enemy.

The forest began to darken as clouds drifted slowly in from the East, and every tree seemed to retreat into the rising gloom. After a good while, when he was hoping to make out the first signs of the river bank, he heard a sound that made him instantly freeze. It was the sound of voices: low, soft and murmuring, some distance away but unmistakable.

He listened intently, crouched down among the bushes, his hand on his dagger. He could tell that there were several men at least, and they were headed across his line of march. They were moving easily, he could hear laughter now, and the clanking and jangle of armour and weapons. There was no fear in their approach.

And then he saw a juniper sway, and suddenly they were in view: Liutizen warriors, five of them, all armed with sword, shield and spear. Some of them wore scale armour hauberks, all of them had iron and leather helmets. Two of them wore the gold torques of ringbearers.

Less than twenty paces separated them from Markward's hiding place, when their leader suddenly stopped and held up his hand. In an instant the five of them disappeared from view as though the forest floor had opened up and swallowed them. There was not a sound, not a chink of metal, not the least muffled curse or creak of leather harness. All was still, silent and waiting.

Markward bit his bottom lip hard, and resisted the temptation to drop lower in among the bushes. He knew that the least movement would give him away, and that with Liutizen so close the merest sigh or intake of breath could be fatal.

An ant wandered across a leaf inches from his eyes. A lacewing floated by, and a thin drizzle began to drift down through the branches.

He began to count. He counted the number of leaves he could see on a branch of hazel. He counted the number of hairs on the back of his left hand. Then, on his right. And then, he counted the water droplets gathering on the polished leather of his shield. And still he waited. He waited until the droplets came together and then ran down the curving face of his shield, before dripping off the rim and onto the ground. And he counted them as they dripped.

'When you need to keep still', as the old hunter from Ruhhaus had once told him, 'Count, count and count again.'

But still there was no movement from the Liutizen. Had they seen him? Or heard him? Or even smelt him? Perhaps their silence was no more than the wary instinct of these woodland folk in pursuit of their prey.

He counted the days march from the Weissburg to Dresdany, and then from the Elbe to the Marshland. And back again. He counted the days he took to march from Eckerheim to the King's banner at Goslar on that first time he rode away to serve the Salian Prince. And then he stopped counting, for all at once his head was filled with nothing but Elsa, and all the memories that he had come so far to forget. For a moment the forest whirled away in the sight and scent of her tossing hair and shining eyes and . . .

The Liutizen leader stood up, rising like a stag from bracken. He looked about him. He was tall and muscular with a bronze and leather baldric double-crossed over his chest. His shaggy, straw coloured hair, braided in front of his ears, framed a lean and high-boned face. He stared hard at the spot where Markward crouched, with pale blue eyes that seemed to look straight through the thick, sheltering foliage and Markward felt for sure that he had been discovered. But then a bird – it was a heron – suddenly flapped from a branch over to his left and dived awkwardly away among the trees. There was a pause.

'Sa!' called the Liutizen warrior, and the others got to their feet laughing. And then, with one last careful look, they headed off, their clipped and rapid language softened by chuckles and the easy banter all soldiers know. Soon they had disappeared, and the forest was silent once more.

'Saved by an angel!' said Markward to himself, as he slowly straightened and stood. He felt stiff, and tired, his sword arm shook – but he knew that the Elbe must be by now very close – the heron had shown him that much. It had also flown away towards the west where he supposed the river to be.

Nevertheless, he decided to return to Branulf and Bernhardt. They would be wondering where he was, and the day, now overcast and raining, was drawing in. He headed back, moving as quietly as he could in case the patrol he had seen was circling back. He was also worried that there might be other groups of Liutizen about. Whatever happened now, he and the others would not be able to take the main path back to the Elbe. As close as they were, it would be madness to try and go any further along that way. Instead they would strike well north and then, when the going seemed good, they would head west again, and hope to make the Elbe without meeting any Liutzen along the way.

It took him longer than he expected to get back to where he had left Bernhardt and Branulf. It was already growing dark, and he nearly lost his way in the gathering shadows. They stood to greet him, with smiles of relief, but said little – just beckoning him over to a small hide of bracken and laurel branches they had woven together on the edge of the clearing.

They exchanged news in cautious whispers, looking about them all the time. Bernhardt said that little had happened. Once they had heard what sounded like someone cry out, and another reply, but it was too far away to tell for sure. An old grey wolf had also happened by, but made off into the scrub when he caught sight of them. Otherwise, nothing.

Some birds seemed to have returned, but not many – just a thrush or two, and a wood pigeon that kept calling from somewhere amid a stand of larches just beyond the clearing.

Markward frowned. 'Well, it's not safe here', he said. 'We will move out now, and hope to reach the river by morning.'

'At night? In this forest?' said Bernhardt. 'It will be as black as pitch. How will we find our way?'

'I'm not sure', replied Markward, 'but I've a fair idea I can find my way back to where I was this afternoon, and then it's just a matter of going north and then west when the time seems right.'

'And if we get lost?'

'Well, then we just go to ground for the night, and work our way through in the morning.'

Bernhardt was silent for a while, and then nodded. Branulf shrugged and went to get the horse. Moments later they were on their way.

At first there was a little moonlight filtering through the forest canopy, and for a time they made good progress. But the forest at night was a frightening place. Branulf tried not to think of the tales of hobgoblins and weird beasts his grandmother had told him all those years ago. Even the branches seemed to reach out to him from the darkness as they pushed their way through the undergrowth. Every so often they heard the sharp cry of some forest creature, and once an owl glided silently by. Otherwise, they seemed to be alone in the vastness of the great woodland. Soon, Branulf could not even see his own feet, and had lost sight of Bernhardt who was somewhere ahead of him. It was though he was walking in the midst of a black cloud trapped deep within the bowels of the earth, and that the more he walked the darker it became until finally he would be unable to walk at all. The very air seemed to have a thick, heavy quality of blackness about it, and he felt a rising sense of panic that he might somehow choke. Then suddenly a branch flicked back and struck him in the face, shaking him out of his fear.

'Are you all right?' whispered Bernhardt from out of the nothingness ahead.

'Yes, I think so,' Branulf answered , and this time he glimpsed a faint movement up ahead, which he took to be the feet of the blacksmith. Taking a deep breath, he stumbled on, praying hard to all the saints his mother used to call upon and curse, that soon they might find the way which would lead them safely to the Elbe.

It wasn't long before they came to the clearing the Liutizen had crossed. It glowed with a dull silver softness as the moonlight filtered down through the branches. The weather was clearing once more.

Branulf rubbed his eyes, relieved to be able to see again. But there was no pause. Markward signalled, and they were off, this time heading northwards into the night.

Twice they stopped. Twice Branulf flung himself down and fell asleep instantly. Twice he was shaken roughly awake, and twice he staggered to his feet before going on. He knew that Bernhardt was struggling to keep up. The blacksmith said nothing, but gasped with pain every so often as branches struck his wounds or brambles clawed at his arms and face. He offered Bernhardt his shoulder, but the other muttered a refusal and carried on. Soon Branulf kept bumping into him as he slowed to no more than a halting limp, until finally he tripped and fell. Markward stopped and came back.

'Nearly there,' he said. 'Look up!'

Wearily the others lifted their heads. Above, through the blackness of the forest roof, the first faint tinges of a grey dawn were showing. They rested awhile. Markward checked Bernhardt's wounds as best he could, and then helped him to his feet.

'Lean on me,' he said. Bernhardt grimaced, but nodded his thanks.

Markward then gestured to Branulf. 'Take the horse. He'll show you the way. He smells water already, but don't let him bolt.'

Again they began to walk, this time Branulf taking the lead with the horse, and Markward following with Bernhardt, and supporting him as best he could. The going was still difficult, with closely growing furze and brambles to push through, and the ever-present elms and oaks on all sides. But the dawn was on its way, and the more they marched the more they could see. And then as the dull grey light rolled back the shadows, Branulf became excited and began to call out that he could see alders and willows ahead. Markward cursed, and hissed at him to hold his tongue. Nevertheless, he felt a surge of relief. The alders could only mean one thing: they were very close to water meadow or marsh, and the willows told him that a river was nearby: almost certainly the Elbe. Unless they had wandered in circles all night, it meant that they were nearly home.

Bernhardt was by now straining to stay upright. More and more he sank against Markward's shoulder, held by the Eckerheimer's firm grip. He sensed that his wounds were bleeding again, and his head began to swim as he fought back the nausea and exhaustion.

'Not far now', said Markward. 'A bowshot and we're there.'

Dawn broke slowly over Eckerheim. A thin, cold drizzle drifted in over the hills in grey curtains, and the cattle brought down to the lower meadows huddled against the glistening hedgerows. Elsa was up early. She and Katrin were off to glean in the outfields that lay beyond the millstream. Their heavy grey shawls were wrapped about them as they crossed the muddy glebe land and made their way down towards the stream. Neither of them spoke. It was early, they were tired, and the news that the levy was late, feared lost, hung heavy on their hearts.

Someone hailed them, and they both looked up. It was Elspeth hurrying after them, a wicker basket bouncing against her knees and the hood of her cloak all flung back.

'I'm glad I caught you!' She smiled as she came up to them all red-faced and puffing. They let her catch her breath.

'What's the matter? You've heard something?' asked Katrin at last.

'No, no.' Elspeth shook her head. 'It's just I wanted company at least part of the way. I'm going to the woods for leaves, berries, roots, anything I can find. The wisewoman asked me. Said she wants them for healing.'

'For healing?'

'Aye, and fresh too. She said she wanted nothing dried. Has to be fresh. Fresh leaves for fresh wounds she said.'

Katrin and Elsa looked at each other. 'The wisewoman knows something then', Katrin said.

Elspeth clicked her tongue. 'Maybe so. She's fey all right, and seems to know when the cattle plague's about and what to do about it, but I'm not so sure she can see over those hills to Dresdany and the Elbe.'

'She's guessing,' said Elsa with a toss of her head. 'There's no second sight in her. She's just guessing. The levy could come at any time. Everyone knows that.' The others stood waiting awkwardly. The drizzle strengthened and the water drops stood thickly on their cloaks and shawls.

'Come on!' said Katrin finally. 'Can't stand here all day. We'll glean till the forenoon, and then stop by on the way home at the mill.'

The Elbe was running high, but it was not in flood. It swirled about the roots of the clustering willows, and lapped and gurgled easily against the low, grassy banks. The grey-green waters stretched out through the morning mist towards the western shore and the land of the Saxons: Home!

Markward stood and looked out over the river. At last they had arrived, and had come safely to within sight of the hills and valleys they had dreamt of reaching for so many days. But how were they to cross? He turned. Bernhardt was sitting, half-lying against a tree. He looked pale and drawn. The blood was seeping through his bandages, and the stump of his arm looked red and inflamed. At least he was asleep, though he moaned in his sleep, and sweat covered his brow.

Branulf was standing next to the horse, his hand on its muzzle, whispering in its ear. Markward nodded: the boy was becoming a man, and a man worth bringing home. He turned back to the river. They could never cross here: too deep, too wide, too fast flowing. The eddies twisted and skeined as far as he could see, and he knew that here at least the river bed would be muddy and treacherous. The horse could swim, but it could not fight the current for long. They would all be swept away.

They would all drown. Bernhardt first. Unless. . . Markward rubbed his chin, and then scratched his head, as he always did when he was perplexed. He studied the river, walked a pace or two, stopped, then turned to look at the forest – then back again towards the river. 'It might just work ,' he said.

Several hours later – nervous, hastening, glancing hours, and the raft was ready. It was a crudely made raft: saplings, fallen branches, rushes and two birch logs, all lashed together with whatever they could find or fashion. Branulf and Markward hauled it to the edge of the river bank and stood back.

'Do you think it will float?' Branulf asked, unslinging his bow and quiver, and placing them on the raft.

'It will have to,' replied Markward, 'Or we are all lost.' He went and knelt beside Bernhardt. The blacksmith's breathing was shallow, and his skin now grey and waxen. Markward sniffed the wounds. 'Still clean at least,' he said. 'Help me with him.' Together, they dragged Bernhardt onto the raft and then slid it gently into the stream, Branulf jumped into the river to steady it, and cried out as the waters came up over his chest.

'Easy, now!' whispered Markward. 'Hold it steady – see there! Where the stern pole should go.' Branulf clung on, slipped once, found his feet and then swung the head of the raft back against the shore.

'Good!' said Markward. 'Now clamber up, and we'll see if she'll take the weight.'

Branulf was just trying for the third time to haul himself up, and was about to suggest that he try from the bank, when an arrow flew over his shoulder and splashed into the river.

Markward whirled around. Another arrow skimmed by him. And then another. He crouched down behind his shield, and winced as he felt the thump and bite of a shaft striking against the leather face.

'Go!' he yelled, and scrambling back on his haunches kicked against the raft so that it moved out into the stream. Branulf ducked down on the lee side of the raft as it bobbed away in the current, carrying the unconscious Bernhardt downstream.

'The flow will take you to Meissen!' Markward yelled again, and then grunted as two arrows struck his shield almost at the same time, one of them driving through the bide and linden wood, and nearly pinning his arm.

His horse had trotted off among the trees to the north, and with the shield across his back, he ran there now as fast as he could, ducking and weaving as the arrows hissed about him.

'They're close!' he thought to himself. 'Why didn't they just creep in and finish us off with swords and clubs?'

Gasping, he reached his horse, and took hold of the bridle. It reared up screaming. An arrow had struck it in the neck. Plunging and kicking, the wounded animal tore free from his grasp, and galloped away into the forest. Markward was vaguely aware of figures rushing towards him, and guttural shouts of triumph. He loosed his sword, stumbled backwards against a tree and struck out wildly as the first attacker came at him. The clash of steel cleared his mind as it had always done before. Now he could see. Now he could think. He even noticed, in a moment of time, that they were coming at him, all strung out, one after the other. They were confident. Sure of the kill. Hochtal flashed before him.

He swept the Liutizen's sword down as his opponent over-reached, stamped on the blade with one foot, and struck hard with the pommel of his sword into the unprotected face. There was a crunching of bone, and the man went down, his forehead misshapen and bloody.

A cry of rage came from the next warrior, and Markward had just enough time to swing up his shield so that the barbed spear point jagged across its rim. He lunged with his sword, and the Liutizen dodged back, spear levelled – but as he did so his foot caught against a root, sending him sprawling. With all his strength, Markward struck home where neck meets shoulder, then panting and wide-eyed squared round to meet his last opponent.

This was a seasoned warrior, older than the others, but lean and hard, with scars across his chest and cheek bone, and a cool look in his eye. He glanced back to where he had cast down his bow and quiver, sniffed twice, kicked at the ground and then swung up his great bearded axe in both hands. He advanced on Markward with steady, even strides – no hint of madness in his coming on. As he closed he began to whirl the axe in a scything figure of eight motion, making it sing and whoosh against the air. He was stripped bare to the waist, but wore leather breeches, and on his arms torques of bronze and gold. A sword and scabbard of spatha- length hung at his hip, and his long grey-blond hair was tied back in a pony tail. This was a ring-bearer, a chieftain's man, a carl of the high hall.

Markward licked his lips and swallowed nervously. He had fought such men before, but always in the fury and confusion of the shield wall, the battle-line and the pell-mell fight where it was always easy to get in the low blow, and always possible to duck behind a friendly shield and make good your escape. Here it was different: it was man on man, tusk to tusk, and what friends he had were fled.

The great axe swung nearer and nearer. The feet, light and strong, danced across the turf. The ice cool eyes, never blinking, stared at him through the blur of steel. Markward knew that to attempt to parry the axe with sword or shield would bring certain death. The eighteen inch blade of the axe was sufficient to shatter a sword, split a shield and kill the man behind it – all in one blow. Nor was evading the axe a simple matter. The movement of the weapon in the hands of a skillful enemy meant that it could easily sweep back and forth to cover and cut off any feinting movements. He could of course run, but that meant turning his back – an action that invited swift punishment from a warrior who could hurl an axe as well as he could wield one.

With a muttered prayer, Markward unslung his shield and let it fall to the ground. It was useless to him against such a weapon. Now he took his sword in both hands, and presented it at high guard. The Liutizen laughed and came closer. He was now no more than three paces away, and tensing for the final flourish which would knock the sword out of Markward's hand, and then split him skull to hip on the return swing.

At that moment – as the eyes of the Liutizen widened and his nostrils flared – Markward leapt to one side in a half-crouch and cut towards the man's ankles. His sword blade missed and bit the turf, but it was enough to force the other to step wide to avoid the cut and regain his balance. As he swung the axe again, Markward closed. The blade of the Saxon sword met the ash wood haft of the Liutzen axe with a hollow 'chunk'. It cut clean through, so that the head of the axe spun over his shoulder and thudded into the ground behind him.

Both men instinctively danced back, and before Markward could gain an advantage, the Liutizen had drawn his sword and closed again.

The woods rang as blade to blade the two men fought: circling, dodging, striking, and moving to parry. Markward could feel himself tiring, but he knew that his opponent was also weary of the fight and keen to finish it. This Liutizen warrior was a master of his trade – a fine swordsman, and no doubt the winner in many shield to shield encounters. Like Markward he was fighting two handed, but his sword was long in the blade, with a fine thrusting point, as well as the usual cutting edges. He lunged, parried, swept and backcut in a smooth flowing rhythm, but there was power in his sword strokes, and when the blades met, Markward felt the shuddering force of each blow. The young Saxon needed an opening, but there seemed little prospect, so controlled and skilful was his enemy's attack. His heart sank as more and more he took in, and understood the mettle of this man. And then, all at once, just as he began to see himself fallen in this place and coughing out his life on the trampled turf, there came an opportunity. A drop of sweat from the Liutizen's brow seemed to get in his eye making him blink, and duck his head. It was a movement that was over in an instant, but it was all that Markward wanted. It broke the deadly rhythm. For a heartbeat it opened up a gap in the blows that rained upon the Eckerheimer. Instead of meeting the sword cut, Markward was able to swerve inside it. As the blade hissed harmlessly by, he thrust his own sword full at the face of the Liutizen, who fell backwards trying to miss the sudden death blow. The sword blade grazed his cheek, and the hilt knocked him to the ground. Before he could regain his feet, Markward's sword was levelled at his throat, the point resting on the Adam's apple.

There was a moment when all seemed to tremble on the edge of that sword. The man clenched his teeth and closed his eyes, his whole body braced for what he knew must surely come. Markward looked down at him, and saw only a farmer – an old, weather-beaten farmer lying helpless on the torn and bloody grass. There could be no joy in such a killing, no feeling of relief, and no reason. He stepped slowly back, releasing the point, and letting his sword drop. For a time the man lay rigid and still. Then he opened his eyes, and squinted up into the light. He remained like that for some time – motionless, staring – then clenched and unclenched his hand as though feeling for his sword which lay well beyond his reach.

Markward signed for him to get up, and watched as the other got warily and painfully to his feet. They stared at each other, still breathing deeply from the fight. With his sword levelled, Markward pointed at himself: 'Eckerheim', he said. The other frowned then nodded. 'Kessiner', he said in a rough guttural reply, and stood, half stooped, waiting for the final thrust.

'Go!' said Markward suddenly. 'Go now!' He pointed towards the woods and the southern reach of the river. 'Go!'

Slowly it dawned on the Liutizen what was meant. He shook his head, as if in disbelief, made as if to go, and then glanced at his sword. Markward grunted an assent, and the man scrambled across, picked up the weapon and made for the edge of the clearing. Suddenly he stopped, turned, gave a half smile, and a kind of vague salute, then disappeared into the trees.

All was quiet. Markward stood, exhausted, sword clenched in one hand. He threw his head back and gulped in the cool fresh air. His whole frame seemed to shake, and he noticed that he could not stop sweating, but he was filled with dull sense of surprise that he was still alive, still standing after the swiftness and savagery of the last few moments. He had fought, and he had survived. Everything seemed crystal clear to him – shining, bright and brimming with beauty and hope. He was alive!

He never saw the fourth Liutizen: a wanderer, ragged and gaunt, prowling like a wolf on the footsteps of those he shadowed. He was a bowman, cautious and cunning, with a good eye for the cruel and hidden shot.

He had watched the end of the fight, smirked to see the beaten warrior given the shame of quarter, and then carefully nocked an arrow as the Saxon turned away and drank in the trembling air.

Markward heard the string hum, but he did not have time to even flinch.

The arrow flew and found its mark, driving near halfway to the fletchings as it pierced flesh and bone.

Spinning round, he saw a Liutizen, bow in hand, pitch forward from the undergrowth, an arrow protruding from his chest.

Almost at the same time there was a cry from the other side of the clearing, and boy appeared, grinning and brandishing a bow.

Markward blinked in amazement:

'Branulf!'

Shouldering his weapon, and looking down awkwardly, Branulf shambled towards Markward. He stepped around the bodies of the two Liutizen, and gazed at the man he had just killed. His grin faded.

'I came back,' he said.

'Praise God, you did!' replied Markward taking him by one hand, and slapping him on the back. 'I was a dead man.'

'I saw him as I came out into the clearing. No time to warn you. Just took a shot.'

Markward smiled. 'Well, it's the shot of a master bowman, and I am forever in your debt.' He noticed he had stopped shaking, and the sweat was beginning to dry on his brow. 'Where's Bernhardt? The raft?'

'That's why I'm here. We were drifting away down stream, and making good progress, but then the raft snagged an overhanging branch, and we swung into the bank. I was trying to free it, when Bernhardt seemed to come to himself. He sort of half sat up and said "Where's Markward?"'

'Well, I told him, and he told me I had to go back and find you. I tried arguing, but he began to shout and I was afraid his shouting would finish him off for sure – so I lashed the raft safe, grabbed my bow and headed back here.'

Markward nodded. 'And you found me just in time. Still, we need to head back to Bernhardt now.'

'What about your horse?'

'Wounded. Galloped off. It's away in the woods somewhere. Probably dead.'

Branulf's face fell. 'That was a good horse. I liked that horse.'

'Aye. He was a good friend to me. Never let me down.'

'I never heard you call him by a name.'

Markward smiled. 'Oh, he had a name all right. I used to whisper it to him all the time. Lean over and whisper it into his ear. Especially when the ride was long or difficult or dangerous. I'd just whisper his name. He liked that. It made him flick his ears.'

They began to walk back the way Branulf had come, stopping only to check the dead Liutizen for trinkets or coins. They had left the clearing about thirty paces behind when Branulf spoke again:

'What did you call it then?'

'You mean my horse?'

'Aye.'

'I called him, Thursday. And before you ask it's the day I bought him from a horse dealer in Fulda. It was before the Friesian campaign and he was the first horse I'd ever owned. I'd ridden a few before that – on the farms around Eckerheim, and once or twice on the march to Friesia – but I'd never owned one. Not until 'Thursday'.

They found Thursday lying dead among some bracken near a stand of silver birches. Markward gently pulled out the arrow and snapped it.

'There's an arrow that will kill no more', he said, dropping the pieces to the ground. He stood over the horse, said something Branulf could not make out, and then stooping down took the imperial banner from under the saddle.

'Come on!' he said.

THE MEISSENERS

They found Bernhardt where Branulf had left him – stretched out on the raft, which rocked and bobbed gently in the swirl of the river flow. He was asleep, his hand clutching a water bottle, and his head resting on a folded cloak.

'His fever seems less,' said Markward. 'The river cools it, but we need to get him downstream to Meissen as soon as we can.'

Branulf clambered onto the raft, which dipped and almost became awash, but then righted itself.

'No room for me,' muttered Markward, but I can cling on, as you did before. If the river runs like this all the way, it should not take us long to reach Meissen.' He took off baldric, scabbard, hauberk and cloak, along with his dagger and wallet. Together with the imperial banner, his shield and Branulf's weapons, he placed them on the raft. Water was seeping up between the timbers and close-packed rushes, but the raft was river-worthy and would not easily sink.

Shouting to Branulf to take hold of the steering pole, he released the tether from the alder branch, and pushed the raft out into the stream.

The current was unexpectedly strong, and there was a moment of panic as the raft drifted away from him, but he plunged forward and caught hold of it, and felt the pull of the river against his chest and legs.

'Can you hold on?' called Branulf as he leaned on the pole to swing the raft further out into the stream.

'I'll have to,' smiled Markward. 'I can't swim.'

Branulf gave a gasp of surprise, but Markward hauled himself up on his elbows and gave a short laugh. 'Don't worry! I've no thought in me to be letting go, and I'm hoping Meissen is just a bend or two down the way. We should be there soon. Just keep to the middle of the river and start to angle across when I tell you.'

The great river carried them southwards under clearing skies and a fresh Summer breeze. To the East lay the deep, dark, impenetrable green of the Liutizen forest. To the West, the gentler fields and meadows of the Saxon shore.

Markward was tempted to try and make landfall as soon as possible, and to feel safe ground beneath his feet – but he knew that without Thursday there was no hope of getting Bernhardt safely to Meissen. The blacksmith looked deathly pale, though the fever had subsided, and he was slipping into a deep sleep, broken only by a fitful tossing and moaning. Occasionally his eyes flickered and seemed to open, but there was precious little life in the eyes, and they quickly closed again.

Branulf was getting anxious. He kept looking down at Bernhardt, and then glancing across to the western shore, while wrestling with the steering pole to keep the raft on course.

'You're doing well!' Markward called out. 'A real river boatman.'

The boy gave a nervous nod and half a smile. 'Much longer do you think?'

Markward shook his head. 'We must be there soon. This raft is doing a good pace, and we've already rounded one bend. I wouldn't be surprised if we catch sight of the castle when we reach that turn up ahead.'

A while later later they came to the turn – a low bush covered cliff pushing out from the Saxon side of the river. The flow swept them towards it, and Branulf had to fight to stay clear of the choppy water which told of rocks and shoals and hidden sandbanks. The raft bucked momentarily as it edged the rapids, and Markward reached to steady Bernhardt. Again the raft lurched and dipped, twisting against the steering oar and making Branulf cry out. But suddenly they had made the turn and were in quieter waters once more.

'See!' shouted Branulf. 'See!'

Not far distant, almost directly ahead, and on the western bank was the dark outline of a fortress: Meissen.

With a gasp of relief, Markward gazed at the fortress. He had only been guessing that they might be near to Meissen, and now all at once the castle and town was there in front of them.

His next thought was that the town may have fallen to the Liutizen, but as they approached there was no sign of attack or disaster. There were people working in the fields – some stopped and waved, and the only smoke came from the hearth fires of the crucks and bothies gathered in small groups along the bank, and across the grassy slopes. And then the sunlight caught the armour and weapons of guards on the ramparts of the fortress, and flapping above them on the top-most tower he could at last make out the great lion banner of the Meissener lords.

'It's all right!' he said to Branulf. 'We can land here safely. It's all right.'

The flow of the river brought the raft in towards the western shore, and they drifted steadily along until they were close upon the jetties and landing stages of the town. There were folk there, buying and selling, and bringing in goods from the countryside as well as baskets of fish from the little boats and wherries that crowded the port. The raft was scarcely noticed as it began to bump among the craft, but then a ferryman called out, and next a porter – and soon it seemed as if everyone had looked up, paused in their work and were shouting, chattering and pointing at the strange arrivals.

Someone reached out from a small boat and took hold of the raft – and then stocky barrel-chested fisherman scrambled to end of a jetty and used a gaff and rope to bring it in and secure it to the wooden piles.

'Well met!' he said, in his gruff, full bellied Saxon tongue. 'What brings you here?'

'We're from the imperial army,' replied Markward, surprised that he could stand up in the shallows. 'We've come from upstream, south of Dresdany.'

The fisherman turned and cupping his hands shouted to the onlookers: 'They're from the Markgraf's army!'

An excited murmur ran through the crowded shore, and many of them pressed forward to hear more.

But a sergeant lounging against the jetty post pushed ahead and held up his hand. 'Hold!' Reluctantly they all obeyed, and the sergeant signed for Markward to climb up onto the jetty. With a brief word to Branulf to keep watch over Bernhardt, he grabbed his sword, his shield and the imperial banner and clambered up onto the wooden walkway. The sergeant stepped forward and smiled, casting a professional eye over the young Eckerheimer. Then he slowly nodded and rubbed his unshaven chin. 'You bring a message from the Markgraf?'

'We bring news of the Army.'

The sergeant frowned. 'You will need to speak to my lady of Meissen then. She is castellan while my lord is away.'

'I first need help for my comrade here, and shelter and a promise of . . .'

'Yes, yes, all of that! There is a healer in the town, and we will lodge you all in the castle. But come now, we must see my lady.'

Markward stood his ground. 'My comrade needs help now.'

Their eyes locked. There was a pause, then the sergeant shrugged. 'Oskar!' he called over his shoulder. A young mop-haired soldier, in a ragged shirt of mail got quickly up from the barrel he was sitting on, and gave a nervous bow. 'Oskar, you and Helmut help this fellow off the raft, and send that idler Franz to run down to the tinker's quarter and find the healer and bring her here. Understood?'

The soldier bowed again. 'Understood, sergeant.'

But still Markward would not leave. Instead he climbed down onto the raft and began, with Branulf, to lift Bernhardt onto the jetty. The two soldiers soon came to help, and at last the sergeant gave a grunt of resignation, and shoving Oskar aside took Bernhardt in his massive arms and carried him clear. He knelt and with a certain care laid the blacksmith down, propping his head with his own leather gloves and helmet.

'Thanks, friend,' said Markward.

The sergeant stood. 'You'll thank me by bearing your news to the castle – now.'

Leaving Branulf to wait with Bernhardt and the two soldiers, Markward set off with the sergeant who pushed his way through the crowd as a man might push through a wheatfield. They gave way, muttering and cursing, and calling out for news, then folded back to cluster about this wounded man from the river and the young lad with the bow.

The castle at Meissen stared down from atop a slope of terraced vineyards, and low-walled fields. A winding path led to the gate and its flanking towers, and the outer walls of smooth-dressed stone shone in the brightness of the midday sun.

Markward was glad of both the sun, and the climb for he hoped to be at least passing dry before he had to be presented to the lady castellan. He could not think it possible, no matter how bad the news, to give it while standing in a dripping pool of river water. Meanwhile the sergeant talked unconcernedly as they climbed the path. He cursed the taxes of the king, laughed at the rumours of plagues and spat at his own mention of barbarian raiders. He said that there had already been some talk of numbers of stragglers or deserters from the army, who had slipped across the river well to the south. Markward held his peace, and leant forward into the slope. As the shadow of the keep fell across his back, and they neared the barbican, he began to think of what he might say to the one who now ruled such a fortress town.

The guards on the gate gave way, and they entered into the heart of the castle. There was a courtyard, another gate, a high walled bailey, doors, a winding staircase, an open corridor and then at last the great hall. They paused outside while a servant brought word to the lady of Meissen, and then they were shown in.

A large, beamed roof arched above them, and the white plastered walls were hung with tapestries. A fire, flanked by sleeping dogs, smouldered in the open hearth to one side, and at the end of the hall, on a raised dais sat the castellan. She was seated on a large, high-backed wooden chair, crested by a shield with a black lion rampant on a golden field. The chair appeared perhaps too large for her, but she sat erect, motionless and regal, dressed in a kirtle of pure white, embroidered with gold and pale blue entwined leaves. A cloak of blue hung over her shoulders and draped across the chair.

A page boy standing at the foot of the dais waved them forward, and then ducked away through a side door.

Markward advanced a little uncertainly, and knelt before the lady, keenly aware of his own wild and unkempt state – and her cool and slender beauty.

'You bring word of my husband?' Her pale green eyes gazed at him intently, and there was a slight tremor to her voice.

'My lady,' he began, feeling the words catch in the back of his throat. 'The Army is . . . the Army is . . .' He started again: 'I bring word that the Army . . .'

'You bring word that the Army is lost.' Her eyes still fixed on him, her slender white hands gripped, then released the carved arm rests of the great chair.

He stayed kneeling, lowered his head and nodded.

There was a silence. One of the dogs got up, yawned and came slowly over to the sergeant. From somewhere in the castle, perhaps the kitchens there was a call, a muffled reply and the faint clatter of pans. Then silence once more.

Markward looked up, and saw beauty framed with sorrow, saw the flaxen hair that hung in golden waves about her face. She was as still and white as a church-front statue. There was light and strength in her eyes.

'He swallowed hard: ' Aye, my lady, the Army is lost.'

'And my lord of Meissen?' Once more the hands gripped the arm rests, and the knuckles whitened. Again, Markward could scarcely speak. He saw the love she had for her husband. He saw it in her hands and in her eyes, and he heard it in her voice. It was a great love. He breathed deep, and spoke:

'Dead, my lady.'

She gave a short, convulsive sob, her head jerked forward, and her hands gripped the arm rests as though they would enter the very wood. Somehow she recovered herself, drew herself upright and

stared at the sky through the high round window at the other end of
the hall. Then, as the very glimmer of a faint hope entered her heart,
she asked in a faltering whisper: 'You saw him die?'

'I found him dead, my lady. He fell in the forest.'

With this it seemed as if her spirit withered. She sank back in the
great chair. She wept: silent tears which rolled down her cheeks while
she gazed across the stillness of the hall, and saw nothing but the
dark forests of the Elbe and the body of her husband.

At last she spoke again, her voice flat and lifeless.

'I thank you captain for your news, though the tidings are perhaps
heavier than I can bear this day. You must be weary, hungry and
perhaps in some pain after your journey. We must see to your
comfort. And to those who came with you.' She waved her hand
towards the servant at the door. He bowed and took half a pace
forward.

'Osbert! See to these men.' Her voice trailed away, and she closed
her eyes.

'I thank you, my lady', replied Markward, filling the silence. 'I
return this banner', he said. 'It seemed good to bring it home.' He
laid it at her feet.

Again she gathered herself. 'You will speak with me again,
tomorrow, at the third hour. Sir Egbert, captain of the guard, and my
two sons will be here as well. You can explain to them all that I do
not understand. Until then . . .' She gave a slight, tired, wave of her
hand, and watched him leave, scarcely acknowledging his anxious
bows and confused salute. For a time she remained seated, and then
slowly stood, and got down from the dais.

From nowhere, a young woman was by her side, one hand resting
gently on her sleeve. It was Aelga, childhood friend, and lady of the
chamber. They went to the solar. The lady castellan sat on the low
padded bench, while Helga fussed about her, brushing her hair and
tying it back. Her cloak was unfastened and folded, and a cup of
honey mead was pressed into her hand. Staring ahead, she raised the
cup to her lips and drank once.

And then as if something had broken inside her:

she gave a single cry, tore at her hair, then rocked back and forth groaning and driving her fists against her eyes while Aelga held her close.

Far below in the courtyard, Markward stood with the sergeant and let the sun fall across his face.

'I should be getting down to my friends,' he said.

'Na!' said the sergeant quietly. 'Stay here, and I will bring them to you. The young lad first, and then when the healer has finished we'll bring the other on up.'

Markward nodded. 'They are Branulf and Bernhardt, and I am Markward. We are all of Eckerheim.'

The sergeant smiled. 'And I am of Meissen. Peter the Tanner they call me, but I have not stripped skins for many a year. My father still keeps a tannery at Kurzfeld. You know it?'

'No.'

'Hah! And I have not heard of Eckerheim, neither. Still, you are safe now, and you are welcome, and you may take your ease here in the sun. I'll get you something to eat and drink, and then be on my way.'

As he turned to go, Markward touched him on the arm: 'Has no one else come back?'

The sergeant shook his head: 'From the Army, you mean? None this way. Not a one till you came, and no word nor rumour, save what I told you on the way up. There must be others, somewhere, who escaped but nothing so far except those few who crossed to the south. But the priests will pray, and we all will hope. Perhaps more will return.' He hesitated as though he was going to ask something, but then seemed to think better of it, turned on his heel and was gone.

Suddenly, Markward felt very tired. His shoulder ached, his head hurt, and his clothes chaffed against his skin. He leaned against the rough stone wall and felt its warmth against his back. And then he sat. Food, drink, some clean dry clothes and a bed of fresh straw: that would be good, he said to himself.

When he awoke Peter the Tanner was looking down at him where he lay at the base of the tower wall.

'Ah, friend! Wake up, now. You have not yet eaten, nor washed, nor looked to any of all that we might offer you.' He was grinning.

Markward gazed bleary-eyed about him. 'I slept.'

'Aye, you did. And the cook said you stink so much, he wouldn't wake you – but he always had a girl's nose, so I wouldn't be bothered by that. Anyway, it seemed best to leave you lie. Bernhardt – is that his name? – is still at the healer's. He's all right, but he'll need to rest up for a bit. Your Branulf has been up here awhile. He's washed, watered and fed, and now he's talking to the serving girls in the kitchen, telling them tall tales about all he did across the Elbe.'

Markward smiled. 'Come sit beside me, Peter of Meissen, and tell me about this place.'

The sergeant sat down, and idly picked up a pebble, rolling it between his fingers. 'Here's a good place. You and your friends are safe here, right enough young Markward.'

'It feels safe.'

'Aye. We've big, strong walls here, and the men to keep them. Those devils over there come to catch us out every Spring. Just as the days lift and the snows roll back, they come. But we're always awake to them. We can smell 'em, see? We know them, and they know us. We're like brothers really. Bad brothers with bad blood between us, but born of the same river. We are Elbe folk.' He glanced to see if Markward was still listening and then went on:

'So they come for us and we smell 'em coming, and give them a knock, and send them back across the river with a bloody nose.'

'Always?'

'Always! Well, nearly always. They come across with the dawn mist ye see. In their little boats. With the dawn. Out of the mist. Black shadows with long knives. But we are always waiting. Meissen never sleeps. And sometimes we too cross the Elbe, and sometimes . . .' He stared at the pebble in the palm of his hand, and then tossed it into the dust. 'My brother, Willi, he went with the levy. He had no horse or shield, but he could swing a sword, so they took him.'

'They took many such from our valley.'

'Aye, but think of this: me a soldier and him a farmer – and still they take him away from plough and family, and leave me here to guard the town.'

The sergeant took his drinking bottle from his belt and offered it to Markward. 'He's a good man, my brother. You don't remember him do you? Big fellow, bushy black beard. Always laughing.'

'I'm sorry.'

'Na! Don't worry. It was crazy to ask.'

'There were so many of us, Peter. I scouted ahead most of the time, or marched with the Eckerheimers.'

'Aye, understood. I had to ask, that's all. We miss him, and his wife fears the worst.' He drew in the dust with a stick, and then threw the stick across the yard so that it bounced off the well-head.

The sun strayed behind a cloud, and a cooling breeze stirred the courtyard. Markward got to his feet. 'The day draws on.'

'It does. And I have left you here long enough! Come now, and take some food and wine, or my lady of Meissen will have me cleaning out the stables with the yard hands.'

Later that day, with the sun westering behind a broken horizon a rider set off for the Weissburg. He rode one horse and led another. There were no posting stages for at least two days, and he would have to find what forage and shelter he could among the scattered hamlets and farms that lay along his route. He rode armed, with kite shield and lance, and the Meissener pennon flapping at its point. And wrapped around his waist he wore the ragged imperial banner. In three days he hoped to bring the news that no man wanted to hear, and all men feared to know.

But already the rumours were beginning to spread down the river in coracles and flat-boats, along the cart tracks to bothy and cruck, and across the wandering slopes where goatherds kept their charges and shepherds led their sheep: 'The Army is lost. All are slain, save a scattering: a few at Meissen and a company or two near Dresdany.'

But how or why, none could say – all that was known was that two men and a boy had floated into Meisssen on a raft, and they had told of the destruction of the Markgraf's great host – or so it was said.

That night the guard was doubled on the gates to the town, and men kept watch at every jetty and wharf for a mile either side of Meissen. In the inns and hostelries townsfolk muttered that if the Army was beaten and destroyed, then surely the Liutizen would come in strength, and all of Saxony would feel the edge of their swords.

Sir Egbert, stared into the lees of his wine cup, as he sat in the Great Hall. He was grim, but not given over to defeat and disaster.

'They will not come,' he said to those who sat around him. 'They have drunk deep enough for a season. They came to us, and we bloodied them; we went to them and they cut us down. There's enough slaughter in that tale for winter songs and feasting. Next year they may begin the dance again, but not within the twelve month — I'll warrant that.'

'Then why the watch?' asked Leofric, one of Lord Meissener's sons from across the trestle table.

'Because it is right to do so,' answered Sir Egbert, brushing back his greying moustaches. 'Just as it is right for you and your brother to sit here on the lower table, until your mother calls one of you to the chair your father ruled from.'

Leofric belched and smiled. 'Sir Egbert, one of us is a simpleton, and the other has the mind and manner of a priest. Whom shall our poor mother choose?'

'The one who can fight,' replied Sir Egbert with an irritated glance, and he got to his feet. 'Tomorrow you are expected here along with your brother. We will talk with the young captain who came to us today. Your mother will be looking to us. She will need . . .'

'Aye, aye — I know my lord.' Leofric's face had lost its insolent look. 'My mother's heart is clean broke through. It's a wonder she can think beyond her grief.'

Egbert nodded. 'If she doesn't she will go mad. Your father was everything to her, and now he's gone. And all for nought.'

There was an uneasy silence. And then one of the young retainers at the end of the table spoke up. 'Sire, we have lost a good number of our best men to the Liutizen. Can we hold with so few against so many?'

Egbert gave a short laugh, but his eyes were full of sorrow: 'My friend, we have to hold. What did my Lord Ludwig always say: "With stout hearts and thick walls, a few good men can turn a host from Hell itself." The young soldier nodded, but unconvinced, returned frowning to his beer. A heavy bearded companion slapped him on the back, and the rest began to talk among themselves once more as Sir Egbert left the hall.

Markward and Branulf slept that night in the kitchens. Peter the Tanner roused them with the news that Bernhardt had survived the night and the Healer was beginning to think he would make a good recovery. They took breakfast, and then strolled down to the town in the morning sun, bought some food and drink for Bernhardt who still slept, paid the healer for another three days, and then returned to the castle. A trumpet sounded on the ramparts: it was the hour before noon, and the Lady of Meissen was waiting for them in the Great Hall.

She greeted them with that pale and still reserve that was strangely beautiful. 'Like winter sun on snowy fields,' said Markward later, drawing a puzzled look from the sergeant.

Markward spoke of the march beyond the Elbe. He spoke of the disaster he had come upon, the fight that Bernhardt and Branulf had survived, and the long journey back to the river.

She listened intently while her sons, Sir Egbert, three old warlords and the court chaplain looked on.

When he had finished, she nodded slowly, thanked him, and asked: 'My husband – he died well?'

'He did my lady. I found him in the midst of his fallen knights. It seemed to me he had died a warrior's death.'

'You brought me no token. A ring perhaps?'

'They stripped the dead, my lady: rings, lockets, everything!' He blurted out the words, though all he could see was the duke's head on a spear shaft, and the tangled bodies all around.

She studied him for a long time, then: 'No matter. He sleeps. My lord sleeps. And you, captain, brought home a banner. When a banner comes home, all is not lost.' Muttering something no one could make out, she lapsed into silence. At length, her son Leofric took half a pace forward:

'Captain,' he said. 'How do you think the Army fought? Was it a fight, or was it no more than slaughter?'

Markward thought hard. 'We were all strung out, my lord, in line of march. It was hot, the ground was difficult, and then a thunder storm broke over us. It should have been over very quickly. There must have been thousands of them, and they struck without warning. And yet, the dead were lying in the forest for miles.'

'So?'

'Well, my lord- that means that a good part of the army fought its way clear, and was only finally destroyed some distance from the first attack.'

'You think they rallied, then?'

'The Army was broken, my lord – shattered, cut to pieces, but there were many that managed to band together to fight to the last. I could see that when I came upon them. They were lying in heaps, and not all scattered. A good number had formed shield walls, some were in small groups – brothers, cousins, and comrades fighting and dying together – only a few were cut down as they ran.'

'That's good,' said Leofric.

'It's a damnable waste!' growled Sir Egbert. 'So many good men, and they died for nothing.'

There was a low murmur of agreement, and a shaking of heads.

The lady castellan remained motionless, gazing at the great double doors as if at any moment she expected to see them to burst open, and her lord come striding in. And then, as the murmuring subsided, and all was quiet, she cast down her eyes, pushed herself up on the arms of the chair, and stood, hands clasped tightly.

'I will leave you now, gentlemen. There will be much to discuss, and much to decide: the defence of this marcher-town now falls on your shoulders.'

They watched, heads slightly bowed, as she came down from the dais and left the hall, disappearing through the narrow curtained doorway that led to the ward tower.

Leofric gave a drawn out sigh, and clasped his brother by the shoulder: 'Well, Otto! What now? What say you? Will you be taking holy orders, and running off to that monastery at Zwickau. You'd suit a tonsure, and the prayers would be useful.'

Otto glowered, and his dark eyes flashed beneath narrowed eyebrows.

'No time for that, brother! There's blood in the forest, and it cries out for vengeance.'

'And bones to be buried, and good men to be brought home', called out one of the old war-lords, tugging at his sword belt.

'It would be better, my lords,' said Markward, risking an opinion, 'to let the dead lie where they fell for at least a season. The Liutizen hold the eastern bank in some strength, though many have doubtless returned to their villages. We have lost an army. We can ill afford to lose what little is left to us.'

'Careful words,' replied Otto with a sneering tone, 'But there is no trace of honour in them.'

'A pox on your honour!' roared Sir Egbert crashing his fist against the top most step of the dais. 'We will do well if we hold this place, and the villages west of here – and yet you would have us walk straight back into the devil's brew this man, whose sword knows more than yours is like to, barely escaped from.'

Otto reddened but said nothing.

'We hold the ford at Dresdany,' Leofric added quietly, glancing round for approval.

'We hold nothing,' said Sir Egbert. 'The son of Bretislav of Bohemia holds the western bank at Dresdany for our lord emperor, but the eastern shore is still denied to him – a messenger came in this morning. As our young friend here has said, the Liutizen still prowl about on the far shore.'

"So we sit on our backsides and wait?' snapped Otto, still burning from the earlier exchange.

'No,' replied sir Egbert. He looked tired, but there was a steely, even tone to his voice. 'What we do is to get off our backsides and look to the defence of what we still have.' He gestured towards an arrow slit: 'The folk down there are frightened, and rightly so. Most of them have lost a loved one because of this mess, and they look to us now to tell them what to do. And that does not mean, my lord Otto, rushing off into yonder forest for more of the same. It means: strengthening the walls, increasing the watch, and showing our lance-points on the ramparts.'

'Baring our teeth, then!' chuckled old Eadred, a warlord who had not yet spoken.

'Aye!' said Sir Egbert, and there was just the ghost of a smile about his lips. 'We bare our teeth, and hold this place, and pray for better days to come.'

'You did well,' said Peter the Tanner, as they made their way down towards the town, with Branulf trotting along behind them.

'You think so?'

'I know so! You stirred up that young cockerel, Otto, and stood your ground with his brother. Besides, Sir Egbert likes you, and that's a rare compliment in these parts, mark my words.'

Markward shrugged: 'I'm glad to be out of it.'

The sergeant laughed: 'Don't worry! We'll get you home soon enough. My Lady of Meissen has given me instructions – me! – that I am to go with you as far as the Weissburg, as soon as Bernhardt is able to travel.'

'That's good news!'

This time Peter threw back his head and roared with laughter: 'Hahah! Good news for you, maybe, but I tell you it did not go down well with my good wife. Brothilda – that's the name her parents cursed her with. She boxed my ears and told me as she hit me that I had no business to be off galavanting around the countryside when there was so much needing doing around the house.'

'I'm sorry.'

'Sorry? Pah! Think nothing of it! It's a fine plan, and my lovely wife loves me no less for it. Besides I've promised to bring her back some pretty ribbons from the market at Weissburg, and perhaps a trinket or two for our little Marga.' He laughed again, slapped Markward on the back and turned to wink at Branulf who was hurrying to catch up with the joke.

Five days later, with the mist rising over the river, and the sun streaming across the forest and the rooftops of Meissen, they set off. The bells were tolling, filling the morning air with their deep, hollow notes, and in the huddled churches of the town prayers were being said for the dead. When the gold and black banners were dipped on the castle walls, then all hope was given up that any more Meisseners might return from across the Elbe. There were rumours that some cavalry and a few fyrdsmen had managed to escape across the river south of Dresdany, but 'he who sows rumours must reap the facts,' said Peter, and no one had the spirit to argue with him.

It seemed a good day to leave, the more so because Bernhardt though scarred and less one hand, was able to sit a horse easily, and could even carry a shield over one shoulder and wear a sword at his hip. They all rode, even Branulf. The lady castellan had provided them with horses from her own stable, and had equipped them from the castle armouries. She had also given Markward a dirk that once belonged to her husband. It was intricately carved with a lion fighting a serpent.

'Remember me,' she had said, as she placed it in his hand.

They made good progress that day. The road was peaceful, though the way was warm and dusty. The grass grew thick and golden brown in the fields on either side of them, and they could see that the haymaking was long overdue, and knew the reason why. Dark shadowed deer wandered across their path, and once Branulf tried a shot, but they bounded away.

The heat rose in waves from the fields and meadows, and despite the turning of the seasons they were glad when the road led them into the shelter of a forest. Peter took off his leather cap and wiped his brow: 'There are outlaws in these parts', he said, 'And plenty of them, but they are hardly likely to try and chew on us, armed as we are.'

And so they went on, and camped for the night beneath the trees. They roasted a rabbit Branulf had shot with his bow, and talked little and slept much, and rode on in the morning.

At length they came to a part of the forest where the tall elms, chestnuts and oaks fell back, giving way to open groves of silver birch and berry bushes. The sunlight filtered through in pools of bright light, but the dusty road had gone, and they walked their horses across a soft carpet of fresh green grass and fallen leaves.

'I know these woods,' said Peter the Tanner. 'I hunted in them as a lad when my father came this way to sell skins to the folk of Muhlertal and the Weissburg. We would camp here, build a bothy, and go hunting for whatever we could find: rabbit, hare, deer and coney – anything.'

Bernhardt eased his horse back. 'It seems we must have passed this way when we marched to Dresdany, but it doesn't look familiar.'

'Same forest, different reach', replied Peter, 'but we'll strike the main path to the Weissburg soon enough: by nightfall at the latest.' He flicked the reins and was about to move on when there was a stirring of the undergrowth on both sides of the path and a group of armed men stepped out in front of them.

Markward's horse reared, nearly throwing him, while Branulf's danced sideways almost pinning him against a tree. Peter and Bernhardt swung their mounts to the edge of the path, and would have drawn their weapons, but several of the men raised their bows, with arrows nocked and made it clear that any attempt to resist would be fatal.

Their leader was a tall, swarthy man dressed in a grimy brigandine and tunic. He carried a broad sword, resting over one shoulder, while a buckler hung from his hip. He had a long scar over one eye.

'Get down,' he said simply.

They waited, glanced at one another, and then swung out of their saddles. Branulf caught his foot in the stirrup, and nearly fell, but grabbed hold of the bridle and mane just in time.

'Who taught you to break the King's Peace?' asked Peter staring at the men in front of him.

The leader of the band, laughed and spat, and brought his sword down from his shoulder in a careless sweep so that its point missed Peter's neck by a hand's breadth. 'The King's Peace! Here? In this forest? I am king here, and these are my liege men. This is my kingdom, and my law. What say you?'

'I say you are a brigand and a thief, and not fit for any law save the one that would hang you and all your villains from the nearest tree.'

The man's eyes blazed at Peter's insult, and his nostrils flared. He took a pace forward, and his grip tightened on his sword.

'My name is Aylward,' he said, his voice low and trembling. 'And now you will listen to me, and you will know why I am the law here.' He paused. 'I was born a peasant, and raised a peasant, and lived a peasant's life – and kept the king's law as faithfully as any man.'

This time he stopped, and looked away as though his anger might overwhelm him, and then went on: 'I watched a bad harvest and a grasping lord starve my father to death, and cripple my mother with sorrow. I and my brothers kept her, till the plague snatched her to the grave, and then we took our inheritance of the scraps of land the lord would allow us, and kept the ploughing and the sowing and the bringing in of the crops. We married, all three of us, and raised families in the teeth of the law which took the tenth, most of what we earned, and sometimes more than we could offer. But still, we kept the peace, and still we tugged our forelocks to the priest and lord, and still we were the king's good men.'

'And then?' asked Peter.

'And then, there came a day when the king's peace in all its glory came to our village. A wandering band of king's men off to the wars, or returning home – I know not what – came upon us, and took us unawares, and slew, and raped and pillaged, and at the last burnt what they could not carry, and then moved on. And we who were left, were left with nothing. Our lord was away somewhere serving his lord, and the priest scuttled off to hide in a monastery. We had nothing to do but bury our dead, and cry for our lost ones. So we took to this forest before the winter came and killed us all.'

'But when your lord returned?'

'Bah! When our lord returned, he fell into a rage to find his village ruined, and had us all declared outlaws and hunted us like we were deer or wild boar. That is until a lucky shot from Olaf here caught him in the gizzard and stopped his hunting days forever.' He gave a thin, dry laugh, and leaned on the pommel of his sword, studying the four travellers with an expert eye.

There was a long silence. At last Markward spoke:

'But we would pass,' he said, 'and in peace.'

'Aye, I guess you would, but first you will pay a toll because I am lord of this forest and the way ahead belongs to me.'

'We are as you once were, villagers, returning home with what is left of the imperial army that crossed the Elbe.'

'Are ye now? Well, more fool you for joining such a band of fools. Now come! Enough of this chatter. Pay the toll, and then take your leave as free men. You will go on your way lighter but happier, I'll warrant you.'

His men laughed, and eased the tension on their bows.

Markward looked at Peter. 'What do you think?'

The sergeant wrinkled his brow. 'I think we need to know the weight of the toll.'

'Gentlemen, I can help you', broke in the outlaw, with a broad, gap-toothed grin. 'If you three knight errants, and your young squire would care to present us with your horses, swords and mail shirts, then we will be pleased to let you pass.'

'Impossible!' roared Peter. 'You leave us with nothing!'

'I leave you with your lives – which is much more than you will have if you do not pay me now.' He gave a little nod, and those of his men who were armed with swords and clubs gave a kind of low growl and inched forward.'

'Hold!' It was Bernhardt.The leader of the outlaws, taken off guard, checked his men with a careless gesture, and then turned to the blacksmith: 'You would say something Sir One Hand , before I cut you down and leave you for the crows?'

Bernhardt smiled, but his voice shook, and more than once he stumbled over the words. 'I would say this: first, we have come far, and suffered much over these past months – and are therefore not likely to shame ourselves by giving way to men such as yourselves, no matter how keen your cause, and sharp your appetite for robbery. And second: I have someone I have longed to see and be with over many a lost day. I will not let you and your men come between me and this.'

'Oh, bravely spoken. Who taught you, a peasant's son, to mince such pretty words together? A beggar-priest perhaps – or some wandering friar.' He shrugged. 'But no matter, they will not save you.' For a moment he paused, then went on: 'But why should I delay the manner of your passing, since you have played the man and chosen death.'

Suddenly, Bernhardt who had stood watching him, with the palm of his hand turned out in sign of peace, moved, like a hawk against the sun. He whirled a hammer from his belt to his chest in a single lightning movement, and then rested it in the crook of his arm. It was though it had appeared by magic. One of the outlaws swore, and most stepped back apace.

'My knocker,' said Bernhardt quietly, his voice now steady. 'I am a blacksmith by my trade, and a king's man by my duty – and this is my knocker. I levelled near on a score of Liutizen with this beauty before they dragged me down, and I'll level any other man who comes between me and what is mine.'

Aylward the Outlaw blinked once, but held his ground. 'My men could kill you in an instant. One word from me, and six arrows in your chest – it's that simple.'

Bernhardt shrugged. 'Aye, maybe so, but you make one mistake, my friend: you are a fool's pace too close – and don't try to step back now. Before the arrows strike me down I will split you noggin to brisket, as smooth as a sweated pin. Just see if I don't.'

Aylward the Outlaw measured the gap with a single glance, and did not reply. With eyes ablaze he studied the blacksmith. No one else dared move. The birds sang in the branches above them, and the last bees of a late summer droned in the warmth of the day. And when at last one of the outlaws quietly began to bend his bow, a single glance from Bernhardt and a slight movement of the hammer made him release the tension once more.

'Well, here's a fine thing,' whispered Peter as if to himself. 'The day wears on and we are here, all of us, stood like loons in a parsnip field.'

Markward nodded, and looked sideways to see that Branulf was not about to do something reckless, but the boy was standing quite still, his eyes fixed on the outlaws in front of him.

They could all hear the rustling of the leaves as a light wind blew through the forest. It seemed strangely peaceful.

When it seemed to Bernhardt that enough time had passed to count a flock of sheep, Aylward spoke:

'You would strike me and die? I think you have much to lose.'

'I have no wish to die, and when I die I hope it comes as a relief, and not a disappointment. But if today is the day, then so be it, at least I will die well.'

Aylward shook his head, relaxed his grip on his sword, and grinned: 'You are too much for me, blacksmith. Such courage is madness, and such clerking chatter is the stuff of fools, but it does not deserve death, not at my hands. Besides, you have the measure of me with that hammer of yours, and you are not worth the headache. Go, be on your way, and don't look back lest I change my mind.' Then, waiting for a moment, he held out his hand, and Bernhardt, cradling the hammer, took it.

'Thank you, friend', Bernhardt said.

'You call an outlaw, friend?'

'I call a good man, friend', replied Bernhardt, and gently releasing his grip, grasped Aylward by the shoulder. 'There is too much of a good man in you to go round butchering innocent folk. Bad fortune and worse counsel may have driven you into the forest, but that has not changed the man you always were. You make a bad outlaw – there's too much honest blood in you. Go back to being a villager.'

'Ah, where do you find all these words? You prattle on like a Benedictine monk!'

Markward laughed: 'Aye! He has been called that before! If he wasn't a blacksmith shoeing horses and knocking hot iron blanks into hinges and plough-shares, he'd be the village priest.'

'Is that so?' said Aylward stepping back half a pace, 'Well I reckon ye have had a lucky escape, then. Such a priest would talk us all to death.' Markward grimaced but said nothing.

One of the horses whinnied and pawed the ground impatiently. There was a muttering among the other outlaws and some uneasy glances. 'Best be gone', grunted one of them. Aylward nodded, raised his hand in salute, and turning, led his men back into the shadowy green of the forest. In a short time all was quiet once more.

For a time they stood looking at the direction in which the outlaws had gone, then, beginning with Peter, one after the other they climbed back into the saddle and continued on their way. They had gone perhaps no more than five bowshots when Branulf said quietly, 'Lucky escape, that was.'

Bernhardt, riding just ahead, heard him, and turned in the saddle: 'Aye, it was – if by luck you mean the Grace of God.'

'You weren't afraid?'

'I thought we were all dead men. Never been so scared.'

'Not even in the shield wall.'

Bernhardt leaned in the saddle, and pushed a branch clear:

'Not even there. In battle you don't have time to think. That much I've learnt. It's shield on sword and sword on shield: all hammering and confusion. But today, it was different.'

'How so?'

Bernhardt sighed: 'It's this way: you have too much time to think when a fellow steps out in front of you, and points a bow at your heart. You feel fear, like a death-grip, the sort that can choke a man.'

Branulf came alongside Bernhardt as the path widened. 'I reckon you saved us', he said.

Bernhardt grunted: 'I reckon you think too much.'

'No, but you did.'

'I did nothing but stare at the man, and offer him some advice.' Bernhardt eased himself in the saddle, and gazed around. 'The forest is thinning all right. I reckon an hour's ride and we can make camp. Then it's just two more days to the Weissburg.' He surprised himself that he could read the forest so well. All his life in a village, and just three months on the march, and he could talk like a huscarl.

They made camp by a stream. The water ran fresh and clear over the bright pebbles, and young willows lined the grassy banks. As the sun crept down among the tree tops they lit a fire and cooked a carp Branulf had shot ('The luckiest shot I've ever seen', said Peter). The smoke hung in the still evening air and the smell of birch wood reminded them of home. Markward lay down, his head against his saddle and looked up at the fading sky. Soon, the Weissburg, too soon Eckerheim. He was eager to go home, and yet afraid to be there. He wanted to look down from the Tops and see the village and the long meadow beyond. He wanted to skim pebbles in the stream, and lean against the marker stone by the miller's fields and watch the children herd the milch cows. He wanted to feel safe again: to sit by a fire under thatch that did not drip rain and tell tall tales from who knows where, while little Albrecht looked up all wide-eyed, and Mutti smiled at him from her chair beside the hearth. All these things, all these things – and a little brown cup, there in the wallet beneath his hand. Little Brunni! When she had given him that cup, it was a simple world, and he was afraid to leave. Now the world had changed and he was afraid to return.

A branch snapped, and he instinctively turned his head: Bernhardt was breaking wood for the fire, bracing one end under his foot and bending the other with his hand. He looked tired, but the grey pallor of fever had long since gone, and there was a brightness about him.

'You dug us out of a hole back there, Berni.'

'I dug myself', said Bernhardt, surprised to hear the familiar form of his name. 'My mind was empty of everything except Eckerheim.'

Markward propped himself up on one elbow. 'It's not Eckerheim you want.' There was the faintest of edges in his voice, but Bernhardt chose to ignore it: 'People make places, Markward. They always have. I want Eckerheim for its people, not its fields.'

'And one of those people in particular?'

'Aye, perhaps.' Bernhardt threw the sticks on the fire and watched them blaze while Branulf turned the spitted fish. The wind had dropped and the smoke and sparks from the fire whirled upwards to the tree tops. Peter the Tanner was standing on the edge of the clearing, his back to them, etched out against the evening sky. He would take first watch, and then sleep until the last quarter of the night. Today had troubled him, and driven him from the camp fire: he, the sergeant, a citizen of Meissen and a chosen man. Back there on the road, he had stood, jaw dropped and empty headed, while a one armed blacksmith from some poor, flea-hut village had snatched the day. How could it be? Perhaps his wife was right. Perhaps he was too old for soldiering. Perhaps it was time to return to the tanner's vats and the steaming skins.

He brushed an insect away from his face, and listened to the stream running across the pebbles. It would be a good night to keep watch, calm and clear with no hint of rain, and no need to talk to anyone.

He turned as he heard a footstep behind him. It was Bernhardt. The blacksmith came and stood beside him and stared into the shadows.

'Will you eat?' asked Bernhardt.

'I will keep watch.'

'And then?'

'Save me some.'

Bernhardt nodded. 'Two more days to the Weissburg, and then you can be going home to your family.'

Peter shook his head: 'If it wasn't for you, I would not be going anywhere.'

Bernhardt grunted and looked down at his feet. 'If it wasn't for you, I'd never have dared to taunt that fellow.'

Peter looked across at him but said nothing.

'It's true', said Bernhardt, and turning, walked back to the fire.

The following day a horseman rode across the Tops and took the main trackway down to the village of Eckerheim. His horse was lathered in sweat and snorted with relief as it sensed that the journey was nearly over. Despite the cooler weather, it was a hard ride from the Weissburg, and his lord had told him to go with all speed. He was on his way to Fulda, but first he had to bring the news to all the villages and hamlets of the Mark that had sent men to the imperial army.

As he cantered across the outer fields, his pennon flapping in the breeze, folk who were bent and stooped to their toil, straightened up and gazed at him. One or two waved, but mostly they stood stock still and stared. They knew who he must be, and what that pennon meant. He stopped and asked for the bailiff. The bailiff was in the South Meadow – a young lad with a dog pointed him the way, and then ran after the horseman, shouting to friends and anyone who would listen. There were women by the well, and as he rode by they broke off their work and chatter, and watching him, huddled together as though a shadow had swept over them. He walked his horse through the village, and then led it across the little stream and into the South Meadow. There was a tall man, dark and angular, standing in the shade of a beech tree, looking out over the meadow. He saw the horseman and waved a greeting, then began to trudge towards him.

'Well met!' he called, 'I am Eric of Eckerheim, bailiff to this village and to my Lord of Weissburg.'

They approached and shook hands.

'And I am Carl of Meissen, messenger to my lady of Meissen.'

Eric's face fell. 'Your lady of Meissen, not your . . .?'

'My lord is dead, as is yours.' The messenger paused as he saw the weight of his news strike home. And then he went on. 'They fell in the great forest beyond the Elbe. They, and nearly all of the imperial army.'

Eric looked at the fresh-faced young knight with his cropped blond hair and pale blue eyes: 'All of the army?'

'No, not all. Some will have made it back home. It cannot be that all have fallen – there is news from the south - but at the moment we know of only three for sure who survived from the Meissen and the Weissburg musters: two men and a boy, and one of them badly injured.' He held up his hand, as if he knew what Eric was about to ask: 'I cannot tell you from what village. One was a captain, and two from among the levies of Saxony and the Harzland.'

For a time Eric could not speak. At last he spoke:

'All gone!' He walked a few paces, and sat down heavily on a headland. 'This cannot be!'

'I fear it is true. Those who returned brought back what seems to be a faithful account. They say it was a slaughter. Knights, lords, levy, all destroyed, all lost in one battle. In the forest.'

Eric put one hand to his brow then looked up. 'That means we have lost ten good men, no, with Markward, eleven. Eleven families! Dear God! We are crushed! – and this after the fight at Christmastide – and all the losses there, and some from Hochtal too. From Hochtal!'

'I know. You have suffered much. They told me at the Weissburg.'

'And so you came.'

'And so I was sent. Bringing news of defeat from here to Fulda and back to the Weissburg.' The knight frowned at his own words, and bowed his head. 'What men feared, and feared to talk of, they now will know. It is a heavy duty.'

Eric stood up. 'And a weary one, no doubt. You have ridden hard and long, I can see that – and I am forgetting my duties as a host. Come! We will go back to the village and find you food and shelter and stabling for your horse. Then, I will gather the people.'

Carl of Meissen gestured towards the village: 'See! They are gathering already.'

It was Branulf who saw the Weissburg first. He had ridden ahead, knees working furiously and elbows flapping, to see if there was any sign of the deer they had spotted in the first flush of dawn. He rounded a bend in the forest track and came out upon a low rise where the road crested against the top of an open bluff. There beneath him, in the early morning light were the shining battlements and towers of the great white fortress. He gave a yelp of joy, and turned to shout the news, but the others were not yet in view. Steadying his horse, Branulf moved to the edge of the bluff.

The track had now become a dusty road, plunging away down into the valley, twisting and winding until it was lost among a distant grove of trees. There were still some miles to travel, but the air was so clear that the castle and village seemed to lie within a bowshot. Everything was so bright and open and good to his eye. He wanted to throw back his head and sing – but he quickly told himself that he would be laughed at for a girl.

Instead he turned the horse's head about, set his heels to its flanks, and galloped back the way he had come, shouting, 'The Weissburg! The Weissburg!'

He tore around the bend, and nearly crashed pell mell into Peter, swerving just in time and skittering to a halt in a cloud of dust and stones.

The horse, reared up, and threw Branulf neatly into a juniper bush. He emerged, unscathed except for a few scratches, still shouting 'The Weissburg'.

Laughing, the others gathered him up, rescued his horse which had trotted away a short distance and headed off towards the bluff.

Once there, they too stood and stared at the landscape that fell away beneath their feet. For a time he gazed silently out over the valley. Peter suggested that they make camp there, but Markward said it was far too early in the day, and the Weissburg was well within reach. 'By the third quarter at the most', he said as he climbed into the saddle.

Hours later, beyond the third quarter, the silent streets of the village opened up to meet them, and they rode quietly along between the crowded houses and barns and bothies. There was no need to pause — they were intent on reaching the castle which towered above them — but Peter leaned out of his saddle to scratch the head of a shaggy grey hound that came bounding up to meet them, and Markward returned the vague salute of a beaming, broad-bellied innkeeper who seemed to recognise him.

It was late in the afternoon, the sun was warm against their faces, and the last of the earlier clouds had been sent scudding away by the fresh September breeze. As they left the village and took the steep winding path, the castle gleamed and shimmered against the northern sky. Its towers and walls seemed impregnable, and though there were fewer banners and pennons on the wall than they had earlier remembered, the massive gateway was well guarded by two tall, broad-shouldered men at arms, dressed in oiled and polished mail, and bearing the shoulder to calf kite-shields of the Weissburg lords.

As they neared the gates, one of the guards shaded his eyes and peered at them. He said something hurriedly to his companion, and then called out:

'Ho, there! Markward! Markward of Eckerheim!'

Markward, surprised, at first did not reply. The guard came forward and called again: 'It is you! Markward! Back from Liutizenland! You're alive!' He slipped his shield from his shoulder, tossed his spear to the other guard, and took Markward by the hand.

There was grinning, and laughing and slapping of backs. Several other soldiers appeared from the inner guard-house, and a few servants bustling about their duties, headed across the courtyard to see what all the fuss was about. It was some time before Peter the Tanner was able to bring his companions before the castellan in the great hall. There, they explained yet again what had befallen the army even though they well knew that the old warlord who sat before them and listened so patiently, was keenly aware of all that had happened even before they opened their mouths. Still, as he gruffly assured them, it was always best to hear the worst from those who had seen it at first hand. When they had finished their story, he nodded gravely, thanked them for their care and courage, and waved them off to the trencher boards where a meal of bread, cheese, salt pork and rough red wine awaited them.

They set to hungrily, eating in silence, and watched by a whispering group of servants, retainers and idle kitchen hands. Some of the maids had come in from the laundry, and were peering around the doorway, hoping for a glimpse of the travellers and giggling to find most of them so young.

As soon as they could, they asked leave to find lodgings in one of the hostelries in the village. Markward reported to the captain of the guard and honoured the warrant of his feudal oath to continue serving as a soldier of the Weissburg. He made his mark against the rolls of enlistment kept by the castle scribe – a nervous young clerk had taken the place of the chaplain who had died alongside his lord – and promised to report for duty once more after he had been to see his family in Eckerheim.

'Ten days, and no more', muttered the captain, scratching his beard, 'We're short of men as it is, and you will be needed to knock our new recruits into shape. Some of them have apple seed for brains and straw for sinew. Never seen a sword either, most of 'em.'

Markward nodded and smiled his thanks before backing away and heading down the guard-house steps before the captain could change his mind. He found the others gathered on the far side of the courtyard, chatting to some pedlars who had come up from the town. They asked them to point the way to a good inn, and set off down the slope as the last of the sun sank behind the western ridge.

THE HOMECOMING

In the morning they set off for Eckerheim. A grey, drifting drizzle limped in over the far pass and began to fold across the valley.

As they left the village and castle behind them, the path steepened and stretched out over the open fields and moorland. The lowering clouds swirled about them in drenching mists, and their cloaks were soon heavy and sodden. They bent their heads and said less and less until even the restless, chattering Branulf fell silent.

Peter the Tanner had agreed to go with them as far as the high cairn which marked the top of the pass. For a time he had thought of going onto to Eckerheim, but he had already come far, and he knew that his family would be worried. Besides, it was market day in the Weissburg. Even as Peter and the others had left the village, the stalls were being set up and traders were shouting their wares. There would be buying and selling until sunset, and then the market folk would make ready to leave early the following day. He had found group of merchants who were bound for Meissen and he was keen to travel with them. Until then he would wander through the market, and see what his few copper coins might buy to make his good wife smile, and his little girl laugh and clap her hands.

An hour later they reached the high cairn. They stood in the mist and said their farewells. Peter gave a half smile and an awkward salute, then turning his horse rode away back down into the valley. Markward watched him go until he was lost in the gloom, then he too turned and led Bernhardt and Branulf across the narrow ridge and onto the track that led to Eckerheim.

Katrin leant against the trunk of the old beech tree, and teased the lambswool apart with her fingers. Behind her, the sun was dipping below the Tops, and pushing shadows across the fields and meadows. She missed her Lukas. Every evening when the weather was fair, she came to this tree, and looked towards Hochtal, and every evening she missed her Lukas more and more, and loved him as she always had. Eckerheim was now her home. Hochtal was no more. The Liutizen had seen to that. She sighed, and wound the wool onto the distaff, and began to spin it. She missed Lukas so badly, but there was nothing to be done. Lukas was gone, along with all the others who had fallen in the fighting. And now news had come of the loss of the Army, and the loss of the Levy – all beyond the Elbe. And so there would be yet more widows and fatherless children in Eckerheim.

The distaff spun and the wool teased, and her fingers worked tirelessly among the threads. She had a place here in this village, but not a hearth she could call her own, and not a man to cook for and tend to, and feel his warmth next to her on long winter nights. She simply lodged. In the corner of a cruck. It was warm, it was dry and the folk were kind to her, but it was not her own. And she knew come Spring that she would have to move on, and find another family who could give her lodging.

She needed a man to care for her, but who? There was a man that she had been drawn to – had admired him for his strength, and courage, and quiet ways – but she could never love him because he was promised to another. And besides, he had gone with the levy.

The distaff slipped from her hand, and fell among the ferns at the base of the tree. She stooped and picked it up. The wool was flecked and spotted with dirt and fragments of leaves. She cleaned it, taking care over every strand, and was surprised by a few tears that fell and stained the grey white fibres.

The light was fading fast, and she knew that she must get back to the cruck to help with the evening meal. Tomorrow, she and Helga would sit at the loom, but this evening they must cook for the men come in from the fields. There would be lentils, salt pork and cabbage, as well as some herbs from the cottar's garden.

As Katrin came down the path towards the village she caught sight of Elspeth walking with little Hetti. They were going slowly, Elspeth, head bent, talking to the girl who trotted along beside her. Elspeth had lost her man, and a good man too, and they were not yet wed. Elspeth and Rainald – betrothed and never to be wed. And there, little Hetti with her father gone. Elsa too had lost her man. All gone, and so hard to bear. Sorrow upon sorrow, and Autumn fast upon them, and the harvest not yet in.

There was a chill damp in the air. It seemed to rise up from the very ground. Katrin pulled her shawl close about her and hurried on. The village stared at her out of the gloom, the heavy thatched roofs, and plastered walls crowding the shadows and huddling about the hollow streets and alleys.

Sorrow: she had seen it in Elspeth's eyes. And courage too. Elspeth had even tried to smile when they stood at the moot and heard the knight from Meissen, but it was a poor smile, and then the tears had come and she had had to turn away. And so it was for all of them, and poor Eric the bailiff in the midst, standing not knowing what to do or say, and the young knight hesitant, head bowed, and eager to be on his way. Mutti alone had not cried, but she drew Albrecht to one side and knelt down and wrapped her arms about him and kissed him on the head.

Elsa, Helga, all of them besides, stood silently, save Branulf's mother who fell moaning to her knees, pulled her shawl over her head and sobbed, and cried out and clawed at the ground.

Some of the children had wept too, some had clung confused to their mothers, others had hesitated, then ran off to play. Little Brunni just shook her head, brushed her long brown hair back across her shoulders and stood stock still. Even when nearly everyone had gone, starting with the menfolk, and the moot was long over and the knight departed to horse and lodgings, Brunni remained standing. She refused to move, despite all the coaxings, and only left when Mutti came at the last, and whispered in her ear, and led her away.

But that was two days ago, and now all that they could do was bury their grief and get ready for the harvest. The corn was in, and a good crop too, but never enough. And now came the wheat harvest ripening late in the changeable weather. It was full and golden white against the Autumn skies, and in any other year the village would have been pleased to sharpen sickles and scythes and hasten to the fields, but with ten good men and their captain gone it would be a cruel, hard harvest, and Eric would have to drive them from dawn to dusk.

Katrin sighed as she made her way down the dark and mud-dried street, lit only by the faint glow from cooking fires filtering through the sackcloth curtains and ill hung doors. The heavy smell of boiled cabbage and farmyard dung mingled with the smoke of evening. Here and there, she heard snatches of mumbled conversations and the shouts of children drifting on the acrid air. A sudden loneliness surged against her, rising up out of the gloom and making her stagger for just a moment. She hesitated, then went onto her cruck which stood on the corner of the main street, and the cramped and twisting alley that led to the glebe. Pushing back the curtain, she went inside.

There was bustle and heady warmth that made her smile despite herself. Helga looked up from her stool beside the cooking pot, and beckoned her in.

'Come, lass!' she said, 'There's work to do, and all the time to do it.'

She paused and studied Katrin: ' Are ye low still?'

Katrin nodded, and put the distaff and wool to one side. 'It's nothing', she said.

'Aye, and everything', replied Helga. 'Still, we'll carry it all of us, won't we just.' She winked at Katrin who smiled in return, and tucked her hair up under her scarf.

Together, they set to chopping the herbs fine and throwing them in the pot. Soon, they were chatting about good and little things: tutting over the children, and giggling over the silly quarrels or fey remarks that always buzzed about the village well and washing stones.

In a while the men and boys would come trudging along the street from the fields, and already they could hear the sounds of laughter as the young girls chased the chicks and ducks up from the water meadow.

It was harvest day. The sun shone but with less strength now, and it was time for harvest. Already some of the women were in the fields. Already Eric had called the men together. They stood and looked over the crop yet again. Then, at a word from Eric they set to work.

Elsa, who had been baking bread since before the dawn, came late to the West Field. She nodded at the other women, stooped and put her sickle to the grain. For a while she worked, head down, slowly settling into a steady rhythm. It was going to be a long day. Then something made her glance up. Little Albrecht was just visible on the heather hill below the high ridge. He was waving, jumping, half-rolling, slipping and sliding down the slope. The faintest of cries came to her on the east wind as he shouted. Down he came. Down and down. Nearer and nearer. And all at once she saw: there!

Etched out on the ridge against the silver blue sky: three men on horses. No, two! Two men and a boy. She could tell it was a boy – shorter, and slouching in the saddle, not used to the height and weaker in the knees. Two men and a boy! Two men! And one rode as a soldier!

Her heart leapt. She dropped the sickle with a sob and ran. Picked up her skirts and ran as fast as she could across the field. Someone called after her, and she half-turned, almost tripped and pointed wildly in the direction of the ridge. She ran on, brushing through the wheat, her bare feet flying over the stones and clods of earth. Almost before she knew it she was at the low straggling hedge that marked the boundary of the harvest field. She burst through it, her heart pounding, and her hair tumbling from beneath her scarf. There were shouts now, men and women, their voices seeming far away, and for a moment she thought she heard the bailiff's loud call.

Albrecht had reached the bottom of the slope, a brace of bowshots ahead of her. He plunged into a ditch of brambles, and then emerging, veered towards her, crashing through a spinney of young birchwood. Too breathless to shout, he was still waving his arms. But Elsa's eyes were on the ridge. Two men and a boy! Surely not! It could never be. Not after all this time. In all the levies. In all the imperial host. From all of Saxony and beyond. She staggered to a halt, staring and staring. The rich dark colours of the folding heather had swallowed up the riders as they descended the ridge and headed for the lower slopes. She forced down any hope inside her, dared not to hope, snatching at any other story that might make the sudden truth less cruel.

Suddenly Albrecht was beside her, wide-eyed, and gasping out the words:

'It's them, Elsi! It's them! They're home! They're home! Marki, Bernhardt, Branulf! They're home!'

Elsa reeled. The ground seemed to lurch beneath her feet, and she reached out to Albrecht, who grabbed her, and shouted out again: 'Elsi! Elsi! They're home!'

All the village now streamed across the fields, the dogs barking and bounding ahead as they scented the excitement.

Elsa held Albrecht tight, and wept and wept, as she waited and watched, and let the others pass by, some tripping and stumbling in their haste, some trampling the crop, and being roundly bellowed at by Eric. Ulrich the priest came hurrying up, hesitated, put a hand on her shoulder, and then went on with the rest of the villagers. And Cedric, and Hec Haraldsson left their flocks on the lee meadow, and made their across to join the welcome.

But Elspeth did not move. She stood alone with little Hetti at the edge of the village. The names of those come home had drifted in on the cool east wind, and Rainald's name was not among them. She knelt down and hugged Hetti, and told her not to cry, and said tomorrow was another day, and the Good Lord could yet bring her father home. Over and over again, she said it.

For all the village, with joy there had come sorrow. Eric called the moot. All came, and all stood patiently in the pale sun and slight drizzle. Bernhardt, Branulf and Markward stood in their midst and told as best they could of all that they had seen and done. The elders grunted and nodded, then frowned as elders do, and one by one asked the questions that none could answer: Who else had survived? Where were the Liutizen now? What of the king? And who will rule the Mark?

Eric sighed, and frowned, as he always did, then declared the moot closed. With his voice raised he reminded the people that there was still much work to be done before the feasts of Christmastide: the wheat harvest was to be brought in, and there was a good measure of ground to be broken up and new seed to be sown.

The villagers returned to the fields and the harvest, and each day they looked less and less to the Tops. The weather held.

The Death of a King

They were standing, both of them, by the marker stone at the head of the long meadow.

Elsa looked at Markward, fighting back the tears and willing him to look up at her. 'Will you not stay?' she asked.

'I cannot.'

'Cannot or will not?'

Slowly, he raised his head and gazed at her with tired eyes. 'Elsa, you know what has happened. You know how many died and how few of us are left. The Weissburg is all but defenceless.'

'And us, Markward – here in Eckerheim. What is to become of us? How many of us failed to come home?'

He sighed and nodded wearily. 'It's true, but without the Weissburg no one will ever survive in Eckerheim. The Markgraf is dead, and Sir Hubert too, and all of his best men. Knights, sergeants, captains, men at arms, all gone down in those marshes and woods.'

'And so they call you back. And the spirits of the fallen call to your conscience. But what of the living? Your place is here. Stay with us, Marki. Stay and make your home here. The people of the Weissburg will find soldiers enough. The bishop of Magdeburg and Ludwig of Meissen's sons will see to that. Stay here. It's your home. Here with Mutti, and Brunni and little Albrecht.'

'And with you?' He looked into her eyes, and his voice faltered. She returned his gaze for just a moment, then lowered her gaze. 'I am promised to Bernhardt, Marki – you know that.'

He was silent, standing, arms at his sides, fists clenching and unclenching. He longed to take her in his arms and hold her tight and tell her how much he cared for her, and promise her the world, but . . .

'I know, Elsi, I know. He's a good man, and I brought him home to you.'

'As he would have brought you, had he found you dying in a forest', she answered quickly.

He sighed again, and half turned to go, then turning back took half a pace towards Elsa. His heart was pounding now, and he could hardly breath. He swallowed hard: 'If Bernhardt had died, if he had not come home . . .'

Elsa did not answer. She could feel the tears on her cheeks. At last, hesitating, she spoke: 'But he came home, Marki. He came home. And you brought him home, God bless you for it! And now you are leaving.'

'And can you care for me still?'

She burst into tears and turned away, staring back towards the village. He stood, all hollowed out, fighting for something to say. But there was nothing. He was alone.

It seemed to Elsa as if minutes passed. And then all at once a sudden fierce joy rose up inside her, and at last she knew. She whirled around, smiling, then laughing through her tears: 'Marki!'

But there was no reply. He had gone, striding away across the meadow, head down, fists clenched, arms swinging at his side: a faint figure against the Autumn sky.

'Marki!'

She watched him go, and softly called, but he didn't hear her. All that Markward heard was the sound of his own breathing, and his boots swishing through the long grass, and the sheep answering the shepherds as they streamed down off the long, low ridge.

An hour later, he had ridden out of Eckerheim with Little Albrecht trotting beside him, hanging onto the stirrup, until his mother called him home.

By the time Elsa came back to the village and made her way to Mutti's cruck, Markward had long since cleared the tops, and the sun was in the eleventh hour.

She entered the cruck and sat down by the fire. Mutti put down her distaff and came and sat beside her. For a long time neither of them spoke. Outside they could hear Brunni and Albrecht playing with one of the dogs.

'What do I do, Mutti?'

'You marry. That's what we all do. You marry for a roof over your head, soup in the pot, and a man to care for your little ones.'

'Is that all?'

'Is there more, you mean? Aye, there's love. You can marry for love, and that's a fine thing, but faint hope these days for most lassies. Forget your Tristan and Isolde. No ballads in Eckerheim!' Mutti gave a short laugh, and leaned over and stirred the great pot that hung over the fire. 'It's the parents who make the marriages, and the children who suffer them. Still, you do the best you can. Markward's father was a fair enough man, and I loved him more than most, though neither of us could say we chose each other. It was family, you see. His father, my father. His father's land and my father's oxen. An arrangement. The priest said the vows, and there we were, man and wife.'

Elsa took her head scarf off and shook out her hair. 'Why did he go, Mutti?'

'Markward, you mean? He's a man that's why, and sometimes men get an idea in their heads and they can't shake it loose. He should have been a farmer, but he made himself a soldier, and that's that. He's a fool to himself but he's a good man, though I say so myself, and one day he may make some poor girl happy.'

The laughter and the barking from outside grew fainter. 'The old hound has seen a rabbit', said Mutti and she smiled.

Elsa moved closer to the fire and poked it with a stick so that sparks swirled around the pot. 'I should marry Bernhardt', she said.

'You marry Bernhardt, you marry a good man. He will care for you with his one arm and his one eye better than most men with all their bits and pieces.'

'He is a good man, Mutti. I do love him.' She brightened.

'Well then?'

'But Markward . . .'

'Ah, that son of mine! Is that your heart I hear young Elsa, or is that your head, or perhaps . . .'

Elsa blushed and stood to the pot over the fire. 'I will marry Bernhardt, Mutti. I will!'

That evening, with supper done, and all the folks abed, and the flocks all quiet, Elsa went down to the stream, and the washing stone, and stood watching the moon as it lifted over the dark high ridge. Bernhardt found her there, and came and stood beside her. She looked up at him, and smiled, and took his hand, and turned to the moon once more.

'When we are married Berni, we must come here lots and look up at the moon.'

Bernhardt squeezed her hand. 'Elsa.'

'Yes?'

'We need to talk.'

'We're talking now, Berni.' She laughed.

'I know, Elsi, but . . .'

'But what Berni?'

'It's Markward.'

'Markward has gone.'

'No Elsa.'

'Yes, he has. He has gone. He went this afternoon. Surely you know that!' Her voice rose and she began to tremble.

For a time neither of them spoke, then Bernhardt brushed Elsa's hair back where it fell across her cheek. 'He'll never leave you Elsa. When you gave your pledge to me, you never forgot him.'

'What are you saying, Berni?' Her voice rose, full of uncertainty.

'You turned to me out of sorrow, because you thought he had stopped loving you.'

'No, Berni.'

'And you agreed to marry me, because I wanted to marry you – but with Markward there was always something deeper, much deeper, and stronger.'

Elsa opened her mouth to say something, but Bernhardt put a finger to her lips. 'No, please. Let me say on. You love Markward in spite of yourself, and in spite of all those things you saw in him that hurt you, and confused you and made you shout and want to hit him. From the very first I saw it, and tried to forget it, but it has always been there. You loved him and you love him still. He's your man.'

'No Berni, I have chosen you. Markward has gone.' For the second time that day tears began to run down Elsa's cheeks, and she brushed them angrily away. 'We will be married Berni. The priest will marry us and say the blessing and . . .'

'Elsi! Listen to me! Listen to me now . . .'

Four days later, at the morning watch, a guard on the ramparts of the Weissburg noticed a woman standing quite still in front of the main gate. She was looking up at the high tower and gave no heed to the folk who pushed by her on their way in and out of the castle. When his watch had ended, he noticed that she was still there and pointed her out to the sergeant of the guard. The sergeant leaned out over the battlements, studied her for a while and then spat casually onto the glacis. 'Leave her there', he said. 'She's no harm – probably mad as a March hare, but no harm. Pity though, she's a good looker even if her brains are scrabbled.'

When the trumpet sounded for the gates to be closed that evening the woman was still waiting. The guards on the gates had ignored her for much of the day, but finally one of them called out to her. She glanced at them but didn't reply, and stayed where she was. They cursed her idly, and laughed, and then the great gates closed. And still she stood.

'That madwoman is still out there', remarked the sergeant as they sat at meat in the guardhouse. 'What madwoman?' asked Markward. The sergeant laughed, tore off a piece of bread and dipped it in his beer.

'You haven't heard, captain? She's been out there all day, at the front gate. A young girl in a blue kirtle. Good looking too, with hair like flame. But if she doesn't go home soon the priest will take her for a witch and then there'll be trouble.' He wiped his beard with the back of his hand, and belched.

Markward looked up from his trencher of salt pork and bread. 'Hair like flame, you say?'

'Aye', replied the sergeant. 'as red a head as you're like to see in these parts', and he turned again to his meal.

Markward thought for a moment, then pushed the bench back and got slowly to his feet.

'I think I'll take a look around', he said.

When he reached the ramparts above the gate the sun had dipped behind the castle. Deep shadows fell across the entrance way and the woman, standing all alone, was only just visible. But Markward knew in an instant. He fled down the stairs from the wall-walk to the bailey, and ran to the gateway, almost colliding with a servant girl carrying water from the castle well. 'The footgate!' he called to the sentries. 'Open, now!'

'But captain!' They scrambled to attention. One dropped his spear.

'Now, I say!' Startled, they hurried to his command, and he pushed through the gate as they slid the bolts and raised the bar.

She was standing in front of him, slightly swaying, tired and drawn, but her eyes shining. He took a step forward

'I never thought you'd come', he said.

'I always knew . . . I always knew you would!' she replied. As she fell he caught her in his arms.

In Goslar the great bells of the cathedral boomed out over the crowded rooftops of the town.

Henry Salian, third king of that line, and Emperor of all Germany and the lands beyond, saddled his horse assisted by a lone groomsman, and rode out through the gates of the Bodfeld palace and up into the hills towards the woods. A chill wind blew against him, and dark clouds gathered over the tops. It was late in the day, a storm was coming and the good people of Bodfeld and Goslar were hurrying to their homes. But their king rode out and up into the woods alone. And as he rode the rain began to fall, at first a few small drops driven on the wind, then larger, heavier drops that pattered down around him. As he crested the first ridge and cleared the swaying pines the storm broke around him and the rain lashed down in torrents. In a moment he was soaked. He reined his horse in, and watched shivering as the thunder clouds boiled and shook across the ridges.

'What is my reign?' he thought to himself.' And what will men say of it, long after I have gone? They will say it was a reign of storms, plagues, fire and famine. Of failed harvests and sudden floods. Of misery and want. Enough to crack the heart of a king. That's what men will say and monks will write it down.'

He clicked his tongue, and turned his horse's head against the weather.

His mind drifted back to the recent visit of the pope to Bodfeld. Surely that would have been enough to open a window of blessing on this trembling kingdom. It had cost him a fortune! Surely that glittering entourage of prelates, priests and acolytes weighed down with a hundred of the finest holy relics Christendom could buy was enough to turn away the wrath of God.

And yet – a flash of lightning startled the hills, and the thunder crashed about him – and yet, even with all that relic and religion, still more trouble had broken through from the East. Today, news had come from a tattered, horse-spent messenger that his army, his own imperial army had been slaughtered in the forests beyond the Elbe.

The darkness deepened, and the rain swept across the ridges above Goslar in quickening curtains of grey murk.

Staring into it, he thought of the campaigns he had fought over the years: He had lost battles, and he had lost skirmishes, but he had never lost an army. It was a defeat that no amount of relics and wealth and papal blessing could ever cup. He had been defeated. He, the most powerful king in Christendom, had been defeated and hurled back by the barbarian tribes that lay to the East. A sudden pain rose in his chest.

He rode on, against the wind. His cloak hung heavy across his shoulders. His gambeson and tunic, already chill and wet clung to his back.

An army lost!

The rain came down and fell on hair and eyes and skin like arrows on a dying army. It mingled with the tears – the tears of a king – and the rage and sorrow poured out of his soul as the rain streamed down his cloak and across the flanks of his horse. Gone, all gone! All gone down in the lands beyond the Elbe. And all the more pity that he had not gone down with them. As a king should.

He kept riding, head down, on into the teeth of the storm, eastwards across the clouded ridges of the Harzland. Slowly, he felt the fever rise in his chest and grip his heart and throat, and spread across his brow. He knew he must turn back, but blind despair and anger drove him on, even though his horse now staggered and slipped against glistening stones and roots.

The Markgraf of Weissburg was gone, and all but a handful of his knights. The Marches were now defenceless before the Liutizen hordes. He shouted into the wind and hurled his horse down a streaming slope. It stumbled, recovered, stumbled again and slithered through the glistening bracken. His horsemanship held. Somewhere in the midst of his darkness, he remembered what the old knight from Karnthen had taught him all those years ago, and kept to his saddle and rode the last few yards to the base of the slope.

He found himself in a sheltered, grassy fold, hard against the lee of the storm lashed ridge. It was strangely quiet, almost calm and peaceful beneath the howling sky. He breathed deeply, and leant forward in the saddle and patted his horse's neck. The rain was whirling down, but it no longer beat and buffeted him. He would wait here until the storm had passed. Soon it would pass. It would pass and he would ride home, back up the slope, and along the ridge and down through the crowded woods to Goslar. And from there to Bodfeld. He was shivering now with the cold, and the old enemy tightening was its fingers on his throat and chest. Was this how a king dies?.

Home now! Back to his dear Agnes! She would be worrying about him. How she worried these days. Agnes – the sweet princess he had married all those years ago at Besancon. Agnes – daughter of that gruff old duke of Aquitaine. What a wedding! All those jongleurs and jugglers crowding through the doors of the palace. And he, young king that he was, had sent them all away. Too severe! Far too severe. And how they had frowned at his solemn Salian ways. Still the old duke had just looked up from his wine, and shrugged and laughed, and so the moment died.

The rain was easing. The storm in its fury was scudding away to the west. He shook out his cloak, and began to ride back up the slope. The pain increased: sharp, burning, coursing through his chest. Was it muscle, was it deeper? The doctors couldn't say, wouldn't say. But still they fed him foul tasting herbal soups and told him to stay off his horse and keep to his bed. Madness! He a king, and an emperor too. Shut up in bed and hiding away in a chamber when he should be . . .

He reached the top of the slope, and at last the pain eased. The storm had passed, he could see now, and there was a pale light forcing its way through the rolling clouds. Back to the palace. The army was gone, the Markgraf was gone, but he was still king, and the people would be looking to him. Now, more than ever he must be a king. Now, more than ever he must be the man his father taught him to be, and his mother feared he might become. Her gentle Henry: too little steel in his soul, too much mercy in his heart. A priest king, not a warrior king. Still, he had fought his battles, and won a good few besides. And he could swear and spit with the rest of them around the camp fires on the march.

He made his way back along the ridge until he could see the roof tops of Goslar far below in the valley. The day was dying, but there was life in it yet. As in this king. God willing he would make it back to the palace yard at Bodfeld before the night closed in.

Markward and Elsa were married on a fine autumn day in October. They stood under the great spreading oak where the village elders met, and they said their vows before the young priest. All of Eckerheim was there, and a good number of the folk from the Weissburg. The sons of the Markgraf came, and there was even a company of horsemen from Meissen who came bearing greetings from Ludwig's widow. They also came with the news that all was quiet along the Elbe, and all those of the Lost Army that could come home had come home. But the king was dead, of a fever, on the fifth day of the month in Goslar.

Far away in Magedeburg, in the bishop's palace, in the great hall, while the fire crackled in the grate, and the priests and nobles listened, heads lowered, the minstrel sang a lament for the lost army:
'And the soldiers fell like leaves in the lands beyond the Elbe,
And lay them down in driven heaps
Across the forest floor.
Stripped and plundered and left for wolves
Until the passing days whitened all their bones.
And in the proud halls of every Liutizen clan
The rafters rang with the songs of victory
And the joy of men come home to their loved ones.
Their feasts were full of sweet new wine
And horns of beer golden with honey.
But on the western banks of the Elbe
In the Saxon lands
From Dresdany to Meissen, from the Weissburg to Leipzig
Folk drank a bitter cup with shaking hand
And cursed the day a Salian prince had called all Saxony to the muster.'

The sun had mellowed with the early days of October, but at last, with the chills and frosts of November no more than fourteen nights away, the wheat harvest was gathered into the barns and storehouses of Saxony and the Harzland. It had been a long, weary harvest. There were fewer men to work the fields, and the women gleaned hard to see off the bitter months of the short, sharp winter that the wise folk promised.

In Eckerheim the men and women gathered as they had always done to hear the bailiff call the people to the fields for the Autumn planting. There were less for the bailiff to look upon, but there were enough, and the hope was that the rains would come early next year, and the Spring lambs would miss the snow.

And then, a day of great joy in Eckerheim: Rainald came home.

He wandered in over the Tops and down into the valley. He came as though he had been out for no more than a day's hunting, crossing the great West Field, vaulting the wall of the old sheepfold, and splashing across the little stream. And there, by the stream, he took Elspeth in his arms as she stood talking with the women at the washing stone. He kissed her as the women shrieked with surprise and delight, and then stood back and laughed to see his Elspeth gasp. She sat down, stood up, then sat down again before at last she leapt to her feet and flung herself about him crying with joy. Arm in arm and thronged by women and children they walked into the village. There, playing in the street with a puppy was little Hetti. She looked up, shouted, and ran to her father. He hugged her tight then threw her into the air, and caught her, and kissed her and told her all was well. Much later, when the day was done, and all the folk gathered in the barn, he told his story:

He had been captured by the Liutizen before the great battle in the forest, and held for months as a slave – he still wore the rope torque about his neck. Once he had tried to escape, but had been beaten and starved and tethered to a stake for three days and nights to try and break his spirit. After that, he was closely watched, and slept each night tied to an iron ring set into a stone pillar.

Then came a day when the tree-priest decided that sacrifice should be made for the Spring Planting. He, Rainald, was chosen as the slave to be sacrificed. They brought him bound to an altar of rough hewn stones in the centre of a ploughed field, and chanted and sang, and made ready to cut his throat. They offered him a rough beer mulled with herbs to make him drowsy, but in his anger and despair he turned his head aside, and shouted out: 'A free Saxon of Eckerheim!' His voice faltered and he felt ashamed.

There were shouts and jeers – but then the crowd fell silent as a tall figure pushed his way through, and came and stood beside the altar. Rainald looked up to see a war-chief, older than any he had seen in the village before, with long grey blond hair tied in a pony tail, and the golden-bronze torques of a warrior who had seen many battles. There were scars on his chest and cheek bones. He looked down at Rainald where he lay on the stone. 'Na!' he said, and drew out a dagger and cut the bonds and dragged Rainald to his feet.

There was a low growl of anger from the villagers who crowded about him; the tree-priest shouted out, and brandished his alder staff – but the war chief silenced him with a wave of his hand. He then spoke. Rainald could understand nothing of what he said, but he spoke with a strong, clear voice, and all the while stared about him as if challenging those who were listening.   When he had finished speaking he nodded at the priest who shook his staff once and then turned away glowering. The rest of the tribesmen stood back. The war-chief gave a slight smile and gestured at Rainald as if telling him to go. For a moment Rainald looked back at him, and then he began to walk. He went slowly and uncertainly at first, half-expecting at any moment to feel the point of a spear between his shoulders or the thrust of a sword in his back. But nothing happened, so he kept on walking, praying all the while, ears straining for the first sounds of pursuit. When he reached the edge of the forest that fringed the field he risked a glance over his shoulder.

There was the war-chief, clearly visible, standing among his people, watching him. They stood like mist-wraiths, like shadow folk from fireside tales. No one had moved. It was as though they were waiting for him to leave. Rainald turned and plunged into the forest and began his long journey home.

He walked for days. He lived off the countryside, keeping mostly to the forest, and following the setting sun as best he could. Several times he came upon Liutizen settlements and had to skirt around them, hiding whenever he saw people in the fields, and only moving when he was sure that he could not be seen.

Somewhere, somehow, he found a ford north of Dresdany, and waded across, chest high through the shoaling waters.

He made landfall on the western bank at a village he did not know, and could scarcely name, but it was part of the Meissener Mark, and the folk there fed and clothed him and sent him on his way. They said little to him, and seemed almost frightened by his sudden arrival, but they did tell him that the Imperial Army had been defeated in a great battle somewhere in the dark forest on the other side of the river, and only small numbers of survivors had made it back to the Saxon shore.

And so Rainald came home – and the village rejoiced once more. But it was cold comfort for the seven families of seven men who would never be coming home. And yet of all the villages in the Mark, Eckerheim had fared by far the best. Though it was now known that others of the imperial army had survived, many a village had lost all the menfolk who had answered the king's call to arms, and it was said that in some places the crops rotted in the fields because there was no one to bring them in.

And Cedric the shepherd took the way across the tops that leads to a village that had suffered more than most. And there he kept a promise, and there he kept his sheep. And Eadyth loved him more than life itself.

Back in Eckerheim, Elsa and Markward sat at table with the family, and joked and laughed with Albrecht as Mutti and Brunni served the meal that they always cooked after the harvest was ended, and the tithe barn sealed: mutton stew and dumplings, with lentils and cabbage, and coarse black bread.

They ate, they cleared, and they gathered by the fire. Holding their hands to the heat of the flames, the family talked of the day, and the day to come.

After a while, Brunni settled to stitching a tunic, Markward dozed by the fireside and Albrecht took himself off to his bed. For a time Elsa was silent, then she touched Mutti on the sleeve and drew her close.

'Will the raiders be back, Mutti? Will they ever leave us be.'

The old woman smiled, and threw a log on the fire. 'We will always be here, Elsi, and they will always be there. They will push and we will shove. Back and forth. Across the Elbe. And sometimes the crops will burn. And sometimes the villages. But we will always be here, and they will always be there. And always there will be someone to plant the crops again, and to rebuild the villages. Liutizen and Saxon, both sides of the great river.'

'And Eckerheim?'

'Eckerheim has teeth. They know that now. They lost a clan chief here, but they soaked his grave with the blood of an imperial army.

That is revenge enough. I'm thinking they will leave us alone for a good while.'

'And how long is that?'

'Long enough to have children, raise a family, and see them start their own. We've the Weissburg to watch over us as well, and the Liutizen will seek easier pickings before they come back our way, I'm sure of it. Their bellies will have to be flapping against their backbones before they think of us again.'

The two women stared into the flames until the log that Mutti had thrown on was all but burnt to embers.

'You don't hate them, Mutti – the raiders, I mean?'

'I don't hate them. But I hate what they do, and I hate what we have to do in return, and I hate missing young folk in the Spring, that I had seen in the Fall.' Mutti gave a tight-lipped smile, and hugged Elsa close. 'Still, we've all of us come thus far safe, and are like to see out old days under the Good Lord's blessing.'

'And the king's peace.'

'The king's death you mean. The king is dead, and a young king too. Worked himself to death to get peace on these borders, and died knowing that it was all the same as it had ever been.'

'He was a good king.'

'He tried to do good things, as a good king should.'

Elsa nodded, and yawned. 'I'm for bed. The field work begins early on the morrow. Eric said.'

'Aye, I heard him. Well, take your man with you. I'll not have him cluttering up my hearth, and getting in my way.'

Down by the stream, Bernhardt stood and looked up at the moon. A full moon, a harvest moon, rising slowly through the drifting clouds.

There came a sound and a shadow. He turned. It was Katrin.

'I like to come here,' he said to her.

She came and stood beside him, and took his hand.

'There was a stream like this in Hochtal,' she said.

'Do you miss Hochtal, then?'

'I miss my man.'

'Lukas was a good man.'

'And all I had.'

They stood together for a long time. The moon rose higher and higher, and the village slept. A dog barked once, twice, down by the old barn then all was quiet. The stream ran on, and Bernhardt and Katrin watched it as it glistened and bubbled in the moonlight.

'I will never go back to Hochtal,' said Bernhardt at last.

'Nor I,' replied Katrin, and she glanced at the blacksmith.

He ducked his head, and caught his breath. There was a silence.

'I could make you happy, Katrin,' he said.

'You mean . . .'

'I could never be your Lukas. He was and is your first love – I know that. But I could make you happy. I know that. And . . .'

'And I you, sweet Bernhardt! I could make you happy, too.'

They looked at each other, smiling. Katrin brushed away a tear, and trembled slightly as Bernhardt reached out and drew her close then kissed her lightly on the brow.

'One eye, one arm. A poor blacksmith. What can you want with me?' he whispered.

'You have all I could ever want,' said Katrin, smiling through her tears, and she hugged him tight.

In the morning all Eckerheim went to the fields and began the planting. In the evening they sang, while the children played and the young girls danced. And as they danced, the young men called to them from the corners of the village square.

And the old folk sat in the doorways, and tended the fires, while they talked of families and flocks and work to do in the lower fields.

And this would be the way in Eckerheim for more than many a year.

Glossary of Terms

Bailiff: The lord's representative in the village. Usually a peasant himself, he had the responsibility of keeping order in the village, and making sure the seasonal tasks were properly carried out.

Bailey: The courtyard of a castle.

Barbican: A defended gateway.

Brigandine: Body armour made of quilted leather, often studded with metal rivets, and sometimes strengthened with small metal plates sewn into the linings.

Bothy: A simple farmhouse or shepherd's hut.

Casque: A simple, close-fitting iron cap.

Castellan: Someone nominated by a warlord to be in charge of a castle while he is away.

Cruck-house / Cruck: A simple peasant dwelling, usually of wattle and daub, with a thatch roof and often an 'A frame' construction.

Friesians: A coastal / delta people, occupying what is now called Friesia in the northern Netherlands. They were independent, hardy, and not inclined to be part of the German Empire.

Fyrd: The old Saxon name for the Levy.

Gambeson: A quilted woollen garment worn under a mail shirt to cushion blows.

Hauberk: A coat of mail, usually made of interlocking and riveted iron rings. A quilted tunic or 'gambeson' was often worn underneath to provide some warmth and cushion blows.

Hayward: A peasant whose job was to keep the cattle from wandering into the crops and damaging them.

Headland: The bank of earth at the end of fields, formed over the years by the turning of the ploughs.

Inner Fields / Outer fields: Crops were sown on rotation, often at different times of the year, and one of the fields (they could be up to 300 acres in size) was always left fallow. The principle crops were barley, maize or corn, rye and wheat. Hedges were far less in evidence than they are today.

Kirtle: A woman's over garment or dress, usually made of wool.

Kite shield: A large, kite-shaped shield made of wood, covered with leather, and often reinforced with a metal rim and central boss.

Levy: In many areas peasants were required to do military service once a year for up to forty days. This was called the 'levy' (from the French 'Lever' to raise.)

Marcher Lands /Marcher Towns: Border lands and towns.

Markgraf: A warlord, usually ruling over a large area, and swearing allegiance directly to the king or emperor.

Marker Stones: These were used to show boundaries between different areas of land, and to separate out different family holdings.

Muster: The gathering of the Levy.

. Liutizen: A series of fierce pagan tribes living east of the Elbe. For many years they successfully resisted any attempts to subdue them, or draw them into Western Christendom.

Provost: An officer in charge of supplies and provisions in the army.

Tithes: A 10% tax on crops imposed by the church.

Wall-walk: The ramparts of a castle.

ISBN 1425121?9-9

9 781425 121792